NETHERWORLD

A Medieval Romance

By Kathryn Le Veque

Printed by Dragonblade Publishing in the United States of America

Text copyright 2014 by Kathryn Le Veque
Cover copyright 2014 by Kathryn Le Veque

Library of Congress Control #2014-048
ISBN 1500856061

Map illustration copyright 2014 by Kathryn Le Veque

KATHRYN LE VEQUE NOVELS

Lords of Thunder: The de Shera Brotherhood Trilogy
The Thunder Lord
The Thunder Warrior
The Thunder Knight

Time Travel Romance: (Saxon Lords of Hage)
The Crusader
Kingdom Come

<u>**Contemporary Romance:**</u>

Kathlyn Trent/Marcus Burton Series:
Valley of the Shadow
The Eden Factor
Canyon of the Sphinx

The American Heroes Series:
The Lucius Robe
Fires of Autumn
Evenshade
Sea of Dreams
Purgatory

Other Contemporary Romance:
Lady of Heaven
Darkling, I Listen

<u>**Multi-author Collections/Anthologies:**</u>
With Dreams Only of You (USA Today bestseller)
Sirens of the Northern Seas (Viking romance)
Ever My Love (sequel to With Dreams Only Of You) July 2016

Note: All Kathryn's novels are designed to be read as stand-alones, although many have cross-over characters or cross-over family groups. Novels that are grouped together have related characters or family groups.

Series are clearly marked. All series contain the same characters or family groups except the American Heroes Series, which is an anthology with unrelated characters.

There is NO particular chronological order for any of the novels because they can all be read as stand-alones, even the series.

For more information, find it in **A Reader's Guide to the Medieval World of Le Veque.**

Dear Reader,

This book was part of the original "The Collection of Beginnings", which was an anthology of the first three chapters of several novels that I had started but had yet to finish. I asked readers to go to my website and vote for the novel they would like to see completed, and NETHERWORLD was the top pick for the first month of voting. Therefore, I pushed another novel that I was planning on completing aside and finished NETHERWORLD instead. It's time for Keller de Poyer's (a secondary character in THE WHISPERING NIGHT) story to be told, and it's a hell of a story.

That being said, this novel is dedicated to my wonderful readers who take the time and effort to read and voice opinions about my novels. Without you, none of this would be possible. I am deeply grateful to you all!

Thank you!

Love,
Kathryn

TABLE OF CONTENTS

"… but when a mountain foot I reach'd
The valley, that had pierc'd my heart with dread,
I looked aloft, and saw his shoulders broad,
And I entered into the Netherworld…."

~ Excerpt from Dante's Inferno

PROLOGUE

October, Year of Our Lord 1197
Nether Castle, Powys, Wales

THE BLOW TO the jaw sent Gryffyn reeling.

Sprawled on the rough oak planks of the great hall, Gryffyn shook the stars from his eyes and looked up to see the big English knight moving in for another blow.

Keller had fists the size of a man's head, but Gryffyn was fast. He managed to roll out of the way and leapt to his feet although his balance was off and he ended up bashing into the corner of the hearth. But Keller was coming in for another blow and Gryffyn threw himself to his left, away from his sister's enraged husband. He knew, by the look in the man's eye, that he meant to kill him.

Gryffyn tried to lash out a fist at Keller, but the knight was just too fast and too strong. Keller grabbed Gryffyn's fist, twisted, and ended up snapping his wrist. Gryffyn fell to his knees, screaming in pain as Keller stood over him in a huffing and furious stance. His dusky eyes were smoldering with fury.

"So you have been hiding here all along, waiting for the proper moment to strike," Keller hissed. "You are a coward of a man, d'Einen – a wretched and vile coward. Now that I finally have you, I intend to do what should have been done long ago."

Holding his wrist, Gryffyn glared at Keller with eyes as dark as obsidian. "If I am a coward, then you are a fool," he growled. "You cannot stop me. Nether and everything in it belongs to me, including my sister!"

It was the wrong thing to say. Keller reached out and used his fist to hammer on Gryffyn's broken wrist, sending the man into howls of pain. But Keller was immune to it. His focus was both deadly and intense as he watched Gryffyn squirm.

"She is my wife now and I swear, by all that is holy, that you shall never lay another hand on her again," Keller rumbled. "I knew someone was beating her but she would not directly tell me who it was. For all of the pain and humiliation you have cast upon her, she still protected you. God knows why, but she did. How long was this going on before I came, d'Einen? How long have you been beating on helpless women to make you feel more like a man?"

Cradling his wrist against his chest, Gryffyn was in a world of hurt. "You bastard," he grunted. "You come to my castle in all of your haughty, conquering glory and married my sister because my weak and foolish father made a pact with the Devil."

Keller's eyes blazed. "William Marshal has nothing to do with you taking your fists to your sister."

"You only married her to gain a castle. Do not act as if she means something to you!"

"It does not matter if she means something to me." Keller was struggling not to wrap his hands around the man's neck, although he knew, eventually, that it would come to that. It was just a feeling he had. "She is my wife and I will protect her. I will tell you this now, Gryffyn d'Einen, so there is no misunderstanding. If you so much as look at her in a hostile manner again, I will run you through. Make no mistake. If you touch her again, I will kill you."

Gryffyn wasn't used to being questioned or disciplined. He had always done as he pleased. Deep down, he was a spoiled little boy with a spoiled little mind. With a growl, he propelled himself off the floor and charged Keller with all of his furious might. Keller easily reached out a massive fist and caught Gryffyn on the side of the head, knocking the man silly. Gryffyn fell on his bad wrist, collapsed in a heap, and began to bellow.

Keller gazed at the man, not at all sorry for the pain and suffering he was feeling. Had Keller possessed any less self-control, the man would be wallowing in a pool of his own blood. He deserved all of the justified agony and more. In fact, Keller was purposely making the man suffer. He wanted him to feel the pain he had inflicted upon Chrystobel, and upon his family, for untold years. He wanted Gryffyn to feel the humiliation and hurt. As Gryffyn writhed in agony, Keller turned to his wife.

Chrystobel had managed to crawl over to the hearth and now sat propped up against the wall, her dark eyes wide with shock. Keller's appearance at the most opportune time had been startling enough, but watching her husband pound her brother was a vision of violence and retribution that she never thought she would live to see. Gryffyn was finally subdued and Keller was the reason, protecting her as he had sworn to do. He was a man of his word, English or no. The realization was almost more than she could bear and she gazed at the man, seeing him through entirely new eyes.

This wasn't the same knight she had met the day before, the man who had shown little to no warmth. That Keller de Poyer was an efficient, humorless man who, she was sure, had viewed her just as he viewed Nether Castle; as an acquisition. The big knight with the wide shoulders and enormous hands hadn't treated her with anything more than polite respect until this moment in time. Having seen Gryffyn preparing to pounce on her was all Keller needed to unleash his fury against the man, as if Chrystobel meant something to him. As if he was protecting something dear. It had been a truly awesome sight to behold and she was still quite stunned by it all.

As his brother-in-law moaned on the floor several feet away, Keller had eyes only for Chrystobel. She was such a lovely creature. He'd known that from the moment he had first laid eyes on her. But the pain in his heart from a love lost had prevented him from seeing beyond his fear. Fear of feeling, fear of opening himself up again. Chrystobel was a beautiful angel he had never expected to know and now, he could feel himself relenting. He could feel himself warming, perhaps willing to open himself up again. The very moment he had saved her life was the moment he started to let himself feel something.

He crouched down beside her as she sat against the wall, his rugged face, worn by the years and the weather, creased with concern.

"Are you badly injured?" he asked softly.

The buzzing in Chrystobel's head had eased considerably. "Nay," she said softly, gazing into his eyes and feeling hope and relief in her chest such as she had never before experienced. "I am well enough."

Keller's gaze drifted over her head, her face, as if he didn't believe her. "Are you certain?" he asked quietly. "I can send for a physic."

Chrystobel smiled faintly, reaching out to put a hand on his arm in a reassuring gesture. "That is not necessary," she said, sighing quietly. "I will admit that my head does ache a bit, but food and rest will cure me, I am sure."

He stared at her a moment before lifting his enormous hands and gently cupped her face. As Chrystobel looked into his eyes, her heart thumping madly against her ribs, she could feel the emotion pouring from the man. It was as if a dam had burst and everything that had been held back was finally gushing out. Sir Keller de Poyer was cold no more, and it was an astonishing realization.

"I am sorry," he whispered. "I am sorry you had to endure what your brother did to you. But I swear, with God as my witness, that he will never touch you again."

Chrystobel was at a loss for words, her breathing unsteady as his thumbs began to stroke her silken skin. It was the first time he had touched her and her senses were understandably overwhelmed.

"It was simply the way of things, my lord," she murmured. "It has been going on so long that I have known little else."

Keller's face hardened. "No more," he rumbled. "He is a dead man if he so much as looks at you in a way I do not like. Do you believe me?"

Chrystobel nodded, though she hardly dared to truly believe. "Aye."

His gentle smile returned. "Good." He fought off the sudden urge to kiss her, not wanting the first genuine kiss between them to be a public spectacle. He was rather shy and conservative that way. Moreover, there was something more she needed to know, something very serious. He braced himself.

"I must also apologize for something else," he said hesitantly. "Your father...."

Chrystobel cut him off by a nod of the head, tears popping to her eyes. "I know," she whispered. "Gryffyn told me."

"He admitted to killing him?"

"Aye," she confirmed. "The blood on the floor... is it his?"

Keller nodded, watching her sorrowful expression. "Aye," he said quietly. "I am so sorry that I was unable to prevent it."

Chrystobel struggled to control her tears, thinking on her father, the man who was supposed to protect her but never did. Although she was sorry for his loss, she couldn't seem to muster true grief for his passing. Had the man ever prevented Gryffyn from having his own way in all things, perhaps she would have felt differently, but at the moment she felt somewhat guilty that she wasn't more distraught.

"You are not responsible," she said, wiping at her eyes. "You did what you could. You saved me, in fact, and I thank you for that."

Keller's dusky eyes glimmered. "It is one of the better things that I have done in my life."

She smiled at the first truly warm moment between them. "I am particularly grateful for your keen sense of timing," she said. "A few seconds later and I might not have been so grateful. Or alive."

He winked at her and dropped his hands from her face, moving to take her two small hands within his big palms. He kissed them both sweetly, tenderly, as a promise of things to come. Now, it would be different between them. Gryffyn had, if nothing else, accomplished that.

"If you can stand, mayhap we should go and check on your sister,"

Keller said. "I am sure you are anxious to see her."

Chrystobel nodded, glancing at Gryffyn as the man sat up with the Ashby-Kidd twins standing several feet away from him, watching every move the man made.

"I am," she said, eyeing her brother warily. "What are you going to do with him?"

The warmth in Keller's eyes faded as he looked over his shoulder at the Welshman, who was holding his broken wrist awkwardly against his torso. His expression suggested anger, defeat, and defiance. Even with the broken wrist, Keller could still see fight in the man. After a moment, he returned his gaze to Chrystobel.

"Lock him in the vault," he said. "The man has much to atone for so I hope you will trust me to make the appropriate judgment."

"Of course, my lord."

His gaze lingered on her a moment, thoughts turning from Gryffyn back to her. He liked thinking of her much better. "You will call me Keller," he said quietly. "Or husband. I will answer to whatever you choose to call me."

A beautiful smile spread across her face. She had a delightful grin with straight, white teeth and slightly prominent canines. "I would be honored to call you Keller," she said sincerely.

He was just about to release her hands but thought better of it as she spoke. The glimmer returned to his eyes.

"I like hearing you say my name," he said honestly.

Her smile broadened even more, if such a thing was possible. "Then I shall say it again," she whispered. "Keller."

He kissed her hand again, smiling when she giggled. In the midst of this hellish situation, it was a tender moment that saw something of a relationship between them take hold. A spark had ignited, and Keller was again thinking on kissing her lips, privacy be damned, when he heard scuffling behind him. Before he could turn around, something violent and painful rammed into the right side of his torso.

He pitched forward as Chrystobel screamed, struggling to keep him from falling even as he collapsed onto his bum. Horrified, they could both see the dagger jutting from his right side, about a foot below his armpit. And there was a hand on it.

Gryffyn stood behind Keller, his good hand on the hilt of the dirk as he crammed it into the man's flesh. Ripping it from Keller's body, he pushed the man aside and aimed for his sister with the blade held high.

CHAPTER ONE

One day earlier
Powys Region, Wales

"DO YOU SUPPOSE that when God created the earth, he forgot to mention that the sun needed to fall upon Wales as well?"

The question drew low laughter from the group. A column of five hundred English warriors tramped north out of Deheubarth, through Gwynedd and into Powys, traversing the lush green and wild country of Wales. August had seen unseasonably heavy rains, turning the roads to muddy swamps. At the moment, the gray clouds were scattering across the blue expanse of sky, moving to the east as the sea breeze blew strong. The comment came from a young knight because even though traces of blue could be seen among the clouds, it seemed that one was always blotting out the sun.

"God may have made Wales with too much bad weather and too many savages," an older knight commented. Sir William Wellesbourne was a big, blond knight with dark eyes and a quick wit. "But it is William Marshal who has charged us with taming it. Consider this your test of knighthood, young George. Sun be damned."

George Ashby-Kidd grinned sheepishly as his identical twin brother, Aimery, laughed the loudest. They were good-looking young men, newly knighted last year, with personalities as identical as their brown-haired, blue-eyed resemblance. They were quick to the sword, quick of temper, and ambitious. Their father was a long-time retainer of their liege, William Marshal, and very ambitious himself. The boys had been well schooled in knightly aspiration.

As the troops surrounding the knights twittered and snorted, a muzzled charger thundered up from the rear of the column. Wellesbourne quieted the snickering men as their commanding officer rode upon them. Mud sprayed as the big horse slowed from a canter to a nervous trot and the knight flipped up his visor with an enormous mailed hand.

Sir Keller de Poyer inspected his knights, flicking the sweat from his brow as he did so. Even in the cooler temperatures, sweat was running in his eyes. It had been a long day at a clipped pace and he, as well as his men, were showing their fatigue. He knew his men had been laughing; he heard them well down the line. He also knew they would shut up as he drew near. They always did, fearful of his temper as well as his punishment. Keller's knights had learned through trial and error to both fear and respect him. They were all relatively new to his service and he was not, in their experience, a forgiving man.

"We should see our destination within the hour," Keller glanced up at the waning sun as it struggled to peek from behind the gray clouds. "Will, send a rider on to announce our arrival. I would have sup waiting for us when we arrive."

Wellesbourne nodded smartly and motioned to one of the mounted soldiers riding in the ranks behind the knights. The man dug his heels into his horse and shot off down the road, splashing black mud as he went. George's charger became excited when the horse sped past, causing his animal to bolt off the muddy path. He had a devil of a time controlling the horse and bringing him back into the column. Keller rode up beside Wellesbourne, ignoring George and his frenzied charger.

William eyed de Poyer as the man pulled alongside. He'd distantly known Keller for a few years, as they both served William Marshal, but only in the past year had he come into the man's service as garrison commander of Pembroke Castle. It had been a dark time in de Poyer's life. All William knew, and this was strictly from what others had told him, was that Keller had been betrothed to a woman he was deeply in love with. But the woman had left him for another man and Keller had turned from a pleasant, dedicated knight into a withdrawn, quick-tempered malcontent.

Since William and Keller were about the same age and had the same number of years as sworn knights, there was an assumed amount of respect and camaraderie between them. There were times when William saw the warm, witty man come through. He had heard tale, from the old soldiers, that Keller had once been a congenial man known for his fairness and benevolence. He had been very much loved by his men and respected by both ally and enemy alike. As garrison commander of Pembroke Castle for the past several years, he had his share of respect from local Welsh chieftains. William Marshal had depended on him at Pembroke a good deal. But these days, most of the time, de Poyer was strictly professional with no emotion, only black and white in his decision-making. There was no longer any warmth or kindness. Those days departed when his lady-love did.

That made the trip to Nether Castle in the wilds of Powys such a dreaded task. They'd all been feeling it for days now as they traveled from Pembroke Castle into the green vales of Powys. Everyone treated the subject as one would the plague; with fear and avoidance. William hated to even bring it up, but there was no avoiding the reason for their trip. Best to get it out in the open to let whatever storm that would brew as a result to run its course and be done with it before they arrived at their destination.

"I have not yet had the opportunity to congratulate you on your contract," he said casually as the horses plodded along. "The Marshal has rewarded you well for your years of service; a castle of your own and titles. You must be quite pleased."

Keller's jaw ticked as his dark blue eyes moved over the lush green landscape. "I should be."

"But you are not?"

"I was content as garrison commander of Pembroke."

"But to have title and lands of your own is every man's dream," William pressed. "Lord Carnedd now, is it not? And your property stretches from Banwy River to the Dovey Valley. I hear it is a rich, prosperous land much coveted by Welsh princes."

"Which will make keeping peace all the more difficult."

"Maybe so. But the Welsh overlord is loyal to William Marshal."

"More than likely because the Marshal gifted the man with English lands and coinage," Keller cast William a long glance. "Do not imagine that the man did not receive a handsome reward for surrendering his Welsh lands. He is now a very wealthy English lord, I promise you. And I also promise you that his Welsh neighbors will not take kindly to a garrison of English suddenly sprouting in their midst."

William wriggled his eyebrows. "Perhaps not," he said. "But that is why you have brought five hundred retainers and three knights, with still more on the way. Isn't de Lohr sending some our way?"

De Poyer nodded faintly to the mention of the Earl of Hereford and Worcester, the great Christopher de Lohr, the most powerful Marcher lord in the realm. "The Marshal asked him to send a thousand more men if he can spare them," he replied. "He is supposed to send a few knights along as well."

Wellesbourne nodded confidently. "With a retinue that size, we shall make short work of any resistance the Welsh might display."

"We shall see."

The way Keller uttered the quietly spoken words led William to believe that he wasn't entirely convinced of the English superiority, even with de Lohr reinforcing his numbers. The Welsh this far north could be powerful and cagey. That being the case, William sought to steer the subject away from that particular issue.

"I also hear that one thousand sheep are part of your contract," he said.

"They are indeed," Keller drew in a long, pensive breath. "I suppose

I can always look at the positive; should I grow weary of fighting the Welsh, I can always become a sheep farmer."

William laughed softly. "Cheer up, de Poyer. You are a fortunate man."

Keller's response was to spur his charger away from William and to the front of the column. It was apparent he didn't wish to speak further on the matter and Wellesbourne was sorry that he had chased him off. Keller remained at the front, riding alone, until the tall, dark-stoned bastion of Nether Castle came into view.

At first, it was difficult to tell the castle from the dark clouds that hovered over the mountains. They blended in to each other. Then, the distinct outline became more apparent and the desolate fortress that was Nether Castle distinguished itself from the angry sky. Perched on the crest of an enormous mountain, Nether Castle was a bleak and foreboding place. It could be seen for miles, riding the summit of the mountain like a great preying beast.

A sliver of road could be seen leading up to it, hugging the side of the mountain precariously. The scattered clouds in the sky seemed to be clustering over the castle, great sheets of gray rain falling upon it. The party from Pembroke could see the storm over the castle, brewing for the approaching guests. It made the countenance of the place most uninviting.

Nether Castle was the seat of the Carnedd baronetcy, an expanse of land nestled in the heart of Powys near the Dovey Valley. It was referred to as "The Wilds" because of the dramatic and desolate landscape, far removed from the marcher lordships that dominated the contention between England and Wales.

Nether, however, was a fortress in the center of turbulent lands. Lesser Welsh princes claimed to rule over the lands, which complicated the issue when the Lord of Nether surrendered the castle to William Marshal in exchange for a very small parcel of more prosperous English property. Still, the exchange of lands came with a good deal of haggling in the form of an arranged marriage. The Lord of Nether, Trevyn d'Einen, had made his daughter part of the bargain. It kept a family tie still linked to the property even though it no longer belonged to his family.

None of the Englishmen knew the details of the deal save de Poyer. It wasn't their business, anyway. But there were various whispers of dread and reluctance from the men. But they knew that the dark and stormy castle was their destination, like it or not. George and Aimery looked to seasoned William, but the blond knight's gaze was fixed upon the distant castle in a noncommittal manner. They all knew better than to comment within earshot of de Poyer, who continued to ride alone several feet ahead. Knowing the man's mood as they did, they suspected it was darker than the clouds above.

Little did they know that it was darker even than that. As the army began their ascent up the road, de Poyer suddenly spurred his animal down a small goat path that led off across the base of the hill. It was parallel to the castle. He wasn't heading away from the structure but he wasn't heading towards it, either. Wellesbourne watched him go.

"Where is he going?" George reined his charger next to William.

Wellesbourne shook his head. "I have no idea."

"What should we do?"

"Continue to the castle. He will meet us there."

"Are you sure?"

Wellesbourne wasn't. With a lingering glance at de Poyer as the man ripped across the slick green hillside, he turned to the column of men and began shouting encouragement to motivate them up the muddy road.

CHAPTER TWO

"**S**HE'LL BE GREETING her husband with a bruise on her face," said an older man, well dressed, who was bent over a woman seated at the table in the great hall. She had her hand over the left side of her face as the old man tried to inspect it. He could already see the welt rising and he turned furious dark eyes to the man standing near the hearth with a chalice of wine in his hand. "Why did you do this? She has done nothing to deserve it."

The man with the wine looked lazily at the older man. "She is a woman, is she not?" he fired back. "That is reason enough. And you'll stay out it."

The older man straightened up, his expression nothing short of rage. "I'll not stay out of it," he seethed. "She is my daughter. And you are my son. You have no right to strike her."

Gryffyn d'Einen tossed the chalice into the blazing hearth, hearing the hiss as the liquid hit the fire. His face contorted with anger as he stomped towards his shorter, weaker father.

"Stay out of it," he repeated, shoving a finger into his father's face. "It is none of your affair."

"Strike her again and you will regret it."

Gryffyn lashed out, striking his father with a closed fist in the jaw. The man went reeling as the woman jumped up from the table, going to the aid of the older man.

"Gryffyn, no!" she cried. "Leave him alone!"

Gryffyn swung on his younger sister. "Have you not learned your lesson?" he reached out and grabbed her hair, viciously yanking the silken blond strands. "If I need to…."

He was cut off by a servant standing in the doorway of the great hall. "My lord," the old servant delivered in a trembling tone. "We have received a rider."

Gryffyn's wrath was diverted from his sister, his dark eyes focusing on the cowering servant. "Who is it?"

"The English, my lord." The servant was moving out of the door even as he delivered the message. Everyone at Nether Castle feared Gryffyn, especially when he was in the midst of a rage. "The party from Pembroke will be here within the hour. They demand their supper and a priest upon their arrival."

Gryffyn released his sister's hair, hardly noticing when she ran to their father to help the man off the floor.

"Is the messenger still here?" he demanded.

The servant bobbed his scraggly head nervously. "Aye, m'lord."

"Send him to me quickly."

"Aye, m'lord."

The man fled. Now out of striking range, Gryffyn's sister and father watched him with a good deal of trepidation. A big man, Gryffyn was violent and unstable. What happened this afternoon had happened a hundred times before. Gryffyn did not care who he struck in anger or annoyance; his father, his sister or a servant were all the same to him. There was no telling his mood from moment to moment.

Chrystobel d'Einen knew that all too well. Her cheek was red as a result of a simple misspoken word to her volatile brother. She didn't even know what it was. One moment they were speaking, the next moment he snapped. It had been thus for as long as she could recall. She spent a good deal of time avoiding the man and the pain he inflicted. It was one of the darker secrets they endured in the place the locals called the Nether World.

"What of Izlyn?" she whispered to her father. "I will not allow her to stay in the vault one moment longer. She has done nothing to warrant being caged in that awful place."

"Shush," Trevyn d'Einen put his fingers to his lips in a hushing motion. He didn't want Gryffyn to hear their conversation. "She has done nothing except to have been mute all of these years. That is enough for your brother."

Tears threatened Chrystobel but she fought them. "God damn him to...."

Trevyn shushed her again. "I will release your sister, have no fear. Your brother will be occupied with the English and his thoughts will not be on your little sister. I would suggest that you see to the meal and stay clear of your brother for the time being."

Chrystobel nodded. "Aye, Father," she murmured. Her gaze lingered on her brother a moment before returning her attention to her father and lowering her voice. "Perhaps you should also clear the hall."

Trevyn shook his head, rubbing his jaw where his son had struck him. "In a moment," he said with more bravery than he felt. "You will go and see to the meal."

Something in Chrystobel's gaze begged her father to leave with her, but the man refused to go. This was his hall, after all, and he would not be chased out by his bullying son. Chrystobel knew this. With a soft sigh of resignation, she turned back to her brother.

"Do you have any requests for supper, Gryffyn?" she asked politely.

Gryffyn had reclaimed the chalice so carelessly tossed aside and was in the process of pouring himself more wine. His mood shift was instantaneous, back to an almost pleasant countenance.

"If the parsnips are bitter you shall feel my wrath," he said steadily. "Do we have honey?"

"Aye."

"Then I would have honey cakes with walnuts."

"As you wish."

With a last glance at her father, Chrystobel quit the hall just as an unfamiliar soldier entered. She steered well away from the man, hardly giving him a glance as she quit the great hall and headed for the kitchens on the opposite side of the keep.

There was a storm brewing overhead and she glanced up as a few stray raindrops pelted her face. They felt cool and soothing on her red cheek which, she knew from experience, would not fade before the English arrived. Since she was well aware that she would be meeting her future husband upon that event, she silently cursed her brother for his beastly actions. She was always silently cursing him but that was as far as it went. Anything more and he might seriously hurt her. She could not take the chance.

So she struggled to move past the latest slap her brother had brought against her and focus on the meal. Now the English were coming and Nether Castle would be garrisoned for William Marshal. Gryffyn had been furious that his father had consigned their ancestral home to the English, but with the promise of richer English lands and coinage, Gryffyn's anger had soothed. Still, he wasn't entirely happy about the English at Nether Castle. His mood swings had been worse since his father had struck the deal. Chrystobel felt some resentment that Gryffyn was so incensed about the deal when she had every right to be the incensed party in the proposal. She was the one, after all, who had been made part of the bargain.

The thunder rolled overhead and a few more drops pelted her face. Chrystobel crossed through the smaller inner wall that sectioned off the kitchen yard from the rest of the castle. She could see the kitchen straight ahead, a structure with a roof and three walls. One entire side of it was open to the elements, but it was a cozy and functional place nonetheless. As she approached, the slender cook with only one good eye informed her that the meal was well underway. A sheep was being turned on a big spit, fat from the carcass dripping into the open flame and creating bursts of flame. Chrystobel spoke to the one-eyed cook long enough to inform the woman that Gryffyn had requested honey cakes with walnuts. The woman listened but seemed more interested in inspecting Chrystobel's red cheek.

It wasn't bad enough that her brother struck her but that the servants, long-time pledges of the d'Einen household, could not be discreet about the marks she bore. Most of them had known Chrystobel since she had been born. They had watched the little bully Gryffyn grow into the bigger, stronger bully who seemed to take delight in taking his frustrations out on his sisters. The eldest, Chrystobel, was a glorious goddess of beauty while the younger girl, Izlyn, was a mute; sweet, silent, lovely little Izlyn. They were all extremely protective of the girls and they had all paid the price at one time or another. Gryffyn viewed it as interference in his world and he would not tolerate it from anyone, not even their father. Trevyn was the recipient of his son's wrath as well.

Chrystobel left the fretting cook, not wanting to get sucked up into the woman's emotional turmoil. Her first impulse was to leave the kitchen yard and go back to the hall to make sure the room was prepared for the English, but she remembered that her brother was there the last time she saw him and she did not want to run into the man again. She couldn't take another welted cheek. The postern gate was to her left, tucked into the wall of the kitchen yard, and she made way for it immediately.

The tunnel that passed through the twelve-foot thick outer wall led to an iron door that was implanted into the exterior edge of the wall. She threw the three bolts on the inside of the gate and shoved it open, emerging into the rocky area outside the great walls of Nether. The castle had been built on a rocky mountain that had been somewhat graded down so that a structure could be built on the strategic pad. And strategic it was. The castle commanded a spectacular view over the surrounding countryside, surrounded by a sheer cliff on the north side, mountains on the east side, and a steep slope on the south side. The west was the entry, facing a mountain road called the Nether Pass. It was dramatic scenery at its best, a mountain fortress nestled deep in the wilds of Wales.

Chrystobel was well aware of the location of her home. She loved the isolation, the green, the pure beauty of her valley to the south. She stood on the edge of the steep slope, her gaze falling over the vast valley below, her thoughts wandering from her welted cheek, to her sister, and to the husband she would be meeting this day. She had always been the pragmatic sort. Trouble was, she wasn't so sure she wanted to make peace with the idea of an English husband. She'd known about it for weeks but that didn't make it any easier to accept. It would be so much easier to simply wind her way down the mountain trails and wander off into oblivion.

Something caught her attention off to the left and she could see a wounded rabbit picking its way down the rocky crevice known as the Gorge of the Dead. It was really the fancy name for the moat that had been hacked out over a hundred years ago by her ancestors who had built Nether Castle. It was a deep, rocky and treacherous pit where the bodies of the enemy were once thrown. But there was a path that cut across it and she followed the path, watching the little creature as it limped its way across the rocky trail. When she reached the bottom of the gorge, she came close to catching it but it scampered away on three good legs. She followed.

The path came up on the other end of the gorge and wound its way down the lush, green slope. It was about three hundred feet down to the valley below and Chrystobel took the path carefully, keeping an eye out for the rabbit as the wind whipped her about. She ended up grabbing her long blond hair in a bunch and holding it tight because the winds had teased it into a frenzy. The raindrops had increased and she now found herself in a full-blown rainstorm. Knowing she needed to return to the castle whether or not she wanted to, she turned around on the muddy slope and promptly lost her footing.

Down the hill she slid.

CB

KELLER SAW HER coming.

At first, he wasn't sure what it was. The rain was somewhat blinding him but he could see something sliding down at him from the slope above. He reined his charger to a halt on the narrow path as the object came closer and he soon realized that it was a woman. She was trying frantically to stop her momentum but she was gaining speed by the second. Keller knew that if he didn't stop her, she would slide a very long way down to the valley below. It wouldn't kill her but it would surely be an uncomfortable and frightening trip. Dismounting his charger, he put himself on an intercept course.

He managed to grab the woman just as she slipped past him. He had ahold of her arm. She shrieked when he grabbed her and her body snapped with the abrupt halt, but Keller had a strong grip. The woman threw up her other hand and grabbed hold of him as he pulled her up and onto the path. Even then, she didn't let go of him. She struggled to catch her breath, still holding him with a death grip.

"My thanks," she breathed heavily, pushing the hair from her eyes. "How fortunate that you were here to save me."

Keller gazed down at the woman. She was petite with gold-colored hair that fell in great silken sheets. In spite of the fact that the rain had dampened it, it was the most beautiful hair he had ever seen. But when she shoved the hair from her face, he was doubly-intrigued. Her face could only be described as exquisite. She looked up at him with great brown eyes, big and round with a fringe of dusky lashes. Her features were delicate and lovely, her cheeks red from the weather. For a moment, he was speechless. It actually took him a moment to move past the wonder of her beauty to realize she had spoken to him.

"I would say it was most fortunate," he replied, tearing his gaze away from her to look up the slope. "Where did you come from?"

She struggled to stand and he held on to her a moment while she steadied herself. "Up there," she pointed to the obvious. "I was chasing a wounded rabbit."

"For supper, no doubt."

She gave him a lopsided grin. "Not really. I felt sorry for the poor little thing."

"And you were going to heal it rather than eat it?"

"That was my intention."

"Seems like an incredible waste of effort." Keller took his hands from her because she seemed steadier. Still, his gaze moved over her. He couldn't help it. She was magnificent. "You are from the castle."

Chrystobel returned his gaze, curious about him now that her fright had eased. "I am," she replied. "And you are with the Marshal's men."

"How would you know that?"

"Because you are not from Wales. I can tell by the way you speak, your manner of dress, your fine charger, your...."

He held up a hand to silence her, though it was done in a light-hearted way. "I can see you are a bright woman. Clumsy perhaps, but bright."

She laughed softly, displaying a beautiful set of white teeth with slightly prominent canines. Keller was instantly captivated.

"I am not always clumsy," she informed him, her brown eyes warm with humor.

Keller regarded her a moment. In truth, he couldn't seem to stop staring at her. "*Beth ydy'ch enw chi?*"

Her delicately arched eyebrows lifted with surprise. "Your Welsh is perfect," she commented. "To answer your question, I am the Lady Chrystobel d'Einen of Nether Castle. May I know your name also, my lord?"

Keller stared at her, the surprise of her identity not lost on him. His first reaction was one of resistance followed just as quickly by one of great interest. The two responses tumbled over in his mind, crashing into one another until all he felt was confusion. But the lady was expecting an answer and he struggled to give her one that didn't sound too extreme one way or the other.

"I am Sir Keller de Poyer," he replied after a moment.

He was positive she would know the name, the stranger who was to become her husband, and was somewhat surprised when she did not react. She continued to gaze at him with a politely friendly look on her face.

"How long will you be part of the English contingent posted at Nether Castle?" she asked.

He was puzzled by her response and he was also strangely offended. He cocked his head. "Does my name not mean anything to you?"

The polite smile was fading. "No, my lord, it does not. Should it?"

He scratched beneath his visor. "Aye, it probably should. It is the name of your husband."

That bit of information received a reaction. Her smile faded completely and her eyes widened. "You... you are my husband?"

He nodded. "Now tell me what you were really doing out here. Were you running away?"

She appeared struck. "Why would I run?"

"I should think that would be fairly obvious." When she continued to look deeply confused, he elaborated. "From me. From our marriage."

She shook her head emphatically. "No, my lord. It is as I told you. I was chasing a wounded rabbit and slipped. There is a trail upslope," she pointed up the mountainside, "that leads from the postern gate of Nether."

He glanced up the side of the mountain, seeing a small sliver of black as it cut through the green of the slope. His gaze returned to the petite, beautiful woman in front of him. If he could admit one thing to himself at that moment it would be that he was glad she was lovely. It made this honor forced upon him a little easier to bear. He realized he was a little less reluctant than he was just moments earlier. Additionally, he was glad that she had not been attempting to run away. Even if he had been...well, almost.

"Very well," his gaze moved up and down her muddy body. From what he could see, it was as exquisite as the rest of her. "Let us return you to the castle and get you into some dry clothing before you catch chill. It would not do for the bride to be ill on the event of her wedding."

Still reeling from the fact that her mystery savior was, in fact, her betrothed, Chrystobel obediently began to move down the muddy path, heading towards the distant road. Keller carefully turned his horse around and began to lead the beast after her.

He watched her lowered head, her slumped shoulders, thinking that perhaps he had been too harsh in accusing her of running away. But it had been the first thing that had popped into his mind and he knew, from past experience, that his manner with women had never been particularly smooth. He was apt to say the wrong thing more than the right. He did not want to start this marriage out on the wrong note.

"My lady," he said, watching her pause and turn around. He walked up to her, gazing down into her chapped face. "I apologize if I offended you by asking if you were running away. I did not mean to insult your honor."

She cocked her head slightly, wiping the rain from her brow. "You did not. But I was truthful with you; I was not running."

"I believe you."

"I do, however, have a question for you, my lord."

"What is it?"

"What were *you* doing here? The castle entrance is not this direction."

He just looked at her. There was a faint glimmer in the dark eyes as he pondered his reply. "I was chasing a wounded rabbit."

"For supper?"

"Hopefully you will provide something more substantial than that."

Her smile was back. She had a very easy, and very lovely, smile. "Indeed I will, my lord."

It was clear she did not believe his evasive answer but she gave him the courtesy of not questioning him further. It made Keller feel worse about dodging her query. She had been truthful where he had not. To be honest, he wasn't sure why he had taken the muddy path along the mountainside. It seemed like a good idea at the time to help clear his head to prepare for the inevitable. But now he felt guilty about it.

His guilt, however, did nothing to either ease or reinforce the confusion he felt as he followed Chrystobel's gently swaying hips all the way back to Nether Pass.

CHAPTER THREE

H<small>E IS A</small> *very big man.*

That was Chrystobel's first thought when she saw de Poyer, without his helm and most of his armor, in the great hall for supper. He had come with a cluster of English knights, haughty men with a haughty manner and big weapons. They were all big and sturdy, war machines for William Marshal's conquest of Wales. She wasn't sure she liked them in the halls of Nether, yet she had little choice. She had instructed the servants to begin serving food as soon as the knights entered the hall and they did so with flighty efficiency.

De Poyer didn't sit right away even though his men did. As Chrystobel watched from an alcove, de Poyer moved to the hearth to inspect it, pacing the room slowly as his gaze moved over every facet of the hall as if biting it off, chewing it, and digesting it. He had a very intense gaze. His perusal of his new acquisition gave Chrystobel a chance to inspect him. As she had initially noticed, he was a large man with a big, muscular body. He had enormously wide shoulders and arms. He wasn't obviously handsome but he had rugged, strong features that she found intriguing. He had dark, dusky eyes and closed-cropped dark hair with flecks of gray near the temples. She wondered how old he was. He wasn't young but he wasn't particularly old. It seemed to her that he was a man who had seen much in life because his manner seemed oddly weary.

A servant swept past her through the alcove, coming from the small exterior door that led off towards the kitchens, and nearly dropped a platter of boiled apples as she went. The woman panicked because she thought Gryffyn, who wasn't even in the hall yet, might have heard the commotion. He did not tolerate clumsiness. Chrystobel caught the platter before it could crash and took it out into the hall herself. No use in hiding herself any longer.

She headed straight for the dais where the knights were collecting. She counted four in all, including de Poyer. Setting the tray down, she dared to glance up and noticed that a big blond knight was studying her intently. Startled when their eyes met, she bowed quickly and turned away, only to run straight into Keller.

He had seen her emerge with the platter of apples and made his way over to the table. Dry and cleaned up from her trip through the mud, he was not surprised to see how lovely she truly was. Her blond hair fell well past her buttocks, the hair around her face pulled back and secured behind her head. She was clad in a rough linen surcoat of a faded cranberry color with a woven tassel rope about her gently flaring hips. When their eyes met, he was intrigued anew by the beauty of her face. But along with that beauty, he noticed a dark shading along her left cheekbone. It was clearly a bruise. His dark eyes inspected her cheek with the same intensity as they inspected the hall. Keller de Poyer was a man who missed nothing.

"You hurt yourself tumbling down the hill today, my lady," he commented. "I am sorry I could not save you sooner to prevent it."

She truly had no idea what he was talking about. Her big brown eyes were a little lost as she gazed back at him.

"My lord?"

He tilted his chin in the direction of her cheek even as his eyes focused on the swollen area. "Your face," he clarified, somewhat softer. "You bruised it when you fell."

Her hand flew to her face and she lowered her gaze with uncertainty. "I...," she tried to move away from him, out from under his intense stare. "I am sorry if my appearance is unseemly, my lord."

He reached out and grabbed her wrist with a massive hand. Even without the gauntlets he usually wore, his hand was three times the size of hers. "You are hardly unseemly," he pulled her back towards him and dropped his hand when he was sure she wasn't going to try and move away again. "I would introduce you to the knights who are now in control of Nether. Good knights, this is Lady Chrystobel d'Einen, chatelaine of Nether Castle," he eyed the men around him somewhat awkwardly. "She is the future Lady de Poyer."

Wellesbourne was the first man to greet her. He did so politely. "My lady, Sir William Wellesbourne at your service."

Still embarrassed about her bruised cheek, it was a struggle for Chrystobel to acknowledge the big blond knight. He was handsome and with a very deep voice. The two shorter knights on Wellesbourne's other side came at her with the gentle force of a raging blizzard. They almost knocked her off her feet with their rush.

"I am Sir George Ashby-Kidd," George grabbed her hand before his brother could get to it. "And this is my dastardly brother, Sir Aimery. You should make all effort to stay away from him. He's a fool."

George grinned as he kissed her hand, while Aimery scowled at him and yanked her hand away before his brother could finish kissing it. Not to kiss the same place his brother had, he flipped her hand over and deposited a rather lingering kiss on the inside of her wrist.

"Sir Aimery Ashby-Kidd, my lady, your devoted servant," he said. "If there is anyone to watch out for, it is my brother. He has the tongue of a serpent."

Chrystobel was taken aback by the bold young knights and their idea of gallantry. Wellesbourne slapped Aimery on the back of the head and took the lady's hand away.

"Good God," he growled, pulling her away. "Idiots, both of you. Go sit down before you make complete jackasses of yourselves."

Keller watched as Wellesbourne took Chrystobel to the other side of the dais, politely seating her and making sure she had an adequate amount of wine. George and Aimery were caught up arguing with each other, leaping on the serving wench when she brought more wine and nearly knocking the woman to the ground. They tended to drink in excess and tonight was to be no exception. But Keller stood back, watching the scene before him, absorbing it. Wellesbourne was much more comfortable with women than he was and he observed the man as he made small talk with Chrystobel. Since William was already married to a woman he adored, Keller presumed, correctly, that Wellesbourne knew much more about conversing with women than he did. Keller would make sure to study his mannerisms and try to emulate them.

Keller's gaze was drawn to Chrystobel. She was an exquisite woman and his initial observation of her had not been wrong. Truth be told, as his interest in her grew, so did his intimidation. He was forty-one years old. She was barely twenty. She was young and beautiful and he began to think it rather tragic that she had been forced to marry an old man. But, on the other hand, he thought it a rather positive situation for him. Perhaps she was just what he needed after a love lost. Perhaps he should at least give her that chance. There could be nothing worse for the woman to be married to an old man whose heart was made of stone.

Taking a deep breath for courage, he made his way over to the dais and sat on the opposite side of Chrystobel. As the storm outside began to thunder and more men from his Corps wandered into the hall in preparation of supper, Keller poured himself a chalice of wine and sat silently as Wellesbourne told Chrystobel of a trip he and his wife took to Paris after they were married.

"I have only been as far as Aberystwyth," she told William. "I have spent my entire life at Nether."

William could see Keller's face on the other side of Chrystobel. "Perhaps your husband will take you to London and Paris someday," he said, glancing at the man. "It is a trip every young woman should make at least once in her life."

Chrystobel turned to Keller, looking at him for the first time at close range. His eyes were a very dark shade of blue. It was an interesting color she had never seen before. He had a long, straight nose and a granite-square jaw. But she could see up close that his skin was weathered and rough, a man who had seen much of the elements and hard times in his life. Still, it added a certain character to him. It was not unattractive in the least. She smiled faintly when he fixed on her with his intense blue eyes.

"If Sir Keller decides that I am worthy of a trip to London and Paris, I would indeed be honored," she said after a moment. "Certainly I would like to hear tale of any travels he has made also."

Keller gazed back at her porcelain face, feeling an odd thumping in his chest. He remembered that thumping, once, and it had led to heartbreak. He should have fought the sensation but found that he could not. In spite of his reservations, he rather liked it. The heart of stone was beginning to show cracks.

"If a wedding trip is your wish, then I am sure it can be arranged," he said. "As for my travels, I have been many places in the course of my duties."

"Do you have a favorite destination, my lord?" she asked politely.

He thought a moment, his eyes steady on her. "I saw lands devoid of green when I went to The Levant," he began. "Land with sand as far as the eye could see. And men with skin as black as tar. But it was warm there, far warmer than England or Wales."

Chrystobel's brown eyes widened. "You went on Richard's Crusade?"

He nodded, as if not at all impressed with himself. "I was with the king when he captured Cyprus," he said without a hint of pride in his tone. "I was in command of the first of four garrisons charged with holding the island for Richard and the French king, Philip Augustus. The island was a place of warm weather almost the entire year. I enjoyed it immensely."

Chrystobel was still lingering on the fact that he had gone on crusade with King Richard. She had never met anyone who had actually participated on the legendary crusade that ended five years earlier. He did not seem at all impressed with himself but she certainly was.

"Forgive me, my lord, if this is not an appropriate subject to speak of," she said respectfully. "But for a girl who has hardly ventured out of her home, I find the fact that you fought in the Holy Land fascinating. Could I beg you to tell me more stories of your adventures?"

Keller hadn't talked of his duty in The Levant since almost the day he had returned. He didn't like to talk about the friends he had lost or the struggles he had endured. They had been unimaginably brutal and difficult. But gazing into Chrystobel's eager face, he found that he could not deny her request.

"Well," he settled back with his wine, thinking a moment. More soldiers clamored into the hall and begin filling up the place with noise and stench, but he didn't notice. He was focused on Chrystobel's enthusiastic expression. "The first true battle I saw was outside of a city called Apollonia. It was the first time I saw camels."

Her eyebrows lifted. "Camels?"

He tried to outline the shape of the animal with his hands. " 'Tis a strange creature with humps on its back, long legs and big lips. The savages in the Holy Land even sleep with the beasts sometimes. They are treated like pets."

She was properly awed. "A camel," she repeated the odd name, listening to the sound of it. "Do you eat it?"

He shook his head. "No," he moved to pour himself more wine as he warmed to the conversation. "The savages ride them, milk them, even race them. They can go for months without drinking water, which is a good thing considering the land does not see rain for months at a time."

"Truly?" she was impressed with the animal's ability to go without water. "What does it eat?"

"Grass, grain," Keller looked around. "Speaking of eat, are we to be served? My men have been on the road since before dawn."

Chrystobel suddenly leapt up. "My apologies, my lord. I was so swept up in conversation that I... forgive me. I shall see to it immediately."

She fled as if the devil himself had just made a request of her. Both Keller and William watched her race off with some astonishment. Wellesbourne turned to Keller.

"What in the world did you say that would make her run like that?" he wondered out loud. "She was so...."

"Fearful," Keller said before William could finish. He thought on her odd reaction a moment before putting it out of his mind. Women, as he'd always known, were strange creatures. He didn't understand them. He downed a healthy swallow of wine, lingering thoughtfully over the rim. "So what do you think of the place?"

Wellesbourne turned his attention away from the spooked lady to the hall around them. "Impressive. But where is Nether's liege?"

Keller scratched his face and shrugged. "Who knows?" he had more wine. "The man did not greet us when we arrived. Unless he is dead or incapacitated, I am not sure what his excuse is."

"Do you suppose he's hiding?"

"Bad manners either way."

Wellesbourne pursed his lips. "No matter what deal The Marshal made with him, I still say we should be on our guard."

The sentence wasn't yet out of his mouth before they both began to hear a great commotion, rising in the distance like a storm. It wasn't long before everyone in the hall heard it also and the servants began to scatter. Keller and William turned in the direction of the hall entry, waiting for the storm to announce itself.

It wasn't long in coming.

CHAPTER FOUR

T HE ENTRY DOOR suddenly blew open and slammed back on its
hinges as a big man with blond hair and piercing brown eyes
entered the room, bellowing loudly for wine. The servants, already in a
panic, fell over themselves to fulfill his request. He slapped a woman
who handed him a half-empty goblet, insulted that it was not completely full. As another woman rushed forward to fill the cup, the man
continued across the floor towards the dais. His expression was both
curious and hostile as he eyed the strangers seated at his table.

Keller and William instinctively rose to their feet as the man approached. It was a bit of an odd standoff as the young man came to a
halt next to the table, his gaze openly inspecting the two knights. They
gazed back steadily in return. After a moment of intense dissection by
both parties, like dominant cocks preparing for a fight, the young man
finally removed his rain-soaked cloak and tossed it off to the nearest
cowering servant.

"I am Gryffyn d'Einen," he announced. "Who is de Poyer?"

Keller didn't like the man's manner or stance from the very second
he entered the hall. There was something arrogant and vain and dark
about him. Although handsome and tall, there was something about the
man that sang of distaste. Keller couldn't put his finger on it but he
could sense it. It put him on his guard.

"I am de Poyer," he replied. "Is Trevyn d'Einen your father?"

"He is."

"Where is he?"

Gryffyn cocked an arrogant eyebrow. "Indisposed at the moment," he sat down, eyeing the knights when they continued to stand. "Do you intend to eat standing up?"

Wellesbourne emitted something of a disapproving growl, looking to Keller for a reaction. Keller's only reaction was to slowly sit, his eyes riveted to the brash young man. Servants began falling all over themselves in an attempt to serve Gryffyn before anyone else.

"So," Gryffyn was the first one at the table to receive a meal in spite of the fact there were guests. "You are to be my sister's husband, are you not? Then there are things you should know about her. She is sassy and willful. She is also quite disobedient. I hope you are prepared to beat some sense into her."

The more Gryffyn talked, the more Keller didn't like him. "She has shown none of those qualities since we have become acquainted," he replied evenly. "But you, on the other hand, have so far displayed all of that and more."

Gryffyn stopped shoving bread into his mouth and frowned terribly. "What do you mean?" he demanded with his mouth full. "We have only just met."

Keller gazed steadily at the man. "Neither you nor your father were in the bailey to greet us when we arrived. That, my lord, is a serious breach of hospitality. We have been here over two hours and you've not shown your face until now. When you do, you slap the servants and show a complete lack of courtesy to your guests by eating before they have even been served. More than that, you slander your sister in front of a roomful of strangers. Does this clarify my statement?"

Gryffyn stopped chewing. His face was lined with outrage, his mouth pressed into a thin, hard line.

"You have little room to speak of bad manners serving a man who is a murderer and a thief," he snarled. "You are here because William Marshal wishes to conquer Wales, so you'll steal my lands and call it a treaty and rape my sister and call it a marriage. It is not I who have shown appalling manners but you and every man like you."

By this time, Wellesbourne was on his feet and seriously considering thrashing the young Welshman. George and Aimery had also heard the last part of Gryffyn's slanderous speech and were posturing furiously, awaiting the word to move forward and pounce. But Keller remained seated, his eyes fixed on the young man. He had no intention of moving a muscle.

"I wonder what is worse?" Keller ventured calmly. "The murdering thief who makes the offer or the man who knowingly accepts it? You are not penniless or destitute as the result of The Marshal's proposal. You made a deal with the Devil and are richer for it, so your protests are empty."

Gryffyn was so angry that he was pale. Like a predator sighting prey, his gaze narrowed dangerously at Keller, sizing him up. "I did not make a deal with William Marshal. My father did."

"But you will benefit, will you not? Lands in Wiltshire, as I recall."

Gryffyn's pale cheeks washed with a hint of color. "I want to take my sister with me when we go."

"Your sister stays."

Gryffyn's jaw flexed and his eyes widened with displeasure. Keller remained characteristically calm, expecting the next volley of insults.

"Why?" Gryffyn demanded. "She will be nothing but a whore to you."

"She will be my wife and the Lady of Nether. She stays."

Gryffyn wasn't used to having his wishes denied. He clenched his jaw, bared his teeth, and hurled his cup against the wall over Keller's head. Deep purple wine splashed on the walls, the cup clattered noisily to the floor, but Keller still refused to move. His gaze was fixed on Gryffyn, realizing the man would not move against him but it would not stop him from throwing a temper tantrum. In the brief conversation that they had, and in the few actions from Gryffyn, Keller realized he was dealing with a very spoiled, very petulant man. And that knowledge gave Keller the distinct advantage.

"You whoreskin," Gryffyn hissed. "I should throw you from Nether right now."

Keller fought to keep the grin off his face. He didn't know why, but he sincerely felt like laughing. "Make one move and I shall inform the Marshal. Your land grant will be rescinded and I will keep your castle anyway. You and your father will be penniless and homeless. Is this in any way unclear?"

Before Gryffyn could reply, Chrystobel entered the hall with several servants trailing after her bearing huge platters of food. She had been given no warning of what was transpiring in the hall and rushed straight to the table with a trencher in her hand. It was intended for Keller but she had to pass near her brother first and Gryffyn threw out a hand, toppling the trencher and spraying it all over his sister.

The action brought Keller to his feet. He vaulted over the table, grabbing Chrystobel before she could slip and fall onto her face in the mess of food that Gryffyn had created. Wellesbourne flew over the table and clobbered Gryffyn, hurling the man to the ground. As William and Gryffyn began throwing brutal punches, Keller picked up Chrystobel and swept her out of the combat zone. George and Aimery suddenly jumped into the fight and in little time, Gryffyn was barely conscious on the dirt floor of the great hall. William, George and Aimery had made short work of him.

Keller placed Chrystobel gently on the bench at the end of the table, far from the brawling knights. Covered with meat and gravy, her dark eyes were wide at the sight of her brother wallowing on the ground. George and Aimery got in a couple of good kicks to the belly before Wellesbourne pulled them off and turned them back to the table. William, in fact, didn't look any worse for the wear. He seemed rather jovial as he, too, turned back to the table and called for his meal. The serving wenches, still stunned from Gryffyn's beating, struggled to move past their shock and put the food on the table.

"Are you well?" Keller asked Chrystobel. "Did he injure you?"

She tore her gaze off Gryffyn, looking up at Keller with the widest eyes he had ever seen. "You...," she gasped, swallowing hard to collect herself. She put her hand to her throat as if holding herself together. "Your men struck him."

Keller's expression was like stone. "He could have seriously injured you. What he received was appropriate punishment."

Tears gathered in her eyes and Keller wasn't sure why. He'd never been very good at gauging women and was suddenly fearful he had done something to displease her.

"I apologize if swift justice has upset you," he wasn't sure what else to say. "Are you sure you are unharmed?"

She nodded, struggling not to weep as she watched her brother wallow on the ground. "I will go and retrieve your meal immediately."

She suddenly bolted up, moving swiftly across the room and disappeared through the door that led to the kitchens beyond. Keller stood there a moment, wondering why she again fled so swiftly and suspected he had failed to make a gracious impression upon his new bride by beating up her brother. No wonder the woman fled.

Just as he turned back to Gryffyn, now struggling to sit up, an older man and a very young woman entered the hall through the main door. The man was looking to Keller first, at a distance, but quickly beheld Gryffyn rolling about on the floor. His eyes widened.

"Gryffyn?" he looked both perplexed and oddly pleased. "What has happened?"

Keller intercepted the man before Gryffyn could reply. "Who are you?"

The man came to a stop, holding the hand of the young woman who, upon closer reflection, could not have been more than twelve or thirteen years of age. She was very small, blond, and quite lovely. Keller could see the resemblance between the young woman and his betrothed. He suspected the relationship before it was made clear.

"I am Trevyn d'Einen, Lord of Nether Castle," the man bowed shortly, suddenly looking stricken as he stood straight. "That is to say, I used to be the Lord of Nether. This is my youngest daughter, Lady Izlyn d'Einen."

Keller's gaze fell on the small woman. She was a delicate beauty, blond hair with big brown eyes, but not nearly the stunning beauty that her sister was. He couldn't help but notice she would not meet his eye. In fact, she looked terrified. He could see that she was trembling. Certainly the event of English at Nether was a frightening prospect, but it seemed to Keller that there was more to it. The girl appeared positively ill with fright and he knew he couldn't be all to blame for it. After a moment's inspection, Keller nodded faintly.

"I am Keller de Poyer," he said. "By decree of William Marshal with whom you have shared a bargain, I am now lord of Nether Castle and husband to your daughter, Chrystobel. Why were you not in the bailey to greet us upon our arrival?"

Keller had never been one for tact. He came straight to the point and woe to the recipient who did not appreciate his forthrightness. Trevyn looked rather shaken by the question, struggling to form an answer as Gryffyn bellowed from his position on the floor.

"He shall not behave as an obedient dog, greeting the master when he returns," he snarled, half-conscious.

"Gryffyn, please," Trevyn held out a hand to silence his son, looking to Keller with a mixture of apology and fear. "Forgive him, my lord. He is not himself today."

Keller didn't bother looking at Gryffyn. "From the behavior that your son has displayed since his entering the hall, I would say that he is exactly himself today," he replied, his dark eyes on the old man with the white hair. "You did not answer my question. Why did you not greet us upon our arrival?"

Trevyn seemed to pull the small girl beside him closer. "Because I was tending Izlyn, my lord. She is… is not feeling well this day."

Keller looked at the pale young girl as Gryffyn spouted off again. "I will punish you for releasing her from the vault, old man. She is a disobedient wench that must be taught a lesson. You did not have my permission to free her."

Izlyn's little face crumpled into tears and she buried her face in her father's tunic. Keller, disturbed by Gryffyn's ranting, turned to look at the man as he struggled to his feet.

"Am I to understand that you are speaking of this child?" he asked with puzzlement. He couldn't help it.

Gryffyn's balance was gone and he stood up only to list heavily to one side. He ended up seated on the nearest bench that flanked the great table.

"That is none of your affair," he growled. "She is my sister and I shall do with her as I please."

Keller had done an admirable job of keeping his temper even and his manner disinterested since his arrival. It was simply the way he was, in all things and especially in light of a new situation. But even he was starting to lose patience with a man he was coming to perceive as arrogant, brutal and dangerous. He faced Gryffyn fully and put his enormous hands on his hips.

"Answer me," he rumbled. "Did you put this child in the vault?"

Gryffyn refused to look at him. He saw a chalice over his right shoulder and decided that was more interesting. As he reached for it, Wellesbourne snatched it out of his reached and threw it against the wall. Wine sprayed on the wall as the cup clattered to the floor, the message obvious. Gryffyn bared his teeth at William, who simply lifted an eyebrow in reply. The test of wills was in full swing.

"She is a stubborn, disobedient wench and must be taught manners," Gryffyn whirled on Keller, snarling. "This not your house or hold, de Poyer. This family belongs to me and I will do with them as I see fit. You will not question me."

Keller's dark eyes glittered. "Nether Castle and all who reside within her became my holding a month ago when the treaty was signed," he found that it was a struggle to keep his temper down. "Your sisters, your father and you belong to me now and will do as I say. Is this is any way unclear?"

Gryffyn lurched to his feet, walking unsteadily towards the entry door. He waved an unsteady hand at Keller as if to block him out, moving past his father and sister, who stepped out of his way to give him a wide berth. They watched him stagger from the entrance like a drunken man.

Once outside, Gryffyn crossed paths with Chrystobel, who was emerging from the kitchens with another trencher for Keller. Furious, irrational, Gryffyn made his way towards his sister, who was completely unaware of the man's rage. He came upon her in such a manner that gave her little time to defend herself. One moment, she was preparing to deliver food and in the next, Gryffyn had her around the neck. Keller's second trencher fell into the mud. No one heard Chrystobel's cries as Gryffyn disappeared with her into the stables.

Back in the hall, the thick stone walls drowned out any noises from the bailey. With Gryffyn gone, Trevyn returned his focus to Keller.

"My apologies, my lord," he said, suddenly looking very old and very defeated. "Gryffyn is not indicative of every person at Nether. There are those of us who welcome you as an ally and would not show you such disrespect."

Keller studied the man a moment, trying to gauge both the man's character and sincerity. Being the garrison commander at Pembroke Castle for five years, he'd known his share of Welsh warlords. He knew how they thought and how, like the English, they could be deceptive. He would be on his guard.

"We shall see," he replied vaguely, changing subjects because he had nothing more to say about Gryffyn. "I sent a missive ahead of our arrival. Is the priest here?"

Trevyn nodded. "I am told he is in the kitchens eating his meal, my lord."

"Bring him to the hall. Your daughter and I will be married immediately to seal the treaty and be done with it."

The command sounded harsh coming from his lips. It was a business arrangement and would be treated as such. Trevyn sent a servant for the both the priest and Chrystobel. The priest was easily located but Chrystobel was not. She was found an hour later outside of the stables, sitting in the mud with her hands over her face.

CB

KELLER HAD BEEN standing in the doorway of Chrystobel's bower for the better part of a half hour. He stood just inside the door, his enormous arms crossed as he silently watched the activity surrounding his betrothed.

After William had found her in the mud by the stables, he had brought the dazed and bleeding woman to her bower. Young Izlyn tried her best to clean Chrystobel's face, wiping the blood away from her lip and cleaning off the mud, and servants dashed in and out of the chamber with hot water and linens in an effort to help. Trevyn had disappeared, as had Gryffyn, and the more Keller watched the activity, the more suspicious he became. People were smacked around, disappearing even, and generally terrified. The situation was odd and growing more odd, and he eventually reached his limit of patience.

He finally ordered the servants out with a brusque command, looking to George and Aimery, just outside the door on the landing, to ensure that his command was carried out. William was stalking the castle, looking for both Trevyn and Gryffyn. Most of the family seemed to have vanished the moment Chrystobel was discovered. Keller doubted it was coincidence. When the servants scattered like frightened chickens, herded from the chamber by the Ashby-Kidd twins, Keller closed the door behind them.

It was oddly and suddenly quiet from the commotion as he faced Chrystobel and her wide-eyed sister. Both ladies were sitting on the bed, looking up at Keller as if he were the devil himself and preparing to demand their souls. Keller regarded the frightened women for a moment, eventually closing the distance between them. His gaze never left Chrystobel's face. What he saw, and what he had observed initially, greatly disturbed him and he was attempting to determine how best to pursue the situation.

When he reached the bed, he sat down next to Chrystobel, his significant weight rocking the bed. Little Izlyn nearly slipped off, holding on to her sister for support. Silently, he held out a hand to Izlyn, who was still holding a rag and a small bowl of warm water. She looked at him with enormous eyes, having no idea what he meant, until he gently reached out and took the bowl from her. Collecting the rag, he dipped it into the warm water and carefully wiped away the blood from the cut on Chrystobel's lip.

Chrystobel sat stock-still as he wiped away the remnants of the mess and inspected her cut at close range. Her sister had done a good job of cleaning off the majority of the blood and dirt, so Keller eventually set the bowl and rag aside. When his focus returned to her, his dark eyes were intense.

"What happened?" he asked softly.

His voice was deep, raspy, and strangely soothing. Chrystobel didn't even know the man yet she sensed an innate gentleness from him, something buried deep and hidden. He had wiped her cut with the lightest of touches. A man with hands the size of his should not be so gentle or delicate. But he was. It was disarming, fascinating. Chrystobel met his gaze for a moment before averting her eyes.

"I… I slipped and fell, my lord," she lied.

"You slipped?"

"Aye, my lord."

"And fell on your face?"

"Aye, my lord."

He continued to gaze at her as she stared at the hands in her lap. She had the most glorious beauty, something he was more intrigued with by the moment. Her lashes were thick and feathery, sweeping against her cheeks when she blinked. He noted the bruise on her cheek, her split lip, and he even saw blood on her scalp. When he reached out to inspect the bloody spot on her blond hair, she flinched but he put a big hand on her arm to still her. Carefully, he inspected the split on her scalp. Then his eyes moved down to her ear and he could see a bit of dark blood in the canal. Inspecting further, he noticed that her neck was bruised.

Chrystobel couldn't see him but she could certainly feel and hear him. She could feel his eyes upon her, inspecting every inch of her, knowing she was lying about what had happened. She knew he would question her on it and she was terrified for that moment. Still, she had to stay strong. She could not let him know the truth. It was her shame alone to bear and she did not want her future husband judging her by such weaknesses, or by their dark family secrets.

She heard him sigh heavily. "Did you fall on your neck?" he asked quietly.

Chrystobel looked at him, confused and wary. "My… my lord?"

Keller lifted his chin in the direction of her neck. "Your neck is bruised."

Her hands flew to her neck nervously as if to hide what he had already seen. "I must have hit it somehow," she replied, her voice weak and soft. "I am sorry that my appearance has been so unsuitable. I will make all effort to make myself presentable."

Keller suddenly grasped her by the chin and forced her to look at him. When their eyes met, Chrystobel felt an exciting jolt, as if his eyes had somehow reached out to grab her. It was like a lightning strike, quickly come, quickly gone. Her breathing began to come in quick little gasps for reasons she could not understand.

"You will stop saying that," he growled softly. "You are not unseemly nor are you unsuitable. You are the loveliest woman I have had the fortune to lay eyes upon so I do not want to hear those words from your lips again. But I would know why you feel it necessary to lie to me."

She looked shocked, blinking rapidly and trying to pull away from him. But he would have no part of it. He grabbed her by the arms with those enormous hands and refused to let her move.

"I… I do not know what you mean," she lied again, hating herself for it but unwilling to divulge the truth.

"Aye, you do," he said calmly, watching her face flush pink. "Who did this to you? And do not tell me that you fell because I do not believe you."

Chrystobel's heart thumped painfully against her ribs, the strength from the man's grip both terrifying and thrilling her. She struggled to pull away, bumping into Izlyn in the process. The youngest d'Einen sibling burst into tears.

Keller looked at the young girl, concerned. "Why is she weeping?" he asked.

Chrystobel craned her neck back to look at her sister, watching the girl put her hands over her face. It was difficult to get a good look at her because Keller had her in an iron grip and she was unable to twist around sufficiently. She tried to pull from his grasp but it was impossible. The man had hands of steel.

"Izlyn?" she asked softly. "Why are you weeping, sweetheart?"

The young girl didn't answer her, bawling into her hands. Chrystobel turned back to Keller, her expression pleading.

"Please," she begged softly. "Let me comfort her. She is frightened."

"Of what?"

Chrystobel's lovely brow rippled. "Of... of you, my lord. She is easily frightened."

Keller gazed at her intently a moment longer before releasing her from his grasp. Chrystobel turned to her sister and put her arms around her, kissing her head.

"All is well, sweetheart," she said softly. "You need not be afraid."

The girl continued to cry and Chrystobel put her hands on the pretty young face, forcing Izlyn to look at her. She smiled encouragingly to the girl. "Look at me," she commanded gently. "See that I am unharmed? Sir Keller has not harmed me. All is well, I promise. Stop weeping."

Keller watched the exchange carefully. His detailed ear digested every sigh, every whisper, every expression and sound. He had spent his life reading people and attempting to deduce their thoughts. In his profession, it was mandatory if he wanted to live a long and healthy life. He was coming to see that there was something beneath the surface of this family that he was not being told. He could see it in their faces and in their actions. Although he was coming to suspect what it was, still, he wanted to hear the truth from their lips.

"What did I do to frighten her?" he asked quietly.

Chrystobel turned to look at him. "It is difficult to know," she said. "Izlyn is very delicate. She weeps often."

"Why?"

Chrystobel shrugged, looking back to her little sister. "It is the only way she can communicate. She cannot speak, so she weeps."

Keller watched as Chrystobel dried the last of her sister's tears. He could see in those small actions that she was a very compassionate and caring individual. He could feel his interest in her deepening, unable to resist.

"Was she born mute?" he asked.

Chrystobel shook her head. "Nay," she looked at him. "As a baby, I remember her speaking a few words. Then, when she was about two years old, she simply stopped speaking. She has not uttered a word since."

Keller didn't know why he was beginning to feel some strange emotional pull towards these women. He shouldn't have and he knew it. Perhaps it was because he would soon be related to them both or perhaps it was because they looked so pale and helpless at the moment. Perhaps it was because they now belonged to him, as did everything else at Nether. He watched them both with his intense dark eyes.

"Why did your brother put her in the vault?" he asked.

Chrystobel's head snapped to him as if startled by the question. She looked back to Izlyn, almost fearfully, struggling over an answer. She wasn't a particularly good liar and the truth, before she could stop it, came out in pieces.

"Because... because she will not speak to him," she almost choked over the words, horrified that they came out but unable to stop them. "It frustrates him and he punishes her for her disobedience."

Keller couldn't help it. His brows drew together and he looked at the pair as if they had gone mad.

"Because she does not *speak* to him?" he repeated, his tone bordering on incredulous. "Is this the truth?"

Chrystobel's gaze was on her sister. She could hear the outrage in Keller's tone, afraid it was directed at her. "Aye, my lord," she said, more hesitantly. "He feels that she is being stubborn and if he punishes her enough, then perhaps it will compel her to speak. He has told her that if she tells him that she does not wish to be put in the vault, he will not do it."

Keller stood up, his sheer size and massive presence causing Izlyn to collapse into her sister's embrace as the two sisters gazed up at him fearfully. His expression was calm although the dark eyes were glittering with something emotional, something deep. He began to pop his knuckles through his heavy leather gloves as if the process would help him think more clearly. It was obvious that he was pondering the situation. He looked from one fearful face to the other and back again.

"That will not happen again," he finally said. "It is apparent to me that Gryffyn d'Einen has wrought much distress upon this place and I do not appreciate nor respect men who wreak havoc simply for havoc's sake. Lady Chrystobel, I will ask you a question and you will be truthful. Did your brother put those bruises on your neck and was it he who split your lip?"

Chrystobel's eyes were wide with fright. She opened her mouth as if to reply, looking at her sister as she did so, and then suddenly shut her mouth. She didn't know Keller well enough to trust him with the truth. She was fearful of what would happen to her or to Izlyn should Gryffyn find out that she told of his foul deeds. At the moment, fear of her brother outweighed the fear of her new husband. Unable to look at Keller, she looked to her lap.

"I...," she began softly. "I am not sure...."

"The truth, lady."

He had interrupted her stammering and she grew flustered. "I… I do not remember," she whispered painfully, still looking at her lap. "I was walking across the bailey and… and perhaps I tripped. I do not remember."

Keller stared at her. He didn't like being lied to and since he wasn't any good when it came to communicating with women, it produced a bad combination in a situation like this. He couldn't decide whether he was furious or disappointed that she would not tell him the truth, which turned his demeanor to stone. His coldness was apparent. Reaching down, he took her hand in his massive gloved one and pulled her up from the bed.

"Come along, then," he muttered. "There is a priest in the hall waiting to perform the wedding sacrament."

He had her on her feet and Chrystobel visibly blanched. "But…," she stammered. "I am not appropriately dressed to receive the sacrament, my lord. At least allow me to change from these dirty clothes."

Keller's gaze moved over her body, noting the shapely figure beneath the surcoat. "God does not care how clean you are, my lady."

Horrified that he was not going to allow her to change into a clean frock and at least brush her hair, she grabbed Izlyn in a gesture of panic and perhaps comfort. Keller dragged both women from the chamber.

He realized, as he hit the bailey outside, that he was angry. Angry that the woman he was to marry would not give him the truth to a direct question. If she would not tell him the truth about a matter such as this, he couldn't imagine what else she would hide or lie to him about.

Perhaps he should not have believed her when she said she was chasing a wounded rabbit down the slopes of Nether. Perhaps she really had been running away. If she wanted a marriage in name only, then he would be happy to oblige her. It would save him from becoming emotionally invested in yet another woman who would break his carefully-protected heart.

CHAPTER FIVE

O F EVERYTHING CHRYSTOBEL had ever imagined her wedding to be, the actual experience was something quite different.

In the smoky, smelly hall of Nether, standing before a priest who smelled of urine and ale, she became Lady de Poyer. Izlyn clung to her during the mass and her father stood a few feet away with a rather sickened expression on his face. In fact, it made Chrystobel angry to see the expression on her father's face since the man had knowingly entered into the contract that would use her as a pawn in his deadly game of tactics with William Marshal. She didn't understand his visible show of remorse, late as it was, but it was of no matter. The wedding sacrament had been hastily, and sloppily, completed, and in short order Sir Keller became her husband.

Still in her muddied and bloodied dress, she'd turned a chaste cheek to Keller at the conclusion of the final blessing and he had deposited a swift kiss upon it to seal their marriage. It had been such a cold kiss, with no warmth about it, but Chrystobel hadn't expected anything less. The man who had dragged her from her bower in her dirty clothes had not been warm in the least. He had been business-like and abrupt, and with those small gestures, he had set the tone for their marriage. Try as she might to maintain a pragmatic attitude, her heart sank at the thought. She had hoped there would be some fondness between them, however small.

She didn't blame de Poyer, however. He had asked for the truth about her injuries and she had lied to him. Worse yet, he had known it. She could tell by the expression on his face. Nay, she didn't expect anything from him but coldness and indifference. In truth, it was all she was worth. She felt sorry for the man, gaining a wife who wasn't much of a prize. But he'd acquired a castle and property in the process, so she hoped that would make up for a worthless spouse.

As she stood there with Izlyn pressed against her and pondered her uncertain future, she watched Keller as the man dismissed the priest. Paying a few coins to the man, he then called his knights to him and they huddled in a private conference. There was something intriguing about the man she had just married, in spite of his coldness, and she watched his profile, strong and proud, as he spoke with his men. He was calm and relaxed for the most part but she could tell by his expression that the subject upon which he spoke was serious indeed. Wellesbourne and the Ashby-Kidd twins were serious, too, and Chrystobel wondered what had them looking so grim, which seemed rather odd in the wake of a wedding. When Keller's knights quickly disbursed and went along their way, they all seemed to have the look of a hunter about them. The mode was professional and the eyes were steely. They were hunting for something, or someone, and a hunch told her that it might be Gryffyn.

Her brother hadn't been present at the wedding and Chrystobel was grateful for small mercies because had he come, surely it wouldn't have been the sedate ceremony she had experienced. It would have been one of apprehension and anger. Still, he was somewhere on the grounds, plotting his next move no doubt, and Chrystobel was certain that her new husband wished to know the man's whereabouts.

When de Poyer approached Trevyn and asked if he knew both the location and intentions of his son, Chrystobel watched her father lie to the man, bold-faced. Trevyn indeed knew his son's location and more than likely of his intentions, but he wasn't going to tell the English knight. Whether it was to protect Gryffyn or protect Keller, Chrystobel couldn't tell. Sometimes her father had rather conflicting loyalties, as exampled by this wedding, and he both hated and loved his son. Trevyn was a torn man inside and there were times when Chrystobel tried not to hate him for it. Their family, in general, was in turmoil.

As Chrystobel mulled over her father's allegiances, she was somewhat startled when Keller suddenly broke away from the man and headed in her direction. Trevyn trailed after the English commander as they approached her.

"It is time to retire for the night, my lady," Keller said in an indifferent tone. "Bid your father and sister a good sleep so that we can be on our way."

Chrystobel struggled not to show her apprehension. *It is time to retire.* God's Bones, she knew what that meant, but it was imperative that she not display any hint of anxiety in the presence of her brittle sister, so she hugged the girl tightly, kissed her on the forehead, and passed her over to her father. Izlyn didn't go easily, however, and Chrystobel spent several minutes convincing the girl that all would be well and that she would see her in the morning. Izlyn, fearful to be away from the only mother she had ever known and fearful for the terrible world in general, was in tears.

Chrystobel could feel Keller standing beside her, the heavy weight of his gaze as he observed the situation. She thought she felt his disapproval but she could not be entirely sure. In fact, she wasn't sure about anything and she struggled to keep an even head about her. The past few hours had been very disorienting in many ways. As she made sure her father had hold of Izlyn, she turned to Keller.

"When you arrived, I instructed the servants to clean out my father's chamber of his possessions," she said. "I hope it is prepared to your liking."

Keller's emotionless gaze was upon her. "Then they should move your things into it, since you and I will be sharing it," he told her. "Did you instruct them to do that as well?"

Chrystobel shook her head unsteadily. "Nay, my lord," she replied.

"I did not know that I would be a married woman by this evening."

"Then mayhap we should retire to your chamber for the night," he said. "Mayhap you would be more comfortable there until we can arrange the master's chamber to accommodate the both of us."

Chrystobel wasn't sure what to say so she nodded hesitantly. "If that is your wish, my lord."

Keller politely reached out to take her by the elbow and began pulling her towards the door. Chrystobel was stiff, and uneasy, but she didn't resist. As she had initially observed, he had very big hands, anyway, so she doubted she could have resisted in any case. He simply would have overwhelmed her and dragged her to the door. She fell into step beside him, her thoughts inevitably wandering to what the evening would bring. It was difficult not to feel a swamping sense of embarrassment and anxiety, and as she struggled against it, Keller spoke.

"Mayhap you will tell me something of this castle as we make our way to the keep," he said, his manner still rather cold. "I did not see much of it upon my arrival, in truth. I went from the bailey to this hall, and other than being in the keep earlier, I've not seen much of that which is now mine."

Chrystobel paused as Keller pulled open the heavy oak and iron panel. "I would be pleased, my lord," she said, hoping that he might forgive her lies to him earlier if they were to share a pleasant conversation. They had yet to truly have one, but more than that, her nervousness loosened her tongue. "Would you like for my father to accompany us? He knows more of the castle's defenses than I do. I am sure you are very interested in those and I cannot tell you anything about them."

Keller cast her a glance, his intense gaze piercing her soul as he peered down his nose at her. "I will speak with your father another time," he said. "I would rather not have a chaperone on my wedding night."

Chrystobel flushed a dull red, lowering her head as they moved out into the gentle night beyond. It was cold but not unbearable, and she was thankful for the darkness, covering the heat of her cheeks. His comment seemed most forward, bold even, but realizing he was her husband, she rationalized that he could say whatever he wanted to her. It was his right. This cold English knight was now her family, as strange as that thought seemed. Taking a deep breath, she began to point out some of the areas of interest around the bailey.

"Nether Castle was built more than one hundred years ago by the kings of Arwystu," she said. "It was not built of wood as most were back then, but of the great stone you will see on the hills to the east. The fortress was built with the intention of watching their northern neighbors, the Cefeliog. The original name was *Annwyn*, which means the Otherworld or the place where spirits dwell. Living here as we do, we are somewhat isolated and sometimes it does indeed feel as if we are in the Otherworld. The lands in this region are mysterious and full of magic. But it was the Normans who gave the castle the name that you know it by – Nether."

Keller was listening to her story with interest. More than that, he was particularly interested in her honeyed voice. She had a delicate timber with a slight lisp, which he found charming. He was quickly coming to realize that he liked to hear her speak in gentle dulcet tones. He'd known it from the beginning but now it was coming to have more impact. The walls he had built up around himself, or at least tried to, since the woman had lied about her injuries were inevitably crumbling. It was evident that he couldn't maintain his indifference to her for long. There was something about her that softened him whether or not he wanted to.

"Then you do not call the castle Nether?" he asked. "What do you call it?"

Chrystobel shook her head. "We do indeed call it Nether Castle," she said. "My grandfather called it by that name and so do we."

Keller's gaze was thoughtfully on his feet as they crossed the middle of the muddy bailey. "Nether means far away or well behind," he said, glancing up to the tall, imposing walls that enclosed them. "This place is indeed far removed from most civilization. I understand why the Normans who first came to Wales gave it that name."

Chrystobel glanced up at him, seeing that the man was still looking thoughtfully at his feet. She couldn't tell if his cold mood was easing but she continued nonetheless. "When you arrived, you passed over a drawbridge that covers our moat," she said, then cocked her head thoughtfully. "It is really more of a pit than a moat, and it bears the name the Gorge of the Dead because back when the castle was first built, bodies of enemies were tossed in it. They were left there to rot."

Keller wriggled his eyebrows in an understanding gesture. "It makes perfect sense, then, to call it the Gorge of the Dead," he said. "Go on."

Chrystobel did. "You have already been in the keep, which has six big rooms to it," she went on, pointing at the big, square structure looming in front of them. "There are three floors to it and two rooms to each floor. We also have three big towers, as I am sure you have noticed."

Keller came to a halt and Chrystobel along with him. He paused to look at the three enormous towers that were built into the southeast, southwest, and northwest corners of the curtain wall. The towers were nearly as large as the keep itself, "D" shaped in structure, and built from the same dark-veined, gray stone that comprised the rest of the castle.

"These towers could be seen from miles away," he said. "When we were approaching from the valley to the south, they were the first things we saw."

Chrystobel nodded as she pointed to the southeast tower. "That is Tower Twilight," she said. "It is houses the married soldiers and servants. The tower next to it, the southwest tower, is called Tower Night and it houses the armor and weapons. The northeast tower is Tower Day, and it houses our unmarried men or any visitors we may have. Your men will be housed there."

Keller turned to look at her. "I have five hundred men with me and as big as that tower is, it will not be able to house all of them," he said. "My knights will be rearranging the accommodations to suit us. I would assume your people have been told to cooperate."

Chrystobel wasn't so sure she liked that statement. It sounded as if the Welsh occupants were beneath the English who were here to take control. But the truth was that they *were* beneath the English. Nether belonged to them now, and everyone within her, including Chrystobel. She nodded in response to his statement.

"Aye, my lord," she said. "They will be compliant."

Keller's eyes glittered at her in the weak moonlight. "Including you?"

"It is my duty to be compliant."

"You were not earlier."

"What do you mean?"

"When I asked you who had left you bloodied. You lied to me."

Chrystobel abruptly lowered her gaze, her manner suddenly nervous. She had been quite calm until Keller brought up the incident in her bower. Now, she didn't know what to say. She had sincerely hoped that subject wouldn't come up but Keller had cleverly introduced it into their conversation. Off-guard, his sly action both irritated and embarrassed her. She didn't like being embarrassed.

"It is not polite to accuse a lady of lying," she told him with more boldness than she had exhibited since their introduction. "A man of courtesy and tact would not question a lady's answer in any fashion."

Even as she said it, she cringed. It was an instinctive reaction, waiting for a hand to come flying out at her. That was what usually happened when she showed any amount of insolence, at least when Gryffyn was around. The flinching reaction was drilled into her brain, the result of too many slaps from a man who was full of them.

But Keller didn't react as Gryffyn often did. In fact, he did exactly the opposite. He stared at her a moment as if surprised by her response before actually cracking a smile.

"I have never been a tactful man but I have been known to be a courteous one," he said as he popped his knuckles in a fidgeting gesture. "I should not have called you a liar."

"How would *you* have reacted had someone called you a liar?"

"Not very well, to be sure. You were far more gracious in the face of slander than I would have been."

Chrystobel eyed him, curious at his change in manner, especially the knuckle-popping. Suddenly, he didn't look like the cold, imposing English knight. Now, there was a measure of humanity to him, a real man with human ticks. His guard, somehow, had gone down with the course of the conversation and it was an unexpected twist. Her gaze lingered on him.

"In fairness," she said, "I supposed it was a natural question, but it was still rude of you to dispute my reply."

Keller conceded the fact. "Indeed it was," he said. "You told me that your injuries occurred when you fell and I should have accepted that."

"It would have been the polite thing to do."

A smile played on his lips. "You are correct. I apologize for calling you a liar."

The man has a handsome smile, she thought. He had big white teeth and massive dimples in each cheek, carving big ruts through his face. More than that, she noticed that rather than rise to a verbal confrontation, he seemed to back down, to ease up his cold and stiff manner. It was a startling realization, as if the man didn't want to upset her with a combative conversation. In what world was it possible that the man would be respectful enough not to argue with her? She wondered.

"I accept your apology," she said, noting that his dusky eyes were still glimmering at her. It was a warm glimmer. "But in the future, should I give you an answer, I would like to have the courtesy of not being called a liar."

"As you wish," he said. "But may I ask a question?"

"You may."

"Will you tell me what really happened?"

Chrystobel gazed at him steadily. In truth, she was debating what to tell him. He had just apologized for calling her a liar even though she was. Still, there were secrets at Nether, dark and terrible secrets that she was embarrassed to admit to a man she'd only known a few hours. Even if the man *was* her husband. After a few moments of looking into his dusky eyes, all-knowing eyes that most certainly saw through her feeble attempt at avoiding the truth, she averted her gaze. She simply wasn't brave enough to look him in the eye whilst she lied to him again. He was asking for the truth and she hadn't the courage to tell him.

"It was of no consequence," she murmured. "I am well enough and that is all you should be concerned with. Now, what more would you like to know about Nether that I can tell you? Would you like to know about our herds of sheep? We have several large herds. They graze to the north of the castle, upon the slopes of the Cemmae mountains. The herds are our primary source of income and are so well regarded that our soldiers stand guard over the flocks in the fields."

Keller was well aware that she was shifting the subject. It was very clear that she didn't wish to discuss her injuries. Twice he had asked her and twice she had avoided giving him an answer. That same sense of self-protection that kept him bottled up and cold threatened to overshadow the conversation at her refusal to answer his question but he fought it. Perhaps she had her reasons for not divulging the truth even though Keller suspected what the truth was. That loud, obnoxious, rude brother had everything to do with it, he was certain. But for some reason she was protecting him.

But in hindsight, he understood why. The English were the enemy in her eyes, even an English husband. She had been taught not to trust them and he could see that it was going to be difficult to convince her otherwise. She had to learn that he was far more trustworthy than her boorish brother, but something like that would take time and he was impatient. With a sigh, one that conveyed his displeasure in her evasive answer, he nonetheless followed her lead. She wished to discuss sheep. He would allow her the privilege of turning the conversation.

"Come tomorrow, I will post my own men on the herds," he told her. "If they are truly that valuable, then I do not need your father's men absconding with them simply to keep them out of my reach. I will place my assets under my control."

Chrystobel wasn't surprised at the answer but she struggled not to become offended by it. "My father's men are trustworthy, I assure you," she said. "They would not steal the sheep."

He looked at her, that hard edge returning to his eyes. "Your father's men are loyal to him and, consequently, to Wales," he said. "I mean no offense when I say I would rather have Nether's assets, all of them, under my control. It is the prudent thing to do."

Chrystobel didn't argue the point, suspecting he was more than likely right, especially with Gryffyn so resistant to the situation in general. She knew that his disquiet had upset her father's men. They had been upset since the day they had been told that soon they would have English overlords. Perhaps Keller was more astute to the mindset of Nether's men than she gave him credit for. He was a knight, after all, and a seasoned one. He knew better than she did in matters of war and rebellion. She was about to reply to his statement when a shout from the Tower Twilight caught their attention.

Keller and Chrystobel turned to see Aimery make his way towards them. The young knight was running, his mail making grating sounds as he moved. It echoed oddly off the cold stone walls surrounding them. He slowed when he came upon them, kicking up mud from his dirty boots. The mud landed on Chrystobel's skirt.

"My lord," Aimery was breathless as he addressed Keller. "Someone has made an attempt on my brother's life. You must come."

Keller had Chrystobel by the arm as he began to follow Aimery across the ward in the direction of the great shadowed Tower Twilight. It made for a massive silhouette against the star-strewn sky.

"What happened?" he demanded.

Aimery was visibly upset but trying not to show it. "We were patrolling the grounds as you had ordered," he said, turning to look at Keller even as he led the way. "It was a crossbow. The arrow caught my brother in the arm."

Keller should have been pleased to hear that the damage wasn't worse, but all he could manage to feel was rage at a coward who would hide in the shadows and shoot arrows at the English knights.

"Is he badly injured?" he asked.

"Nay, my lord."

"Where did the projectile come from?"

"The wall, my lord."

Keller glanced up at the parapets where men with torches patrolled the night. "Where is William?"

"He is with my brother now."

Keller didn't ask any more questions. *And so it comes*, he thought to himself. *The Welsh welcomes are beginning.* As they neared the entry, which was also part of the great curtain wall, he could see Wellesbourne and George standing at the darkened opening. A great smell of dampness filled the air, as if someone had opened a tomb. As Keller approached, he realized that the smell was coming from the tower itself. It smelled like death. He fixed on George.

"Why are you standing here?" he nearly barked. "I thought you were injured?"

George was holding his left arm, bent, against his chest. He looked rather pale, even in the shadows. "I am well enough, my lord," he assured Keller. "It is just a flesh wound."

Keller stared at the young knight a moment before turning to William. As soon as he looked at the man, the knight held up the offending arrow in his right hand.

"He is correctly, mostly," he said. "It buried itself, but not deeply enough to damage anything. I was able to easily remove it."

Keller took the arrow from William and examined the tip. He held it up somewhat so it could catch what little light there was. After a moment, he glanced at William.

"Bodkin tipped," he muttered, referring to the broad triangle shape. "Only a man of wealth would have launched this. Men of lesser means would have simply used a sharpened stick without the metal tip."

William nodded, his eyes perusing the complex. "Agreed," he said.

His gaze finally came to rest on Chrystobel, standing next to Keller. She was looking rather shocked by the event and William focused intently on her. "What would you know of archers and errant arrows, my lady? How many archers does your father employ at night?"

Chrystobel was instantly on the defensive. "My father does not have archers upon the wall at night."

"Yet someone shot this arrow into young George's arm," William said steadily. "That arrow is from a fine and expensive quiver, as evidenced by the metal tip and the goose feather fletchings. A man of some wealth owned this arrow."

By this time, Chrystobel was gazing at the man as if he were, indeed, the enemy. He was interrogating her as if she was certainly his enemy and her resentment grew.

"I do not know anything about arrows or fletchings," she said. "My father has twenty archers and all of them are fairly well armed but they do not stand watch at night."

William could see that she was frightened but he didn't back down. "Does your brother own a crossbow?"

"I do not know what my brother owns and I do not care."

She was shaken and angry with her reply. William's gaze lingered on her a moment before turning to Keller. "Mayhap we should find out what the man owns."

Keller had been watching the exchange with his usual intense focus. He didn't miss a sign or a twitch throughout the exchange and he was fairly convinced that his new wife was truthful when she said she knew nothing of the attack. But that didn't solve the mystery of their attacker and Keller knew it was time to show his might. If he did not answer this incident strongly, then it could be perceived as weakness. He still had Chrystobel by the arm as he spoke to Wellesbourne.

"Roust the castle," he said. "I want every man, woman, and child brought to the bailey and placed under guard. Clean this castle out, Will. Is that clear?"

William was already nodding firmly, snapping his fingers to the

Ashby-Kidd twins. "Summon the men," he commanded softly. "Have the sergeants break them into groups of ten or more. I will take a group into the keep and you two take the towers. If anyone resists, kill them."

Chrystobel gasped but the English knights didn't dispute the harsh order, nor did they particularly react to the command other than to follow it. An attack had been made against them and they had to show that such attempts would be harshly met. As William, George, and Aimery charged off, Keller turned for the keep and pulled Chrystobel along with him.

"Does that order go for me as well?" she asked fearfully as he dragged her along. "I was truthful when I told you that I did not know about my brother. I do not know if he owns a crossbow."

Keller didn't look at her. He was scanning the walls for another arrow that might try to strike him as well.

"I believe you," he said. "But we must get under cover. If someone is aiming for English knights, they might accidently hit you if they are aiming for me."

Chrystobel yelped, instinctively flinched and ducking her head down as she skipped along beside him. By the time they reached the keep, they were practically running. Chrystobel raced up the exterior stairs and bolted in through the door, followed by Keller, both of them swallowed up by the dark innards of the great stone structure. Before they could take the stairs, however, Chrystobel turned to him.

"What about my sister?" she asked anxiously. "Must she be held under guard out in the bailey like a common criminal?"

Keller shook his head. "Nay," he replied. "I will have her brought to you. You two may remain together, in your chamber, until we sort this through."

"But what about my father?"

"I will question him personally."

Although still apprehensive, Chrystobel was satisfied by his answers enough so that she willingly took the narrow stairs to the next level where her bower was. Keller followed her into the chamber, one he had been in a scant hour before. The bed was still messy and the bowl of water and linen rag that Izlyn had been using to tend her sister's bloodied mouth were still on the table.

Keller looked around the room, noting the small size of the bed. He couldn't help but think that it would make consummating their marriage a bit tricky, for he wasn't entirely sure they could both fit on the bed side by side. He might have to spend all night lying on top of her, which wasn't an entirely terrible thought. A soft body against his rough flesh was something he'd not felt in years. The mere thought was enough to cause him to break into a sweat.

But he shook those visions from his mind, as tempting as they were, to focus on the moment at hand. Chrystobel was over by the hearth now, stoking it, to ward off the chill of the room.

"My lady," Keller said, meeting her gaze when she turned to look at him. "I asked you a question today, twice, which you refused to answer, but hear me now: I will ask you this question and you will not avoid it. You will not lie to me, either. I expect nothing less than total truth from you or we will have a very difficult relationship from this moment forward. Is this in any way unclear to you?"

Chrystobel was looking at him with a mixture of fear and dread. "It is clear, my lord."

Keller's gaze lingered on her. "Very well," he said after a moment. "You will tell me if you believe your brother is behind the arrow that injured my knight."

Chrystobel hesitated. "If you are asking me if I believe him capable of such a thing, then the answer is yes," she replied. "He is indeed capable of the action."

"Do you believe he did it?"

She shrugged unsteadily. "That is difficult to say," she said carefully, not wanting to anger or provoke him. "He might have had someone else do it for him. At times, Gryffyn likes to bully others into carrying out his unsavory tasks. Other times, he will simply do it himself. It mostly depends on what kind of mood he is in."

"Does he have men at Nether who serve him directly?"

Chrystobel shook her head. Somehow, she didn't feel much like defending her brother against this latest onslaught. If she did, it would go badly for her, she could tell. She struggled not to think herself a traitor for divulging what she could.

"He does not have men who serve him directly, but there are men who will only listen to him," she said quietly. "There are at least six of them – Dewey, Glyn, Owain, Hwyel, Moeig, and Meustyn. They are soldiers, not knights, and they will do my brother's bidding without hesitation."

"Where are these men now?"

"More than likely in Tower Day in their quarters."

Keller was somewhat pleased that she was being forthcoming with information about her brother even though the sensible part of him, the professional knight, told him not to trust her completely. They were still, in many ways, enemies and although he didn't believe she would deliberately mislead him, it would be prudent of him to at least be somewhat cautious of her information.

"Does your father have any knights?" he asked.

"Two," she replied. "Older men. They will not be much trouble to you."

"What are their names?"

"Sir Wynne and Sir Rhun."

"And where are they?"

She shrugged. "More than likely in bed," she said. "They are old, as I mentioned, and tend to retire at sunset. You would find them in Tower Twilight."

Keller digested the information. It was the most forthcoming and talkative she had been since their introduction. He still couldn't decide how much to trust or believe her, but at this point he was willing to take a little on faith. He had little choice.

"I thank you for conveying your knowledge," he finally said. "Now you will tell me where you think your brother is. A lair where he would hide, mayhap?"

Chrystobel nodded. "The top level of Tower Twilight," she said. "It is his private domain."

"Tower Twilight is where George was injured."

"I know."

Keller's gaze lingered on her a moment but she met his eyes without reserve. It gave him more confidence, knowing that liars usually had difficulty making eye contact. She had not looked him in the eye when she had given him the weak explanation of her injuries earlier. That fact alone told him that, this time, she was telling the truth. He was quickly coming to see that his wife could not easily lie, which was something of a relief. With a nod of his head, to thank her for her truthfulness, he turned for the door.

"Remain here," he told her. "Do not leave this room for any reason. Is that clear?"

"It is, my lord."

"I will return your sister to you."

"My thanks, my lord." Keller was nearly through the door when she called out to him. "My lord?"

He paused to look at her. "Aye?"

Chrystobel appeared nervous, uncertain. She made her way towards him in slow, halting steps, as if fearful to speak. But she forced the words out.

"You...," she began, swallowed, and then started once more. "You will not tell my brother that I told you where you might find him, will you?"

Something just short of rage pulsed through Keller and he came back into the chamber, closing the door behind him. "Why would you ask that?"

Chrystobel struggled not to look away from his piercing gaze, suddenly regretful that she had said anything at all. Now, surely, he would begin to suspect things. "Because," she stammered. "Because... he would become very angry and take his anger out on those around him."

Keller cocked an eyebrow. "You?"

She couldn't help it now. He was shooting bolts of fire out of those dusky eyes so she looked at the ground. "Anyone," she said softly.

Keller walked over to her and put the fingers of his right hand under her chin, forcing her head up. He forced her to look at him, staring into her eyes with his searing and intense gaze. The bolts of fire were growing more intense.

"*You?*" he demanded in a whisper.

There was something so heated and liquid about his gaze, fire bolts reaching in to grab whatever soul and heart she had inside of her, yanking them out and holding them with gentle power and molten fire. She could see everything inside of her now hovering in the air between them as clearly as if he were holding all of it in both hands. She could see fear and vulnerability and interest, interest in him as both a man and as her husband. He must surely have sensed it. It was as if she no longer had any control over her mind, her free will vanishing within the power of his dark blue gaze. After a moment, she could only nod helplessly.

"It is possible."

She spoke the words so softly that he barely heard her, but hear he did. Fury such as he had never known boiled up within Keller to the point that it was actually making him sweat. He'd known all along that it had been Gryffyn attacking Chrystobel, but to hear the confirmation, as vague as it was, nearly drove him insane. No man was going to take his fists to a woman, and most especially not his wife, and live to tell the tale. He dropped his hand from her chin and grabbed her by the arms, nearly crushing her as he fought off the innate sense of disgust.

"No more," he hissed. "Do you hear me? It will never again happen. I will find your brother and I will make that abundantly clear to him."

He was speaking through clenched teeth, frightening her, and Chrystobel's eyes filled with tears.

"Nay," she whispered. "You must not. He will vent his rage on Izlyn and my father. You must not challenge Gryffyn!"

Keller watched tears spill down her cheeks. He could literally feel the fear from the woman. He realized that he wanted very much to comfort her, perhaps draw her against him, hugging her and initiating that comforting human contact to convey both his sympathy and his sorrow for her plight. But somehow, he couldn't do it. The last woman he comforted had put his heart beneath her shoe and crushed it. Nay, he wasn't ready to hold Chrystobel yet, to feel her warm body against his. He seriously wondered if he ever would be. With a heavy sigh, he dropped his hands, hating Gryffyn d'Einen more with every breath he took.

"Not only will I challenge him, but I will win," he said. "You need no longer fear for your sister or father, Lady de Poyer. You are my wife now and your family is now under my protection. Your brother's reign of terror is over."

With that, he turned on his heel and quit the chamber, leaving Chrystobel struggling not to sob. Was it possible it was true? Was it possible the English knight would actually become their savior and end their terror once and for all?

She was about to find out.

CHAPTER SIX

N OT SURPRISINGLY, THE inhabitants of Nether Castle did not easily obey the English orders to muster in the bailey. In fact, they had a fight on their hands with some of the soldiers. Keller and his men had to strip them of their weapons, forcing them out into the bitterly cold night with nothing to defend themselves with. Like conquered men, they were unhappy and uneasy.

The servants, however, showed no resistance and collected in a frightened huddle near the kitchen yard as the rebellious soldiers were corralled into several groups in the bailey. Keller didn't want them to be all in one bunch because there was strength in numbers should they decide to rebel. Therefore, there were six separate groups of men, all of them sitting in the mud with their hands on their head. Five hundred English soldiers against less than three hundred Welsh was no match at all. Nether was subdued.

But Gryffyn was not among the subjugated. Keller had managed to locate the six men that Chrystobel had named as Gryffyn's henchmen, and he had also located the two old knights, who were treated better than anyone else and allowed to stand rather than sit. They showed absolutely no resistance and Keller showed them a measure of respect for that behavior. But Gryffyn was nowhere to be found and as William held the Welsh hostage in the bailey, Keller took George, Aimery, and one hundred of his men in a feverish search of the castle. He was determined to find Gryffyn if he had to take the castle apart stone by stone.

It made for a loud and hectic search. Doors banged and men shouted. As Keller and his men tore through Nether's towers, Chrystobel and Izlyn sat in Chrystobel's bower, listening to the commotion. Izlyn had been brought up to Chrystobel before the bedlam started, a scared little girl needing the comfort of her elder sister. William had delivered the child and he was polite to Chrystobel but not overly friendly. She was coming to suspect that he didn't trust her because she had denied knowing anything about the arrow. Even though she'd told the truth, his behavior had upset her, but she wouldn't dwell on it. She had Izlyn to focus on now, and focus she did.

They could hear the shouts and cries floating in through the three big lancet windows in the chamber, and Chrystobel eventually secured the oil cloth drapes to help block out the noise as well as the chilling temperature. The hearth was blazing brightly, the chamber warm and inviting, and Chrystobel washed both her and her sister with water scented with violets, washing away the mud and cares of the day.

The violets had come from a garden that Chrystobel and Izlyn tended, creating pleasant memories in a world that had little, and they grew flowers and herbs in the rocky, and very moist, soil. While the cooks and kitchen servants tended the vegetable garden in the kitchen yard, Chrystobel's walled garden was near the north side of the keep and consisted exclusively of flowering plants, herbs, and two apple trees that produced tiny but tasty apples. It had been her mother's garden long ago and it was something the girls continued to tend. More than a garden, it was a haven of joy for them, a light in their darkened world.

Over the years, the garden had collected a variety of rose plants, lilies, violets, basil, and great bushes of rosemary. Chrystobel's mother, Lady Elyn, had managed to cultivate lavender, even in the cold climate and rocky soil, and the bushes grew big and wild with well-established roots. The lavender oil was precious and used in soaps, oils, and medicines, and the garden itself was almost as prized as the sheep that provided Nether with its income and stability.

The scent of violets was heavy in the air as Chrystobel and Izlyn finished bathing and dressed in heavy sleeping shifts. Chrystobel braided her sister's hair and finally put the girl to bed, covering her up with fluffy coverlets. As the child slept dreamlessly, Chrystobel sat by the hearth in a chair made of oak, with curved rails along the bottom so that it rocked gently, and gazed pensively into the fire. Now that the day had calmed and she and Izlyn were both safe and warm, her thoughts drifted to the man she had married.

Keller de Poyer. The English knight was now her husband. She kept seeing his dusky blue eyes and strong features, rolling them over in her mind. Up until six months ago, she'd had no knowledge of the man and, in fact, had been accepting gifts from the local chieftain, Colvyn ap Gwynwynwyn, a bastard grandson of the last man who claimed the Powys throne. It was perhaps assumed that she would marry Colvyn, even though the man was known to have an entire stable of lovers, and she didn't particularly find the man attractive or even interesting. He was short, dark, and rugged, and saw a wife as merely another possession. He'd as much as told her that. She wondered if de Poyer saw her as just another possession, too, just like Nether Castle.

It was hard to know someone after only having been acquainted with him for a few hours, but in that time she had seen that Keller was vastly intelligent, wise, and rather stiff. Aye, he was indeed stiff, as if he didn't know how to smile or enjoy himself. She'd seen him crack a smile, briefly, and it was a very handsome gesture. But then the smile had vanished and he was back to his stiff, intimidating self. It was quite clear that the man had an emotional wall around him, a wall that protected the soul beneath. She wondered if the wall was so strong because it was protecting something very soft and delicate. There had been moments, briefly, where she had seen something in the depths of those dusky eyes that bespoke of all things untold and vulnerable. It seemed strange to think of the powerful English knight as vulnerable.

As she sat by the fire and pondered the character of her new husband, there was a knock on the chamber door. Before she could rise and open it, the panel flew open and Gryffyn appeared. He blew into the chamber, slamming the door behind him and bolting it. Chrystobel was so startled that she leapt out of her chair and, tripping over the leg, ended up on the floor. Gryffyn hardly noticed, however. He raced past her and carefully peeled back the oiled cloth, peering at the activity in the bailey below.

Chrystobel picked herself up, brushing off her knees. "What are you doing here?" she demanded, fighting down her panic. "You mustn't stay here. My husband will be back any minute."

Gryffyn whirled on her. "Husband?" he spat. "So you have already married the loathsome swine?"

"I have," she replied. "Father tried to find you to tell you of the ceremony, but he was unable to locate you."

Gryffyn avoided commenting on his whereabouts during her wedding. "De Poyer is nothing but a thieving bastard!" he barked. "He has no right to be here!"

Chrystobel had seen her brother in rages like this before. His control would soon leave him and he would punch her senseless, so she made sure to stay well away from the man and his unpredictable fists. In fact, the only thing to do was to agree with him, humor him, anything to keep him from pummeling her and Izlyn in his fury over the English.

Terrified, she had to do what was necessary to protect both her and her sister. It was a submissive behavior she'd utilized for many years in the face of her abusive brother; sometimes it worked and sometimes it didn't. She prayed it would work this time. She had to show she was on his side, to agree with a barbaric man in the hopes he would go along his way and not harm her. The game of terror had begun.

"I know," she agreed quickly. "But I was forced to marry him. I did not want to."

That seemed to ease Gryffyn somewhat. He began smacking a fist against his open palm, agitated. "To the Devil with him and the rest of his *Saesneg* soldiers," he grumbled. "The first arrow did not work but there will be more. If they want my castle, they will have to fight for it. There will be hazard and rebellion every second of the day!"

Chrystobel tried not to appear too shocked by his admission. *So the arrow had indeed come from him!* She very much wanted to appear as if she was on his side, anything to get the man out of her chamber without blood being drawn. The longer he remained here, the more chance there would be of him becoming violent. *Get him out!*

"Of course, Gryffyn," she said patiently. "Anything you say. But you cannot remain here. He has already been back twice. If he finds you here, it would be very bad for you."

Gryffyn was in the process of mentally dismembering the man he now considered to be his arch enemy, de Poyer, but he paused when his sister's words sank deep. He looked at her, abruptly, his expression nothing short of venomous.

"He cannot best me," he declared. "He had his demons pummel me earlier, but wait until I get the man alone. I will tear him apart!"

Chrystobel agreed steadily. "Of course you will," she said. "I have seen what you can do. You are much more powerful than he is. Now, get out of here and go hide someplace where he will never find you. To the storage vaults, mayhap; there are many places to hide there."

Gryffyn ignored her suggestion, at least outwardly. Inside, however, his distorted mind was working furiously. He was like a caged beast, pacing around and knocking over furniture, so much so that he awoke Izlyn. When the girl rubbed her eyes sleepily and then saw her brother, she began to weep. Gryffyn looked at the girl, infuriated.

"And you!" he barked, pointing a finger at her. "Tell me that I have your support or I shall punish you severely!"

Chrystobel raced to her sister's side, falling onto the bed and throwing her arms around the girl. "You do not have time for her," she insisted, her voice rising with panic. "Gryffyn, you must leave now. If they find you, they will kill you!"

Gryffyn marched over to the bed and reached out, grabbing

Chrystobel by her hair. As she cried out in pain, he yanked her away from Izlyn and onto the floor. On her knees before her brother, his fingers brutally entwined in her hair, she gasped when he yanked her head upwards so that she was gazing into his menacing face. Gryffyn yanked her hair again just because he liked to hear her yelp. The sounds of pain always gave him pleasure.

"You are loyal to him, aren't you?" he hissed.

Chrystobel was gasping and weeping with pain. "Nay!" she cried.

"Admit it!"

"Nay!" she wept. "Please, Gryffyn, let me go!"

Gryffyn didn't comply. He held her hair tightly, his wretched mind mulling over a variety of scenarios involving his sister and the enemy knight. True, she had never shown any real excitement for marrying the *Saesneg*. In fact, she had been openly reluctant to do so. She was a bigger pawn in this situation than any of them. Therefore, Gryffyn eased his stance slightly... but only slightly. At the moment, he was concocting a scheme that would very much involve his sister. He needed her to save him. He needed her to save them all. There was a very simply way to put an end to the *Saesneg* reign of Nether.

"Then you will prove your loyalty," he rumbled, digging into his leather vest and producing a small, sharp dagger. When Chrystobel cried out, terrified he was going to use it on her, he yanked her hair again to both control and still her. "When your husband comes to share your bed, you will use this dagger on him. When the man least expects it, thrust it into his back and kill him. Do you understand?"

Chrystobel was weeping uncontrollably but she nodded. Gryffyn yanked her hair one last time as he thrust the dirk at her, placing it into her shaking hands. Then he let go of her hair and watched her fall to the floor. His gaze, furious only moments before, was now strangely impassive as he looked at his sister huddled in a terrified heap.

"It is your duty as a Welshman to kill the English vermin," he told her. "If you do not, then I will know you are a traitor and I will kill you the first chance I get. Once you are dead, I will kill Izlyn and Father as well. I will leave no one in this family alive, so you hold everyone's lives in your hand. Kill your husband or I will kill you. Is this in any way unclear?"

Sobbing, Chrystobel nodded her head. "It... it 'tis."

Gryffyn felt very powerful at that moment, pleased with his plan to kill de Poyer. As usual, he would have someone else do his dirty work for him. This time, it would be his sister.

"Good," he grunted. "I will be down in the storage vaults. You are correct. It is the best place to hide. I will await word of your success."

He meant it as a threat and she took it as one. Chrystobel remained in a ball on the floor, her face against the wooden planks, hearing Gryffyn as he stomped to her chamber door and swiftly quit the chamber. Like a violent storm, Gryffyn had swept along the land, leaving a trail of devastation in his wake. But the moment he vacated, the sudden silence was both comforting and eerie.

Once he was gone, Chrystobel jumped up and ran to the door, throwing the iron bolt so that he could not come back inside. Then she collapsed against the door, weeping and frightened. All she'd ever known from the man was terror, since she had been a small girl. He continued to put the fear of the devil in her, a primal instinct that had been instilled in her long ago. It therefore took her several moments before she was able to calm sufficiently.

Still sniffling, she pushed away from the door and made her way back to Izlyn, who had lain back down in the bed and pulled the coverlets fearfully over her head. The little girl was trembling, too, and Chrystobel lay down next to her, snuggling with the child to comfort her. All the while, Chrystobel was very torn with the course her life would take over the next few hours. She was terrified of Gryffyn, enough so that she was actually considering doing his bidding. She knew her brother well enough to know he meant what he said. He would kill them all should she fail.

But in the next breath, her new husband had sworn to protect her. She didn't know the man and she didn't yet trust his word – should she believe him? Or should she do her brother's will simply to keep her family alive? Her entire life had been filled with these moments, threats of murder from a man who delighted in spreading panic. She was so very sick of the fear, so perhaps it was time to do something about it.

The dirk was still in her hand and she opened her palm to look at it, gleaming dully in the weak firelight. Perhaps it was time to take a leap of faith to save her father and her sister, to trust a man she had only known a matter of hours. She was coming to feel as if Keller de Poyer was her only hope, an English enemy who had sworn to defend her. Nay, she could no longer subject herself and her family to Gryffyn's tyranny because to do so, ultimately, would only cause their deaths. This she knew as certainly as she lived and breathed. Someday, someway, Gryffyn would kill them all.

It was time to take a stand.

CƷ

IT WAS AN hour or two before dawn by the time Keller made his way back to Chrystobel's chamber. Over six hours of searching had failed to produce Gryffyn, so he put his men on shifts to watch over the Welsh inhabitants of Nether. Half went to bed while the other half remained awake and vigilant, guarding the unhappy Welsh.

The more the minutes passed, the more enraged he was about Gryffyn's absence. He was coming to think that the man had fled the castle, which would have been the right thing to do. Gryffyn was more intelligent than he gave him credit for if that was the case, and as Keller made his way up to Chrystobel's chamber, he struggled to push aside thoughts of the man. He didn't want to carry that poison over into the lady's chamber. He didn't want that vile man on his mind when he looked at her.

The keep was dark and quiet at this hour as he reached the second floor landing. There were two chambers on this floor and he went to the chamber on the left, the one that overlooked the southern portion of the bailey. Lifting the latch, he gave a shove but the door was bolted.

He knocked softly.

It took a moment for him to hear movement. He could hear feet on the floor, coming closer. Chrystobel's voice hissed at him from the other side of the panel.

"Who comes?" she demanded.

"It is your husband, Lady de Poyer."

He could hear the iron bolt being thrown, grating against the wood. The door opened slightly, but only enough to allow Chrystobel out. Keller was forced to step back as she came onto the landing, closing the chamber door behind her. He couldn't help but notice that she was in a sleeping shift with a heavy shawl draped around her shoulders. A sleeping shift made him think of a bed, and a bed made him think of consummating their marriage. She also smelled of flowers, something he found quite alluring. He was still dwelling on the scent of violets when she began to speak, jolting him out of his somewhat lustful thoughts.

"Izlyn is asleep and I did not wish to wake her with our conversation," she whispered. "I must speak with you."

Keller could sense her grim mood. "How may I be of service?"

Chrystobel looked up at him, her brown eyes deep and bottomless. It was evident that there was much on her mind, a thousand questions without adequate answers. He was coming to see that the woman had no ability to hide her emotions. They were written all over her face. After a moment, she sighed faintly.

"Did you find my brother?" she asked.

"Nay."

She grunted softly. "Nor will you, I suppose," she muttered. "My lord, I must ask you something and I would beg you to be truthful."

"I always am."

She was very hesitant and the words came out in spurts. "You... you are a stranger here," she said nervously. "I have only known you a few hours, yet you are my husband. I do not know you as a man of character or honor yet. I can only assume such things because of your rank. You said earlier that Gryffyn's violence towards us would be no more and I very much hope... that is to say, I want to believe you. But there are things you do not know."

Keller took her statement very seriously. He crossed his big arms, bracing his legs apart as he settled in for the conversation. "I suspect there is a great deal I do not know about this place and about you," he said. "But the question is whether or not you intend to tell me, or if you intend on keeping secrets."

She looked both surprised and offended. "It is not secrets I keep but family realities," she said. "This is *my* family and there are things...."

He interrupted her. "I told you earlier than you and your family belongs to me now," he said. "I am your family and it is my right to know what goes on here. What is it that you are not telling me?"

Her nervousness was growing worse. "All families have issues that they do not wish to share with outsiders," she said. "You, my lord, are an outsider."

"I am your husband."

"But I do not *know* you."

"If you continue to keep secrets, you will never come to know me and I will always be a stranger to you. Is that what you truly wish?"

Nay, she didn't. Chrystobel looked at him, his intense gaze and intelligent face, and realized that he made a good deal of sense. He was her husband, and would be forever, and it was time to build the bridges of trust unless she wanted a miserable marriage. She would have to make the first move because she very much wanted his help and she wanted to believe him when he said he would defend her. With a deep breath for courage, she opened her mouth to speak but tears popped to her eyes instead. It was fear, pure and simple. She had to fight through it.

"Gryffyn came to me earlier this evening," she said, her voice tight with emotion. Then she held up her right hand, the one clutching the dirk Gryffyn had given her, and extended it to Keller. "He told me I had to kill you. He told me that if I did not, he would consider me a traitor and kill me and Izlyn and my father. He said he would kill us all if I did not abide by his command."

Keller eyed her a moment before taking the dirk. It was small, but sharp enough to do damage. He inspected it a moment, struggling not to feel an inordinate amount of hatred towards Gryffyn. Emotions were misplaced in warfare, and this was definitely war. Gryffyn had challenged him since nearly the moment he had entered the walls of Nether, and now the game was increasing in intensity. It was growing deadly.

Gryffyn was including his sister in his games, instructing the woman to murder on his behalf. The fact that she had divulged her brother's scheme told Keller that she wasn't allying herself with her brother, which relieved him tremendously. She could have very easily obeyed him, but she hadn't. Instead, she had come to Keller for help. He knew she had done it more out of fear of her brother than of her loyalty to her new husband, but it didn't matter. Trust went both ways, and now it was time for him to earn her trust. She was placing her faith in him and he would not fail.

"Why did you not send word to me in the bailey that he had come to you?" he asked calmly.

Chrystobel shook her head. "How?" she asked. "You have taken all of the servants away and I could not leave Izzie alone. I knew you would come to me, eventually. But there is more you should know."

"What is that?"

Chrystobel felt terrible telling him such things, ashamed at her brother's appalling behavior. "He admitted to being behind the attempt on your knight's life," she said. "From what I could gather, he meant the arrow for you."

Keller wasn't surprised to hear that. Rather than be angry about it, he thought the entire circumstance ridiculous. It was a coward of a man who stood in the shadows and directed others to do his deadly deeds only to fail at them.

"I am sure it was but, like a fool, he entrusted other fools to do what he should have done himself," he said almost philosophically, glancing up at her to see her genuinely contrite expression. He felt rather sorry for her. "Do you know where your brother is now?"

She nodded. "He is in the storage vaults," she said helpfully, relieved that he wasn't taking her brother's nasty behavior out on her. "There are many places to hide in there but only one way in or out. You will find the door to the stores on the level beneath this chamber, cut into the floor of the small feasting hall that my father sometimes uses."

Keller nodded, absorbing the information, and turned to leave. Chrystobel, however, reached out to grasp his arm.

"Please," she begged softly, blinking back tears. "He means what he says. When he discovers I have betrayed him, he will kill me."

Keller put a big hand over her small one, feeling her warmth as it seared through his glove. For a moment, he was so caught up in her magnificent eyes that he almost forgot what he was going to say. Quickly, he regrouped.

"Nay, he will not," he said quietly. "I will send my men up here to guard your chamber. No one will get past them, and once I catch your brother, he will understand the meaning of my wrath. I swear he will never be a threat to you or your family again, my lady. I will not betray your faith."

Chrystobel believed every word. There was something about the man that was deeply sincere. She nodded her head.

"I believe you."

He took her hand and, removing it from his arm, kissed it softly before letting it go. "Return to your chamber, now," he instructed. "Bolt the door and do not open it for anyone but me or my knights. Is that clear?"

Chrystobel was still reeling from the kiss to her hand but managed to nod. "It is."

He smiled faintly at her as he pointed to the door. "Go inside," he told her. "I will not leave until I hear the bolt thrown."

Chrystobel somehow managed to make it back into her chamber, dutifully locking the door as he had instructed. She leaned against the door, listening to his boot falls fade down the stairs, before looking at the hand he had kissed. She could still feel his lips against her flesh, a gesture that had made her heart race and her knees tremble. There was something overwhelmingly powerful about the man, something she had never before experienced. All she knew was that his presence was growing stronger by the minute.

She should have been rightfully nervous about trusting him to subdue her brother. She should have been terrified that all would not go as planned and that Keller would fail her in spite of his declaration. She knew what her brother was capable of. She had yet to know what Keller was capable of. Perhaps he would be weaker or less cunning than Gryffyn, but somehow, she didn't think so. Keller de Poyer was anything but weak. She hoped that her brother had finally met his match.

Gazing down at her hand, the one Keller had kissed, she could only pray that she was right.

CHAPTER SEVEN

THE PROCESS OF rousting Gryffyn from the storage vaults hadn't been an easy one.

Keller had taken all three of his knights and thirty of his men to accomplish the task. Entering the keep with his big numbers, he sent ten of his soldiers up to guard Chrystobel's door while taking the rest with him to the storage vaults on the lower ground level of the keep.

It was dark and crowded in the vaults below and Keller decided the best method would be to drive the fox to the house, as it were, so he sent the knights down to begin the hunt. Gladly, William, George, and Aimery descended the ladders with their broadswords in hand as Keller stood at the top of the ladder with his soldiers. The knights began to beat on, tip over, or shake everything they came across, creating a huge racket. The game that Gryffyn was so intent on playing was now turning against him as the group of angry Englishmen intended to make sport of him. At least, that was the hope.

As dawn began to appear on the eastern horizon, turning the sky shades of purple and pink, Keller's knights wrought havoc in the storage vaults of Nether. There were bales of cream-colored wool bound with rope that they plunged their broadswords into and barrels of barley that were opened and stirred with sharp weapons. There were a great deal of stores and the knights were methodical, starting at one corner of the room and moving forward in a wave so as to drive

Gryffyn out of his hiding place and to the ladder where Keller was waiting for him.

This went on steadily for an hour until it became apparent that Gryffyn was not in the storage vault. When William was finished with the last barrel of apples, he finally appeared at the base of the ladder, gazing up at Keller at the top.

"He is not here," he said, sighing with some exhaustion. "Are you sure this is where she said to look for him?"

Keller nodded. "Aye," he said, a creeping sense of displeasure coming over him. "Are you sure there are no alcoves or hidden rooms he could be in?"

William looked around the darkened storage area as George and Aimery continued to poke around. "Nothing," he said. "Mayhap he left before we got here."

Keller lifted his dark eyebrows in resignation. "That is possible."

"That is the only explanation unless she lied to you."

Keller shook his head. "I do not think so," he said. "I will, however, question her again while you go speak with the father. See what Trevyn knows about his son."

William leaned on the ladder, looking up at him. "He knew nothing when we questioned him earlier," he said. "I am not sure a few hours will make a difference in what he knows."

"It might," Keller said. "Mayhap the son has left Nether altogether. Ask the father if the man has any friends or allies around here that would take him in."

William nodded wearily, calling off the Ashby-Kidd twins as Keller made his way up to his wife's bower only to be told by his soldiers that the woman and her sister were sleeping soundly, exhausted from the excitement of the night. After a moment's indecision, he left her to sleep and instead joined William to hunt out Trevyn. In the briskly cold dawn of a new day, they found Trevyn in the great hall, breaking his fast in a cold room before a darkened, sooty hearth that had been dead for hours.

The hall smelled heavily of smoke and animals as Keller and William entered. Hungry dogs were clustered around Trevyn as the man picked apart cold meat and stale bread for his meal. He glanced up when the English knights approached.

"There are no servants to prepare a meal," he said. "You still have them held captive in the bailey."

He sounded somewhat disgruntled but Keller didn't react to what could have been interpreted as a rebuke. "Where is your son?" he asked, his voice a cold as steel. "And do not tell me that you have no knowledge of his whereabouts. I believed you once but I will not believe you again because he appeared to Lady de Poyer a few hours ago, so he is indeed somewhere within these grounds. Tell me what you know or you will not like my reaction."

Trevyn looked at him, his dark eyes dulled with age and fatigue. "What can I tell you?" he asked, perturbed. "My son does what he pleases, wherever he pleases. If he is not in his tower room or here in the hall, then he could be a thousand other places. I simply do not know."

"You do not know or you will not tell us?" William asked, propping a big boot up on the bench and leaning on his knee. He was exhausted and growing increasingly agitated with the fact that no one seemed to know where Gryffyn was hiding. "He is your *son*, old man, and presumably under your control. Why does everyone around here act as if that bastard is the lord of Nether? That title would have formerly been held by you, in case you were not aware. Now you are subject to Sir Keller de Poyer, Lord Carnedd, premier knight of William Marshal, and Lord Protector of the King's interest in Powys. Whatever fear you hold for your son, it would be wise for you to fear de Poyer more. Now, tell us where Gryffyn is so we can release the servants and finish with these foolish games."

Trevyn looked between de Poyer and Wellesbourne, his dark eyes circled and his features taut. Angrily, he slammed his bread and meat to the table.

"I told you before that I did not know where Gryffyn was and I will tell you the same thing now," he said, frustrated. "The man has a mind of his own. I do not pretend to know it."

Keller was watching Trevyn carefully. Unlike Chrystobel, the old man was a bit more adept at lying. He could tell, and the realization infuriated him.

"If you knew where he was, would you tell me?" he asked steadily.

Trevyn faltered. "Mayhap," he said, averting his gaze and looking to his bread once more. "Mayhap not. What do you intend to do to him?"

Keller was finished interrogating the old man. He had to make a point and his patience, usually limited even in the best of circumstances, was gone. He reached down and ripped the bread from Trevyn's hand, tossing it to the dogs. When the old man swiped for the meat, Keller swept it completely off the table. As it landed on the floor, the dogs had a grand feast. When Trevyn looked up at Keller, astonished, fearful and enraged, Keller met the aged gaze with an expression of complete control.

"Your son is an uncivilized brute," he growled at the old man. "I have no idea how long he has been beating you and your daughters, but I tell you now that those days are finished. I am here now and Gryffyn will obey me or he will pay the consequences."

Trevyn visibly paled. "Who told you such things?" he nearly choked. "Did Chrystobel tell you that he beat us?"

Keller was fighting down a righteous sense of fury. "She has not told me directly," he said, "but I would have to be a fool not to have figured it out. Moreover, Gryffyn threatened to kill all of you if she did not murder me to prove her loyalty. What manner of beast have you raised, d'Einen?"

Trevyn was struggling. He had a difficult time maintaining eye contact, knowing de Poyer's words were true but unable to acknowledge it. Like his daughter, he had been living with it for so long that it was simply the way of things. Now, he was being questioned about something he had no answer for. It was too uncomfortable to admit that he'd lost control of his son long ago. Shaking his head, he simply looked away.

"I do not know what you mean," he muttered. "My son is strong and intelligent."

"Your son is an animal," Keller countered. "If you do not help me locate him, then I cannot protect you against him. If you will not do it for yourself, at least do it for your daughters. I cannot believe that you, as their father, stand by while your son abuses them. Are you truly such a weakling?"

Trevyn's head snapped to Keller, his mouth working as if he had something to say. It was evident by his expression that there was much anger, and much fear, in his heart.

"I agreed to William Marshal's terms," he said, "the crux of which did not give you permission to demean and insult me and my family. You know not of what you speak!"

Keller cocked a dark eyebrow. He was deliberately trying to provoke the man into an emotional confession, hoping they could glean information about Gryffyn from it.

"I am not sure how the truth can be considered demeaning," he said. "Do you fear your son so much that you would do anything to protect him? What about protecting your daughters? Don't they deserve your protection also?"

Trevyn hissed at him and tried to stand up, but William slammed the old man back down into his chair. Trevyn took a swipe at William, who easily dodged the strike. He rammed his hands down onto Trevyn's shoulders, holding him fast as Keller leaned into his face.

"You are a weak and pathetic excuse for a father," he hissed. "You have two beautiful daughters and all you can do is allow your son to abuse them. You are a coward of a man, unworthy of the lovely women you have fathered. You are supposed to protect them, you fool, or are you too afraid to do it? You should have woman parts between your legs because you surely do not deserve to be called a man."

Trevyn's face was a deep, dull red and sweat beaded on his forehead in spite of the cool temperature of the room. "You do not understand!" he barked.

Keller slammed his big fists on the table, causing Trevyn to jump at the violent movement. "Then explain it to me," he demanded. "Explain to me why your daughters live in fear of their brother. Explain to me why you allow the man to do as he pleases. Explain to me all of this because as surely as I stand here, I cannot fathom a father's failure to do his duty."

Trevyn glared at him with a deadly hatred. Angry as he was, he wasn't stupid. He knew he was outmanned by the two English knights. Nothing they had said was untrue. They had verbalized the same thoughts Trevyn had been thinking of himself for many years and the more he mulled their words over in his mind, the more his hatred began to turn inwardly. He was an embittered and torn man.

"I made a promise," he finally muttered.

Keller leaned in to hear him better. "What promise?" he asked. "To whom?"

Trevyn shook his head, looking at his lap. "To my wife," he said quietly. "She perished of childbirth fever shortly after Izlyn was born. She made me promise... she could never bring herself to discipline the boy, you see, and she made me promise not to lift a hand to him. She could control him whereas I could not, so it was never an issue until he became older and then... he is my only son. He is allowed to do as he pleases."

Keller drew in a long, calming breath, glancing at William to see the man's reaction. William appeared both puzzled and disgusted, so Keller pressed Trevyn.

"But he terrorizes your entire family," Keller said, unsure of his personal feelings with regard to the man's answer. "Why do you permit this?"

Trevyn merely shook his head. "He was a lively boy when he was young," he said. "He was mischievous but not naughty. But somehow as he grew older, the foul streak arose. I had promised my wife not to strike or discipline him, so I let him do as he pleased. Now… there is no way to stop it. I promised my wife, after all."

Keller stared at the man a moment before looking to William. The big blond knight met Keller's gaze before removing his hands from Trevyn's shoulders. Having a wife for as long as he had, William understood Trevyn's point of view more than most. He plopped his big body down on the bench and faced the man.

"I can understand that you promised your wife not to strike him," he said, his tone considerably less hostile, "but in making this promise, do you realize what you've done? You've allowed the man to run wild and terrorize all of you. I am sure that is not what your wife had in mind when she made you promise not to strike him."

Trevyn was still staring at his lap. "Mayhap," he agreed quietly. Then, he lifted his head and looked at Keller. "But it has come to this. Gryffyn knows no fear or boundaries. He takes what he wants, he does what he wants, and even though he is my son I have grown to hate him over the years as one would hate an enemy. Do you know why I brokered this deal with William Marshal? Giving him my castle and lands? It was not to know peace with the English. Nay, that was not the reason. It was so that my son could not inherit these lands that have belonged to my family for generations. Instead, Gryffyn will inherit lands in England, a country he hates intensely."

It was a shocking admission. Keller's rage at the old man had calmed significantly by the time Trevyn was finished. In fact, he understood his reasoning completely.

"But you made your daughter part of this deal," he pointed out softly. "You offered to marry her to an Englishman of the Marshal's choosing."

Trevyn nodded. "I know," he said. "I wanted it that way. At least it would remain somewhat in the family if Chrystobel married the new lord of Nether. At least my grandchildren would inherit it, but not my grandchildren through my son. I do not want that line to have anything to do with what is so beloved by the d'Einens. I pray every night that my son will die without having issue and that his evil ways will die out with him. The House of d'Einen is a good family, my lord. But Gryffyn has tainted the name."

Keller sighed loudly, glancing over at William for the man's reaction. William looked at Keller as if to say *how can we become angry with him now?* Keller finally cleared his throat softly.

"Where is your son?" he asked quietly. "I do not want to kill the man. I only wish to locate him."

Trevyn shook his head. "He has more than likely left the fortress," he said, sounding defeated. "He has a friend he cavorts with, a local lord named Colvyn ap Gwynwynwyn. The man lives at Castell Mallwyd, about a half day's ride from here."

"And you believe he went there?"

"It is possible."

Keller glanced at William again, both men knowing that there wasn't much more to be said on the subject. It was assumed that Gryffyn had left the fortress. After a moment, Keller rose from his seat, as did William. The knights began to move away from the table, heading for the hall entry.

"You will tell me if he returns," Keller said to Trevyn. "Meanwhile, my soldiers will be manning this castle and her walls. Your soldiers, particularly since they are loyal to your son, will be kept elsewhere and watched over by my men. Today, the English will assume the full mantle of Nether Castle."

Trevyn merely nodded, resignation in his tone. "As you say."

Keller's gaze lingered on him. "And you, my lord?" he asked quietly. "Will I have your loyalty as well?"

Trevyn was looking at his lap again. "I cannot say I am readily an English subject," he said. "At least, not yet. But I promise you that you will have no trouble from me."

"For now, I will accept that."

Without another word, Keller and William quit the hall, closing the door behind them. Once the door was shut and the room returned to the cold, dark, and cavernous chamber, leaving Trevyn quite alone, the old man signed heavily and buried his face in his hands. After a moment, a noise that sounded suspiciously like a sob burst from his lips, first one and then another. He kept his hands over his eyes, silently weeping, as a panel near the hearth shifted and a figure emerged.

Gryffyn appeared in the shadows, his gaze on his father. He had been hiding in the passage used by the servants to travel to and from the kitchen area, a secondary passage that was submerged in the thickness of the walls of the great hall. Unless one was a native of Nether, the passage was easily concealed and therefore not easily known. But Trevyn knew about it and he also knew that Gryffyn was hiding in it, listening to the entire conversation with the English. As he wept, he wept for himself. He was the coward de Poyer had accused him of being.

"Excellent, Father," Gryffyn said quietly. "Now they will let their guard down. They will not be looking for me within the fortress any longer."

Trevyn wiped at his eyes. "You heard what they said," he muttered. "You told your sister to kill her husband. How could you do such a thing?"

Gryffyn's features hardened. "How could she *not* do such a thing?" he countered savagely. "The foolish bitch has betrayed me and she will pay. I will kill her before this day his finished."

Trevyn continued wiping at his eyes. "If you do, her husband will kill you," he said. "You heard the man. He is already protective of her."

Gryffyn was near the table. In a flash, he marched to his father and clubbed the man in the jaw, sending him to the floor. Gryffyn grabbed the knife on the table, the one used to cut the bread, and pounced on his father as the man struggled on the wooden floor. Holding the knife to his father's throat, he snarled into the man's face.

"I will kill her," he repeated, hissing. "Chrystobel has disobeyed me and for that, she will pay with her life. Izlyn, too, because she does not deserve to live, the imperfect and foul child that she is. She is an embarrassment to the d'Einen name. I will be done with these women who disobey me and then I will be done with you because you brokered this contract that would see the English assume my inheritance. I should have killed you when you negotiated the deal behind my back but I did not. I heard you tell those *Saesneg* bastards why you gave away my legacy. You hate me and I hate you. Now, I will take back what is rightfully mine and rid Nether of the English scum forever."

Trevyn struggled for his life. "Gryffyn, nay!" he cried. "I did not mean what I said about you! I only said it for their benefit!"

Gryffyn wasn't listening. He was bent on destruction. Taking the bread knife, he plunged it into his father's chest, stabbing the man deep into his heart. As Trevyn lay dying on the floor, his deep red blood bleeding out onto the wood, Gryffyn wrapped the old man's hand around the knife to make it appear as if he had taken his own life. The way Trevyn had rolled onto his side, Gryffyn easily propped the hand up against the knife hilt and kept it in place. As Gryffyn pushed himself off his father, he rolled the old man over even more, driving the knife deeper.

Trevyn d'Einen, former Lord Carnedd, lived the last few seconds of his life breathing in the dirt off the floor of the great hall as his son slinked back into the recesses of the hidden passage. Gryffyn's black, vile heart could only understand one thing at a time, one abhorrent emotion above all else. He couldn't even think that his father was dead by his hand. Nay, that was not in his realm of thought. At the moment, all he could feel was betrayal. His sister had betrayed him and she would pay with her life. Returning to the hidden passageway near the hearth, he sank back into the shadows to make his plans.

His next target was Chrystobel.

☙

AFTER HIS DISCUSSION with Trevyn, Keller had returned to the crowd of Nether inhabitants and gave orders to release them, and that included the servants. He stood in the cold, bright bailey, discussing the schedule of the day as his men assumed their new posts and the servants flooded back into the kitchens, keep, and hall. Screams from the servants returning to the great hall and finding the bloodied corpse of Trevyn d'Einen alarmed the English knights, sending all four of them racing into the hall to find a scene of death before them.

Unfortunately, some of the servants had seen Keller and William emerge from the great hall just before Trevyn's body had been discovered, so the rumors began to fly fast and furious that Trevyn had been murdered by the new lord of Nether. George and Aimery heard the whisperings and yelled at the servants, which upset them more. A good deal of weeping and commotion went on around them as Keller and William tried to sort through the chaos and figure out what had happened. The first thing Keller did was have George and Aimery herd the hysterical servants out of the hall.

When the weeping subsided and an eerie silence settled, Keller was able to think more clearly. As he gazed down at the body, it appeared as if the man had killed himself because of the hand against the knife hilt and the way the body was laying, but to Keller, the scene was puzzling at best. He had spoken to the man only minutes earlier and he had seemed well enough. Certainly not upset enough to take his life. It was a most puzzling circumstance and a disturbing one as well.

"This does not make any sense," he said as he stood over the body. "D'Einen did not seem depressed enough to take his own life, and certainly not by stabbing himself with a bread knife. The blade is dull and it would have taken a great deal of force to push it through skin and bone."

William was kneeling beside the corpse, shaking his head with bewilderment. "It would not have been a simple or painless way to die," he said, inspecting the knife shoved deep into Trevyn's chest. "But if someone else did this, who would it be? All of the occupants of Nether were under guard one way or the other. There was no one else around."

Keller's dusky eyes were grim. "No one that we *know* of," he said quietly. "It is entirely possible that there was someone else wandering this fortress that we did not know of."

William was still looking at the body. "That is possible," he agreed. "Do you have any ideas about it?"

"Mayhap Gryffyn has not left the fortress as was speculated."

William looked up at him, the light of realization going on in his eyes. "Mayhap he was here all along," he concurred, standing up and brushing his hands off on his breeches. "You said that he tried to coerce Lady de Poyer into killing you. Is it possible he thought his father was a traitor as well? Enough to drive him to murder the man?"

Keller shrugged his shoulders, looking down at the cooling corpse. "We have had one altercation with the man and it was enough to tell me that he is unpredictable and brutal," he said, keeping his voice lowered so the servants wouldn't hear him. "It is quite possible he is hiding here at Nether, evading our searches, and waiting for the proper time to strike."

William listened seriously. He pondered the situation, his gaze moving back to the corpse of Trevyn. "Then mayhap we have been going about this all wrong," he said after a moment. "Gryffyn has lived here his entire life and would know where to hide to evade us. We could search for years and still never find him, so instead of going in search of him, we must bring him to *us*."

Keller's eyebrows lifted. "A trap?"

"Indeed."

Keller liked the idea. In fact, it made a good deal of sense. "He wants me dead," he said. "It would make the most sense to use me as bait."

William shook his head. "Nay, it would not," he replied softly. "You said that your wife told you that Gryffyn would kill his entire family if she did not do his bidding. It is quite possible that Gryffyn has already started that task, first with his father and next with his sisters. It would make the most sense to use one of them as bait and since the little one is so skittish, it would make the most sense to use your wife."

Keller hastened to disagree. "He admitted that the arrow that struck

George was meant for me," he reminded William. "I told you what Lady de Poyer said to that regard, so the man is indeed out to kill me. I say let him try."

Again, William shook his head. "That would not be wise, Keller," he said. "Think on it this way; as we have seen, Gryffyn would not attack you man to man. Rather than do that, he relied on an arrow, so it would seem he is not confident in a confrontation of brute strength against brute strength. He is much more apt to attack a weaker person physically, your wife for example, because it makes him feel more powerful. She makes him feel omnipotent and you are a challenge to that sense of power. Therefore, she is the better bait because he will come to her, knowing he can best her."

Keller had gone from giving his full support to the scheme to drawing back considerably. The thought of Chrystobel in danger nearly threw him into fits. "But she is a mere woman," he said, trying to make a strong case for his refusal when he knew, deep down, that William was correct. Gryffyn was a coward in every sense of the word and would more than likely attack a woman before he would attack a full-grown man. "She is afraid of her brother as it is. How can we expect her to lay a trap for the man?"

William cleared his throat softly. "Stop thinking like a husband," he muttered. "If my wife was expected to lay a trap for her murderous brother, I would say the same thing, but the truth is that Lady de Poyer makes the perfect bait. We will be around her at all times so she will be well protected, but if Gryffyn has killed his father, it would make the most sense that his sister is next. That is exactly what he threatened to do, is it not?"

Keller wanted to argue with him; he truly did, but he found it difficult to muster a convincing case. He was so torn that he could hardly think straight. Why was he so reluctant to put Chrystobel in danger? Could it possibly be because he actually cared for her somehow and cared what happened to her? *Impossible*, he told himself sternly. Still, the thought lingered.

"I must think on it," he finally said, unable to look William in the eye because he was certain that the man could see his turmoil. "Set the posts for the day and get some sleep yourself. I will see you later."

He turned to leave but William grasped his arm. "Wait," William said. "I know you are not keen on the idea of making your wife a target, but we have little choice. At this very moment, Gryffyn d'Einen is running loose somewhere in this fortress after having murdered his father. He may very well be watching us right now. In any case, I will not sleep soundly until the man is caught and I doubt you will, either."

Keller almost brushed the man off but he refrained, mostly because he was right. He and Wellesbourne had never been particularly close but that had been Keller's fault. He didn't want to get close to anyone again, but the past day or two had seen that attitude waver somewhat. Wellesbourne was an excellent knight, excellent counsel, and more than that, he felt as if the man was offering his friendship. Perhaps it was time for Keller to reconsider his harsh stance against emotional attachments and open himself up. But it was difficult.

"Nay, I will not," he agreed quietly. "I fear that you are more than likely correct in your suggestion."

William breathed a sigh of relief that Keller was actually agreeing with him. That had never really happened since William had known him. The man didn't take suggestions well so it was a surprise to realize that he was accepting this one. De Poyer was being almost... congenial. Aye, that was the word William was looking for. He'd hardly seen that from the man, either. Perhaps his stiff liege was finally easing.

"We could use more assistance with this situation," William said, dropping his hand from Keller's arm. "When are de Lohr's reinforcements set to arrive?"

Keller scratched his scalp in a weary gesture. "It was my understanding that they were a few days behind us at most, so unless bad weather has delayed them, I would expect to see them very soon." He stopped scratching his head and sighed wearily. His fatigue was catching up with him. "Put the senior sergeants in command while the knights get a few hours of sleep. I want my men patrolling every inch of this fortress and most especially the keep where the ladies are. And get Trevyn out of here before his daughters see him like this. That would not be good for their morale."

William nodded. "Aye, my lord."

There was a friendly expression on William's face, one that compelled Keller to behave similarly. He counted himself lucky to have Wellesbourne under his command so he gave William a brief, awkward smile as he turned and headed out of the great hall with Trevyn's blood on the floor and its dirty hearth. Already, his thoughts were turning to Chrystobel. He realized that he very much wanted to see her.

The morning was deepening as he crossed the muddy bailey towards the keep, the sky above brilliant blue as a brisk breeze swept across the land. Gusty winds not only chased fat, puffy clouds across the sky, but it also kicked about leaves and clutter in the ward. Everywhere Keller looked he could see his soldiers; upon the walls, milling in the bailey, or near the towers. He even saw the Ashby-Kidd brothers over near Tower Night, standing in conversation near the entry.

Keller was satisfied to see such a heavy English presence but he knew, as he lived and breathed, that Gryffyn d'Einen was somewhere, watching and waiting. It was an uneasy feeling he had, but one he intended to remedy quickly. With that in mind, he headed in the direction of George and Aimery to relay his orders – rest for the knights with the senior sergeants in command, and the hope that de Lohr's reinforcements would soon arrive.

William had been correct. Keller wouldn't sleep easy until his wife's murderous brother was caught.

CHAPTER EIGHT

C HRYSTOBEL HAD HEARD the sobbing in her dreams, eventually awakening her from a deep sleep. She gradually became aware that there was a sobbing woman in the landing outside of her chamber and as she listened more closely, she recognized the woman's voice. It was a kitchen servant, one that had served Nether for many years. She was a flighty woman but not usually given to hysterics, which concerned Chrystobel. Rising wearily from her bed as morning sunlight streamed in through cracks in the oilcloth, she was careful not to disturb Izlyn as she made her way across the cold floor to the chamber door and unbolted it.

The serving woman was being held at bay by several English soldiers, all of them crowded onto the landing and guarding Chrystobel's door. They seemed unsure what to do with the agitated woman, but when Chrystobel appeared in the doorway, the woman began screeching about Trevyn d'Einen's death at the hands of the English.

Horrified, Chrystobel came out onto the landing to demand what she meant, completely ignorant of the fact that she was still in her sleeping shift in front of ten pairs of curious male eyes. But the serving woman seemed incapable of doing anything other than weep, telling Chrystobel between gasps that the *marchog Saesneg* had murdered the lord. *The English knight has killed your father!* The servant was babbling in Welsh, something the English soldiers couldn't understand, and what she was telling Chrystobel was dreadful and sickening. Overwhelmed, Chrystobel slumped against the wall, listening in utter shock.

It's not true! She put her hands to her head as if to block out the horror. She couldn't take the woman's screaming any longer, piercing her brain like a thousand shards of steel, cutting into her very flesh. She bolted for the stairs but, finally realizing she was only wearing a shift, turned for her chamber and raced into the room to find some proper clothing. She ended up snatching the first suitable garment she came to, a heavy robe made from leather and wool, with great belled sleeves, and she pulled it on and fastened the ties at the waist. Pulling on the closest pair of shoes, which happened to be Izlyn's small leather slippers, she raced for the door just as her little sister sat up in bed.

Izlyn made a sound, something close to a little cry, and Chrystobel froze at the chamber door, turning to the girl. Izlyn was rubbing her eyes sleepily and Chrystobel went to the girl, pulling her into her arms. She hugged her, warm and soft and cozy.

"I must leave for a moment, Izzie," she said, kissing the girl on the head and struggling to keep a calm manner. "I shall return shortly but I want you to remain here. Please?"

She held the little girl's face between her hands, nodding encouragingly, but Izlyn was tired, and a bit disoriented, and shook her head unhappily. Chrystobel's manner grew firm.

"Aye, you will," she said steadily. "Lay back down and rest. I will return with bread and butter and sweet fruit, I promise."

Sweet fruit were the magic words as far as Izlyn was concerned. She loved the fruit compote the cook would make with apples and cinnamon and honey, so with the lure of her sister returning with such treats, she lay back down and did what she was told. Chrystobel smiled at her sister as she stood up from the bed and headed to the door.

"Stay here," she instructed firmly. "I do not want you running about with English soldiers in the castle, so you must remain here. I will return shortly, I promise."

Izlyn nodded, pulling the covers up over her head at the mention of the English soldiers, but it was good enough for Chrystobel. She knew her sister wouldn't leave the room, for the child tended to be fearful enough without such things as strange men lurking about, so Chrystobel quit the chamber and shut the door behind her only to come face to face with at least eight English soldiers on the landing.

She eyed the soldiers somewhat warily for a moment, just as they were eyeing her. Each one was so uncertain of the other, the English in enemy lands and the Welsh facing men who were bent on conquest. But Chrystobel pushed her natural fear aside because it was a standoff at the moment. They were wasting precious time.

"What do you know about this madness of my husband killing my father?" she demanded. "Who would spread such lies?"

An older soldier stepped forward. "I do not know, my lady," he replied. "We have been here all night. We've not heard anything about it."

Chrystobel gathered her skirts. "Then I am going to find my father," she said. "You will remain here and guard my sister."

An older soldier shook his head. "We were instructed to watch over you *and* your sister, Lady de Poyer," he said. "If you are going to find your father, then I will escort you."

Chrystobel frowned. "I do not believe that is necessary."

The soldier wouldn't budge. "It is the lord's orders, my lady."

Chrystobel eyed the man. She knew why Keller had given the orders and she was frankly thankful for the protection. If she thought about it, she knew the man was correct in not letting her out alone. Gryffyn was about somewhere and she did not want to be caught without protection from his violent tendencies. Therefore, she asked the obvious question.

"Has my brother been located yet?" she inquired.

The soldier shook his head. "Not to my knowledge, my lady."

With that confirmation, Chrystobel was convinced that it would be wise to take an escort with her. Although she rightly feared English soldiers, she knew Keller would not have assigned untrustworthy men to watch over her. Gesturing for the soldier to follow her, she descended the stairs to the entry level below.

It was dark and cold on this level, but bits of morning sun struggled through the gloom, streaming through cracks in the entry door to create a brilliant smattering of light against the entry floor. It was surprisingly clear of servants. She didn't hear a soul stirring but she paid it little mind. Chrystobel lifted the iron latch on the heavy oak panel and pulled open the door.

It was cold and bright in the ward beyond. There were many strange soldiers moving about, English soldiers, and she pulled her robe more tightly about her body as she descended the stone steps that led down to the ward. It was muddy and slippery, and there were big puddles of water at the base of the keep from where the overnight dew had collected on the structure and then trickled down the stone.

Once on the floor of the bailey, she tried not to slip in the mud as she made her way towards the great hall. She could see servants milling about over by the kitchen and off to her right, she could see that the stable servants were busy feeding the horses. She could smell the barley dust in the cold morning air. Everything seemed busy and normal enough, certainly not the chaos that the serving woman had indicated. With the English soldier trailing after her, she drew close to the great hall and nearly ran straight into William as he exited.

William was just leaving the hall after having had Trevyn's body removed. Startled at the unexpected sight of Lady de Poyer, he put out a hand to stop her forward progression.

"My lady," he greeted, his voice calm and even in spite of his surprise. "Where are you going on this fine day?"

Chrystobel gazed steadily at the big blond knight. "I am looking for my father," she said. "Have you seen him?"

William hesitated. "Aye, I have seen him," he replied. "Where is your husband? When last we spoke, he intended to seek you out."

Chrystobel shrugged, feeling impatient. "I have not seen him," she said. "Where is my father?"

William didn't want to tell her what he knew. That was Keller's privilege. Therefore, he did the only thing he could do, he stalled.

"It is possible that I saw him with your husband," he said. Well, it wasn't much of a lie. He *had* seen Keller and Trevyn together as Keller knelt over the old man's corpse. That was technically seeing them together, wasn't it? "Wait here in the sunshine and I will find your husband and send him to you."

He seemed terribly polite for a man who had been mildly rude to her most of the night. She would have wondered about his sudden change in behavior if she hadn't been so preoccupied with finding her father.

"I will come with you," she said. "I do not...."

William cut her off, holding up his hands to prevent her from following him as he began to move away. He had no idea where he could find Keller and he didn't want the woman trailing after him, so he began heading in the direction of the gatehouse of Nether.

"Nay, Lady de Poyer," he said, very nearly insisting. "Remain here so that I may find you easily. I do not know where your husband is and I do not wish to drag you all over the grounds, so stay here and I will return as quickly as I can."

He passed a glance at the soldier standing behind her as if to silently emphasize that the man keep her in that particular location. The soldier received the silent message clearly, going so far as to nod as William headed off towards the gatehouse. Chrystobel watched him go with her hands on her hips, wondering why the man was nearly running away from her. Now his odd behavior was causing her to notice. Watching him race off, she finally shook her head.

"Why would he want me to stand here in the cold?" she wondered, mostly to herself. "I can just as easily wait for him in the hall. It would not be too far for him to go in order to find me."

Since the soldier escorting her had been in the keep all night, he had no idea what had transpired in the great hall or what lay in store for them. When Chrystobel moved to the massive entry door that led into the great hall, he simply followed. He didn't want to stand out in the cold, either, and he doubted he could have persuaded the lady to remain out in the cold light of day. Trailing after her, he passed through the door just behind her, listening to her gasp the moment she entered the hall.

There was a big puddle of blood on the floor near the feasting table. Even though the hall was dark, without a fire in the hearth or anything to light the dimness of the room, she could still see the blood at the end of the long table. Frightened, Chrystobel ran towards it, standing over the puddle and trying not to become ill at the sight of it.

"What happened here?" she demanded to anyone who could answer her. With no reply, she began looking around frantically. "What happened? Who was injured here?"

The only person she could see was the soldier standing next to her and he had no answers to provide. But that didn't stop Chrystobel from pointing to the blood.

"What happened?" she asked the man. "Find someone who can tell me why there is blood on this floor!"

The soldier shook his head. "I will not leave you, Lady de Poyer," he insisted, then he, too, began to look around. "There must be a servant nearby who can tell you what happened."

Chrystobel's gaze was drawn back to the blood on the floor. It was beginning to make her rather nauseous. The sight and smell of blood always did.

"God's Bones," she hissed. "What could have happened here? It looks as if someone was terribly injured."

The soldier simply nodded, eyeing the blood as he moved away, wandering to the eastern end of the room where a side door led out to the bailey. He thought perhaps to find a servant there but all he managed to find was a trail of blood. It was evident that they carried the person who left the puddle on the floor out in this direction. As the soldier looked around at the dark and empty servant's alcove, he shrugged and headed back into the hall.

Chrystobel was still standing over the bloody floor, most concerned at the sight. She noticed the soldier coming from the east end of the room, however, and she turned to him.

"Is there no one back there?" she asked.

The soldier shook his head. "Nay, my lady."

Chrystobel thought it was very strange that there were no servants in the hall at this early hour. In fact, the entire circumstance was beginning to concern her. As the soldier passed by the darkened hearth, she pointed to it.

"Wait," she told him, watching him stop. "There is a passageway next to the hearth. Push open the wall to the left of the hearth and see if there is anyone in the passage. Sometimes the servants use it to come in from the kitchen yard."

The soldier turned obediently to the hearth, peering at the stone wall on either side of it. Since it was so dark, it took him a moment to see unmortared seams along the left side of the hearth and he gave a shove, watching part of the wall swing back on great iron hinges. But it was the last thing he would ever see as a figure suddenly materialized from the darkened passage and plunged a knife into his belly.

Chrystobel saw the soldier go down, falling into the passageway so that she could only see his legs sticking out. She was curious, concerned, until she saw Gryffyn emerge, stepping over the supine body of the soldier with a bloodied dirk in his hand. Then, it was as if all rational thought left her. A cry of terror erupted from her lips just as Gryffyn looked at her, his dark eyes filled with hatred and murder.

Chrystobel screamed again, louder than before, and ran for the hall door, but Gryffyn was faster. He grabbed her before she could reach the exit, yanking her away from the panel so that she fell onto the floor. Once she was down, he kicked her in the leg just because he could. He wanted to see her cry.

"You little bitch," he snarled, stalking her as she wept and struggled to crawl away. "You betrayed me! I told you what would happen if you betrayed me!"

Chrystobel was beyond panic. Her greatest fear was now a reality before her and she was nearly frozen with terror.

"Please, Gryffyn!" she cried. "Please do not kill me!"

Gryffyn was beyond fury. He was in the realm of madness as he watched his sister struggle across the wooden planks. When she tried to get to her feet, he hit her on the head, so hard that she fell back to the floor, only half-conscious. It pleased Gryffyn immensely. Now, she would make an easy target for him, easier than their father had made. He could hardly believe the luck of finding her without more than one escort. It had been a stupid thing for her to do, but he knew her to be stupid. As he gazed down at the struggling woman, the only thing he could feel was an overwhelming sense of satisfaction that he would have his way, one last time, as he pulled the sharp blade of his dirk across her tender throat.

"I told you what I would do if you did not prove your loyalty to me," he rumbled. "You have always been foolish, Chrystobel. I tried to discipline you, to mold you, but you were stubborn. *Too* stubborn. Now see what it will cost you."

Chrystobel was barely conscious, struggling to shake off the buzzing in her head, but she could hear him, somewhat. She was full of fear and sorrow.

"Nay," she breathed, struggling to lift her head. "Gryffyn, you… you must not. Please do not."

Gryffyn gazed unemotionally at the woman he had grown up with. She was his sister, that was true, but only by blood. She meant nothing to him, no more than the dogs in the great hall did. She was a possession and little else. He felt absolutely nothing as he listened to her plead for her life. In fact, he liked to hear her plead. It excited him.

"After I kill you, Izlyn is next," he said, looking at the bloodied dirk in his hand. "She is a defective creature. She should have been drowned at birth."

Chrystobel was in tears as she turned onto her belly and began clawing at the floor, dragging herself along as she tried to get away from him. The world was spinning and the floor rocking unsteadily, but she could not give up. She had to fight.

"God help me," she gasped, clutching at the floor and breaking her nails down to the nub. "*God help me!*"

Gryffyn heard the pleas as she cried into the darkness, but her prayers were meaningless to him. All that mattered was that he accomplish his task and return to hiding, waiting for the opportunity to kill again. He watched his sister drag herself across the floor, passing through part of the bloody puddle as she went. It created dark streaks across the wood, dragged along by her heavy robe.

"That is Father's blood, you know," he said casually. "I told you I would kill him if you betrayed me and I did. How does it feel, Chrystobel, knowing that you killed your father? It is your fault I had to do it. If you had only killed de Poyer like I told you to, none of this would have happened."

Chrystobel was sobbing openly now, grieved for their father and terrified that her life was coming to an end. There was so much she had yet to do and see. Her world had been relatively small, as she'd told Keller when she'd first met him. He had promised to take her to Paris and now that would never happen. Perhaps someday they might even grow fond of one another, or even have children, and now she wouldn't know the joy of either event. She was so very crushed, knowing any dreams she ever had were about to come to an end.

Behind her, she could hear Gryffyn's boot falls approaching. He was coming to kill her and there wasn't a thing she could do about it. The room was still swaying and she was struggling to get to her feet without success. But there was one thing she could do. She could scream as loud as she could and pray someone heard her. Pray someone heard her before Gryffyn slit her throat and she could scream no more.

The boot falls were coming closer. *Death* was coming closer. Chrystobel began screaming at the top of her lungs.

ᙦ

"YOUR WIFE IS near the great hall," William sounded breathless as he spoke. "She is looking for her father, Keller."

Keller had been just inside the doorway of Tower Night, speaking with George and Aimery about the state of Nether's armory, when William found him. He'd only meant to speak to the twins about the security of the fortress with Gryffyn on the loose but he had been distracted by the Welsh weaponry. It was rather impressive. But with William's appearance, he was jolted back to the reality at hand and immediately craned his neck out of the doorway in search of Chrystobel. It was a bright day and he squinted in the light, searching for signs of his wife. But she was nowhere to be found and looked to William, puzzled.

"Where did you leave her?" he asked. "I do not see her."

William, too, began searching the area for any sign of the petite woman with the long blond hair. "I told her to wait by the great hall," he said, putting his hand up to shield his eyes from the sun. "I told her I would bring you to her."

Keller came out of the tower, heading in the direction of the great hall. "You said that she asked for her father?" he asked William. "By God's Bloody Rood... what a damnable mess this is. What did you tell her?"

William was marching along beside him. "She wanted to know if I had seen him," he replied. "I was not going to tell her the truth. I told her to remain by the hall entry and that I would bring you to her. *You* can do the telling."

Keller was still looking around even as he made his way to the great hall's entry, a massive oak panel that was braced with a great iron cage for stability and protection. He was increasingly concerned that he couldn't seem to locate her in the big expanse of the bailey.

"Do you suppose she went looking for Trevyn?" he wondered, turning to look at William. "You had him removed from the hall, didn't you?"

William nodded. "I had some soldiers take him away," he replied. "They said they would take him to the storage area near the stables until we could decide what to do with him."

Keller sighed sharply. "I do not want her stumbling upon anyone who can tell her what happened," he muttered. Then he hissed a curse. "I should have gone directly to her chamber when I left the hall but I paused to speak with George and Aimery. Then we started discussing the inventory in the armory. I sincerely hope my foolish delay does not cost me more than just the time spent."

William was looking over to the keep, straining for a glimpse of a blond head. "She could not have gone far," he said. "Do you suppose she went back to her chamber?"

Keller pointed in the direction of the keep. "Go and see," he instructed. "I will see if she is in the hall. In fact...."

He was cut off by the faint sound of a scream. It was muted, and vague, and he came to an abrupt halt, looking around the bailey as if to discover the source.

"Did you hear that?" he asked William, curiously.

Wellesbourne nodded. He, too, was looking around the bailey for the origins of the distant scream. "I did," he said. "It sounded like a woman."

Keller was on edge. "Where did it come from?" he demanded. Then, he pushed William in the direction of the keep. "See if it came from the keep. *Run.*"

William was off, racing across the mucky bailey, as Keller turned in the direction of Tower Night. George and Aimery were still standing in the doorway and he motioned to them.

"Kidds!" he bellowed. "To me!"

The twins came running, their youthful energy cracking in the early morning air, the feisty young men looking for excitement. Keller opened his mouth to speak when another scream, this one very loud and frightening, pierced the air.

Keller whirled in the direction of the great hall. It seemed to come from there. He broke into a sprint, closing the distance to the great hall in a matter of seconds. The Ashby-Kidd twins were on his heels, all of them barreling into the great hall. George and Aimery were moving so fast that Aimery actually tripped over George and crashed to his knees. What they saw immediately upon entering the dark and smelly chamber shocked them all to the bone.

Keller was throwing himself at Gryffyn before he even realized he was moving.

CHAPTER NINE

T HE BLOW TO the jaw sent Gryffyn reeling.

Sprawled on the rough oak planks of the great hall, Gryffyn shook the stars from his eyes and looked up to see the big English knight moving in for another blow.

Keller had fists the size of a man's head, but Gryffyn was fast. He managed to roll out of the way and leap to his feet although his balance was off and he ended up bashing into the corner of the hearth. But Keller was coming in for another blow and Gryffyn threw himself to his left, away from his sister's enraged husband. He knew, by the look in the man's eye, that he meant to kill him.

Gryffyn tried to lash out a fist at Keller, but the knight was just too fast and too strong. Keller grabbed Gryffyn's fist, twisted, and ended up snapping his wrist. Gryffyn fell to his knees, screaming in pain as Keller stood over him in a huffing and furious stance. His dusky eyes were smoldering with fury.

"So you have been hiding here all along, waiting for the proper moment to strike," Keller hissed. "You are a coward of a man, d'Einen – a wretched and vile coward. Now that I finally have you, I intend to do what should have been done long ago."

Holding his wrist, Gryffyn glared at Keller with eyes as dark as obsidian. "If I am a coward, then you are a fool," he growled. "You cannot stop me. Nether and everything in it belongs to me, including my sister!"

It was the wrong thing to say. Keller reached out and used his fist to hammer on Gryffyn's broken wrist, sending the man into howls of pain. But Keller was immune to it. His focus was both deadly and intense as he watched Gryffyn squirm.

"She is my wife now and I swear, by all that is holy, that you shall never lay another hand on her again," Keller rumbled. "I knew someone was beating her but she would not directly tell me who it was. For all of the pain and humiliation you have cast upon her, she still protected you. God knows why, but she did. How long was this going on before I came, d'Einen? How long have you been beating on helpless women to make you feel more like a man?"

Cradling his wrist against his chest, Gryffyn was in a world of hurt. "You bastard," he grunted. "You come to my castle in all of your haughty, conquering glory and married my sister because my weak and foolish father made a pact with the Devil."

Keller's eyes blazed. "William Marshal has nothing to do with you taking your fists to your sister."

"You only married her to gain a castle. Do not act as if she means something to you!"

"It does not matter if she means something to me." Keller was struggling not to wrap his hands around the man's neck, although he knew, eventually, that it would come to that. It was just a feeling he had. "She is my wife and I will protect her. I will tell you this now, Gryffyn d'Einen, so there is no misunderstanding. If you so much as look at her in a hostile manner again, I will run you through. Make no mistake. If you touch her again, I will kill you."

Gryffyn wasn't used to being questioned or disciplined. He had always done as he pleased. Deep down, he was a spoiled little boy with a spoiled little mind. With a growl, he propelled himself off the floor and charged Keller with all of his furious might. Keller easily reached out a massive fist and caught Gryffyn on the side of the head, knocking the man silly. Gryffyn fell on his bad wrist, collapsed in a heap, and began to bellow.

Keller gazed at the man, not at all sorry for the pain and suffering he was feeling. Had Keller possessed any less self-control, the man would be wallowing in a pool of his own blood. He deserved all of the justified agony and more. In fact, Keller was purposely making the man suffer. He wanted him to feel the pain he had inflicted upon Chrystobel, and upon his family, for untold years. He wanted Gryffyn to feel the humiliation and hurt. As Gryffyn writhed in agony, Keller turned to his wife.

Chrystobel had managed to crawl over to the hearth and now sat propped up against the wall, her dark eyes wide with shock. Keller's appearance at the most opportune time had been startling enough, but watching her husband pound her brother was a vision of violence and retribution that she never thought she would live to see. Gryffyn was finally subdued and Keller was the reason, protecting her as he had sworn to do. He was a man of his word, English or no. The realization was almost more than she could bear and she gazed at the man, seeing him through entirely new eyes.

This wasn't the same knight she had met the day before, the man who had shown little to no warmth. That Keller de Poyer was an efficient, humorless man who, she was sure, had viewed her just as he viewed Nether Castle; as an acquisition. The big knight with the wide shoulders and enormous hands hadn't treated her with anything more than polite respect until this moment in time. Having seen Gryffyn preparing to pounce on her was all Keller needed to unleash his fury against the man, as if Chrystobel meant something to him. As if he was protecting something dear. It had been a truly awesome sight to behold and she was still quite stunned by it all.

As his brother-in-law moaned on the floor several feet away, Keller had eyes only for Chrystobel. She was such a lovely creature. He'd known that from the moment he had first laid eyes on her. But the pain in his heart from a love lost had prevented him from seeing beyond his fear. Fear of feeling, fear of opening himself up again. Chrystobel was a beautiful angel he had never expected to know and now, he could feel himself relenting. He could feel himself warming, perhaps willing to open himself up again. The very moment he had saved her life was the moment he started to let himself feel something.

He crouched down beside her as she sat against the wall, his rugged face, worn by the years and the weather, creased with concern.

"Are you badly injured?" he asked softly.

The buzzing in Chrystobel's head had eased considerably. "Nay," she said softly, gazing into his eyes and feeling hope and relief in her chest such as she had never before experienced. "I am well enough."

Keller's gaze drifted over her head, her face, as if he didn't believe her. "Are you certain?" he asked quietly. "I can send for a physic."

Chrystobel smiled faintly, reaching out to put a hand on his arm in a reassuring gesture. "That is not necessary," she said, sighing quietly. "I will admit that my head does ache a bit, but food and rest will cure me, I am sure."

He stared at her a moment before lifting his enormous hands and gently cupped her face. As Chrystobel looked into his eyes, her heart thumping madly against her ribs, she could feel the emotion pouring from the man. It was as if a dam had burst and everything that had been held back was finally gushing out. Sir Keller de Poyer was cold no more, and it was an astonishing realization.

"I am sorry," he whispered. "I am sorry you had to endure what your brother did to you. But I swear, with God as my witness, that he will never touch you again."

Chrystobel was at a loss for words, her breathing unsteady as his thumbs began to stroke her silken skin. It was the first time he had touched her and her senses were understandably overwhelmed.

"It was simply the way of things, my lord," she murmured. "It has been going on so long that I have known little else."

Keller's face hardened. "No more," he rumbled. "He is a dead man if he so much as looks at you in a way I do not like. Do you believe me?"

Chrystobel nodded, though she hardly dared to truly believe. "Aye."

His gentle smile returned. "Good." He fought off the sudden urge to kiss her, not wanting the first genuine kiss between them to be a public spectacle. He was rather shy and conservative that way. Moreover, there was something more she needed to know, something very serious. He braced himself.

"I must also apologize for something else," he said hesitantly. "Your father...."

Chrystobel cut him off by a nod of the head, tears popping to her eyes. "I know," she whispered. "Gryffyn told me."

"He admitted to killing him?"

"Aye," she confirmed. "The blood on the floor... is it his?"

Keller nodded, watching her sorrowful expression. "Aye," he said quietly. "I am so sorry that I was unable to prevent it."

Chrystobel struggled to control her tears, thinking on her father, the man who was supposed to protect her but never did. Although she was sorry for his loss, she couldn't seem to muster true grief for his passing. Had the man ever prevented Gryffyn from having his own way in all things, perhaps she would have felt differently, but at the moment she felt somewhat guilty that she wasn't more distraught.

"You are not responsible," she said, wiping at her eyes. "You did what you could. You saved me, in fact, and I thank you for that."

Keller's dusky eyes glimmered. "It is one of the better things that I have done in my life."

She smiled at the first truly warm moment between them. "I am particularly grateful for your keen sense of timing," she said. "A few seconds later and I might not have been so grateful. Or alive."

He winked at her and dropped his hands from her face, moving to take her two small hands within his big palms. He kissed them both sweetly, tenderly, as a promise of things to come. Now, it would be different between them. Gryffyn had, if nothing else, accomplished that.

"If you can stand, mayhap we should go and check on your sister," Keller said. "I am sure you are anxious to see her."

Chrystobel nodded, glancing at Gryffyn as the man sat up with the

Ashby-Kidd twins standing several feet away from him, watching every move the man made.

"I am," she said, eyeing her brother warily. "What are you going to do with him?"

The warmth in Keller's eyes faded as he looked over his shoulder at the Welshman, who was holding his broken wrist awkwardly against his torso. His expression suggested anger, defeat, and defiance. Even with the broken wrist, Keller could still see fight in the man. After a moment, he returned his gaze to Chrystobel.

"Lock him in the vault," he said. "The man has much to atone for so I hope you will trust me to make the appropriate judgment."

"Of course, my lord."

His gaze lingered on her a moment, thoughts turning from Gryffyn back to her. He liked thinking of her much better. "You will call me Keller," he said quietly. "Or husband. I will answer to whatever you choose to call me."

A beautiful smile spread across her face. She had a delightful grin with straight, white teeth and slightly prominent canines. "I would be honored to call you Keller," she said sincerely.

He was just about to release her hands but thought better of it as she spoke. The glimmer returned to his eyes.

"I like hearing you say my name," he said honestly.

Her smile broadened even more, if such a thing was possible. "Then I shall say it again," she whispered. "Keller."

He kissed her hand again, smiling when she giggled. In the midst of this hellish situation, it was a tender moment that saw something of a relationship between them take hold. A spark had ignited, and Keller was again thinking on kissing her lips, privacy be damned, when he heard scuffling behind him. Before he could turn around, something violent and painful rammed into the right side of his torso.

He pitched forward as Chrystobel screamed, struggling to keep him from falling even as he collapsed onto his bum. Horrified, they could both see the dagger jutting from his right side, about a foot below his armpit. And there was a hand on it.

Gryffyn stood behind Keller, his good hand on the hilt of the dirk as he crammed it into the man's flesh. Ripping it from Keller's body, he pushed the man aside and aimed for his sister with the blade held high, but Chrystobel threw herself sideways, out of his line of fire, and Gryffyn's blade came down on the wall behind her.

Screaming, Chrystobel was barely out of the way when the Ashby-Kidd twins pounced on Gryffyn. It was a bad fight from the onset, with fists flying, feet kicking and Keller somewhere underneath it all. The knife that had gored Keller fell to the floor in the process and Gryffyn began to howl as his broken wrist was further injured.

Chrystobel, meanwhile, had lurched to her feet, trying to keep free of the fighting men as she skirted the battle, attempting to find Keller in the chaos. It was difficult because all four of them were rolling about, throwing punches and grunting, and she could see a thin trail of blood on the stone that must have been from Keller. Horrified, she attempted to stay clear of the fight.

"Keller?" she cried. "God's Bones, *Keller!*"

He didn't answer but she could see that he had Gryffyn by his good arm, twisting it. It was as much as he could do given the position he found himself in, laying on his chest with three other men on top of him. George had Gryffyn around the neck while Aimery was fighting off the effect of a kick straight to the face. As Aimery fell back, hand to a bloodied nose, Gryffyn reared his head back and head-butted George. As George staggered, Gryffyn rolled off of Keller and scrambled to his feet, falling to his knees before scrambling up again.

It looked like a panicked flight of a man who knew his life expectancy was only counted in minutes now. Deep down, Gryffyn was a coward. He knew he was out-manned and the eventual outcome would not be in his favor. He had to get away from the knights who were intent on killing him. He ran straight to the hearth and shoved open the servant door, bolting through it as George, followed by a bleeding Aimery, went in pursuit. Chrystobel could hear the scuffling and shouting as they ran off.

With the fight having moved on without him, Keller was struggling to push himself up off the floor as Chrystobel raced to his side, trying to steady the man. Horrified, she could see deep red blood staining the right side of his tunic and leaking onto his mail.

"Keller," she gasped. "Stay down. Let me look at your injury."

He shook his head as he attempted to get to his feet. "Later," he grunted. "I must go after your brother."

Chrystobel had her hand on his shoulders, trying to keep him from rising. "You are in no condition to go after him," she said, sounding as if she were scolding. "Your knights are in pursuit. He will not get away."

Keller was on his knees, looking up at her and realizing she was more than likely correct. He trusted George and Aimery to subdue Gryffyn. More than that, he didn't feel particularly well. If he were to go after Gryffyn, he would only be a hindrance. Frustrated, he sighed heavily.

"Then I should find Wellesbourne at the very least," he said. "He must know what has happened."

"We will find him in a moment," Chrystobel insisted. "You must let me tend your wound."

Keller didn't seem particularly concerned about it. "It is not too severe," he said, although his lips were pale with shock. "I would wager that a few stitches should take care of it."

He was trying to stand up and no amount of pushing could force him to remain down, so Chrystobel got him by the arm and pulled him over to the bench next to the feasting table. He sat heavily as she pulled away layers of clothing and mail to get to the puncture wound. Keller tried to hold her off but she wouldn't be dissuaded. Eventually, he gave up trying and sat there as she finally revealed the wound. He heard her sigh heavily at the sight.

"It does not seem to be bleeding too heavily," she said, concern in her tone, "but I need to sew it up right away. Can you make it up to my chamber?"

Keller nodded, suddenly feeling very weary. He hadn't slept in almost two days and his fatigue, now compounded by the injury, was catching up to him. So he stood up as Chrystobel positioned herself next to him, slinging his big left arm over her slender shoulders. She was very determined to assist him and he was touched by her resolve. He couldn't remember the last time a woman had showed him such concern.

"I must find Wellesbourne," he repeated as they slowly moved for the hall entry. "He must know what has happened."

"Then we will send one of your men for him," Chrystobel replied steadily. "You'll not go on the hunt for him."

"Not even a little?"

"Not even a little."

He fought off a grin at her firm tone but didn't argue with her. He rather liked a woman who wasn't afraid to deny him, so he kept his mouth shut as they moved out into the bright bailey beyond. As they walked across the mud, carefully, heading for the keep, they could hear shouting off to the right where the kitchen yard was located. Soldiers were breaking their posts and running in the direction of the yard. Keller watched them run, wondering what was so vital that had them breaking posts. But as he watched his men, a thought occurred to him.

"That passageway that is next to the hearth," he ventured. "Where does it lead?"

Chrystobel was watching the ground where they walked, careful to keep them both out of the slippery mud. "It is used by the servants," she said. "It leads to the kitchen yard. Gryffyn must have been hiding in it."

He looked at her lowered head. "And you did not think to tell me that there was such a passage where he may hide?"

She felt rather guilty. "It is such a common passage," she said truthfully. "It never crossed my mind. The passage is used constantly so I never imagined he would hide there, but he did, and when I entered the hall to wait for you, he was waiting. He killed the soldier that was my escort and then tried to kill me also."

Keller sighed. Frankly, he didn't want to think what could have happened had he been a few seconds later into the hall, so he pushed those thoughts aside as he turned once more towards the commotion in the distance.

"So your brother and my knights ran through the passage and ended up in the kitchen yard," he said. "That must be what all of the chaos is about. Mayhap they have your brother cornered."

"Mayhap."

The more they walked to the keep, the better the angle towards the kitchen yard. Keller could eventually see the wall that surrounded the yard and the open gate that led into the area, but not much more. Men were shouting and someone was bringing horses from the stable, which soldiers quickly mounted. They tore off through the gate and on into the kitchen yard.

"Where are my men going with horses?" Keller wondered aloud.

Chrystobel kept her focus on the ground. "There is a postern gate there that leads to the slopes beyond," she said quietly. "Mayhap my brother slipped through it and they are going in pursuit."

Keller turned to look at her, recalling a mention of a postern gate from their first acquaintance. "The same postern gate you used yesterday when you were chasing the injured rabbit?"

"Aye."

Keller grunted, visibly unhappy. "That gate should have been locked and guarded," he grumbled. "Someone will have to reckon for this mistake if, in fact, your brother was able to escape."

Chrystobel didn't say any more, fearful that he might become angry with her somehow. She continued to help him across the bailey, dodging the puddles and kicking away the dogs. As they neared the keep William emerged, his eyes growing wide at the sight of Chrystobel helping an obviously injured Keller. He rushed forward to assist.

"What happened?" William demanded.

Keller ended up leaning on the man heavily. He had been keeping his weight off of Chrystobel so he wouldn't topple her over but found he could no longer suffer the strain. He gripped William as the man struggled to steady him.

"Gryffyn was in the hall," Keller said. "He managed to catch me with his dirk. George and Aimery are in pursuit, over near the kitchen yard, I believe."

"My brother stabbed him," Chrystobel clarified since Keller seemed inclined to make light of what was a very harrowing incident. "He has a wound in his back."

William gazed at Keller with great concern. "How bad is it?"

"It is bad!" Chrystobel answered for him. "He seems to think that he only needs a stitch or two, but it was a deep gash. He should rest today at least so the bleeding will stop."

William was rather amused that Chrystobel seemed to be doing all of the talking, forcing Keller to stand there and wriggle his eyebrows in submission. In fact, it was a rather stunning situation because William knew Keller de Poyer to be anything but submissive. Yet with this woman, now his wife, that was exactly what he seemed to be. It was odd behavior coming from the usually humorless and rigid man. But, then again, the past two days had seen some remarkable behavior from him. Perhaps it was as William had mused. Perhaps, somehow, the man was learning to be human and the walls of protection were crumbling.

"Lady de Poyer will see to my wound," Keller told William, "but I want you to take charge of the capture of Gryffyn. The man is deadly and needs to be dealt with. Put him in the gatehouse and await further instructions from me."

William acknowledged the order but continued to aid Chrystobel in assisting Keller into the keep. The man took the narrow stairs slowly to the second level where several of his soldiers were still gathered to protect the door of Chrystobel's chamber. It seemed rather useless to have them all there now, so Keller ordered them away, all but two, and the men disbanded. William followed them with the promise that he would send word to Keller once Gryffyn was secured.

Satisfied, but increasingly weak, Keller followed Chrystobel into her comfortable chamber where Izlyn was now sitting next to the fire, playing with some sticks on the ground in front of her. When she looked up and saw her sister and the English knight, she ran to the other end of the room and cowered against the wall.

"Izzie," Chrystobel tried to soothe her sister as she helped Keller to sit on the bed. "Sir Keller is injured and I will need your help. Will you do this for me, please?"

Izlyn remained on the other side of the room but managed to nod. Chrystobel smiled at her sister. "Thank you, sweetheart," she said. "Now, I am going to need some very hot water and clean linen. I will also need for you to bring me my sewing kit."

It took Izlyn a moment to come away from the wall and, hesitantly, move to the big wardrobe. She pulled open the doors, revealing the neatly-stacked items inside; shawls, shoes, belts, and other boxes containing possessions. As Izlyn retrieved the sewing kit, Chrystobel began removing Keller's clothing, very carefully. His heavy green and yellow Pembroke tunic was first.

"Will one of your soldiers escort Izlyn to retrieve the hot water?" she asked, gingerly pulling the tunic over his head. "I need to cleanse the wound."

Keller grunted as it pained him to lift his right arm. "I will send one of my men for it," he said. "With all that his happening around the fortress, it would be safer if she remained here."

Chrystobel nodded and, once the tunic was off, went to the chamber door and opened it. A soldier stuck his head inside in response to Keller's summons and the man was soon off on a mission to retrieve hot water. When the man was gone, Chrystobel returned to her patient.

His tunic was in a pile on the bed beside him as she stood back, inspecting the mail coat for the best way to remove it. Keller surmised what she was doing.

"The best way to remove the mail is for me to bend at the waist as you pull it over my head," he told her as he stood up, towering over her by head and shoulders. "I will bend over and you can pull."

Chrystobel had never removed a knight's mail before, so this was an entirely new project for her. In fact, she felt a little giddy and daring, undressing her new husband, even if it was only moderately so. Keller bent over and extended his arms, grunting because his back pained him, and instructed her to take hold of the shoulders first. She did and pulled, moving the mail over his big body incrementally. The mail was ungiving and wanted to bunch up like a log jam in places, so Chrystobel found herself working it in sections. Keller, in excruciating pain with the angle of his body, never uttered more than soft encouragement to her.

It was a new experience for them both. Keller could only see her lower body as she worked with the mail, which would have come off much easier with the help of someone who knew how to do it, but Keller was showing remarkable patience for a man who usually had none. When Izlyn brought over the sewing kit and set it upon the table next to the bed, the young girl actually attempted to help her sister with the task, and soon Keller had two rather weak females pulling at his mail in all the wrong places. They tugged and shifted, and all they managed to do was bunch it up round his head and shoulders so that the weight of it was nearly bending him in half. Chrystobel could see what they had done and she was mortified.

"It is stuck," she gasped, tugging on the arms with all her might. "God's Bones, I managed to twist you up in your own mail coat."

Keller was in a bad way with the mail. "It might help if you try to move the arms off first," he said patiently. "The rest should follow."

At Chrystobel's instruction, Izlyn took one arm and she took the other. There was a good deal of grunting and groaning going on as the two women struggled to pull the mail coat off, and somewhere in the midst of it, Keller found himself grinning at the activities. Izlyn was literally jumping up and down as she pulled, dramatically struggling with the heavy mail, and Keller had to bite off the giggles at her antics. It was really quite humorous to watch and it was the most animated that he'd seen the child since he had first met her.

He was watching Izlyn's great struggles when Chrystobel's portion of the mail suddenly slipped free and Keller went right along with it. He lost his balance and pitched forward, sending them both to the ground. His full body weight came down and Keller ended up on top of her, gazing into her painful expression.

"God's Bloody Rood," he grunted, bracing his hands on either side of her and pushing himself up. "Are you well? Did I hurt you?"

Chrystobel groaned softly as his weight lifted from her. "You did not hurt me," she said, rubbing the back of her head where it had hit the floor. "I am well. Are you? I did not hurt you, did I?"

Keller rolled back on his haunches, grasping Chrystobel by both arms and pulling her to a sitting position. "I am well enough," he said, glancing at Izlyn, who was standing a few feet away with a fearful expression on her face. "'Twas your sister and her amazing strength that did this. She is a fearsome wench."

A smile bloomed on Chrystobel's lips and she looked at her sister, who was looking rather confused by Keller's statement. "Aye, that she is," she agreed, rising to her feet and helping Keller as he struggled to his. "She is very fearsome, indeed."

Keller eyed the younger girl as he pulled the rest of his mail coat off. "Do you think the fearsome wench can find me a chair to put this coat on?" he asked. "It should be left to dry."

Chrystobel turned to her sister, who had heard the request. She still appeared rather fearful and confused, but she dutifully went on the hunt for a chair. There was one near the hearth and she dragged it over, presenting it to Keller with the greatest timidity.

Keller took it and thanked her politely, which almost sent her cowering to the wall again because the man had spoken directly to her. But she didn't get too far. In fact, her curiosity was overcoming her fear of the great English knight. He hadn't been cruel to her and he certainly hadn't been cruel to her sister, so her nervous edge was easing somewhat. She began to creep closer to the bed but backed up when Keller noticed her movement. When he looked away, she would resume inching forward.

Keller was aware of Izlyn's game. He was trying very hard not to smile as she shuffled discreetly in his direction. Every time he looked at her, she would stop, pretending that she was doing nothing more than casually standing there, but then he would look away and he could hear her shuffling feet again. He looked at her quickly one time and she nearly fell over in her haste to come to a stop. It was a cute little diversion and he was content to play along, but in truth, there was something more prevalent on Keller's mind.

As Chrystobel helped him remove his padded tunic, revealing the naked and muscular torso beneath, it began to occur to him that he was now only half-dressed with two women in the room, one being his new wife whom he had yet to have marital relations with. He was an inherently shy man, reserved, and had never been particularly comfortable with opposite sex. He knew some men were content to walk around in the nude no matter what the circumstances, but he wasn't one of them. He was, kindly put, a prude.

Consequently, he hadn't had his first sexual experience until he was a seasoned knight, twenty-seven years of age to be exact, and that experience had occurred in a tavern because he had been exhausted and drunk after a battle march. A serving wench had taken advantage of his state and he'd soon found himself in bed with not one but two women. They had both pleasured him and he'd ended up having sex with both of them, one after the other, and the women told him repeatedly that he had the biggest member they had ever seen. It was supposed to make him feel manly but it just made him feel self-conscious.

He'd awoken the next morning with both women snuggled up next to him, feeling rather shocked and embarrassed at his wild behavior. He'd slipped out of the tavern half-dressed because he hadn't wanted to wake them, putting on the rest of his clothing and protection while on the road. His colleagues had made great sport of his embarrassment and, to this day, it made his cheeks flame to think on that shame. He'd been the butt of jokes for months afterwards. *Have you heard about de Poyer? The man has such a mighty rod that it takes two women at once to satisfy him! Beware your sisters and daughters around him, for he'll take his pleasure with them and blow the top of their heads off with his virility!*

God, he'd just wanted to die of shame from all of the ribald comments. Those same knights who had taunted him ended up in his command years later and he made sure they felt his wrath. But fourteen years later, he was no more comfortable with women than he had been those years ago. He'd had a few more sexual encounters since then, with paid women, but they had been few and far between. Consequently, he wasn't very experienced with intimacy and as he sat on the bed, his naked torso exposed, he found that he was actually embarrassed. Perhaps it wouldn't have been so bad if the younger girl wasn't there, but as it was, he was vastly uncomfortable. But he couldn't very well send the child away. Meanwhile, he tried not to appear too uneasy as he sat there and popped his knuckles absently.

"It would be better if you lie on your belly," Chrystobel's soft voice broke him from his train of thought. "Would it be too painful for you to do that?"

"It would not," he said softly. "If it makes tending the wound easier for you, I am happy to comply."

Chrystobel smiled at his kind words as Keller stopped cracking his knuckles and rolled onto this stomach, his face buried in coverlets that smelled of violets. He could feel Chrystobel's gentle fingers on his back, the tender touch of an angel soothing him. Thoughts of discomfort and embarrassment faded, and he was asleep before he realized it.

It was the first time in two days that he felt at ease enough to sleep.

CHAPTER TEN

Castell Mallwyd
Lair of Colvyn ap Gwynwynwyn

S ITUATED DEEP IN Powys among some of the most dramatic scenery in all of Wales, Castell Mallwyd sat amongst a series of foothills, riding the crest of one of the tallest hills like a great figurehead at the bow of a mighty ship. It could be seen for miles, perched atop its towering hill, and the castle was difficult to reach even in the best of conditions. In winter, it was nearly impossible.

The castle belonged to Colvyn ap Gwynwynwyn, the illegitimate son of the last king of Powys, Gwynwynwyn ap Owain. His father had been very old when he had been conceived, his mother being the fourteen-year-old granddaughter of one of Gwynwynwyn's advisors. His mother had died in childbirth with him and in order to avoid a devastating and costly civil war within his kingdom, Gwynwynwyn had given the advisor a castle and lands of his own, property that now belonged to Colvyn.

But it was a dirty place, with crumbling stone, skinny dogs, and a great hall that could only contain twenty people at the most. A great pit in the middle of the dilapidated hall served as its fire pit, with smoke escaping through holes in a roof that needed to be repaired. Colvyn didn't spend much time in the hall. He preferred the gatehouse where he had a sturdy room with a good roof and a hearth, and a buxom servant woman to fill his bed. But on this late night in October, he found himself sitting in his hall, watching Gryffyn d'Einen slurp down a thin stew made from rabbits and field mice, and watered ale.

The man had come to Castell Mallwyd earlier in the day, exhausted and nearly hysterical. He rode a horse bearing English tack, which was puzzling to Colvyn until Gryffyn began spouting his story in between ravenous bites. Then, it all started to come out.

The English had taken over Nether Castle. Trevyn d'Einen had been killed in the battle and Gryffyn's sisters had been taken hostage, including Chrystobel, whom Colvyn had his eye on. It was disturbing news to say the least, and Colvyn sat and listened to Gryffyn, who seemed genuinely upset about the English onslaught. Gryffyn had barely escaped with his life, and was only able to do so after stealing an English soldier's horse. The more Gryffyn spoke, the more concerned – and doubtful – Colvyn became.

"Why Nether?" Colvyn demanded. "It is not as if the castle is in the marches and is of contention between the Welsh and the English. It is thirty bloody miles from the marches, so to attack Nether makes no sense at all."

Gryffyn slurped down the last of the watery stew. The flavor had been terrible but it was warm, and that was all that mattered. "William Marshal desires it," he told Colvyn. "The man desires a foothold in Powys and now he has it."

"A foothold for what?"

Gryffyn sucked the scraps of meat from his bowl and tossed it aside, watching the dogs fight each other for the privilege of licking it.

"Long have the Normans desired to conquer Wales," he said, eyeing the short, dark man across the table from him. "You know this. They have already conquered southern Wales and now they move north. Today it will be Nether; tomorrow, mayhap it will be Castell Mallwyd. You must send word to your *teulu* for more men so that we can take Nether back and vanquish the English from our region. If we do not strike now and strike fast, all will be lost."

It was an impassioned plea but Colvyn, unlike Gryffyn, was not quick to react. He was more methodical, and frankly, the story seemed a little far-fetched. He'd never heard of English attacking a fortress this deep into Wales, at least not without good reason. Conquest of the region, especially with winter bearing down on them, seemed odd. All skepticism aside, however, it was not an entire unlikely prospect. The English had been known to do stranger things. Torn between real possibilities and Gryffyn's dramatics, he sighed heavily.

"There is some truth in what you say," he replied. "I can think of no other reason for the *Saesneg* to attack Nether other than it must be a part of a greater plan. Mayhap of conquest, as you said. And you say your father was killed in the attack?"

Gryffyn nodded, appearing properly grieved. "The *Saesneg* warriors killed him because he resisted," he replied. "Then they took my sisters as a prize."

"But you escaped?"

"Only by the grace of God was I able to," Gryffyn said, sounding properly convincing. "They tried to restrain me but I was able to break free. See this broken wrist? This is proof of their brutality."

He was holding up his heavily bandaged wrist, one that Colvyn's soldiers had set because Colvyn didn't have a physic. His castle was too poor for that. Eyeing the wrist, Colvyn digested the story. He had known Gryffyn d'Einen for many years and they were friends, although Gryffyn at times had tested that friendship. He was a nasty man with a brutal streak and there were times that Colvyn had been disgusted by his actions.

Once, on a visit to Nether, he caught Gryffyn slapping Chrystobel, but Gryffyn had come up with a very plausible and convenient excuse for the action, and Chrystobel had kept her mouth shut out of fear. She'd neither condemned nor defended her brother, but the incident had left a bad taste in Colvyn's mouth. Still, men had a right to discipline their women and Gryffyn was no exception. Colvyn gave him the courtesy of not questioning him further on the matter, even when he saw Chrystobel the next day with an eye swollen shut.

However, facts were facts – Gryffyn had never shown any real concern for his family, so his story of his family at the hands of the English seemed questionable. Colvyn had been listening to it for over an hour. With that in mind, Colvyn contemplated his next volley of questions.

"That may be true," he said. "They are a brutal race. But why have you come to me for help? You hold no real love or affection for your family, Gryffyn. Do you panic because the English seek to steal your legacy? Surely you do not wish for me to save your family from their clutches. They are probably better off with their *Saesneg* captors than they are with you."

As he laughed quietly into his cup, Gryffyn struggled not to become enraged. If he did, Colvyn would throw him out and he would have nowhere to go. More than that, if he offended the man, he would lose his only real ally. Therefore, it was imperative to convince Colvyn that the English were bent on conquest of the region. There was no other way to force Colvyn to rally his men and, consequently, his very large *teulu*. The Gwynwynwyn *teulu* had hundreds of members at the very least. With that in mind, he decided to go for the man's heart. It was the only way to get what he wanted and Gryffyn was a man who did not like to be denied his wants.

"They took Chrystobel," he said. "We have no way of knowing what they have done to her in the time I have been gone. Rape and brutality is commonplace with them. Will you leave her to their clutches or will you help her?"

Colvyn's general disinterest began to fracture. He was very fond of Chrystobel. He'd made no secret of that. He'd sent her gifts and messages for the past six months with the intention of asking for her hand in marriage at some point. The thought of the woman being a captive of *Saesneg* filth had his genuine concern.

"They have probably already marked her," he muttered. "Like the dogs they are, they have marked her as their own. She is too beautiful to be left untouched. As fond as I am of her, I will not accept *Saesneg* leavings."

Gryffyn appeared stricken. "Then you will not help her?"

Colvyn eyed the man. It was evident that he wanted help very badly but Colvyn wasn't apt to give it so readily. Unlike many of his fellow Welshmen, he wasn't particularly hot-headed. He was rather methodical and weighed all options before attacking. He set his cup aside, gazing intensely at Gryffyn.

"This is not my fight," he said. "If I help you, then the *Saesneg* might come after me, too. It is true that Castell Mallwyd is difficult to reach, but it is not impossible and this place could not stand a siege. It would fall, and I cannot say I am willing to risk that."

Gryffyn's first reaction was to scream at the man but he bit his tongue. He knew it would not do any good. He would be stupid to berate him. Taking a deep breath, he downed what was left of the watered ale in his cup, coughing up the dregs in the bottom that managed to make it into his throat. He had to make this worth Colvyn's time and effort; *think, man, think!* He mulled over the man's response. Since playing on his sympathies as far as Chrystobel was concerned hadn't worked, he tried another tactic – a more profitable tactic.

"I understand," he finally muttered, moving to pour himself more wine with his awkward left hand. "If I were in your position, then I might say the same thing. But the fact remains that I need your help to oust the *Saesneg* and I will pay for the privilege. With my father gone, I am now in control of Nether's wealth and you know as well as I do that there is a good deal of it. I will pay you handsomely for your assistance in removing the *Saesneg* and if my sister is untouched by them, you can have her, too. Will you at least think on it?"

Colvyn had to admit that Gryffyn's proposal had his attention. Even if he was the bastard son of the last king of Powys, the truth was that any family fortune had gone to the legitimate offspring. All Colvyn had was a broken-down fortress and limited income. He mulled over the proposal. His conviction to not involve himself in Gryffyn's battle was fading at the lure of being paid for his manpower.

He knew Nether was very wealthy. It had herds of sheep, orchards, and coveted lands. Perhaps he should rethink his refusal to lend assistance. As much as he didn't want to, he found himself doing just that.

"How much?" he finally asked.

Gryffyn grinned, knowing he had the man's interest and, with the right answer, his help. "Half of everything I have," he replied without hesitation.

Colvyn was stunned. "*Half?*" he repeated. "Do you swear this to me?"

"I will write it in blood if I must."

Colvyn thought on that a moment, realizing with sickening certainty that he was about to involve himself in another man's fight because the lure of money was just too great. He found that he couldn't refuse.

"Not in blood," he said. "But I will have it in writing and I shall give the document to my kin. If I help you chase off the *Saesneg* and you fail to pay, they will bring everything they have down around Nether and take all of it. Is this in any way unclear?"

Gryffyn nodded his head slowly, his dark eyes glittering wickedly. "It is perfectly clear."

"And I will have Chrystobel, too."

"Aye... Chrystobel, too. You can even have Izlyn just for sport."

Colvyn simply sat and eyed the man. He was afraid to say anything more. He was afraid he'd said too much already, because it seemed as if he had indeed committed himself to Gryffyn's cause. For a price.

He wondered if that price would ultimately prove to be too high.

CB

Nether Castle

KELLER WASN'T HAPPY in the least. In fact, he was damn well furious. Standing in the solar in Nether's keep, the one with the door cut into the floor that led down into the storage area, he faced William, George,

Aimery, and several senior sergeants. He had eleven men altogether, and all of them were in the chamber because all of them were, to varying degrees, responsible for a significant failure. They were all bracing themselves for de Poyer's rage.

"You let that bastard escape," Keller growled, eyeing the men around him. "One man against how many English? Is he really that cunning or are all of you really so bloody incompetent?"

William cleared his throat softly. "In fairness, d'Einen seems to be quite cunning," he said. "He escaped George and Aimery by throwing a large rock at George's head and nearly braining the man. George barely escaped unscathed, and Aimery was already injured at that point. It made it difficult to keep up with the man. By the time the horses were brought out, d'Einen was in hiding and he knocked one of the soldiers off his horse and stole the beast. After that, we gave chase but lost him in the mountains to the south. We could not risk pursuing him any further."

Keller's jaw was ticking as he listened to William. He had fallen asleep the day before and had slept all day and all night because Chrystobel wouldn't allow anyone to awaken him, not even when William came to tell him about Gryffyn's escape. Therefore, the man had been gone nearly an entire day by the time Keller awoke, refreshed and feeling very well indeed, until William told him what had happened. By then, Keller's legendary temper had been unleashed.

"Spare me your explanations," he snapped softly, holding up a hand to quiet William. "The fact remains that d'Einen escaped. Three hundred Englishmen could not capture one lone Welshmen and that is a shameful statistic. If the Marshal ever found out, we would all be consigned to scullery duty. This failure is inexcusable."

William glanced at the men who were stoically receiving their verbal beating. "In speaking with some of d'Einen's men, they have offered to assist us in locating him," he said. "But I would advise caution, my lord. These men are Welsh, and loyal to the House of d'Einen, so it would not be my inclination to trust them. I have already sent scouts to pick up Gryffyn's trail, so we should know something more by tonight."

Keller's expression was wrought with disgust. He was furious with their ineptitude and with the fact that he had slept through the crisis. Truth be told, he was perhaps more angry at himself than anything. He had allowed himself to be lulled into a deep and dreamless sleep. *Never again,* he vowed. *I will never let myself be so at ease ever again.* After a moment, he looked away from the men crowding the chamber.

"Get out of here," he told the group. "Go back to your duties and stay out of my way. All but my knights, you will remain."

The senior soldiers filed out silently, quitting the chamber and eventually the keep altogether. Keller waited until he heard the entry door shut before looking at his three knights.

"I am having a serious difficulty grasping this," he said, rubbing at his eyes in an exasperated gesture. "I cannot fathom how you let that man escape. Well? I am waiting for an explanation that makes sense because right now, all I can see is three massive failures standing before me. How on earth did you achieve your current posts when you were capable of such failure?"

Aimery, with a swollen nose and two black eyes, spoke softly. "It was inexcusable, my lord," he agreed. "I apologize for myself because I should not have let my injury slow me down as it did. I should have…."

George cut his brother off. "He could hardly see, my lord," he told Keller, watching his brother's indignant expression. "He fell down twice running behind me and the third time, he was in the kitchen yard and slipped in the mud. He went right into the butcher block and knocked himself giddy. D'Einen had already passed through the postern gate at that point so I ordered several soldiers to pursue the man so that I could help my brother. The failure is all mine, as I should not have returned to aid my brother. I am willing to accept your punishment."

Aimery's mouth was hanging open in outrage as he glared at his brother. "It was *my* fault," he declared, turning to Keller. "You must punish me *first.*"

George scowled at his brother. "Shut your pie hole, you fool!" he hissed. "You were in no condition to capture d'Einen, so I am the one who must be punished! It was my fault!"

"It was *my* fault!"

William opened his mouth to shut them both up but Aimery threw a punch at his brother and they both went down, tumbling over a table and crashing to the ground. William began yelling at them, moving to pull them apart, as Keller just stood there and rolled his eyes. He realized, to his surprise, that he was very close to grinning at the foolery of the Ashby-Kidd brothers. He'd seen them pull this kind of idiocy before and he'd always yelled at them, frustrated at their behavior. But at this moment, all he could feel was amusement, especially when Wellesbourne began tossing them about.

"Enough!" William roared, grabbing George by the neck and throwing him off his brother. "Sweet Bleeding Christ, Aimery, get off the damn ground. What is the matter with you, behaving like that?"

Aimery was furious as William yanked him to his feet. "George only backed off the pursuit of d'Einen because of me," he insisted angrily. "It is not right for him to take the blame when it was clearly my fault."

Keller put up his hands. "Shut your mouths, all of you," he snapped. "God's Bloody Rood, what a stable of knights I have. Throwing punches and demanding to be blamed for a failure? I have half a mind to lash you to the vault and beat you all senseless. Yet as much as it would give me hours of endless joy to do that, I must refrain. The fact of the matter is now that d'Einen has escaped us, we must locate him. That is our task at hand."

George and Aimery managed to calm themselves, but it was a struggle. William slapped George on the head and directed the young man across the chamber, well away from his brother. When William was sure they weren't going to charge each other again, he turned to Keller.

"As I told you, I have sent scouts out to pick up d'Einen's trail," he said quietly. "But I must ask this question; do you truly care if the man is returned? If he is gone, then the trouble he creates is gone, including the threat to your wife and her sister. Nether will be a more peaceful place, one would hope."

Keller, too, was calming after his initial rage. The antics of the Ashby-Kidd brothers had managed to loosen him a bit. In fact, he was coming to appreciate these men who served under him. They were competent in spite of what he had said, and they were genuinely dedicated to his service. He'd spent the past two months trying not to get close to them, to let them into his world and into his thoughts, but he was coming to think that the wall he'd put up around himself to protect his damaged heart had been too big a wall. It was lonely being isolated like that. Chrystobel had already succeeded in knocking down some of that wall. Perhaps he needed to lower it further to include the men that served him. Especially Wellesbourne; he suspected the man would make a fine friend. With a heavy sigh, he turned away and sought out the nearest chair.

"And I would agree with you except for one thing," he said, easing his big body onto the oak frame chair with the rigid back. "It is my fear that d'Einen has gone off to rouse trouble against us. His father mentioned that he was friends with a local lord. What if he goes to that lord and manages to rouse the man against us? At least if he is locked up in the vault here at Nether, he cannot create trouble."

William agreed, somewhat. "I still say he's better off away from Nether," he said, scratching his blond head in a weary gesture. "But I will tell you what the scouts say when they return. Mayhap he has not gone too far and capturing him will not be an issue."

Keller sat back against the chair, shifting when the wound in his back pained him. He shifted around a few more times until he could find a comfortable position.

"Mayhap," he agreed softly as he moved around. Once he was comfortable, he cast William a long glance. "I understand that you tried to tell me of this situation last night but Lady de Poyer would not wake me. Is this true?"

William looked at him. "Who told you that?"

"I did," George said helpfully from the other side of the room.

William gave George a rather exasperated expression before returning his focus to Keller. He hadn't told Keller of Chrystobel's intercession when he had gone to rouse the man, fearful that her actions would bring her husband's anger against her.

"She said that you were injured and exhausted," he said. "I told her that it was an urgent matter but she said unless the Romans were pillaging the castle and murdering people in their beds, she was not going to wake you. She was very firm about it."

"And you naturally complied."

"I had little choice."

Keller suspected as much. He held William's gaze for a moment before exhaling heavily and looking away. "I suppose that if I am angry with anyone, it should be her," he muttered. "But I cannot bring myself to do it."

William could see that the man was calming and he was thankful. "She was only thinking of your health," he said. "You *were* injured and you had not slept in two days."

Keller pondered his wife's protective instinct. He'd never known anyone to be protective over him, ever, and he wasn't sure how he felt about it. He felt humbled, but he also felt suspicious. Why should someone care for him so much that they would be willing to protect him? He cleared his throat softly, uncomfortably.

"This is something very new for me," he admitted quietly. "Is this how a woman normally behaves? That is to say, are you sure she was only thinking of me?"

William fought off a grin. "Of course I am," he said. "She certainly wasn't doing it to be cruel."

Keller seemed rather perplexed by the thought. "Women can be domineering," he said. "I have seen it. Are you sure she wasn't trying to dominate me?"

William couldn't help the smile. "God's Bones, de Poyer, of course not," he said. "She was doing what you would have done in the same circumstance. Would you not have tried to protect the woman if she was lying there, injured and sleeping?"

"Of course I would have."

"Then you can understand what she was trying to accomplish. She was protecting her husband, and that happens to be *you*."

It was a foreign concept. As he sat there and pondered the fact that his wife was evidently concerned for him, a soldier entered the solar. Keller, and the other knights, turned to focus on the man who was singularly fixed on Keller.

"What is it?" Keller asked.

"An army approaches, my lord," the soldier said.

Keller's brow furrowed as he stood up stiffly from his chair. "What army?" he asked. "Are they flying colors?"

The soldier nodded. "De Lohr pennants, my lord," he replied. "Blue and yellow."

Keller looked at William, satisfaction in his expression. "Our reinforcements are here," he said. William was already moving, shooing George and Aimery out of the solar as Keller followed, speaking to the soldier as he went. "Open the gates and send out riders to greet them."

The soldier fled as Keller continued on his normal pace, heading for the keep entry, but as he passed the stairs that led to the upper floor, he came to a stop. He looked at the stairs, narrow dark stone leading up a narrow dark passage, and thought of Chrystobel on the floor above him. As lady of the keep, it was her job to make arrangements for visitors, so Keller headed up the stairs to inform her of their arrival. By the time he reached the chamber door, he realized he was actually a little giddy at the thought of seeing her. He made sure to smooth at his hair, a weak attempt at grooming, before knocking on the door.

Rapping softly, he waited a few seconds before lifting the latch and opening the door. As the panel swung open, he immediately spied Chrystobel sitting by the hearth with some kind of sewing in her lap. Izlyn was sitting at her feet, playing with sticks from the kindling. It would seem that building with sticks was her favorite pastime, as Keller had seen her do it before. Chrystobel smiled brightly at him when their eyes met.

"Greetings, husband," she said. "Are you finished meeting with your men?"

Keller stepped into the room. "Aye," he replied, unwilling to elaborate on the subject he and his men had discussed. When he'd left his wife, he'd only told her that he was meeting with his men and nothing more. "We were interrupted by the announcement of approaching visitors. I've come to tell you to expect several more men for the evening's meal."

Chrystobel set her sewing aside and stood up. She was dressed in a surcoat of dark green wool that fit her delicious figure snuggly. In fact, she looked alluring and beautiful, and he couldn't take his eyes off her shapely torso and gently flaring hips as she approached him.

"Of course," she said seriously. "I will make sure there is enough food for all."

Keller's dusky gaze lingered on her. "Thank you," he said, his mind returning to what William had said as he looked at her. *She was protecting you.* He felt like the most fortunate man in the world but in the same breath, he couldn't believe that such a glorious creature could actually feel something for him. The thought only made him feel giddier. "I believe these visitors will be staying with us for some time. They are English knights, sent to reinforce my ranks, so if you could prepare a spot in the keep for them to sleep, I would be grateful."

Chrystobel smiled again, her expression open and friendly. "I will make sure they are comfortable," she said. "Is there anything else you wish?"

It was such a sweet question. Keller felt like an idiot because everything about her seemed to make him feel weak. The walls of defense he'd kept up, so practiced around him, had fallen and he could feel himself opening up again. It was terrifying and thrilling all at the same time.

"Nay," he said, shaking his head. "I will be with our visitors, so please send a servant should you need me."

He turned for the door but Chrystobel put her hand on his arm, stopping him. "Wait, please," she said, smiling timidly when he turned to look at her. "I was wondering if I might speak with you for a moment. I will be brief, I promise."

Keller nodded. "Of course," he said. "What is your wish?"

Chrystobel cleared her throat softly, perhaps a bit nervously, and glanced at her sister before speaking. "My brother," she said, her tone very soft. "Has he been located? Is he finally locked up?"

Keller realized she didn't want to upset Izlyn with such talk, so he motioned for her to follow him out onto the landing. Once outside of the chamber on the dark and dank landing, he closed the door behind them quietly.

"Your brother escaped Nether yesterday," he said, his voice quiet. "I understand that Wellesbourne came to speak to me last night about it but that you sent him away."

Chrystobel nodded, trying not to appear too contrite. "I did," she said. "You were sleeping so soundly that I did not want to wake you. Did I do wrong?"

Keller smiled faintly, shaking his head. "You did not," he said. "Wellesbourne wanted to tell me about your brother escaping Nether. We have sent scouts to follow his trail."

Chrystobel looked at him, worried. "Will you bring him back?"

Keller shrugged. "William pointed out to me that to have him away from the castle means peace for us all," he said. "But there is a larger part of me that wants to bring him back to face justice for the murder of your father, among other things."

Chrystobel thought seriously on both points. In fact, she looked rather bewildered. "Away from Nether?" she murmured, more to herself than to him. "I... I have rarely known him to be away from Nether. He has always been here, lurking about."

Keller studied her intently, seeing both fear and relief in her expression. It occurred to him that she should have some say in all of this, considering how much of it directly affected her. For so long she'd had no control over her brother. Now, Keller would give her some of that control back.

"What would be your desire?" he asked softly. "Do you want me to bring him back here and punish him or do you want me to let him keep running, so long as he stays far away from here?"

Chrystobel looked at him, surprised he would ask her such a question. She took it very seriously. "I...I do not know," she said. "I never thought... that is to say, I never believed I would ever know a life without living in fear of my brother. It does not seem real."

Keller watched her befuddled expression, daring to reach out and brush her fingers with his own. The mere touch between them sent bolts of excitement racing through his big body and when she latched on to his fingers, holding them tightly, he actually thought he might swoon. Everything in his chest welled up so that he could hardly breathe.

"It is real," he replied. "You will never again have to fear the man so long as I am alive. If you want me to track him down and punish him for killing your father, I will. But if you simply want to let the man run off forever, out of your sight and out of your mind, then I understand. I will leave the choice to you."

Chrystobel clutched his fingers with both hands, feeling his warmth and strength. It was an overwhelming sensation, one that made her heart race with joy. As she gazed up into the man's dark blue eyes, all she could feel was pure and blissful attraction. He may not have been the most handsome man she had ever seen, but he had a rugged beauty that was beyond compare. She was so caught up in the soft pout of his smooth lips and the square cut of his jaw that she nearly forgot to reply to his statement.

"Punishing him will not bring my father back," she whispered. "I simply want him away, Keller. I never thought I would know this opportunity but now that is here, I do not want to see him ever again and I do not want to think of him ever again. I want to erase him from my mind completely. If Gryffyn is running, let him run. Let him run forever as long as it is away from Nether."

Keller nodded in agreement, lifting her hands to kiss them sweetly. "If that is your wish," he said softly. "But if I ever see the man again, make no mistake. I will kill him. If he ever returns to Nether, he is a dead man."

Chrystobel nodded, feeling warm and safe and protected by his declaration. "Of course, Keller," she said. "I support whatever you will do to that regard."

"I appreciate that."

She was gazing up at him still but it was apparent there was much on her mind. "About my father," she ventured, her expression gradually becoming distressed. "We must bury him. Where is he?"

Keller squeezed her hands gently. "We put took him to the stables yesterday but I do not know if he has been moved," he said. "I will discover where he is and then we can plan his mass. Where would you bury him?"

Her eyes grew moist, thinking about her father, her regrets with him, her sorrows. "My mother is buried at St. Peter's in Machynlleth," she said. "It is a few miles to the west. I will send word to the priests to make arrangements for my father."

"I will do it," Keller replied. "I will ride into town on the morrow and make the arrangements, unless… unless you would like to accompany me?"

Chrystobel's expression brightened. "Aye, I would like that," she said. "Moreover, I think I should. You spoke excellent Welsh to me when we first met, but are you able to carry on a conversation with it?"

"Yr wyf yn," he said in perfect Welsh. "Pam ydych chi'n gofyn?" *I am. Why do you ask?*

Chrystobel grinned. "Because I believe the priests only speak Welsh," she said, cocking her head. "How is it that you speak my language so well?"

He shrugged. "I was the garrison commander at Pembroke Castle for many years," he told her. "I learned Welsh long ago in order to effectively deal with the local chieftains. I can probably speak it better than you can."

Chrystobel laughed. "I do not think so," she said. "I learned it at birth. I did not learn English until I was six years old, when I went to foster at Chirk Castle. And then, I had to learn it quickly because the lord's wife only spoke English."

He was grinning at her. "I am sure you were a good student."

Chrystobel smiled modestly, her hands still holding on to his fingers, feeling giddy and silly in his presence now. The conversation was flowing so wonderfully, better than it ever had in spite of the subjects of her father and brother, and she was thrilled. When Keller wasn't being cold and distant, he had a hint of charm in his manner that was boyish and sweet.

"I tried," she said, realizing the dialogue was coming to a close and not wanting it to. But there were tasks to be accomplished and she gave his big hand a squeeze. "I suppose I should go and make preparations for your visitors now. May I travel unescorted now that my brother is no longer a threat?"

Keller didn't see any harm in it. "You and your sister may both travel unescorted," he said. Then, his thoughts began to linger on the sister, the small and silent child who seemed so terrified of everything. "Tell me… how long did your brother lock her in the vault because she is mute?"

Chrystobel's smile faded. "Years," she said softly. "My father did not send Izlyn to foster because she would not speak, so she has always lived here at Nether. I have educated her as best I can from what I was taught at Chirk, and my father educated her as well. She is an intelligent girl and can read and write Welsh, French, and English, but the fact that she was bright only fueled my brother's rage towards her. He was convinced that in her lack of speech, she was simply being stubborn. She would spend days in the vault on end, at least until my father would release her, but Gryffyn would grow angry with her again and lock her back up. She has been in and out of the vault weekly since she was eight years of age."

Keller was grim. "How old is she now?"

"She has seen twelve years as of last month."

Keller breathed lightly. "Then she will benefit the most from your missing brother," he said. "Mayhap she will finally begin to enjoy life a little, as a young girl should."

Chrystobel thought of her little sister, of her horrific life up until that point, and her eyes grew moist. "I sincerely pray for that."

"It is my intention to make sure you both enjoy life now that I am here."

Chrystobel smiled gratefully and Keller kissed her hands again, but he didn't stop there. Her lips were soft and inviting, and he gently slanted his mouth over hers, suckling her lips gently. Her response was timid at first, but very quickly, she gave in to his attention and the kisses became more powerful as she wrapped her arms around his neck. Keller pulled her against him, his torso against hers, as his kisses turned to fire. She was incredibly soft and warm, and the feel of her in his arms roused him like nothing he had ever known. He never realized a kiss was supposed to be this sweet or this alluring. At this moment, it was the most powerful thing he had ever experienced. She was the most powerful thing he had ever known.

But that blissful moment was cut short when the chamber door next to them rattled. Suddenly, Keller was standing a few feet away from Chrystobel as the door opened and Izlyn stood in the doorway. He didn't even know how he got there. All he knew was that the door movement had startled him as if he had been a silly stable boy stealing a kiss from a serving maid, fearful he'd been caught doing something clandestine. When he realized how he had reacted, he felt like a bloody idiot.

Keller looked over at Chrystobel, who seemed flushed and dazed as she took her sister by the hand and told the girl that they had visitors to prepare for. She smiled at Keller as she disappeared into the lower levels to make arrangements for their guests, and Keller followed at a distance, his wits still not completely gathered. Their kiss had left him scatterbrained to say the least, and it was a full minute before he even remembered the task that lay ahead of him. He had visitors to greet, great knights from the stable of de Lohr.

Still lingering in the effects of that heated kiss, he headed out to meet them.

CHAPTER ELEVEN

S IR GART FORBES was an enormous man with piercing green eyes, a bald-shaved head, and hugely wide shoulders. And the man didn't walk. he stalked. He had the look of a hunter about him and he literally stalked as he dismounted his charger and went to greet Keller. Their handshake was so powerful that it would have toppled a lesser man, but Keller simply grinned. A heavy-handed handshake was Gart's way of declaring one was worthy of his attention.

Sir Rhys du Bois, the second knight to wearily dismount his charger, didn't have the look of a hunter. He had the look of a trained killer. Nearly as tall as his hunter counterpart, he was broader and more muscular, with black hair and brilliant blue eyes. Every woman whose gaze was fortunate enough to fall upon Rhys du Bois would swear he was the most handsome man in all the world, which was mostly true. He was a fine example of male beauty coupled with intelligence and skill.

Keller, however, saw beyond the Adonis-like knight and the stalking hunter. He saw his old friends. Rhys grinned as he took Keller's hand when Gart finally released it, and Keller shook the man's hand firmly. He'd known the men since he had been a young man, newly knighted in the service of the aged Henry II, and they had kept in touch with each other even though he'd not seen them in over a year. They were a most welcome sight.

"So de Lohr sent you two?" Keller said, shaking his head. "What happened? Did he run out of excellent knights to send?"

Rhys laughed softly. "No one wanted to come so we had to draw lots," he said. "Gart and I lost."

Keller was grinning, smiling more than he had in months. "You serve Christopher and Gart serves his brother David," he said, looking between the two of them. "You normally do not serve together. How is it you ended up as a motley pair?"

Gart was pulling off one of his massive leather gloves, his trained gaze moving around the bailey as he did so. "The de Lohr war machine is involved in the baron's revolt against John," he said. "We were spared to come to Wales because Christopher fears that while most of the English barons are preoccupied with civil unrest, the Welsh might decide it is a perfect time to create problems. He wants us here, with you, in case that happens."

Keller's smile faded. "I've not seen Richard in a few years," he said. "I was with him all through the great quest to The Levant, but once he gifted me to William Marshal, I was sent to Wales and in Wales I have remained. This has not been my choice to be in this land of endless mountains and pewter skies."

Gart and Rhys knew that. Keller had been a very great knight for Richard and was much decorated for his heroism in the Holy Land. To tuck this great knight far away in the wilds was nothing short of criminal. Keller was someone they both greatly respected.

"William Marshal must have a purpose for putting you here," Rhys said. "He is not foolish. I am sure he wants you here for the same reason de Lohr has sent us to support you. With England eating itself up from the inside, if the Welsh decide to take advantage of the chaos, it would be very bad not to have a foothold here."

Keller knew that all too well but he still wasn't happy about it in spite of the fact that he now had an impressive castle, titles, and a beautiful wife. But it was not in his nature to complain. He was a knight and knights did as they were told.

"I just came from Southern Wales," he finally said. "It is calm for the most part. I heard no stirrings of revolt."

Gart grunted. "All the Welsh do is revolt," he muttered. "The Scots, too. And the French. Can no one simply do what they are told these days by those who demand to rule them?"

Keller was back to grinning. "You have spent enough time in the wars in France to know the answer to that," he said. "No one wants to be subjugated these days."

"Speaking of subjugated," Rhys said as he peeled back his hauberk, revealing the sticky black hair beneath. "How has it been for you around here? Any excitement?"

Keller just looked at him. *Where to start?* After a moment, he simply shook his head. "Let us go into the great hall and I will tell you the madness that has been commonplace here since my arrival."

Gart looked interested. "Madness?" he repeated. "Have we missed something?"

Keller could only lift his eyebrows. "That would be a simple way of putting it."

Ϩ

CHRYSTOBEL PRESENTED A lovely meal for Nether's newest guests. After being introduced to Sir Gart Forbes and Sir Rhys du Bois, she had run back to the kitchens were the servants were preparing a great feast. Great pitchers of ale, made from barley from their own fields, appeared on the tables and were quickly consumed by the two big knights and over one hundred senior soldiers they had brought with them into the great hall. The rest of the English mingled with Keller's forces to the north side of the bailey and near the gatehouse, swelling the ranks of the English to almost eight hundred men. Nether was a big place and was able to accommodate the crowd, but the d'Einen soldiers were rather outnumbered. The sight of so many English made them nervous.

When Chrystobel sent the ale to the hall, she also made sure to send barrels of ale out to the soldiers in the bailey, English *and* Welsh. She didn't want to neglect any of Nether's inhabitants, and especially the Welshmen who were not overrun by the English. Meanwhile, the cook and two of the kitchen servants began making loaf after loaf of dense brown bread and, piping hot, the loaves were sent out in waves to the great hall and troops outside. Butter went with the loaves, giving the men something to eat while the cook worked on re-heating roast mutton and covering it with a rosemary-peppercorn gravy made from the rosemary in Chrystobel's garden. As the mutton was being sauced, an old kitchen servant was making a great, hearty stew made from dried peas, barley, and carrots over an open flame in the kitchen yard in an iron pot big enough for a man to bathe in. The stew was thick and delicious, seasoned with onions and precious salt, and soon everyone was partaking of the mutton and of the stew. It was a glorious feast, indeed.

With everything running smoothly, Chrystobel stood in the corner of the hall, watching her husband, William, George, Aimery, and the two enormous English knights as they devoured the meal. The hall was rather lively, being so crowded, alive with conversation and filled with smoke from the hearth and the wanderings of hungry dogs. Men were laughing and talking everywhere.

At the end of the long feasting table sat Keller and the other knights, having a serious conversation from what Chrystobel could see, which was why she hadn't joined them. She assumed, correctly, that they had a great deal to talk about so she focused on her kitchen duties to ensure that everyone had enough to eat. She wasn't comfortable enough, or bold enough, to join the knights' conversation.

The feasting and the conversation went for most of the day and on into the early evening. Everyone seemed quite caught up in their conversation and ale. As the evening meal approached, the cook prepared a large quantity of mice pies – literally, pies filled with cooked, de-boned mice, onions, turnips, carrots, beans, and garlic, baked until the crust of the pie was a deep golden brown. Mice were very plentiful at Nether and the cook had managed to find a way to utilize the pests, cooking them into a tasty pie. Like rabbit or any other rodent, the Welsh cooks made use of what they could find and the result, in this case, was a clever and delicious result.

By the time the mice pies rolled out for the diners, Chrystobel took a couple of the male servants and went to the keep, down in the bowels of the stores where they kept their hoard of alcohol. They had a small brewery near the kitchens where they made ale using the barley grown on Nether lands, but they also made cider fermented with apples, cherry juice, honey, and peppercorns. It was a very potent cider with a powerful kick, hence, it was only brought out for special occasions. Otherwise, it was left to continue aging in the cold, dark stores, growing more potent by the day. Every time they brought out the bottles, there seemed to be more of a punch to it.

As the evening deepened, more alcohol was distributed. The ale, as it was more plentiful, was given to the troops supping in the bailey while Chrystobel took big bottles of the powerful cider into the hall. The servants distributed the bottles onto the tables and, on top of the ale that the men had been drinking most of the afternoon, the introduction of the cider turned most of them into drunken fools not a half-hour later. The legendary cider packed a more powerful punch that normal being ingested on top of the ale. In fact, things began to veer out of control after the mice pies were gone and the cider was in steady supply.

Back in the corner of the hall, Chrystobel could see that the feast was turning into wild drunken debauchery. The men were now playing games of chance, gambling on the tabletops as they drank, or betting each other that one could jump off of the feasting table higher and farther than another man could. Then, someone would vomit, and then ten more men would vomit, spraying it all over the wall and floor nearby. More laughter about it, then urination would follow. Men would pass out on the floor.

Open-mouthed, Chrystobel watched the increased activities with great concern and some awe. She'd never seen such drunkenness. Izlyn, who had been helping in the kitchens, heard the commotion going on and came to stand next to her sister, wide-eyed at the spectacle. Holding hands tightly, they stood and watched with shock and bewilderment as George, as drunk as a giddy fool, jumped on top of the feasting table and began singing ribald songs.

"There once was an old whore named Rose,
    Who would lick off the tips of your toes!
In passion, 'tis odd, she would swear that, by God,
    A tree was as big as your rod!"

The men roared with glee, singing the chorus of the song as loud as they could. They weren't really singing. In fact, they were shouting and slamming their wooden cups against the floor, the wall, or the table. George was dancing around on the table, drunkenly kicking cups and trenchers onto the floor, including Gart's. Frustrated, Gart reached up and yanked him down. George ended up in a pile on the floor as Aimery, even drunker than his brother, leapt up in his place. He launched into a well-known song, much repeated in inns and taverns throughout England and Wales.

"A young man came to Tilly Nodden,
    His heart so full and pure.
Upon the step of Tilly Nodden,
    His wants would find no cure."

When it came to the chorus, Aimery lifted his hands to encourage every man to sing with him. Soon, the hall of Nether was filled with the sounds of English voices, all joined in drunken revelry.

"Aye! Tilly, Tilly, my goddess near,
    Can ye spare me a glance from those eyes?
My Tilly, sweet Tilly, be my lover so dear,
    I'm a-wantin' a slap of those thighs!"

The men laughed uproariously, mostly because Aimery was bouncing around on the table, doing a jig like an idiot. But he slowed long enough to sing the last verse with the greatest flourish.

"Then our young man, his life less grand,
Since the day he met our Tilly.
His love for her nearly drove him daft,
When he discover'd not a puss, but a shaft!"

Cups pounded on the tables and walls loudly as men shouted a refrain of the chorus. Aimery leapt down from the table, pulled his brother up from the floor, and began dancing with him, crazily, around the head table while the soldiers screamed encouragement. The two of them held each other in an embrace as they danced a wild jig around the room, suddenly coming to a stop when they spied Chrystobel and Izlyn. Aimery pointed at the pair.

"Look!" he cried. "The two most beautiful women in all of Wales!"

The entire room turned to look at Chrystobel and Izlyn, standing against the wall, and before they could run off, George and Aimery had them cornered.

"Come and dance with me, Lady de Poyer," Aimery begged. "It is a night for celebration!"

Chrystobel was torn between fear and humor with Aimery's drunken antics. He had her by the wrist and she was trying to pull away.

"Nay," she insisted. "I do not dance."

"What?" Aimery bellowed, outraged. "A beautiful woman who does not dance? It is a crime! A tragedy! An *outrage!*"

Chrystobel was shaking her head even as he tried to drag her away from the wall. "Nay," she said, more firmly. "I do *not* dance. Please let me go."

Aimery wasn't trying to be cruel. He was simply drunk and had little self-control. To his right, George had managed to grab Izlyn, who was paralyzed with fear as the man held on to her. When Chrystobel looked over and saw the expression of terror on her sister's face, something within her snapped. Izlyn was petrified and George didn't seem to notice. All Chrystobel could hear or see were visions of Gryffyn as he grabbed Izlyn to haul her away to the vault while she had been helpless to intervene. How many nights had she lain awake, weeping because she couldn't help her sister? But this was different. Gryffyn wasn't here and Chrystobel wasn't helpless in the least. She could defend her baby sister, however small the gesture, against a drunken knight. Yanking her arm away from Aimery, she reached over and slapped George across the face.

"Let her go!" she roared, clutching her sister fiercely against her. "Can you not see that she does not wish to dance?"

Izlyn broke into sobs as Chrystobel rushed the girl off, bolting from the hall. Keller, having been over on the opposite side of the room, barely caught the commotion. All he saw was Chrystobel slapping George and his protective instincts began running wild.

Pushing himself away from the table, he was trying to figure out why he was so dizzy as he headed over to where George and Aimery were standing. He was mad enough to kill and it began to occur to him that that he might be slightly drunk. Everyone else was, and he was coming to think he was no exception. There was no other explanation for the tilting room and his surging fury. He was never any good when he imbibed too much so he was usually very careful about it, but he seemed to have lost track of how much drink he had ingested this night. He seemed fine until he started drinking that powerful cider, and then....

By the time he reached George, his fury had gained full steam. He grabbed the young knight by the shoulder and spun him around to face him.

"What did you say to Lady de Poyer to cause her to slap you like that?" he snarled. "Well?"

George's eyes opened wide with both fear and surprise. "N-nothing, my lord," he insisted. "I only asked her sister to dance but she did not want to!"

Aimery was nodding fervently, confirming what George was telling his liege. Frustrated, angry, Keller looked between the two young knights.

"You will never again touch my wife or her sister," he growled. "Do you comprehend me?"

George and Aimery nodded seriously. "Never again, my lord," George assured him. "We apologize."

That wasn't good enough for Keller. He thumped George's chest with a big hand. "You know what Gryffyn d'Einen did to those women," he said, his voice low and threatening. "You know what hell he put them through, how he beat and humiliated them. By God's Bloody Rood, you should have more sense than to grab women who have known little else but abuse. You'll scare them to death!"

George readily agreed. "We are deeply sorry, my lord," he repeated. "Should we go apologize to your lady wife and her sister?"

Keller eyed the two knights, knowing they were mostly harmless, and suddenly feeling rather foolish for becoming so angry with them. It was the alcohol forcing his manner.

"Nay," he grumbled, pushing past them. "I will go and make sure they are well. You just stay away from them."

George and Aimery watched Keller stagger from the hall, heading out through the darkened bailey towards the keep. As they stood there and wondered what more they should do to make amends to Lady de Poyer, from across the room, William, Rhys, and Gart were watching.

The older knights were fairly drunk themselves. Gart, in fact, was having a difficult time remaining upright. The tabletop kept trying to rise up and hit him in the face. Rhys was more exhausted than anything, but William was just plain liquidated. Everything about him was liquidated and sloshy. He watched Keller rough up George before leaving the hall. When the man was gone, he turned to Gart.

"I think that I should follow him to make sure all is well," he muttered, putting his feet under him in the hopes of being able to stand up and not tip over. "He does not do well when he has had too much to drink."

Gart was holding on to the tabletop for balance, even though he was seated. "Before you go, tell us the truth of the matter now that de Poyer is out of earshot," he said. "I have been wanting to ask you this since we arrived. Was it true that Keller was betrothed to Garren le Mon's widow?"

William nodded gingerly. Too much movement would have him toppling over. "The Marshal gifted de Poyer with le Mon's widow," he confirmed. "It was reported the le Mon perished in the battle for Lincoln Castle, but that was erroneous information, for Garren le Mon did not die. From what I was told, Keller was fairly in love with the Lady le Mon and her two children. He was looking forward to a beautiful family and when le Mon returned, it nearly destroyed him."

Gart grunted in response to the sorrowful story. "I know Garren," he said quietly. "I, too, was at the battle at Lincoln Castle. Garren was in command of Richard's troops during the siege, in fact. But then someone stole le Mon's armor and got himself killed, so it was naturally assumed that it was le Mon himself. Thank God it was not true. Garren is a good man."

"Indeed his is," Rhys agreed. "I was at that battle, also, and well remember the rumors of le Mon's death. Garren is a much decorated and much respected knight, but then again, so is Keller. The man should have never let his feelings get involved with a marital contract. Wives are not meant to be loved."

Gart eyed his blue-eyed friend. "So you do not plan to love your wife when you marry?"

Rhys was stalwart. "I do not plan to marry," he said firmly. "In our profession, wives are a hindrance."

"Keller has a wife," Gart reminded him.

Rhys was firm in his opinion. "The wife came with the castle," he said. "If I was gifted with such a castle, then I'd take the wife, too. That does not mean I have to fall all over myself, fawning with adoration for the woman. 'Tis foolish, I say. It is demeaning to a man."

Gart grinned, unusual for the usually stone-faced knight. "I will remind you of that the day you marry," he said. "I will tell your wife not to expect any affection from you."

Rhys could see that Gart was teasing him. "The woman would be wise to simply do what I told her to do, when I told her to do it," he said, feigning a rigid manner. "That is all a woman is good for, anyway."

Gart opened his mouth but William stopped him from replying. "Idiots, both of you," he said. "I have a wife whom I adore and I would not have it any other way. Now, if you two louts will excuse me, I am going to make sure Keller doesn't make an arse out of himself in front of his new wife."

Gart reached up to grab him before he could move away. "De Poyer must make his own way in this marriage," he said. "He cannot have you bailing him out of trouble at every turn. He must learn on his own."

William sighed heavily. "Under normal circumstances I would agree with you," he said, "but you sat here all afternoon listening to de Poyer tell you about his wife's brother and how the man beat both of the sisters and abused the family. Furthermore, you saw what just happened – everyone is very sensitive about the situation in general and Keller is so socially inept that I'm not entirely sure he knows how to deal with skittish women. He might send them off into fits and then we would have a disaster on our hands."

Gart looked up at him, lifting his eyebrows. "I will repeat what I just said," he muttered. "The man must learn. You must let him find his own way in this marriage."

He was right. Reluctantly, William sat back down but refused Gart's offer of more cider. He'd had enough. So the three knights sat there, reliving memories from when they had all served King Richard in The Levant, telling story after story, laughing at the humorous situations and reveling in the glory of others. Odd how the death, disease, and destruction of the Third Crusade didn't enter in to their conversation;

at the moment, they could only remember the good times. Perhaps it was the alcohol, perhaps not. Fond memories and warm sands were all they could seem to recall.

It was a good evening of proud and touching recollection.

CHAPTER TWELVE

KELLER COULD HEAR the soft voices as he approached his wife's chamber in the keep. He could hear Chrystobel speaking to Izlyn. As he stood at the door, listening to the soft hissing, it began to occur to him that he'd yet to consummate his marriage and he was a bit perturbed that his wife's twelve-year-old sister was in the chamber. He simply wanted to be alone with the woman to do what was his legal and moral right. He didn't want, or need, an audience. It was a selfish thought and he knew it, but thanks to the alcohol in his veins, he didn't particularly care. Hand on the latch, he quietly opened the door.

The chamber was warm, the only light in the room being cast from the flickering fire. The walls, the furnishings, and the people undulated in shades of orange and yellow. As he entered the room and quietly closed the door, his gaze found Chrystobel and Izlyn over by Chrystobel's big bed. Izlyn was lying down, covered up, and Chrystobel was sitting up beside her. When her gaze met with Keller's, she smiled.

"Why have you left your guests?" she asked him. "Is something amiss?"

Keller shook his head as he made his way to the bed, his gaze lingering on his beautiful wife. God, the alcohol was making him crazy because all he could think of was separating her from her clothing and having his way with her. Those thoughts were entirely foreign to him and he felt rather like a fiend for having them. He forced himself to shake off the lustful urges.

"Nothing is amiss," he said quietly. "I came to see if you and your sister were well. I saw what happened in the hall with George and thought to check on you."

Chrystobel's smile faded. "I am very sorry that I struck your knight," she said remorsefully. "But he would not let go of Izlyn and she was quite frightened."

Keller shook his head. "You need not apologize," he said. "George was drunk. But he did not mean any harm."

Chrystobel hung her head. "I know," she said. "But I could not let him frighten my sister."

Keller gazed at her a moment before turning his attention to Izlyn. The girl was gazing up at him without a hint of fear. In fact, she was looking at him quite openly and he swore he could see the thoughts rolling through her young mind. He put his hands on his hips as he focused on her.

"Lady Izlyn," he addressed her politely. "Can you understand me?"

The girl appeared surprised by the question and immediately looked to her sister for support. When Chrystobel smiled encouragingly, Izlyn's gaze returned to Keller and she nodded her head. Keller continued.

"The young knight who had you by the arm is named Sir George," he said, his hands coming off his hips as he began to pop his knuckles, that habit he seemed to have, which only happened when he was in an uncertain position. "He did not mean any harm. He likes to dance and play, and he wanted to dance and play with you. I realize you have known little comfort from any man other than your father, but I assure you that George and his brother, Aimery, would never hurt you. They would sooner frolic through a field of flowers with you, chasing frogs, than they would harm you. Do you understand what I am telling you?"

Izlyn was gazing back at him with her big, brown eyes. Again, she nodded slowly, and Keller dipped his head in return to acknowledge the fact that they understood one another.

"Then you must never fear them, or any of my knights," he told her. "I am sworn to protect you and so are they. Is that clear?"

Izlyn blinked as if she wasn't quite sure how to respond but eventually, she nodded yet again. She continued to stare up at Keller as the man gazed down upon her. His expression had grown rather gentle.

"Would you like to chase frogs tomorrow?" he asked her. "George and Aimery would be happy to accompany you. Or mayhap you would like to chase birds? Have you ever been out of this castle simply to walk the land?"

Izlyn looked at him as if she had no perception of what he was saying. She looked at Chrystobel as if the woman could clarify his question, and Keller found himself looking at Chrystobel, too.

"She has no concept of what I am asking, does she?" Keller asked softly.

Chrystobel was gazing sadly at her sister. "Nay," she said. "She has never known things such as that."

Keller's gaze returned to the girl on the bed. In her shift, wrapped in linen coverlets upon a mattress stuffed with a mixture of feathers and dried grass, she looked well cared for and content. But that had been far from the truth up until yesterday. Keller's drunken state was making him somewhat emotional about a young girl who had had been locked in the vault by her evil brother and had known little happiness in her short life.

"Things will change," he said, turning away from the bed and moving towards the hearth. It didn't appear nearly stoked enough for him so he took chunks of peat from the iron cage-like container next to the hearth and started throwing the pieces into the fire. "Now that I am here, much will change. I will make sure that Lady Izlyn is allowed to chase birds or frogs, and that you... what is it that you like to do, Chrystobel? Do you have any skills or pursuits?"

Chrystobel couldn't help but notice he was not only being rather talkative, but rather loud. The entire time he had been speaking to Izlyn, he had been popping his knuckles which, she was coming to see, was a nervous habit of his. Now, he kept throwing peat into the fire, arranging it with a poker, and the blaze was starting to pick up.

"I can sew and I can paint, a little," she said. "Though I have not painted in years. My mother had a small box of paints and when I used it up, I never had it replaced."

Crouched by the fire, Keller was watching her as she spoke. "Why not?" he asked. "Do not tell me that your father would not buy you more paints?"

Chrystobel shook her head and moved away from the bed, going to sit on one of the two stiff-backed oak chairs that faced the hearth.

"My brother would not permit it," she said softly. "Gryffyn felt that any money spent should be on him, as the heir. He spent the money on expensive horses. You can find them in our stables. He was fond of big-boned war horses from Flanders even though he'd hardly ever ridden to battle. He liked to collect them."

Keller's brow furrowed. "War horses are extremely expensive," he said. "How many does he have?"

"There are thirteen."

Keller was shocked. "*Thirteen* chargers?"

She shrugged. "I am not exactly sure how many chargers he has, or rounceys, or palfreys," she said. "I believe he has one Spanish Jennet."

Keller was still fairly astonished. "Only wealthy men have collections such as that," he said. "But with your brother gone and with the fact that I am now lord of Nether, his collection now belongs to me and I will duly inspect the animals on the morrow. But we are off the subject. If painting is what you like to do, then when we are in town making arrangements for your father's mass, we will purchase paint supplies for you. Would you like that?"

Chrystobel nodded hesitantly. "Aye," she said. "As I said, I've not painted in years, but I would like to."

Keller stood up from his crouched position and collected the chair next to hers, sitting heavily. Lashing out a big boot, he propped his foot up on the wall next to the hearth and, as he did so, let out a big burp.

There was just too much alcohol in his system for him to do much else at this point. As he nearly rattled the walls with his deep belch, Izlyn began to giggle. Keller craned his neck back to look at her.

"So you think that humorous, do you?" he asked. Then, he swallowed air and emitted a massive belch while speaking the words: "You silly wench, do you think this funny, too?"

Izlyn giggled uncontrollably and even Chrystobel laughed. Keller, grinning, did it again, releasing such a loud belch that he nearly vomited. "Is this what I must do in order to keep you two entertained?" he gasped in a normal tone.

Izlyn was squealing with laughter as Chrystobel stifled her laugher behind her hands. Keller started coughing because the gas had irritated his throat, but he was pleased that the women found it so amusing. It was the first time he'd ever seen them laugh out loud.

"If I do that again, I shall surely spray the contents of my stomach out all over this wall," he said, grinning. "But mayhap I shall give another try later if you both find it so amusing."

Chrystobel waved him off. "I am sure that is not necessary," she said. "But we thank you for your humorous attempts."

Keller's gaze lingered on her. In fact, he couldn't stop staring at her. "You are very beautiful," he said softly.

It was a swift turn of subjects and he was looking at her with a rather seductive smirk on his face. Chrystobel's smile turned from one of genuine happiness to one of modest flattery. "Thank you, my lord."

He lifted his eyebrows. "You are not permitted to call me that," he said. "You are only permitted to call me by my name. But I prefer to be addressed as 'husband'. That's what I am, you know. I am your husband."

Still smiling, she cocked her head. "I know."

"I do not feel like a husband, however."

Her smiled faded. "Why not?"

He shrugged, leaning forward so that his elbows were resting on his knees. "Because I was married yesterday and I still have not come to know my wife as a husband is entitled," he said, eyeing Izlyn as she lay on the bed. "Does she sleep in here with you always?"

Chrystobel knew precisely what he meant and struggled not to become embarrassed or defensive about it. "She does," she replied quietly. "But... but my father's chamber is across the hall and it is bigger than this one. I assumed that we would eventually share that one and that chamber has much more room."

Keller stood up and held out a hand to her. "I would see it now."

Chrystobel appeared somewhat stricken, eyeing her sister on the bed. "Now?" she repeated, taking his hand simply because it was almost directly I her face. "Can... can we at least not wait until Izzie has gone to sleep?"

Keller looked over at the girl, who was wide awake, watching them. "Why?" he asked. "She looks comfortable enough."

Chrystobel stood up, still holding his hand, and glanced at her sister. "Because she will cry if she is left alone," she said softly. "She is afraid of being alone."

Keller accepted that explanation and promptly sat back down. "I see," he said. When Chrystobel went to reclaim her seat, he tugged on her hand. "Not there. Sit with me."

"With you?"

"On my lap."

Somewhat shocked by the suggestion, but also thrilled by it, she went to him and he took her by the waist and pulled her down onto his big thighs. His big arms went around her slender torso as he rested his cheek against her arm, gazing up into her lovely face. Chrystobel could smell the alcohol on his breath.

"So you would like to go to Paris, would you?" he asked.

Chrystobel rather liked being held by his strong arms, even though she was sure it was only the alcohol that had loosened his tongue and his manner. She's never seen the man so unguarded.

"I... I would like to see the city someday," she said timidly. "But I know that it is far away and it is undoubtedly expensive to travel there. I am sure it would be too much trouble."

Keller scowled. "It would *not* be too much trouble," he said. "It is more than likely a few weeks' journey, so it is not too far away. We will also stop in London for a few days so that you may see the sights and mayhap shop in some of their expensive shops."

She looked at him with a measure of bewilderment. "But... but what would I buy?"

He shrugged. "Anything you wish," he said. "You are my wife now and you shall never want for anything ever again. No matter how small or how large your desire, you may have it. I will see to it."

Chrystobel was still looking at him with that same expression of bewilderment. "Large?" she repeated. "What could I want that would be large?"

He was enjoying her closeness. He turned his head slightly so that his nose was against her right arm. He could smell lavender.

"A summer home, a boat, a diamond and ruby necklace," he murmured, his eyes closed as he inhaled the thoroughly alluring scent. "You can have anything you want."

She was awed. "*Any*thing?"

His eyes opened and he looked up at her. "Anything except another husband."

Chrystobel giggled. "I think I shall keep the one I have," she said. "But why would you buy me such riches? I do not need them."

He closed his eyes again and smelled of her deeply, his arms tightening around her. "Need them or not, you shall have them," he said. "If it is money you are worried about, then don't. Nether is only a very small part of my fortune."

"What do you mean?"

He opened his eyes and sighed contentedly, his head against her shoulder as he thought on her question.

"My family is very wealthy," he said quietly. "We are originally from Tours, having come to England in the second wave right after William of Normandy came ashore. I have an ancestor who distinguished himself at the Battle of Hastings and, consequently, was sent to Leicester in the name of the new king. My family has held the title High Sheriff of Leicester for over one hundred years, the station of which my father now holds. It will pass to me when he dies. As for the family's wealth, it is rooted in livestock and yellow cheese. We produce and sell cheese all over England and France, and we have massive livestock holdings. I am the oldest of four children, and the only male, so everything will go to me. Therefore, you may have whatever you wish, whenever you wish. If you ask for the stars, I would be happy to negotiate a price for them."

Chrystobel was truly astonished. "Yet you accepted a contract marriage for a Welshwoman who was not of your station?"

He looked at her. "You *are* of my station," he said. "Nether is quite acceptable, as are you. Or haven't you yet realized that I am rather pleased with this marriage?"

Chrystobel wasn't sure if it was the alcohol fueling his words or if he truly meant them. "But, truly, it seems as if you could have commanded a much finer...."

He cut her off, his manner growing agitated. "I do not want a finer woman," he snapped. "I was once betrothed to a very fine woman, a widow of a great and powerful knight, but she was cold and terrible, no matter what I did. I tried to woo her. God knows, I tried. And those two children she had, too. I managed to woo them quite nicely and the girl and I were good friends. But the woman... the harder I tried, the more she pushed me away. It was an exercise in utter futility. And then, do you know what happened? Her husband had not died after all. He returned, took her and the children away, and left me with empty hands and broken dreams. And that was the end of it."

He was speaking rather animatedly, chattering even, but Chrystobel didn't miss the gist of his words. It began to occur to her now why the man had walled himself up, why he seemed so guarded. At least, he had seemed guarded until now. He'd had his heart broken. She began to feel very sorry for the man.

"That is a terrible story," she said softly, looking upon him with pity. "I cannot imagine how it must have hurt to have someone you love taken away from you."

He looked at her as if startled by the statement. "I did not love her," he clarified. "She was lovely and high born, and she had moments of kindness, but I did not love her. The unfortunate part is that I allowed myself to get close to the children. When they left… well, that *did* pain me, just a little."

Chrystobel felt a great deal of sympathy for him. Timidly, her hands found their way onto his big arm as it embraced her. She patted him gently.

"I am sorry for you," she said gently. "I promise that I will never leave you. I have no husband to come back from the dead, and there are no children to take away."

He looked at her a moment and the emotions across his face seemed to ripple. There was sadness there, and anger, and resignation. There was an entire gambit of emotion and he suddenly stood up, nearly dumping her onto the floor. Off balance by his swift movement, Chrystobel toppled into the nearest chair.

"Nay, you will not leave me, but there are all manner of terrible things that have happened here at Nether," he said, pointing a finger at her. "Your brother beat you silly and you would not tell me who did such terrible things to you. When I asked you, you lied to me repeatedly. And this same bastard brother has abused your sister so much that the child will probably never speak because that whoreskin scared the speech right out of her. And your father – by God's Bloody Rood, do you know what he told me? He allowed your brother to abuse you all because he promised his wife he would never discipline him. Is this really true? Because if that is the case and your mother granted your brother privilege to do whatever he pleased, then I fear your mother was a fool of a woman and she took your father right down with her. How do you think I felt seeing the bruises on your face, knowing it was your brother's doing but being helpless to protect you because you would not trust me? It was as horrible as that shrew of a woman I was betrothed to who scorned me as if I was the lowest form of life. She treated the servants better than she treated me. And now I come here, find a wife I could never have imagined, and it scares me to death to realize that I feel something for you. I feel...."

He suddenly stopped himself, looking at the expression on Chrystobel's face. The look of shock, hope, and of deep sadness stopped him bluntly and Keller began to realize that he had let his emotions run rampant, spouting out of his mouth without a dam to stop them. He was too damn drunk to realize he was saying things he shouldn't. He gazed back at her with more horror and regret than he had ever felt in his life.

"Oh... Chrystobel," he breathed. "I did not mean what I said... please forgive me... I did not mean any of it. I do not know why I said anything at all except... except... except that I cared for a woman and children once, much like you and your sister, and it ended badly. If this ended badly, I am not entirely sure I would recover."

Chrystobel was looking at him with the unguarded depths of sympathy. It came pouring out of her; her eyes, her expression... everything. Reaching out, she grasped his big hand.

"It will not end," she promised softly. "I understand you have been hurt, but I promise I will do all in my power not to hurt you, ever. I... I am sorry I lied to you about Gryffyn, truly, but I did not know you. You were an outsider and what he did... it was so shameful. It was such a terrible thing to admit, even to you."

Keller could feel her hand on his, her warm fingers caressing him, and he wanted so badly to give in to the comfort. Was it possible that she was able to give him comfort, to show him affection? He'd never known such a thing in his entire life. Was it really possible that this glorious creature could find it within her heart to tolerate him? Or, perhaps someday... *more* than tolerate? It was a terrifying, hopeful thought.

Looking into her beautiful face, he suddenly felt very embarrassed and very self-conscious about his outburst. He felt like a fool. Pulling away from her grasp, he headed for the door.

"I must go," he muttered. "I must see to my guests."

Chrystobel ran after him, grabbing him by the arm to stop him from leaving. "Wait," she said. "Please do not leave."

He tried to pull away from her, but not too hard. Not hard enough to really make a difference. "I must," he said, refusing to look her in the eye. "I have not seen Rhys or Gart in over a year and there is much… we have much…."

"You will see them in the morning," Chrystobel said firmly, cutting him off and putting herself between Keller and the door. "I did not see my husband last night and… you said yourself that we have not spent… well, spent time together. You slept through the night with your injury and your weariness. Will you be away from me this night, too?"

Keller was still having difficulty looking at her but, eventually, he had little choice other than looking her in the eye. When their gazes locked, Chrystobel smiled timidly and he could feel himself relent. But he was still horribly embarrassed for his outburst and he was having a difficult time overcoming that.

"Nay," he murmured. "I will not be away this night, too."

"Swear it?"

"I swear."

Chrystobel smiled. "Then go and see your friends if you must, but you will return to me," she said. "In fact, I will prepare my father's chamber for us. We can sleep in there tonight."

He eyed her. "Mayhap there is another chamber we can sleep in," he tried to suggest kindly. "Mayhap it will be too difficult for you to sleep in your father's chamber so soon after his passing."

Chrystobel's smile faded and she glanced over her shoulder at Izlyn to see if the girl was listening. Fortunately, Izlyn seemed to be dozing off. Chrystobel lowered her voice.

"I have had much to think about since my father's death," she said softly. "Although it is true that he is my father and for that reason alone

I will mourn him, the truth is that he was never much of a father to me or to Izlyn. He let Gryffyn beat us, hurt us, and he never did much to stop it. I often begged him to but he would never take action. Eventually, I stopped begging. It was of no use. Is… is it wicked of me to feel more resentment towards him than grief? I cannot seem to help it."

Keller's expression reflected her own. "If it is wicked, then we are sinning together," he said with some regret. "I have harbored a great deal of disgust towards your father and his reasoning for why he did not prevent your brother from wreaking havoc. How does your sister feel about all of this? Have you been able to tell?"

Chrystobel glanced over her shoulder at her sister, back in the shadows of the room. "I believe she feels much the same way I do," she said softly. "Whenever Gryffyn would throw her in the vault, or strike her, more often than not she would come to me for comfort. My father… he would release her from the vault only to stand by and do nothing when Gryffyn would put her back in again. Much like me, she learned not to depend on him. I am sure she feels grief, but I do not know to what extent."

Keller pondered that. Both women with an ineffective father, struggling to come to terms with his death. He was their father, a fixture in their lives… but he was also a failure. It was difficult to know how to feel. After a moment, he let out a quiet breath.

"I suppose to your father, his reasons were sound for what he did," he said. "Mayhap he ultimately feared your brother because your brother beat him as well. But I suppose we will never truly know why he let Gryffyn spread his terror as he did."

Chrystobel shrugged vaguely, in agreement, trying not to linger over the anger she felt towards Trevyn now that he was gone. She was very torn between natural grief and bitterness. Taking a deep breath, perhaps to help her move past the memories, she looked up at Keller.

"Mayhap you are correct," she agreed. "In any case, I will go and prepare his chamber for us now. I will expect you once you have seen to your guests."

Keller nodded and moved past her without so much as a kiss or a hint of affection. She was his wife, after all, and he should have at least shown some consideration, but he found that he was too embarrassed. The woman had been the recipient of his unguarded thoughts and the more he thought about it as he headed out of the keep, the more ashamed he became. Unused to such feelings, he had no idea how to handle them.

When he reached the hall, most of the men had either passed out around the room or left entirely to go sleep off the effects of the powerful cider. George and Aimery were gone, but William, Rhys, and Gart were still sitting where Keller had left them. When they saw the man enter the hall, they waved him over to join them.

Keller, trying to shake off his shame from his outburst with Chrystobel, gladly allowed himself to be swept away with memories from The Levant. He also allowed William to pour him more cider. The combination of embarrassment, old memories, and the cider was too much for him to overcome.

The next thing he realized, he was lifting his head off the feasting table when someone opened the door to the great hall and let the weak morning light filter in. There was drool all over his right cheek and a big puddle on the table beneath him. The moment he tried to move, the pounding anvil in his head started.

It was not going to be a pleasant day.

CHAPTER THIRTEEN

S HE WAS STUPID. Truly, deeply, and terribly stupid. As Chrystobel moved about in what used to be her father's chamber, she was feeling like the biggest fool in the world.

Keller had sworn to return to her last night but he hadn't. The sun was rising and she hadn't seen him since he'd left her chamber the night before. As Chrystobel pulled items out of her father's wardrobe in preparation for storing them in a trunk, she was feeling so terribly embarrassed about everything she'd said the night before. She should have been smarter about it. She should have known that Keller was full of ale and cider, and that all of those things he had said were foolish words to gain her sympathy. He'd even apologized for them, and she had forgiven him. But the truth was in the actions – after telling her of a failed love, after swearing he would return to her later, he had failed to come back at all.

She didn't know where the man was and she didn't care. She'd felt sorry for him as he'd told her of his lost love, but gaining her sympathy had probably been part of his ploy. He'd made her think that he was a poor, lonely soul, but the truth was that he was a liar. He wasn't a man of his word, as he'd broken his promise to return to her, so she could only assume everything else he'd told her had been a lie.

Damn him! She tossed one of her father's tunics into a pile on the ground. Keller had made her believe that he was sympathetic to both her and Izlyn. Finally, a man who would show them both the kindness they'd so lacked in their young lives. But he hadn't meant any of what he'd said. He'd been drunk and running off at the mouth. Hurt, angry, she continued to clean out her father's chamber.

Her back was to the door when she heard boot falls and a soft knock on the panel. Turning around, she caught sight of Keller standing in the doorway in full armor. She looked at him, caught off guard by his sudden appearance, and couldn't help but notice that he looked pale and bleary-eyed. But the moment their eyes met, she thought of him last night as he looked her in the eye and swore he would return to her, and she quickly returned to her project.

"Good morn to you, husband," she said, her voice clipped.

Keller heard her tone. It was cold and angry, just as he knew it would be. He'd put off coming to see her for a solid hour because he was so afraid that she might be angry with him and he'd been correct. She was furious. From her stiff back to her curt words, she was bloody well furious.

"Good morn to you, Lady de Poyer," he said timidly. "My lady... Chrystobel... I am truly sorry I did not return last night. I am sure you are...."

She cut him off, throwing more of her father's items into a pile on the floor. "It does not matter in the least," she said, pulling at a pair of ripped breeches. "I slept in my chamber with my sister and we were quite comfortable. In fact, I am cleaning out this chamber for you so that you may have it. It 'tis a big chamber, and comfortable, and it should be very pleasant for you. I plan to have the servants pull the bed apart and re-stuff the mattress."

Keller could see that she wasn't going to forgive him easily. Why should she? He'd said many things last night, things he was still embarrassed over, and she'd had time to reflect on all he'd said. Perhaps she'd come to realize what an idiot she'd married. Perhaps it really didn't matter to her that he'd not returned – more than likely, she was glad that he hadn't. His heart sank as the nervous knuckle-cracking started.

"I thought this was going to be our chamber?" he asked softly, popping his joints.

Chrystobel laughed, but it wasn't a humorous laugh. It was an angry cackle. "Nay, my lord," she said, gathering all of the things she had thrown on the floor and lifting them up onto the bed. "This will be the master's chamber and you, after all, are the master. I will happily sleep across the hall with my sister so that you can summon me at will. No need for us to share a space."

Keller was feeling worse and worse. "Chrystobel," he said softly, firmly. "I am sorry I did not return last night. I went to see to my friends and ended up drinking more of that devil cider, and after that... I do not remember anything until I woke up this morning. I did not stay away intentionally."

Chrystobel was a woman with no trust in men. She'd been lied to and abused her entire life, so forgiving an innocent like Keller, who truly meant what he said, was nearly impossible for her to comprehend. It was easier not to believe him than to forgive him. He'd already lied to her. In her mind, he'd destroyed her trust.

"You do not need to explain your whereabouts or your reasons," she said, pausing in her task to look him in the eye. "This is a contract marriage and there are no expectations. You are lord and master of Nether and I will respect you as such. I will be at your call as you wish, but do not expect more than that. Do not tell me stories to garner my sympathy because I do not care. I do not care about anything!"

She ripped off the clothing pile and the top layer of linen on the bed to punctuate her angry sentence. Everything when sailing onto the floor. Keller stood there and watched her, feeling the familiar angst welling in his chest. Once, when he had been betrothed to the widow who broke his heart, he felt these same emotions when she callously dismissed him. The old, horrible feelings were sweeping him again. *God, not again*, he thought. *Why do I bring these things down upon me? I cannot go through this again!* He stopped popping his knuckles because he nearly broke a finger in his turmoil.

"I am sorry that I did not keep my promise to return," he said, his voice soft and low. "I feel terrible about it. All I can tell you is that it was unintentional and that I am truly sorry."

Chrystobel's gaze lingered on him a moment before turning to the pile on the floor. "You need not apologize," she said. "It is your right to do as you please."

He sighed sharply. "Do you not believe a man when he says that he is sorry?"

Her head snapped up, the dark eyes fixed on him. "I believed him when he swore he would return last night. Mayhap it is the last time I shall believe anything he says."

It was like a punch to his gut. Keller could tell just by the expression on her face that she was attacking his honor. After a moment, he simply shook his head. "What must I do to prove I am sincere, Chrystobel? I do not want to go the rest of my life at odds with you because of a mistake."

She looked at him a moment, appraisingly, and he swore that he could see the turmoil in the big brown eyes. She was hurt and defensive, he could clearly see it. But she tore her gaze away after a moment and looked back at the pile and, as he watched, planted herself on the floor beside it. She began sifting through it.

"Go about your duties," she told him. "I will make sure your chamber is prepared by tonight."

It was evident she didn't wish to speak to him about it. He groaned inwardly. "I am going into town to make arrangements with the priests for your father's mass," he said quietly. "I thought you wanted to go with me."

Chrystobel shook her head, focused on her task. "You can make the arrangements quite adequately," she said. "I do not need to go with you."

There wasn't any use arguing with her. He could see that plainly. She was essentially shutting him out and he felt horrible about it. But it was probably justified. He had promised to return last night. He didn't blame her for thinking he was not a man of his word. With a lingering gaze at her blond head, he silently quit the chamber and shut the door behind him.

The landing was dimly lit and cold as he turned for the stairs. He had a knot in his stomach from his emotions, coupled with his pounding head. He deserved all of it, he told himself. Every misery he had, he deserved. As he began to descend the stairs, he glanced up and saw Izlyn standing in the doorway to the chamber she shared with her sister. Keller came to a halt.

Izlyn was dressed in a sweet pink-colored linen surcoat with an embroidered apron over it. Her pretty blond hair was pulled into two adorable braids draped over each shoulder. She looked clean, groomed, and well-rested. In fact, the child looked better than he'd ever seen her. He smiled weakly.

"I do not suppose you can tell me how to beg forgiveness from your sister," he muttered wryly.

It had been a somewhat rhetorical question but, to his surprise, Izlyn nodded. Keller was about to continue down the steps but the child's gesture had him pausing.

"You do?" he asked, interested. "She is very angry with me. But I suppose you know that."

Izlyn nodded solemnly. Keller wriggled his eyebrows in defeat. As he shrugged his big shoulders dejectedly and began to move down the steps, Izlyn rushed forward and stuck her hands out. He caught the movement from the corner of his eye, pausing to look up at the pale young woman. As he watched, she rushed over to him and grasped his sleeve, tugging. Keller ended up ascending those few stairs he had just taken and following Izlyn as she pulled him into the chamber she shared with her sister.

Keller was quite curious at her actions. She led him over to one of the chairs near the hearth and pointed to it, indicating for him to sit. He did, uncomfortably, in his heavy armor, watching Izlyn as she went over to a small table that was on the opposite side of the bed. The girl had scraps of what looked like parchment or vellum. She picked up a quill and, dipping it in ink, began scratching onto the parchment. When she was finished, she blew on it to dry the ink and rushed over to him, thrusting the parchment in his face.

Keller had to dodge his head or risk being hit by the parchment. He took it from her, holding it at arm's length to read it because his eyes weren't very good these days. It was often very difficult for him to read. The letter was written very careful, in Welsh:

Roedd hi'n drist pan nad oeddech yn dychwelyd

She was sad when you did not return.

Keller sighed heavily when he finished reading it. He felt like a monster. "I had every intention of returning, I assure you," he told the young girl. "But... by God's Bloody Rood, this is embarrassing, but that cider your sister provided put me to sleep. I fell asleep with my face pressed into the top of the feasting table. The next I realized, it was morning."

He put his hand on his nose and smashed it down to demonstrate his sleeping position, watching Izlyn giggle. She was a pretty little thing when she smiled which, he suspected, was not that often. She snatched the parchment out of his hand and ran back to the table to collect her quill. She scratched a few more words out onto it before blowing furiously on it and racing back to him, thrusting it at him. Keller took the parchment and held it far away from his face to read it.

Mae'n rhaid i chi ddweud wrthi ei fod yn ei bai hi am ei bod
yn rhoi i chi y ddiod

You must tell her it is her fault because she gave you the drink.

Keller smiled wryly after reading it. "Alas, I cannot," he sighed. "I did not have to drink it and I should not have. I cannot blame her for my failings. I wish she would at least accept my apology. Mayhap I need an envoy to soothe the savage beastie."

Izlyn took the parchment away from him but she didn't run over to write. She just stood there and looked at him as if she didn't know what else to say. Much like Keller, she was socially inept. The lack of voice made it so, and the isolation, and in that realization Keller felt a somewhat kindred spirit with Izlyn. He was a bumbling idiot at times, too, as evidenced by the current situation with Chrystobel. He smiled at her and she smiled back. *At least one d'Einen sister is smiling at me*, he thought ironically. Noting the parchment still in her hand gave him an idea.

"Would... would you do something for me, my lady?" he asked. "I would be most grateful."

Izlyn nodded eagerly and ran for the chamber door, but he called her back. "Nay, not that," he said, rising out of the chair as he waved her over. "I was jesting when I said I needed an envoy. I do not want you to go to her on my behalf. Is that what you were going to do?"

Izlyn nodded, looking rather confused because she thought he wanted her to fetch her sister. But Keller put his hand on her slender shoulder.

"You are good at writing," he said. When she nodded firmly, he continued. "I must go to town now and will not have the time to make amends to your sister today, so I was wondering if you would help me."

Izlyn nodded eagerly and Keller patted her shoulder, directing her back over to the table with the pieces of parchment and pewter inkwell that was modeled to look like a flower. As Izlyn collected her quill and rifled through her pieces of parchment in order to find one that didn't have any writing on it, Keller thought about what he wanted to say. It was rather sly, really, using the sister to beg forgiveness from his wife, but at that point, he was willing to do what was necessary to gain her good favor again. He also thought that he might see what stock the merchants in the town had once he'd finished with the priests. He'd been known to lavish gifts on those that warranted it, and even to those who didn't. The widow he'd been betrothed to had accepted many lavish gifts from him. Keller hoped that giving gifts to Chrystobel wouldn't be the same lesson in pointlessness.

As Keller dictated and Izlyn carefully scratched the words, in English this time, upon a piece of yellowed parchment, he sincerely hoped she would read the missive and not burn it in anger. He thought that perhaps she wouldn't destroy it because it might hurt Izlyn's feelings, the creator as well as bearer of the message. In fact, he was counting on it.

Fifteen minutes later and satisfied with the heart-felt missive, he left Izlyn to deliver it while he took William, Rhys, and Aimery with him into the town of Machynlleth, leaving Gart and George behind to see to the castle and her security. He hoped that, when he returned from town, Chrystobel might be more receptive to his presence.

And he would swear a thousand times over that he would never touch that devil cider again as long as he lived.

CB

"THE BLOODY CASTLE is crawling with English!" Colvyn hissed. "You did not tell me there were so many!"

On a rocky, wind-swept crag overlooking Nether Castle in the distance, Gryffyn and Colvyn could see hordes of English soldiers both in and out of the castle. In fact, they were spilling out over the Gorge of the Dead and onto the roadway beyond. Some were setting off in groups, no doubt patrols, while others were lingering around the gatehouse. Gryffyn blinked in both surprise and concern at so many English.

"More must have come," he muttered. "There were not so many when I left yesterday."

Colvyn eyed the English milling in and around Nether Castle. Now, what Gryffyn had told him was starting to make sense. There were far more English than he had imagined. They have a foothold in Wales! Perhaps Gryffyn had been correct. He thought the man was merely being dramatic but by the looks of things, that wasn't the case at all.

There was a hive of English in the heart of Wales and it was most definitely a cause for alarm.

Around them, the wind was picking up and the smell of rain wasn't far off. They could see it over to the west. Gryffyn and Colvyn hunkered down against the rocks, watching the activity in and around Nether. Mostly, they were there so that Gryffyn could prove to Colvyn that the English had indeed overrun the castle.

Based on their observations, Gryffyn hoped that Colvyn would plan some sort of attack or other restless action. If de Poyer wanted to hold Nether, then Gryffyn was going to make it exceedingly difficult for him.

"Well?" he asked Colvyn. "Do you believe me now that they have confiscated Nether?"

Colvyn's dark hair whipped up in the wind as he pulled his rough woolen cloak more tightly around his neck. "Aye," he replied, his dark gaze on the castle. "I believe you. It would seem that we must do something about it."

"Agreed," Gryffyn said as if Colvyn's statement was the most obvious thing in the world. "You must contact your *teulu* for support. We will need many men to regain Nether."

Colvyn pondered that scenario and as he did, there was something that didn't quite make sense to him about this situation. "Nether is built to withstand a siege," he said. "It is surrounded by the Gorge of the Dead and has sheer walls. How did the English manage to take it?"

Gryffyn blinked at the unexpected question. He had lied about the English attacking the fortress simply to force the man's support, so he thought quickly, trying to come up with a plausible fabrication.

"A distraction," he said, working his way through the lie as he went. He'd always been rather good at that sort of thing. "My father was unprepared for their assault and met them at the gatehouse while a group of them came in through the postern gate."

Colvyn's gaze lingered on the distant fortress. "Odd," he muttered. "They do not seem like an invading army. Everything is...*open*. There are soldiers going in and out of the gatehouse as if nothing is amiss."

Gryffyn shrugged as he sat back against the cold slate rocks, huddling for warmth against the cold breeze. "What do they have to worry over?" he grunted. "They have the castle. They have nothing to fear."

Colvyn eyed him. "But they know you escaped."

"I suppose so. They probably do not care."

"But they must presume you would go for help."

Gryffyn shook his head. "Mayhap they would," he said, blowing on his cold hands. "But why would the gatehouse be open if they presumed that?"

It was a clever question, one designed to make it look as if Gryffyn was just as confused about the open castle as Colvyn was. Colvyn's gaze lingered on Gryffyn a moment, mulling over the question, before returning his gaze to the castle. Increasingly, something about this wasn't sitting right with him. True, there were English at Nether, but they were very casual-appearing soldiers for the siege they just put Nether through. More than that, the castle didn't look damaged in the least as it would have had the English bombarded it. Nay, something wasn't right about this entire circumstance. He was coming to think that Gryffyn wasn't telling him everything he knew. Just as he opened his mouth, Gryffyn, who had been studying the castle, suddenly grabbed his arm.

"Look!" he hissed. "See the group of knights riding from the castle?"

Colvyn ducked behind his rock, peering out at the road below. "Aye," he said after a moment. "Heavily armed *Saesneg* warriors."

Gryffyn was watching the group as they headed north on the road. "I count four," he said. "I only saw four knights before I fled. Is it possible all four are leaving the castle? Where could they be going?"

Colvyn shook his head. "I would not know," he said, his gaze tracking the four big knights and at least ten men-at-arms as they thundered down the road. "Mayhap we should follow them to discover their business."

Gryffyn thought on that before his attention turned to the castle. "I have a better idea," he said. "My sisters... they are still in the castle. Mayhap we should try to rescue them while the knights are away."

Colvyn looked at him. "In daylight?" he asked as if Gryffyn had made an utterly foolish suggestion. "We would be too easily seen. It would be madness to try."

"*I* can try."

"But the English soldiers know you, do they not?"

"Not all of them."

Colvyn wasn't so sure that was a good idea. His gaze was intense on Gryffyn. "Why is it important to you to rescue them?" he asked. "I have known you for many years, Gryffyn. Chrystobel and Izlyn have never meant anything to you. Why would you risk yourself to go in after them?"

Gryffyn didn't want to tell him the truth, that he wanted to slip in and kill them both and then blame their murders on the English. It would be a good way to incite rebellion within the Welsh. With the knights away, it was perfect timing and he could hardly believe the good fortune.

"Stay here, then, if it pleases you," Gryffyn said, gathering his cloak as he began to move out from between the rocks. "I am going to see if I can gain entry to Nether."

Colvyn regarded him dubiously. "Not to save your sisters."

Gryffyn cocked a blond eyebrow. "I am not for certain yet," he muttered. "I will know better when I get there."

Colvyn watched him go, quite convinced now that Gryffyn wasn't telling him everything. There was something very secretive and ominous about him. The further the man moved away from him, the more wary he became. Perhaps he shouldn't be here. Perhaps Gryffyn had lured him into danger intentionally.

Still, the English were there for some reason, and Colvyn wanted to know that reason. As Gryffyn made his way down the slippery hill and headed for Nether Castle, Colvyn and a few of his men made their way back to their shaggy ponies, horses that were starting to grow their heavy winter coats, and spurred their mounts after the English riders that had headed off to the north. He wanted to follow their trail and see what business they had.

He was very curious, indeed.

CHAPTER FOURTEEN

And suddenly, I know that it is time to start something new
And trust the magic of a new beginning.
My heart may be broken, but it is not destroyed.
My soul may be injured, but it is not shattered.
When I look at you, I see all things bright and pure.
I see the magic of a new beginning with you.

CHRYSTOBEL HAD READ the note at least ten times. She was reading it again even now, thinking that it was perhaps the most wonderful note she had ever read. It made her feel warm and fluid and giddy inside. Seated on her father's bed, surrounded by a half-packed trunk as she finished storing away the man's possessions, she couldn't take her eyes off the faded yellow parchment. After she'd read it a twelfth time, she looked up at Izlyn.

"You are sure that Keller composed this?" she said, holding up the scrap. "This is your writing. Moreover, it is in English."

Izlyn nodded frantically and made motions that would indicated someone had spoken the words to her and told her to write it. It took Chrystobel a minute or so to figure out what her sister was gesturing about. She looked back at the parchment again.

"These are beautiful words," she admitted. "Truly, he told you to write this to me?"

Izlyn nodded firmly. When Chrystobel looked up at her, the girl grinned and wrapped her arms around her body as if demonstrating something very romantic. Izlyn hugged herself dramatically and Chrystobel grinned.

"You silly little goat," she said. "You like him, don't you?"

Again, Izlyn nodded and Chrystobel sighed heavily. Her face took on a distant expression as she stood up, moving pensively towards one of the three lancet windows in the room. Reaching the window, she leaned against the sill, noting the puffy clouds and damp wind. Thoughts of Keller were heavy on her mind.

"I like him, too," she sighed. "I just wish he had not lied to me."

Izlyn raced from the room. Chrystobel turned in time to see her sister disappear out into the landing. She could hear the girl across the hall in the other chamber, shuffling around. She had no idea what her sister was doing and returned her attention to the landscape beyond the window.

After her rage of the morning, she had calmed somewhat, wondering if perhaps she had been too hard on Keller. Unfortunately, trust was a powerful issue with her. She had so little of it and what little she did have, she had pinned on Keller, only to be disappointed. He'd tried to explain why he had not returned to her but she had been too angry and too stubborn to listen. She had been regretting her behavior somewhat when Izlyn presented her with what she said was a message from Keller. Now, Chrystobel was feeling especially bad for being so unkind to the man. She hoped he would be receptive to speaking with her when he returned from Machynlleth.

Behind her, Izlyn came rushing back into the room with her hands full of scraps of vellum. This was normal with her. Since she could not speak, she wrote her conversations, something that had infuriated Gryffyn because he figured if she could write, then she could speak. Izlyn scooted to her sister and handed her the first of several pieces of parchment in her hand, of all different shapes and sizes. Some even had previous conversations on them crossed out. Chrystobel read the note on the piece of vellum.

Mae'r seidr yn gwneud iddo gysgu. Yr oedd eich bai nad oedd
yn dod yn ôl

The cider made him sleep. It was your fault he did not come back.

Chrystobel's eyebrows rose as she finished reading the note and looked at her sister. "Did he tell you that?"

Izlyn nodded seriously. Then she rifled through the notes on in her hand before she came to the one she wanted and handed it to her sister. There were other notes on the scrap, crossed out, so it took her a moment to find the most current note.

Mae'n ddrwg iawn. Yr ydych yn gwneud iddo drist.

He is very sorry. You made him sad.

Chrystobel finished reading the note and looked to her sister with a good deal of remorse. "I was angry," she said. Then she grew serious. "I... I suppose I did not want to know disappointment with Keller. Izzie, no man has ever been good to us. Father did what he could but it was a weak effort at best. Always weak. And Gryffyn... I swear to you that I will never mention his name again, not ever. You and I survived his torment and I swear that we will move on and have normal lives now. I believe Keller will make that so for us and... and when he promised he would return and then didn't, I suppose I was horribly disappointed. We do not need yet another man to disappoint us and treat us with disrespect."

Izlyn was watching her sister closely. She was an extremely sensitive girl, deep feeling and intuitive. Gryffyn had scarred her badly but he had not ruined her. Even being away from him for so short a time, just a few short hours, had seen her bounce back admirably. With the terror removed from her world, it had made all the difference. She was young and she was resilient. She also understood that her sister was feeling a good deal of turmoil and she wanted to help.

As Chrystobel struggled with her guilt and her burdens, Izlyn shuffled through the scraps of parchment in her hand and picked one, extending it to her sister. Chrystobel took the torn fragment of parchment and read the note.

Rwy'n credu y bydd yn dy garu di

I think he will love you.

Chrystobel shook her head quickly and averted her gaze. "Nay," she muttered. "Please do not say that. It is foolish, do you hear?"

Izlyn smiled knowingly at her sister, suspecting that she had struck a nerve. She knew her sister was growing fond of her new husband. Love was a fool's dream. It was every girl's dream. She went over to Chrystobel and put her arms around her waist, hugging her. Softened, Chrystobel hugged her sister tightly for a moment before quickly pulling away.

"Look at your fingers," she scolded gently. "All stained with ink. Go wash your hands."

Izlyn simply grinned as Chrystobel pushed her away. She pretended to resist, feigning wiping her fingers on the stone walls. Chrystobel finally swatted her harmlessly on the arse.

"*Go*," she insisted, pointing to the chamber across the hall where she knew there was some water and lumpy white soap. "Wash your hands off and then you can come back here and help me."

Izlyn wasn't in any hurry to do what she was told. There was a lightness in the air that hadn't been there before, the joy of a positive future. Keller had done that for them. As she neared the chamber door, she abruptly came to a halt. Chrystobel was returning to her packing when she saw Izlyn jump up and down, pointing frantically to the landing outside. Curious, Chrystobel made her way over to see what had her sister so excited.

As soon as she neared the chamber door, she could hear it. Someone was calling her name, a respectful male voice floating up through the dim stairwell. Peering at Izlyn with some concern, as if the girl could tell her who it was that was summoning her, she exited the chamber and made her way down the steep, narrow steps to the first floor below.

It was a bit brighter on this level because the entry door was open, and George immediately came into view. He was standing near the open door, smiling politely at her, but he wasn't alone. A massive knight with a bald head and enormous shoulders was standing with him. Chrystobel recognized Sir Gart Forbes, a man she had been introduced to the previous night, but she focused on George.

"Greetings, Sir George," she said courteously. "Did you summon me?"

George nodded. "I did, Lady de Poyer," he said. "I did not want to come up to the living level without having been invited, especially with Sir Keller away."

Chrystobel nodded. "Of course," she agreed with his sense of propriety. "What can I do for you?"

George indicated Gart. "You remember Sir Gart?"

Chrystobel nodded, locking gazes with the massive warrior. "Indeed," she said. "Good day to you, Sir Gart."

Gart nodded his head but remained silent. There was something extraordinarily intimidating about the man but she didn't sense evil. She sensed a man who was simply no-nonsense and serious, a very big man with very big weapons. He was English to the core, much like her husband, men she had been taught to hate. Odd thing was, given her experiences with Gryffyn and Keller over the past couple of days, she was coming to see the English as far less dangerous than the Welsh. Still, Gart *was* a bit scary. She returned her attention to George.

"My husband has gone into town to make arrangements for my father's funeral," she said.

George nodded. "I am aware, Lady de Poyer," he replied. "Before he left, Sir Keller asked me to come to you to seek what manner of coffin you wish for your father. He wants to know if there are any craftsmen at the castle who can make one."

Chrystobel cocked her head in thought, coming off the stairs as she thought on her answer. As she moved towards George, Izlyn, who had been standing behind her on the stairs, also came off the steps. Instead of following her sister, however, she seemed very interested in Gart. As the big knight stood politely just inside the doorway, Izlyn walked up to him and inspected him with great interest.

"We have a carpenter who works in the stables," Chrystobel said as Izlyn scrutinized Gart. "He repairs or builds things as needed. Shall I take you to him?"

George shook his head. "I would not want to trouble you, my lady."

Chrystobel waved him off. "No trouble at all," she said. Then she wriggled her eyebrows ironically. "Besides, the man does not speak any English, so I will have to translate unless you speak Welsh."

George shook his head. "I do not, my lady."

Gathering her skirts, Chrystobel preceded the two knights out of the keep, taking the stairs down to the bailey. The smell of rain was heavier in the air now and the wind was brisk. As she began walking across the ward towards the stables, George caught up to her.

"Your father has been stored in the stables, my lady," he told her. "Mayhap… mayhap you should not enter the stalls. What is the name of this man so that I might seek him out?"

Chrystobel turned to look at him. "Wentzy" she said. "He is not difficult to locate. He is missing one eye."

George's eyebrows lifted curiously. "And he is a carpenter?"

"A very *good* carpenter."

As George and Chrystobel discussed the skill of the one-eyed carpenter, Gart trailed several feet behind them, his hawk-like gaze roving the castle grounds. It was a big place with lots of places to hide, he thought. But as he perused the grounds, he couldn't help notice that Lady de Poyer's sister was walking beside him. He tried not to look at her. He hoped that she would go away if he just ignored her. If he spoke to her, surely it would be like feeding a stray animal and he would never be rid of her. Moreover, he had no idea what to say to the girl. He wasn't very good with children. Therefore, Gart did what Gart did best – he ignored.

As they drew near the stables, however, he couldn't help but notice that the girl was moving closer to him. In fact, she was nearly bumping into his right arm as they walked. He could feel her arm brushing against his, so he discreetly moved over to his left to put some distance between them. A few seconds later, he could feel the brushing again as Izlyn moved next to him again. Therefore, he slowed down. *She* slowed down. He sped up, *she* sped up. Finally, he stopped completely and folded his big arms over his chest, pretending to inspect something in the distance. He could see in his peripheral vision that the young girl had come to a halt, too. She was just standing there, hovering, like a gnat. He wanted to swat her.

Irritated and struggling not to show it, he turned to look at her. The moment he did, she smiled brightly at him and, like an idiot, he immediately folded. She was a cute little thing. He smiled back, patted her on the head, and continued towards the stables. He hoped that would satisfy her curiosity. But the girl scampered to catch up with him. Gart sighed heavily and shook his head. He'd managed to attract an admirer and he wasn't too happy about it.

As Gart struggled not to become frustrated with his follower, Izlyn was completely and utterly entranced with the massive bald knight. She had seen him the night before in the great hall as he'd feasted with Sir Keller. In fact, she'd watched him quite a lot. He was very handsome, she thought, and she knew he was kind. She could tell by looking at him. The entire time she'd watched him, he'd never hit anyone like her brother often did, so she knew that meant he must be very nice.

Therefore, like moth to the flame, she was drawn to the enormous English knight with the brooding presence. She decided that she liked him very much. She might even marry him, but she had not decided on that yet. Still, she knew she liked him. As the big knight followed her sister and Sir George towards the stables, Izlyn happily skipped after them.

Little did she know that, from the shadows, her worst nightmare was watching.

CB

HE'D MANAGED TO slip in through the secret tunnel that led from the Gorge of the Dead up to the kitchen, which was built against the northern wall. It was meant to be a secret escape route if the castle was ever overtaken, but Gryffyn used it to gain entrance. The opening in the gorge was hidden by a few strategic rocks, concealed unless one knew where to look. The stairs, carved into the bedrock, were tiny and slippery, and he fell twice as he made his way up the passage and into the kitchen. When the cook saw him, he had strangled her and dragged her body into the passageway so no one would find it. Now, he had full access to the castle and he intended to use it.

He intended to find his sisters.

Knowing Nether as well as he did, he was able to dodge servants as they went about their duties by hiding in alcoves or in niches, away from those who would recognize him. He also had a rough woolen cloak, one he'd borrowed from Colvyn, so he was less recognizable to those who would know his fine dress. He was worried about his boots, however, because they were of the finest leather, so he made sure to dirty them up before proceeding into the castle. He hoped that all of these measures would prevent him from being noticed before he could accomplish his task.

He'd managed to make it from the kitchen to the stables without being noticed. The fact that de Poyer had saturated the castle with his own men worked in Gryffyn's favor. None of the English soldiers recognized him and he was able to move past them relatively unnoticed. Once inside the stables, he climbed up into the loft above and buried himself in the dried grass used to feed and bed the animals. Heart racing with fear and excitement, he planned his next move among the smell of grass and horses.

Stable servants moved around underneath him, tending the horses, and he listened to their inane chatter. Unfortunately, they didn't speak of anything useful so he continued to plot on his own, knowing that whatever he did had to be accomplished before the English knights returned to the castle which, he assumed, would be before nightfall. So he lay there, buried under grass, and waited for the servants to move out so he could leave the stables and make his way to the keep.

But that wasn't an instantaneous happening. In fact, he had no idea how much time had passed while he wait, for he actually fell asleep at some point, exhausted from the mayhem of the past two days. It was a dreamless sleep, like the kind of sleep he had when he was young and without care. The smell of dried grass reminded him of those days. When he finally woke some time later, it was to the sound of Chrystobel's voice.

Startled by the familiar tone, he struggled to gain a view of her and not make too much noise or commotion in the process. Grass was noisy, and crunched, so he eventually lay still because he knew he was creating too much noise and didn't want anyone heading into the loft to see what was causing the disturbance. So he remained immobile and realized he could see part of the stable entry through the slats in the loft. He strained to catch a glimpse of his sister as she spoke to someone about a coffin for Trevyn.

She is here! He thought to himself gleefully as he spied her at the mouth of the stable entry. Already, he could feel her soft flesh in his hands as he squeezed her neck just as he had squeezed the cook's. To think of Chrystobel breathing her last as he gazed into her eyes, watching her life slip away, thrilled him beyond compare.

His hatred seemed to fixate on her more than anyone else, the foolish wench who looked so much like their mother. The bitch had died shortly after Izlyn had been born. He should hate Izlyn more for killing their mother, but he found his hatred focused on Chrystobel because she looked and sounded just like Elyn. Elyn had been the only person Gryffyn had even remotely loved, and when she died, his hatred and anger had become mainplace. It blackened his heart. Anger and hatred towards the world in general, and mostly towards a sister who looked like the woman he had loved and lost. Chrystobel reminded him of his loss on a daily basis.

But no matter, Gryffyn shook himself of his bitter and sweet memories, of a mother he tried not to remember. He hated her now and that was all that mattered. Hated her for dying.

Below him, Chrystobel's voice distracted him again and he peered at her through the slats, listening to her speak to someone regarding funeral services for Trevyn at St. Peter's in Machynlleth. *A funeral*, he thought, as if a great idea had just occurred to him. She would be out of the castle and it would be easier to get to her, stealing her out from under de Poyer's nose. Aye, that would be a much smarter move than trying to corner her here in the castle. In Machynlleth, there would be knights and soldiers about, that is true, but if he employed Colvyn and his personal Welsh guard to assist in the covert operation, men who were sly warriors and who could distract the knights while Gryffyn captured his sister, then success would be guaranteed.

Gryffyn rolled over onto his back, listening to the sound of his sister's voice. Soon, that voice would be silenced. Now, he knew what he had to do. His plans had been laid for him.

He eagerly anticipated the day.

␣

THE PRIESTS AT St. Peter's spoke the harshest Welsh Keller had ever heard. In fact, he wasn't even sure it was Welsh until they spoke a few words that he recognized. After he began to understand their accents, it was easier to have a conversation, and soon he had made arrangements for Trevyn d'Einen's funeral mass to be held on the morrow.

St. Peter's was a lovely old church, low and squat, and built with the gray granite stone that was so prevalent in the Welsh mountains. The priests pointed out Lady d'Einen's crypt and he found himself gazing at the effigy of the woman who gave birth to both Chrystobel and to Gryffyn. How one woman could spawn two diametrically opposed individuals was something of a curiosity for him. Heaven and hell sprang all from this woman, in his opinion, so he wasn't sure if he revered or reviled her.

Seeing Lady d'Einen's effigy caused his thoughts to linger heavily on Chrystobel. He could only pray that her anger would cool and she would eventually forgive him. He wondered if his poem had done any good, if it had accomplished his purpose and managed to cool the fire of fury. He spent a good deal of time praying in that church about it, softly in his mind, even as he carried on a conversation with the priests about Trevyn's funeral. His prayers were for his relationship with his wife, one that he hoped wasn't over before it truly began. He was both eager to return to Nether Castle and terrified of it. Terrified to discover she was still angry with him. Terrified to discover whatever trust that had been building had been lost.

So he braced himself for the possibility, but he also decided to do what he could to ease the woman the only way he knew how – with gifts. Keller was a gift-giver when the mood struck him and had been known to spend copious amounts of money at one time. He'd brought more than enough money with him today. Mayhap if he plied Chrystobel with enough finery, she would soften and forgive him. It was worth a try and, at this point, he felt that he was out of options. He was in groveling mode.

When he was finished making arrangements with the priests and paid them several silver coins for their services, he quit the church with his knights in tow, out into a morning that was becoming increasingly threatened by rain. As he stood next to his charger and tightened up his gloves, Rhys came to stand next to him, gazing up at the angry pewter sky.

"Rain is coming," Rhys said. "But I suppose it does not do anything else here. This entire country smells like a rotten egg."

Keller grinned, glancing up at the sky. "I am sure there are a few people around here who would disagree with you," he said. Then, he started looking around, up and down the muddy street that ran from one end of the town to another. "I must find a goods merchant."

Rhys began looking around, too, because he was. "What do you need?"

Keller's dark eyes focused on the western end of the town where there seemed to be several people milling about, doing business. "Down there," he said, ignoring Rhys' question. "It looks as if there is some commerce going on down there."

He mounted his charger effortlessly, spurring the animal down the street. William, who had already mounted his charger and had not heard the conversation between Rhys and Keller, reined his charger next to Rhys as the man mounted his steed.

"Where is Keller off to?" William asked.

Rhys pointed down the street. "To find a goods merchant."

"Why?"

"He would not tell me."

William's gaze lingered on Keller as the man charged off down the road. "I would suspect a peace offering for Lady de Poyer."

Rhys looked at him. "Did they have a row?"

William shrugged and looked at Rhys. "The man spent the night passed out on the table in a drunken stupor and not with his new wife, which is where he should have been," he said. "If you were Keller's new wife, how would *you* feel about it?"

Rhys grunted heavily and turned his gaze to Keller down the road. "I would be furious."

William nodded in agreement. "As I am sure she is."

"I am *never* getting married."

"Then you are destined for a lonely life, my friend."

They didn't say anything more after that, taking the ten men-at-arms down the road, following Keller, as Aimery brought up the rear. Once they reached the busier part of town with waddle and daub huts, and merchant stalls made of the big granite rocks that were plentiful in the fields and mountain, they slowed their pace and began to inspect their surroundings.

Since Machynlleth was a small village, there wasn't a great selection of merchants and most of those were agricultural or farming. There was a man selling sheep, a few men selling vegetables and big grass baskets of grains. There was also a merchant who had iron pots all stacked up in front of his shop, while inside the shop, there were bundles of heavy woolen fabric and other odds and ends.

It was this merchant that interested Keller. He dismounted his horse and entered the stall, nearly too big to move around in the small space, as outside, the clouds overhead that had been threatening rain most of the day began to let loose of a heavy mist. When that began to happen, the shopkeeper raced past Keller from well back in the stall and began dragging the heavy iron pots inside so they would not rust. He was a small man with a bent back, so Keller politely helped the man pull in all of his pots. When they were finished dragging them into the stall, the man was very grateful to Keller.

"Diolch," he said. "Sut ga 'fod o wasanaeth?"

How may I be of service? The man had a very heavy Welsh accent. Keller replied in his perfect Welsh. "I am looking for a gift for my lady wife," he said. "Would you have anything that a woman might appreciate?"

The merchant cocked his head, perhaps dubiously. "How much are you willing to spend, my lord?"

"More money than you've seen at one time, I assure you."

The merchant didn't doubt him by the way he was dressed or by the fine steed he traveled on. His doubt turned to the thrill of perhaps making a great sale, which were far and few between in this little berg. Swiftly, he turned for the rear of his shop.

"I keep my precious items away from the street," he said. "The villagers cannot afford them and I do not want to invite robbers."

Keller wondered what the man had by way of "precious items". By the looks of the stall, he was certain it wasn't much and prepared himself for disappointment. When the merchant reached the rear of the stall, he fumbled under a pile of goods and pulled forth a medium-sized strong box reinforced with an iron cage. There was a lock on it and he pulled a string of keys out of his pocket and located the one he needed. Turning the tumblers on the big iron lock and sliding the bolt, he opened up the box.

Keller was rather surprised to see what the man had. He pulled forth an emerald and pearl necklace that was exquisitely made, set in dark gold. He also withdrew three or four gold rings, with different colored stones, and also removed another pearl necklace that was set with garnets.

The last item he pulled out was a big, heavy necklace made entirely of gold, with one hooked clasp at the back of the neck, and three strands of golden chain, each chain longer than the previous. When on a woman's neck, it gave the illusion she was wearing three necklaces. Each strand of the necklace was magnificently done. One had purple amethysts, one had sapphires and pearls, and the longest strand had gold beads that were shaped like a cross intermingled with pale green stones. It was absolutely breathtaking and Keller held it up, inspecting it in the weak light.

"Where on earth did you come across items such as this?" he said. "I have seen jewelry like this in large cities with fine merchants. These do not usually come from small villages such as this one."

The merchant watched him scrutinize the jewelry. "I received them in trade from a local noble family."

Keller glanced at the man. "This is very fine work," he said. "It must have cost a small fortune to commission. Who is the family?"

The merchant was eager to tell the tale. "The ap Gwynwynwyn family," he said. "The last kings of Powys. They used to be quite wealthy, but the family has grown more destitute over the years and from time to time has come to me to trade some of their more valuable items for things that they need. The necklace that you are holding bought them four barrels of barley, two sacks of beans, an old sow, and six sheep. They come down from the hills every year, usually with some manner of jewelry as you see, and trade it for sustenance."

Keller glanced at the man. "And this is all from the same family?"

"Aye, my lord."

Keller's gaze returned to the exquisite piece of jewelry. As he gazed at it, he turned his head slightly so he could shout out of the stall.

"Rhys!" he boomed in English. "William! Attend me!"

He was still holding the necklace when the knights appeared, struggling to move their bulk into the shop. Rhys in particular was having a difficult time because he was extraordinarily wide. Keller held up the big necklace in front of them.

"What do you think about this?" he asked. "Do you think any woman would be proud to own it?"

Rhys cocked a dark eyebrow, thinking that he was no judge of jewelry, but William reached out to finger it.

"Magnificent," he said quietly. "I know my wife would love to have it. Are you thinking of purchasing it for Lady de Poyer?"

Keller nodded, looking back at the other jewelry laid out on a bundle of wool fabric. "I am," he said as he picked up the emerald and pearl necklace. "This, too. What do you think?"

William was interested in the goods only because he had a wife that he often purchased things for. Rhys, however, was bored silly.

"It is quite beautiful," William concurred. "I am sure Lady de Poyer would be thrilled with any of it."

Keller was looking at the small gold and garnet necklace, thinking it might be a nice gift for Izlyn. He picked it up to inspect it. "Enough to cause her to forgive a drunkard of a husband?"

William looked at him. "So she is indeed angry with you for drinking too much last night?"

Keller sighed heavily as he set the garnet necklace down. "I pray that is not common knowledge."

"It is not, although I had suspected."

Keller cast the man a sidelong glance. "If I ply her with enough gifts, mayhap she will forgive me."

"Why didn't you just apologize?"

Keller gave him an impatient expression. "I did," he said. "It was not enough."

William fought off a grin. For a man who was as uncertain with women as Keller was, the reality of an angry wife must have been torture. "Then you had better get all of it," he said, pointing to the jewelry. "I would leave nothing to chance."

Keller took his advice. He bought everything the man had, a purchase which came to a staggering amount – 10£ for the big necklace, 4£ for the garnet and pearl necklace, and 4£ 10p for the emerald and pearl necklace. Each ring cost him 2£, and he bought all four – a garnet, a ruby, a blue sapphire, and an emerald. The merchant also threw in three scarves made from a fabric called *albatross*, a very fine fabric from France, and an alabaster phial of perfumed oil that smelled of roses and lavender spikes.

The last purchase he made was something called a "splash" or "waters" (used interchangeably, Keller found) that were fragranced waters distilled with a mixture of water, wine, and herbs that were used for bathing or cleansing the face. The merchant happened to have a corked gourd containing "splash" that had come from Ireland, fragranced with lavender, sage, and clove. It smelled earthy and strong, so he purchased it as well.

Keller ended up paying the man eight gold crowns for his purchases which was, as he had said, the most money the old man had ever seen at once. It was a small fortune. But to Keller, it was worth every last pence as a peace offering to his wife. The jewelry, the "splash", and the perfume, wrapped up in the scarves, went in Keller's saddlebag and he was looking rather eagerly to the returning home to presenting Chrystobel with such beautiful gifts. Keller recollected that she had mentioned that Gryffyn, being the heir, believed any excess funds should be spent on him, meaning Chrystobel and Izlyn more than likely never received anything other than basic necessities. He was very happy to be able to provide them with something that wasn't a necessity.

As he pondered that thought and prepared to mount his charger, something swift and deadly passed over his head, sailed between the two men-at-arms behind him, and hit an innocent peasant standing across the road. The knights turned swiftly to see that the man had been struck by an arrow. It had come from the south, behind the merchant stalls.

There was instant chaos in the air. As the peasant fell to the road and the man's wife began to scream, men came hurling out from between the merchant stalls with weapons raised. Keller had to duck to avoid being decapitated as he unsheathed his broadsword. Using a massive fist, he plowed it into the face of the man who had aimed for his head and, with blood spurting in all directions from a broken nose, shoved the man to the ground next to his horse. Keller's charger, smelling a fight, finished off the man with his heavy, sharp hooves to the head and chest.

Men were screaming in all directions and the fight was bad from the onset. William had been ambushed by two men and had managed to dispatch one, now in a nasty sword fight with the other. His opponent had an old double-headed battle axe, still quite viable, and he was swinging it with some power at William's head while the knight mostly stayed out of his way. The battle axe was a heavier weapon but the sword had more range, so it was only a matter of time until William saw an opening and plunged his blade into the man's ribcage. With both opponents down, he went to help the men-at-arms who were swarmed by fast-moving Welsh and their smaller, but just as deadly, weapons.

Rhys, too, had been attacked by two men at a time but in his case, it had been a foolish tactic by his opponents. Rhys was a rarity in that he fought with dual blades, custom-made broadswords that he carried in a double sheath strapped to his back, so when he was attacked by two men, the dual blades flew into action and in little time he'd had both men put down. Then he went to help Aimery, who had been caught by a spear in the thigh, creating a bright red stream of blood down his left leg. When Rhys leapt into the fight with the dual blades flying, both of Aimery's antagonists wisely fled.

The fight was short but vicious, and in little time, the Welsh were fleeing back into the village, disappearing behind huts or running down alleyways. Keller's men went to chase them but he called them off. It was more important that they return to the safety of Nether rather than try to pursue rebels who knew the land, and hiding places, better than they did. Therefore, the knights mounted swiftly and encouraged the men-at-arms to do the same.

"Return to Nether!" Keller commanded. "Go!"

Men began to scramble and spur their horses back the way they had come. Mud and dirt kicked up, hitting walls and individuals as the horses struggled for traction on the wet road, but soon the group was thundering out of town, racing past St. Peter's church in their haste to get clear of the village.

The road to the east was carved into the side of a sheer, rocky mountain, giving them a good view of the lands below. The mist had turned to rain by the time they hit the open road, however, blurring their vision as they went. As they ran, the knights turned their attention to the town and any sign of the enemy laying chase, but that vision never materialized. Even so, Keller saw no need to let his guard down. He would be in defensive mode all the way home.

They were, after all, in enemy territory. The attack simply reminded them of the fact.

CHAPTER FIFTEEN

"**A**ND YOU ARE surprised that you were attacked by Welsh?" Gart asked. "Surely you expected it, Keller. But what I find interesting is that they found you in that town, at that point in time, and they were fully armed. Rebel militia doesn't usually hang around in villages and especially small villages where their activities cannot be camouflaged."

Keller and the party from Machynlleth were in the great bailey of Nether, having raced the entire way back to the castle in the driving rain. The horses were exhausted, as were the men, and Aimery was dealing with a rather nasty puncture wound on his thigh that would require stitches. Keller watched Aimery very gingerly dismount his charger.

"Then they must have been following us, although I did not see signs of that," he told Gart. "We managed to kill at least six of them and the rest fled."

Gart eyed Rhys as the man joined their conference. "I suppose the dual blades had flesh for supper this day," he said to the man.

Rhys lifted his dark eyebrows. "All that and more," he said. "It was an excellent fight but not nearly long enough. I barely had time to warm to it."

Gart fought off a grin. "That time will come, my fine lad," he said. "I suspect those rebels might report your presence to a bigger militia, and that means we might see trouble here at Nether."

Keller sighed at that thought. He had hoped to avoid trouble in his new home. His saddlebag was in his hand and his eyes moved over the great hall of Nether, with smoke rising from the chimney. He wanted to get inside and out of the rain.

"That was bound to happen sooner or later," he finally said. "It has always been my intention to call a meeting with local chieftains to announce my marriage to Chrystobel, among other things, but it seems now that I must do it right away. I was able to hold the peace, more or less, at Pembroke Castle for seven years, so I am hoping Nether will know the same measure of peace."

Gart nodded his big, wet head. "With you in command, I have confidence that peace will hold," he said. "It was always a mystery to me why a man with your social ineptness could negotiate with the enemy where the rest of us would fail."

Keller shrugged humbly. "I understand them, I suppose."

Gart thought on that for a moment, in brief. "I would believe that, for I have seen the proof," he said. Then he pointed to the keep. "Go inside and get out of this rain. I believe your wife has a feast planned in honor of your return."

Keller looked at him, surprised. "She does?" he asked, hope in his voice. "Is she inside?"

Gart nodded. "I believe so," he said, whistling to nearby soldiers to help take the horses to the stables. "She and her sister are somewhere inside. And do you know the sister followed me around today like a shadow? I couldn't shake the girl."

Keller grinned. "Izlyn followed you about?"

Gart seemed genuinely outraged. "She did," he declared. "I actually had to stay in the gatehouse all afternoon because she would not leave me alone."

Keller chuckled, not at all feeling sorry for Forbes. If there was such a man who struck terror into the heart of all men, it was Gart Forbes. The men-at-arms had a nickname for him, in fact. *Sach*, they called him. It meant "madness" in Celtic, and when Gart was on the field of battle, he literally became mad with bloodlust, so to hear that he had been hiding from a twelve-year-old admirer brought Keller to giggles. He never thought he'd see the day when Gart Forbes would hide from anything.

As Gart remained out in the bailey and disbursed the escort party, Keller headed for the great hall. The rain was pounding so hard that it was difficult to see even a few feet in front of him, so he entered the great hall rather blindly behind William and Aimery. He was hit in the face with the heat and smoke from the room as he nearly staggered through the doorway. Wiping the rain from his eyes, he grasped Aimery by the arm before the lad could wander away.

"Wait," he said. "Before you eat, we must have your wound tended. We must find Lady de Poyer."

William was standing with them, his dark eyes searching the room for Lady de Poyer's blond head. A swift perusal of the hall did not produce her, so he grabbed the next servant that passed him and sent the woman on the run for Lady de Poyer. As they stood there and removed wet gloves and helms, Chrystobel suddenly appeared from the eastern portion of the hall.

She emerged through the smoke and bodies, a goddess of a woman wearing a dark green surcoat that brought out the pale creaminess of her skin. Keller watched her come towards him, his heart fluttering wildly in his chest, wondering how to start the conversation and praying he wouldn't say the wrong thing. He wasn't entirely sure time had eased her anger against him in spite of what Gart had said about planning the meal in honor of his return from Machynlleth. Therefore, he braced himself as she drew close.

When their eyes met, Chrystobel smiled as beautifully as he had ever seen her smile. It was enough to cause his knees to weaken.

"Lady de Poyer," he greeted softly. "You are looking well this evening."

Chrystobel dipped her head graciously. "My thanks, my lord," she said, her dark eyes glittering at her husband. There were a thousand words bottled up there, words that would have to wait until they were alone to be spoken. As if remembering there were more men standing around, she suddenly extended her hand to indicate the feasting table. "If all of you will sit, I will have your meals brought out."

Looking between Keller and Chrystobel, and seeing the longing in their expressions, William sat with a smile on his lips. He felt as if he were intruding on a private moment and made haste to leave. Keller, however, remained behind with Aimery still in his grip. The young knight was pale and weary as Keller indicated his injury to Chrystobel.

"We had a bit of a skirmish in town," he told her, pointing at the bloodied thigh. "Aimery sustained a wound that requires tending. Mayhap you can assist him now."

Chrystobel peered at Aimery's wound with great concern. "Of course," she said, beckoning for them to follow her. "I have my things in my chamber. I will tend him there."

Keller had a grip on Aimery's arm as he watched Chrystobel collect a sheepskin cloak, which was protection from the rain, and pull it over her head. Holding the cloak over her so she would not get wet, and lifting her skirts up to keep them out of the mud, she picked her way across the soaked bailey with Keller and Aimery behind her. The stone steps leading into the keep were slippery and she took them slowly, but once in the keep, she dropped the cloak next to the door and indicated for the two knights to follow her up the stairs. They did, ending up in the smaller chamber she shared with Izlyn.

It was very warm in the room with its comfortable furnishings and brightly snapping fire. She headed for her sewing kit on the opposite side of the chamber.

"I will need to get at the wound," she told them both. "Because the injury is so high on his leg, mayhap he should remove both the mail coat and his breeches."

Aimery looked at Keller, stricken by the fact that the woman had virtually ordered him to disrobe, but Keller stoically indicated for him to remove his tunic. Unhappy, and embarrassed, Aimery removed his tunic and gloves. Next came the helm, which ended up by the door, and then then the mail coat and hauberk. All of it ended up in a pile near the chamber door. But when it came to removing his breeches, the young knight balked.

"The breeches are torn where the spear entered," he said, moving to the nearest chair and indicating the big hole in the leather. "I am sure Lady de Poyer is skilled enough that she can tend my wound without my removing… anything."

Keller could see that the young knight was vastly embarrassed, which was somewhat amusing, so he turned to his wife. "Can you work through the hole?"

Oblivious to the knight's chagrin, Chrystobel peered at the puncture wound through the rather wide opening. "I believe so," she said, crouching down beside him. "I will try to be as swift as possible."

Relieved that he wasn't going to have to remove his clothing in front of Lady de Poyer, Aimery sat perfectly still as she cleansed the puncture wound with wine. When she carefully threaded her needle with cat gut, she glanced over at her husband.

"Was the skirmish in town terrible?" she asked.

Keller, standing near the door, shook his head. "Nay."

Chrystobel had expected more of an answer and she looked over at him as she poised over Aimery's wound. "This is the only injury?"

"It is."

"Who started the fight?"

Keller shook his head. "Not I, Lady de Poyer, I assure you," he said. "We were attacked as we left. We assumed they were Welsh rebels of some kind."

Chrystobel's gaze lingered on him as she bent over and made the first stitch in Aimery's leg. "It is possible but not likely," she said thoughtfully, concentrating on her work. "There are no rebel strongholds in this region unless you include Colvyn ap Gwynwynwyn, but he is poorly supplied and poorly armed. The most he can claim is a strategic castle and an old family name."

Keller thought on that. There was that name again – *Gwynwynwyn*. He'd heard it from the merchant in Machynlleth. Moreover, he'd heard it from Trevyn when the man listed an ally of Gryffyn. *I find it strange that they happened upon you at that particular point in time.* Wasn't that what Gart had said? It was indeed strange, *too* strange. Was it possible that Gryffyn had been following his movements outside of Nether and was behind the attack? If that was true, then it meant Nether was being watched by Gryffyn and whoever he had managed to ally with. Perhaps they were being watched even now. It was an uneasy realization.

"Your father said that he is a friend of Gryffyn's," he said quietly.

She nodded as she placed the second quick stitch. "He is," she concurred. "In fact, he somewhat courted me before my father arranged for a marriage with you."

Keller was startled by the bolts of jealousy that rocketed through his body at that knowledge. The sensations were violent and harsh. But, in the same breath, he shouldn't have been surprised by a courtship towards Chrystobel. She was a beautiful woman and, in truth, should have known many suitors before Keller came along. He found that he wanted to ask her many questions about ap Gwynwynwyn, and the courtship, but he kept his mouth shut as Chrystobel finished putting the remaining stitches in Aimery's leg. He didn't want the young knight hearing what would undoubtedly be a private conversation, so he bided his time until Aimery limped out of the chamber and down the stairs.

Closing the chamber door and bolting it as he heard the knight's footfalls fade away, he turned to watch his wife as she put away her sewing kit. Then his gaze trailed to the saddlebags, laying on a big wooden chest over to his right, and thought on all of the wonderful things he'd brought Chrystobel. The storm outside caught his attention as lightning flashed and he was coming to think that this small, warm chamber was a much better place to be than the stuffy hall across the bailey. It was much more private. Aye, it was a better place, indeed.

"Tell me about Colvyn ap Gwynwynwyn," he said as he began to remove his gloves. "So he courted you, did he?"

Chrystobel looked up from her sewing kit. "Aye," she replied. "It was really only over the course of the past few months. He would send me little gifts such as a leather pouch filled with flower petals or a polished stone he had found and thought was rather pretty. Colvyn is a nice man, but he is rather grim and unexciting. I had no interest in him."

Keller removed his helm, setting it down next to the door. "Then you harbor no feelings for the man?" he asked. "Our marriage did not interrupt a budding love with ap Gwynwynwyn?"

She looked at him, disgusted. "Never!" she hissed. "Colvyn is not someone I could have feelings for, not in the least."

Keller felt markedly better to hear that. In fact, the declaration gave him an abundance of courage. "Am *I* someone you could have feelings for?" he asked softly.

Chrystobel appeared surprised by the question, but just as quickly, a bashful smile spread across her lips and she lowered her gaze so that he could not see her hot cheeks. Keller saw them, anyway.

"Mayhap," she said coyly. "I have hardly known you enough to know for sure."

That was true, but Keller was enchanted by her brightly blushing cheeks. "But you could at least have an inkling as to whether or not I am worthy."

Chrystobel wouldn't look at him. "It is too soon, I tell you."

Keller grinned. "I believe you are someone I could have feelings for," he said softly. "In fact, I am sure of it."

Her head shot up, her dark eyes wide on him. She thought on the poem he'd had Izlyn write, one that spoke of new beginnings. Could it be true? Could he really have feelings for her? Gazing into his dusky blue eyes, she could see the sincerity and hope in them. She could see the man's naked optimism for something he very much wanted to happen. The seed was there. She could feel it. It was a seed that had been planted over the course of the past couple of days, against all odds or expectations. Now, the seed needed to be nurtured.

"I've not yet thanked you for the poem you told Izlyn to write for me," she said softly. "It is the most beautiful poem I have ever read."

He smiled modestly. "I had hoped you would like it," he said. Then, his gaze grew intense. "Chrystobel, I must again extend my deepest apologies for failing to keep my word to you last night. Please know that it was not intentional. I would never intentionally break my word to you. You are my wife and by that station alone you will always have my greatest respect. I would never intentionally do anything to harm or anger you. What I said in the poem was true. In you, I see the magic of a new beginning for us both."

Chrystobel was caught up in the sweet lure of his statement. It was a thrilling and fulfilling thought, and the hurt and anger she had felt earlier in the day vanished like a puff of smoke. She couldn't have remembered it if she tried.

"I... I think I do, too," she said quietly. "Keller, I should not have dismissed you so harshly when you tried to explain what had happened. My sister finally told me. I should have guessed it was the cider that put you to sleep before you could return. I should not have assumed the worst."

Keller rolled his eyes. "That damnable cider," he grunted. "I have never in my life ingested anything so utterly devilish. I will never touch that drink again."

Chrystobel grinned at his dramatic statement. "My father brought it out for only special occasions," she said. "Otherwise, it has been left in stores to continue fermenting. I should have warned you."

Keller shook his head as if shaking off bad memories of the potent drink. "I think we should give it to every enemy of Nether," he said. "That will take care of them quickly enough."

Chrystobel laughed softly, sobering as she met his glimmering gaze. "I am very sorry I became angry with you," she said quietly. "It was unkind of me."

Keller's gaze lingered on her a moment before reaching over for his saddlebags. "You should not have apologized so quickly," he said. "I have brought you gifts and now you have taken away my reason to give them to you. I was going to buy your forgiveness."

Chrystobel laughed but she was also very interested. "Gifts?" she repeated, quickly playing his game. "Very well, then. I have *not* forgiven you, you abominable man. Now, may I have my gifts?"

He grinned, enjoying her sense of humor. "Do you have a mirror?"

Chrystobel nodded, moving for her dressing table and producing a polished bronze mirror. "It belonged to my mother," she said. "Why do you need it?"

His gaze was intense upon her. "I do not need it at all," he said softly. "But you will. Close your eyes."

Chrystobel wanted to question him further but did as she was told. Dutifully closing her eyes, she stood still, ears attuned, as she listened to Keller move about. She could hear him rummaging through something, his big boots moving softly over the wooden floor. She heard him as he moved closer to her and then there was something against her neck, cold and hard, and she was very eager to open her eyes and look at it. She was so eager than she started bouncing around and she heard Keller sigh.

"If you do not hold still, I will never close this hook and you will never get to see it," he scolded gently.

Chrystobel came to a halt but it was difficult for her. She was grinning with excitement. Behind her, Keller finished the clasp and grinned.

"Open your eyes," he whispered.

Chrystobel did. Looking into the mirror, the first thing she saw was the magnificent pearl and emerald necklace, and her eyes widened as a hand flew up to touch the magnificent piece. The smile vanished from her face.

"God's Bones," she exclaimed softly. "For *me*? Truly?"

He came around so he could see her from the front. The emerald necklace coupled with the dark green surcoat she wore was absolutely stunning. He smiled with satisfaction.

"Truly," he said quietly. "Do you like it?"

Chrystobel was still staring at it in the mirror, her fingers moving gently along the pearls. "It is the most beautiful thing I have ever seen," she breathed with great sincerity. "Oh, Keller... for me? *Truly?*"

He laughed softly. "Indeed, it is for you."

Chrystobel simply stared at it, the exquisite workmanship and beauty of it. She was clearly overwhelmed. "To thank you seems so inadequate," she said after a moment. "I wish there was a greater word for my gratitude."

He turned away and went back to his saddle bags, pulling out all of the things he had brought for her. Scarves and jewelry spilled forth along with a corked gourd and an alabaster phial.

"There is more," he said, holding aloft the garnet necklace and the great three-strand necklace. "I purchased these, also. I thought mayhap to give the garnets to Izlyn. Do you think she will like them?"

Chrystobel looked at him in awe. "You... you would give it to her?"

He nodded. "Aye," he said. "Unless you think she will not like it. If that is the case, then I will have to look elsewhere for a present for her."

Chrystobel just stared at him a moment. Then, she looked at the necklaces and her eyes filled with tears. Keller was immediately concerned.

"What is the matter?" he demanded gently, like a man who is fearful of a social misstep. "Did I say something? Why are you...?"

Chrystobel cut him off, shaking her head. Before he could press her, she threw herself at him, arms around his neck, smacking him in the throat even through his hauberk. Off-guard but quite thrilled by the unexpected gesture, he did the only thing he could do. He put his arms around her and held her next to his rain-dampened body. She was soft and sweet and alluring.

"Thank you," she whispered tightly, squeezing his neck so tightly that she would have strangled him were it not for the hauberk creating a barrier. "You are so kind to bring me gifts, but to bring gifts for Izlyn as well… what a generous man you are. Izzie will be thrilled."

Keller was sorely wishing at that moment that he was not wearing his armor. He wanted to feel his wife against him in the worst way. His wife. It still didn't seem real because it was in name only. He'd had yet to progress beyond the social stage and he very much wanted to. As the storm pounded outside, lighting up the sky every so often, he thought that now would be a good time for them to become husband and wife in every sense of the word. Releasing Chrystobel enough so that he could look her in the eye, he cupped her face with his enormous hands and gently slanted his mouth over hers.

Chrystobel didn't resist Keller's kiss. In fact, she had anticipated it, hoped for it, and now that he was upon her, she collapsed against him, her tender lips suckling his. It was warm and wonderful, and being swallowed by his big arms was nothing short of delightful. When he moved to kiss her more deeply, she didn't resist. She responded readily.

When his tongue snaked into her mouth, timidly, she simply allowed herself to experience it. She'd never been kissed like this, not ever, and there was something very naughty and decadent about it. His kisses grew more forceful and she let him have his way, experiencing every sensation with the greatest of pleasure. Her arms went around his neck to hold him fast, hold him against her, and she was startled when he suddenly bent over and swept her into his arms. Big, strong, powerful arms cradled her without effort as he carried her over to the bed and deposited her gently on the mattress.

It began to occur to Chrystobel what was about to happen. The moment was upon them, the moment that should have occurred on the day they married but didn't. Instead of being fearful, she was actually quite curious. She gazed up at Keller expectantly only to see that he was removing his tunic and wet mail, so she thought that perhaps she should remove her clothes also. Wasn't that what one did when consummating a marriage? Although no one had ever really spoken to her about the ways between men and women, at least not seriously, she had heard servants speak on it more than once. Naked flesh against naked flesh, they had said. A man's male member between a woman's legs, causing babies to be born. Aye, she knew all of that. It was time to create a baby, a son for Keller, so she sat up on the mattress and reached behind her, unfastening the stays of the surcoat.

As she stood up to remove it, Keller was already half-undressed. His mail hauberk and tunic had come off, leaving him naked from the waist up. Silently, he reached out to help Chrystobel by lifting her surcoat over her head, leaving her clad only in her shift and stockings. He tossed back the coverlet on the bed and Chrystobel removed her shoes and stockings, completely ignorant of the fact that this was supposed to be an intimate and pleasant experience as much as it was an experience to create a child. No one had ever told her it was supposed to be pleasurable. Therefore, she was looking at it all rather logically. She climbed into the bed, gazing up at him with a mixture of trepidation and anticipation.

"Are we to create a child now?" she asked rather frankly. "If that is the case, then you will have to tell me what to do. I do not know that much about it other than what the servants have told me."

Keller gazed down at her, a smile playing on his lips. "You are already doing all you need to do," he told her. "Getting the woman into the bed is the most difficult part."

She cocked her head curiously. "It is?" she asked, confused. "It is simply a matter of climbing onto the mattress. I fail to see what is so difficult."

Keller scratched his head in a marginally awkward gesture. "It was a jest," he muttered. "Not to worry. I shall take over from here."

"You will let me know if I need to do anything."

"I'll be sure to."

With that, Keller sat down on the edge of the bed, his back to her, and pulled off his big boots. Then, he unfastened his breeches and swiftly pulled them off. He pulled the coverlet up and over him as he slid into the bed, covering himself up to the chest. Chrystobel was still sitting next to him, realizing that he was now completely nude beneath the covers and she was not. Pulling the shift up over her head, she tossed it to the floor whilst pulling the coverlet up to her neck as she lay down beside Keller.

So they lay there, side by side, as she stared up at the ceiling, waiting for him to make the first move. Keller, who had never made love to a woman that he hadn't paid for the privilege, rolled onto his side so he could look at her. Every woman he had bedded had taken the aggressive role and he'd simply gone along for the ride. Given that Chrystobel had never done this before, he was going to have to be the aggressor. He hoped he didn't scare the woman off with his bumbling attempts.

Leaning over, he kissed her naked shoulder, the only thing that was peering out from the top of the coverlet other than her head. Her skin was warm and soft, and she smelled faintly sweet. Then, a big hand snaked under the covers and cupped her left breast, feeling her jump with surprise at his action. Her breast was warm and soft, too, and he was instantly and madly aroused as he fondled her. From one breast to the other, he squeezed gently and caressed, pinching her nipples and feeling her quiver in response. It excited him so much that he buried his head beneath the coverlet, which was still pulled up to her neck, and began suckling her nipples.

His hot, wet mouth on her breasts caused Chrystobel to gasp, first in shock but then in pleasure. She could never have imagined a sensation like this, something that made her entire body tremble and liquid heat to race through her limbs. His mouth was aggressive, moving from breast to breast as his hand kneaded the tender flesh of her belly and upper thighs. His roving hand seemed to be everywhere as he nursed against her breasts which, with her limited knowledge, were only used to nourish babies, but Keller was nursing against them hungrily for his own needs. It was wanton and exciting.

As he continued to suckle her breasts, his roving hand moved to the junction between her legs, pulling her left leg towards him and parting her thighs. A big finger began to stroke the outside of her Venus mound and Chrystobel actually had to put a hand over her mouth because she was startled, embarrassed, and aroused all at the same time. Her head was filled with muddled mists, fogging her brain until she couldn't think a clear thought. All she could see to do was feel, to experience, as Keller grew bolder. Suddenly, the finger that had been stroking her was now inside her, invading her private folds, and she drew her knees up, gasping in response.

Her hissing reaction was all Keller needed to roll is big body on top of hers, his head coming out from beneath the coverlet and his mouth fusing to hers. He kissed her furiously, his tongue forcing her teeth apart as it ravaged her. The finger inside her body, stroking her, was joined by a second finger, thrusting into her, making her wet and heated, before abruptly withdrawing. Keller was still kissing her aggressively when he placed his manhood against her swollen, wet folds and thrust into her virginal body.

It was a sharp and startling action, and Chrystobel tore her mouth away from his, gasping with the pleasure-pain of it. There was a slight stinging sensation but nothing more as he thrust again, seating himself fully into her tender, quivering body. He was a big man, with a very big member, and Chrystobel squirmed beneath him, unaccustomed to a man's body inside of hers. But Keller's senses were heightened, his sense of passion and lust boiling over, and as Chrystobel gasped and squirmed, he began the ancient primal rhythm of mating.

His thrusts were big and painful at first. Unaccustomed as she was, Chrystobel grunted with every thrust, struggling not to gasp aloud at the sensual intrusion. Keller's lips had moved to her neck, her shoulders again, nibbling on her flesh and causing bolts of excitement to race down her limbs. But the more he thrust, the more her body relaxed, and before she realized it, she was coming to respond to him.

Her hands reached for him, timidly, feeling the naked flesh of his body for the first time. He was warm with a fine dark mat of hair that covered his arms and chest. She liked it very much. But as she moved to touch him, she ended up touching herself as well, which brought about an unexpected result. Her hand brushed against her left nipple, which was highly sensitive after Keller's attention, and the moment she touched herself she could feel a wild explosion in her loins that caused her entire body to seize. Her limbs stiffened as ripple after pleasurable ripple radiated upwards from between her legs where Keller was impaling her on his manhood repeatedly. It was like nothing she had ever experienced in her life, causing her eyes to roll back in her head and her breathing to come in shrieking gasps. The more Keller pounded into her, the more heightened the exquisite sensation.

It seemed as if it went on forever when, in fact, it was only a few seconds because the moment Keller realized that she had found her release, there was nothing to hold back his own pleasure. Feeling her body draw at him, throb around him, brought about the greatest climax he had ever experienced. He spilled himself deep into her body, feeling his hot seed as it made her very slick and very wet. He liked the feel of what he had put inside her. In fact, he loved the feel of her altogether. *His wife.* It was the sweetest thing he had ever known.

When the tremors faded away and Keller lay on top of Chrystobel, his head on her breasts, it took very little time for the exhausted and satisfied knight to pass out from sheer contentment. Chrystobel realized it when he began snoring softly, his arms wrapped so tightly around her torso that when she tried to move, in his sleep, his hold on her tightened.

Grinning when she realized he wasn't going to let her go, Chrystobel put her arms around the man's head and shoulders, holding him close against her body and thinking that of all the things she had assumed about coupling, it had been nothing close to the reality of it. The reality had been passion and warmth beyond anything she could have imagined, all stemming from an English knight she had been forced to marry. Two days ago, she had been certain her life, such as it was, was about to take a turn for the worse. That fear couldn't have been further from the truth.

I see the magic of a new beginning with you.

CHAPTER SIXTEEN

I T WAS VERY late when Gart cleared the hall, making sure all of his men had found a place to sleep somewhere inside where it was warm. Rhys had volunteered to take the night watch, mounting the battlements with their spectacular views of the storm-whipped countryside, and William went with him. The Ashby-Kidd twins headed off to sleep off too much ale, leaving Gart the task of buttoning up the hall and keep for the night.

Keller had retired with his wife earlier in the evening and Gart knew he wouldn't be seeing the man until morning. Not that he blamed him. Men with new wives often disappeared from time to time to seek out privacy with their ladies. As Gart strolled across the bailey, rain dripping off his lashes from the storm that was still pounding, he found his gaze wandering off towards the kitchen.

The cook had been killed earlier that day, accidently falling down a flight of stairs that were carved into the bedrock and led to a secret entrance into the castle from the gorge surrounding it. The old woman had been found at the bottom of the stairs with a broken neck, but Gart was fairly convinced that the woman's neck had been broken before she fell because he was certain he saw finger marks on her flesh.

By the time Keller, Rhys, and the other knights had returned, the finger marks were less visible and Rhys wasn't sure he saw what Gart did. Keller had already retired by that time and hadn't been aware of the woman's death as far as Gart knew, unless Keller's wife told him, but such things weren't exactly pillow talk for newlyweds. Therefore, it was left to Gart to be suspicious of the circumstances. Something just didn't sit right with him about it and that, in turn, made him suspicious of Nether in general. Something evil was afoot. He wasn't sure what it was yet, but he could feel it.

Pushing thoughts of the dead cook out of his mind, he took the steps to the keep entry two at a time, eager to get out of the rain. Once inside the keep, it was dark and cold and silent for the most part, the only sound being the rain outside the door. As he headed for the stairs that would take him to the top floor where a warm bed await him, he heard sniffles coming from the small hall directly in front of him.

Curious, Gart followed the sounds. The smaller hall was dark, with a cold and useless hearth. In the darkness he could hear more sniffling and he stepped into the room, eventually spying Izlyn sitting at the end of the small feasting table. She had her arms all wrapped up around her small body, shivering as she sniffled. Curious, and somewhat concerned, Gart moved in her direction.

"My lady?" he asked softly. "Is something amiss?"

Izlyn jumped at the sound of his voice, her dark eyes wide with fright. Gart put up his hands to ease her, seeing that he had succeeded in frightening her.

"I am sorry to startle you," he said quietly. "Why are you weeping? Why aren't you in bed?"

Izlyn looked at him, her lip moving into a pout. She looked both unhappy and angry at the same time. Gart knew from Keller that the girl was mute, so he wasn't sure how to communicate with her any more than what he was already doing. It became a staring game until he finally held a hand out to her.

"May I escort you to your chamber, my lady?" he asked politely. "It is growing late and you should be asleep."

Izlyn hesitantly unwound her arms from around her body and she looked rather uncertain about his question. Finally, she shook her head.

"Why not?" Gart asked. "Aren't you weary?"

Izlyn nodded. Then, she slipped off the bench she had been sitting on and made her way to the darkened hearth. Gart stood a few feet away, watching her as she pulled a piece of kindling out of the wood-box. Taking the stick, she began to scratch around in the soot that was gathered in front of the hearth. Gart thought she might be drawing pictures, which seemed rather odd, but she suddenly stopped scratching and beckoned him closer. Gart took a few steps towards the hearth, looking to the soot because she was pointing insistently at it.

There was writing in the ashes. Bending over, he peered closer to the letters. He was frankly surprised that she could write. Being a woman, and being mute, the odds that she could communicate in any fashion were against her, but evidently she was educated. He squinted at the writing and realized it was in a language he could not read, more than likely Welsh.

"I am sorry," he said, looking at her. "I cannot read this."

Izlyn fell to her knees beside the soot and wiped it smooth. Then, she took a piece of kindling again and scratched out another message. This time, Gart could read it.

The door is locked.

After reading it, he looked at her. "What door?"

Izlyn smoothed out the ashes again and scratched another message as Gart stood over her shoulder and watched.

My chamber.

"Your chamber is locked?" he asked. "Who would lock it? Come with me and I will open the door. I shall kick it down if I have to."

Izlyn shook her head frantically, reaching up to tug on the knee of his breeches before he could get away. Gart paused, watching, as she scratched out another message.

My sister and Sir Keller are inside.

Gart understood quite a bit at that moment. "I see," he said. No, it wouldn't do to break down the door at all. He might get flogged if he did. Gart cleared his throat softly. "Is there another place you can sleep? Surely there is another bed for you."

Izlyn was uncertain. Gart crouched down beside her to be more at her level, feeling rather sorry for the young girl whose entire world was in upheaval. Her father dead, sister married, and she was quite alone. As he gazed at her, he also remembered what Keller had said about the girl and her brother, and how the brother had abused the entire family. Gart couldn't imagine anyone abusing this slight, delicate creature. Even to think about it enraged him.

"I understand that your chamber is with your sister," he said patiently. "However, there are other rooms in this keep. In fact, I have been given a bed on the top floor that I will gladly give to you. Do you want me to take you there?"

Izlyn shook her head, smoothing out the ashes and writing again.

You sleep there.

Gart read it, shaking his head. "I will not sleep there if it means you do not have a bed," he said. "Is there anywhere else you can sleep? Otherwise, you must sleep in my bed. I will insist."

Izlyn started to shake her head but thought better of it. Her expression suggested she had an idea. After a moment, she set the stick aside and stood up. Gart stood up next to her. She gazed up at him with her big brown eyes and this time, he wasn't annoyed by it. She was a sweet little thing. When she held out her hand to him, he took it, swallowing it up in a fist the size of her head. As she walked, he followed along beside her.

Izlyn led Gart up the stairs to the first level. There were two chambers on this level and she went to the door on the right. Lifting the latch, she pushed open the door to reveal a large, roomy chamber with an enormous bed in the middle of it, pushed close to the hearth. The room had been swept clean and three big trunks were neatly lined up along the wall near the door. Izlyn pointed to the big bed.

"You can sleep there?" Gart clarified, looking at the bed, the room in general. "It looks nice and comfortable. This is a very big chamber. Who does it belong to?"

He asked the question, forgetting she couldn't speak to him. But Izlyn scampered over to the hearth, which had been mostly swept out, and found a scrap piece of wood in the woodbox. There were enough ashes that she could make a slate, and she knelt down and began to write.

Papa.

Gart peered over her shoulder to see what she had written. When he saw what she had scribed, he looked around the chamber again. It belonged to the dead father they were burying on the morrow, the one killed by his own son. He wondered if Izlyn knew who had killed her father, more burdens for a young woman whose short life had been full of them. He really did feel a good deal of sympathy for her. More than that, he was coming to feel guilty for hiding from her. Perhaps she had just wanted a friend and he had been cruel about it. He put a big hand fondly on her blond head.

"I will send a servant to prepare the room and build a fire," he said. "I shall return."

As he went for the door, he heard swift pitter-pats of little feet as Izlyn caught up to him and slipped her hand in his. When he looked down to see what the trouble was, she simply smiled up at him. Gart didn't have the heart to force her to remain. She was undoubtedly feeling lost and lonely, as evidenced by the weeping when he'd first come across her, so he permitted her to accompany him as he went in search of a servant, making sure Trevyn's bed was prepared for Izlyn and ensuring there was a fire in the hearth. All this he did for her as she clung to his hand, scurrying after him as he went about his task.

When the room was finally warm and comfortable, he stood by the door with an old female servant, one he had roused from the hall to assist him, and watched Izlyn as she climbed up onto the big bed. When the old woman turned to leave, Gart stopped her.

"You will remain here with her," he said. "If she has any needs, she must have someone to tend them."

The old woman only understood marginal English. She pointed to Izlyn as Gart gestured for her to remain in the room, and the old woman understood after that. As the old woman went to settle in, Gart turned to leave but he was thwarted by a big thump on the floor that sounded as if it was near the bed. By the time he turned around, Izlyn was picking herself off the floor and running towards him. Gart was startled when she threw her arms around his waist and hugged him tightly, fearfully. Gart held his arms aloft, unsure what to do, as Izlyn squeezed his waist. He found himself looking at the old servant woman, at a loss how to respond. The old woman shuffled back over to the door where the two of them were standing. She struggled with her English.

"Afraid," she said, wringing her hands anxiously as she looked to Izlyn. "*Afraid.*"

Gart looked down at the girl clinging to his waist and all he could feel was sorrow and disgust. Disgust for the life she had led and for the terror she surely must have suffered, and sorrow for the fact that she must have surely been fearful of every aspect of life. There were many atrocities in the world and Gart had seen his share, and when he was able to assist, he had. This was an atrocity that he'd not witnessed and only heard of, but still, the effects were obvious. Izlyn didn't even know him, but somehow, she sensed that he would never do her harm, which was the truth. He wouldn't. But he would surely kill anyone who made a move against her ever again. The atrocities, for Izlyn, were over. For as long as Gart was able to, he would make sure of it, and he knew Keller would make sure of it, too.

Unwinding Izlyn's arms from around his waist, he led her over to the big bed and lifted her up, putting her on the mattress. Pulling the coverlet up, he tucked her in as she had never been tucked in by any male member of her family. Gart, a stranger, and a man with little capacity for compassion or mercy, was certainly showing an abundance of it to a lonely, frightened girl. When Izlyn finally fell into an exhausted sleep, it was clutching Gart's big hand. She'd never felt so safe in her life.

The old serving woman spent the night sleeping on the floor next to Izlyn, keeping the young girl company as she slept while her knight in shining armor slept a floor above her, hoping that, one day, he might have a daughter just like sweet little Izlyn.

૭੪

KELLER AWOKE WELL before dawn the next day, startling himself awake because he had been sleeping so deeply that, for a moment, he couldn't remember where he was. He awoke with Chrystobel in his arms, his face buried in the back of her head, and in his disorientation it took him several long moments to not only place the room but the woman in his arms. It was his wife, and he was sleeping in the bed she shared with her sister.

Lifting his head carefully, he looked around the chamber. It was dark, with the fire reduced to glowing embers, and it was still very dark outside and very quiet, so he assumed it was well before the soldiers roused for the morning shift. His gaze moved to Chrystobel, sleeping so peacefully against him, and he smiled faintly as he thought back to their love making. It had been so sweet and delicious, and as he lingered on it, he realized that the event had taken him to an entirely new level of emotion. He had been fond of Chrystobel before, but now... there was something more to it. Kissing her exposed shoulder very, very carefully, he cautiously disengaged himself from her and silently went in search of his clothing.

He found his breeches, boots, and padded tunic, quietly pulling them on as he moved for the chamber door. Next to the door, in a pile, he could see his mail and armor along with his broadsword in its scabbard. When he picked up the hauberk, he noticed that it had rusted somewhat because he hadn't had it cleaned immediately. Collecting everything into his big arms, he unbolted the door with great stealth and slipped from the chamber.

As he stood on the landing outside of Chrystobel's door, he was curious where Izlyn slept since the girl was so attached to her sister. Undoubtedly she returned last night to sleep in her chamber and, finding it bolted, sought out another safe haven to sleep in. He should have been more concerned about the girl and felt badly that he hadn't considered her once he finally had his new wife all to himself. On a hunch, he quietly opened the door across the hall, the master's chamber that Chrystobel had cleaned out for their use, and poked his head in. It was dark in the room but he could clearly see a small figure on the bed. Taking a few steps into the chamber, he recognized Izlyn all wrapped up in a heavy coverlet with an old servant sleeping on the floor at her feet. Smiling faintly at the girl, and glad she was sleeping somewhere safe, he slipped from the room and down to the first floor below.

The rain from the previous night had let up and, as he emerged into the bailey, the sky above was bright with stars. He headed towards the two-storied gatehouse where there seemed to be some activity going on as the guards walked their posts for the night. He was still holding his hauberk and mail coat when he entered the guard house and managed to locate two young squires who were sleeping on the floor. The boys had come in with Gart and Rhys, but Keller confiscated them to clean his mail while he went about his duties of arranging an escort for the funeral mass. One thing in particular he had to do was seek out George to see if a coffin had been made.

So it was busy work in that brief hour before dawn and, somewhere in that hour, he'd managed to find George, whom he put in charge of loading Trevyn d'Einen into his coffin, and Gart, who was just coming out of the keep as the eastern sky began to turn shades of blue and pink. Keller and Gart had a brief conversation about the agenda for the day and when Keller mentioned heading over to the kitchen to ensure the morning meal was being prepared, Gart informed him about the cook's death the day before. Gart also mentioned his concern about the death and, together, the two of them headed over to the kitchen where Keller was shown the secret stairs that led down to the concealed entry in the gorge, the very stairs where the cook allegedly met her death.

Keller very quickly decided he didn't like that entry in the least and left Gart behind in the kitchens to figure out a way to either plug it or protect it. Keller didn't want to leave the castle, thinking it was well protected when, in fact, it had an Achilles' heel.

As Keller returned to the bailey in search of his remaining knights, Rhys and William, who'd had the night watch, came off the battlements and swore they would be able to ride escort for the funeral mass in spite of the fact that they hadn't slept all night, and Keller took them at their word. In the past, he'd known Wellesbourne to be awake for two straight days and perform flawlessly. The man needed little sleep to function. Keller put Rhys and William in charge of forming the party that would escort Trevyn d'Einen's coffin into Machynlleth.

With the knights in motion and the escort party forming, Keller headed back into the keep to rouse his wife and her sister. As he mounted the stairs to the first floor, he could hear scurrying above him and his wife's soft voice. Chrystobel was awake and as he neared the top of the stairs, Izlyn raced from the master's chamber with something in her arms that looked like a dress or coat. Already, the women were awake and organized. He followed the girl into the smaller chamber where she and her sister were evidently very busy.

It was warm and fragrant in the chamber, with a bright fire in the hearth and two fat tapers lit against the early morning dimness. As Keller stood in the doorway, he found he only had eyes for Chrystobel. Like an angel, she looked radiant and beautiful at this early hour and as he gazed at her, thoughts of the previous night came rolling into his mind again. Although Keller was a worldly man who had seen and experienced more than most, he had never experienced a touch like Chrystobel's. There was something about her that seemed to strengthen him and weaken him all at the same time. He couldn't explain it any better than that. All he knew was that, somehow, she had gotten under his skin and he wasn't the least but sorry about it.

As Keller stood there and stared, Chrystobel caught movement out of the corner of her eye and turned to see her husband standing just inside the door. When their eyes met, she smiled sweetly at the man, giddy as she had never been giddy in her life. She had awoken a short time ago, noticing that Keller was gone but taking a few moments to lay in the covers, warm and cozy, recalling the night before when she'd finally become his wife in the literal sense. Keller had touched her body in ways she'd never imagined possible and even as she thought on it, her cheeks grew warm with the recollection of the giddy pleasure he'd given her. It was an entirely new aspect of life she'd never known to exist.

Once averse to the marriage, now she couldn't remember when she hadn't been married and loved every moment of it. Her expression must have given away her thoughts because Keller seemed to have the same warm expression on his face, too.

"Greetings, Lady de Poyer," he said, his voice low and soft. "You are looking lovely this morn."

Chrystobel looked down at the dark green surcoat she was wearing, the same one she had worn yesterday.

"Thank you," she said, a faint blush mottling her cheeks. "And... and you? Are you well this day?"

"Most well now that I have seen you."

Chrystobel grinned shyly, catching a glimpse of Izlyn and noticing the girl was giggling at her rather besotted reaction to Keller's compliment. Irritated with her sister's taunts, she turned her back on the girl as she made her way to Keller.

"I assumed you would want to leave early for Machynlleth," she said. "Izlyn and I shall be ready to travel shortly."

Keller held up a hand to ease her. "Take your time," he said. "I am still preparing the escort and seeing to the security of the castle for the duration of our absence."

Chrystobel nodded. "Then we shall be ready when you are," she said. "I was about to go and see to the morning meal."

"I already have."

Her brow furrowed. "But that is a woman's task," she said, confused. "Why would you do that?"

"So you would not have to," he said, his dusky eyes glittering. "I wanted you to remain warm and cozy in your chamber, and dress at your leisure. I did not want you to bother with mundane things."

Chrystobel's heart was swelling with adoration at his thoughtfulness. In fact, it was swelling with adoration for *him*. "You are very kind to do that," she said, but she soon sobered as thoughts of the kitchen came to mind. "Were you told that the cook was killed yesterday? She took a tumble down a flight of stairs."

Keller nodded. "I was told," he said. "I saw the stairs, too. No one ever mentioned there was a concealed passage that led from the kitchen to the gorge."

Chrystobel nodded. "Indeed there is," she said. "It is meant to be used if the castle is ever compromised. I am sorry I neglected to tell you about it. It simply never crossed my mind."

He understood. "Are there any other passages I should know about?"

She shook her head. "Nay," she replied. "The only points of entry or exit at Nether are the gatehouse, the postern gate, and the passageway. There is nothing else."

He believed her and, not wanting to linger on the negative note of the cook's death, he simply smiled at her and began to remove his gloves.

"That is a good thing," he said. "A castle with too many holes in it is no castle at all. We may as well not have walls if that is the case."

Chrystobel was back to smiling again, giving him a flirtatious little expression as she turned away and headed back over to the bed where she had been mending a rip on the hood of a cloak. Keller grinned at the come-hither countenance on her face then scowled dramatically when he glanced at Izlyn and the girl made a silly face at him. He could hardly believe these were the same two women he had met only three days ago. When fear and terror were removed, it was remarkable how quickly the human soul healed. As he set his gloves aside, his gaze fell on his saddlebags, still where he left them on the big wooden trunk. Next to the bags was the pile of scarves and perfume he'd neglected to give his wife. They were still as he had left them.

"Before I forget," he said, moving over to the pile, "there were more gifts I brought back from town yesterday, but I don't suppose you'd care to see them."

Chrystobel came running, needle and thread still in hand from where she had been mending the cloak. "Of course I want to see them!" she begged. "May I? Please?"

Keller eyed her hopeful face as it was joined by a second hopeful face. Izlyn didn't know about the gifts, or the necklaces, but because her sister was excited, she was excited, too. Keller found himself looking at two very eager ladies. He couldn't help but laugh.

"Very well," he said, reaching down to the pile and drawing forth a beautiful pale-blue scarf made of the light *albatross* material. He extended it to Izlyn. "For you, my lady. I hope you like it."

Izlyn took the scarf that was so delicate it was as if it were made from angel's wings. Glee didn't quite cover her expression. She was positively overjoyed as she fondled it happily, rubbing the soft fabric against her cheek before wrapping it around her neck. As she played with it, Keller handed the remaining two scarves to Chrystobel.

"And these are for you," he said softly. "Wear them in good health."

One scarf was egg-shell colored while the other was a pale green, both of them soft and airy. Chrystobel was thrilled.

"These are beautiful, Keller, truly," she said sincerely. "You are too kind."

Keller merely smiled. "With your new pearl and emerald necklace and that green scarf, you shall look like a queen," he murmured, turning back to the jewelry he'd left on the chest the night before and drawing forth the garnet and pearl necklace. "Izzie, come here. I have something more for you."

Izlyn was dancing around with her beautiful new scarf, waving it in the air, but swiftly ran over to Keller when he called her. It didn't even occur to her that he'd used her nickname, but it certainly occurred to Chrystobel. In fact, she was very touched that he would use the nickname, a family name that intimated affection as if he belonged to them already, and they belonged to him. This man, this enemy, who had been kinder to them than any of their kin had ever been.

As Izlyn ran up to him to see what he had for her, she didn't expect the exquisite necklace that he held up in the light. In fact, it rather confused her until he motioned for her to turn around so he could put the necklace on her. Chrystobel went to retrieve her polished bronze mirror and she held it up for her sister as Keller placed the necklace on her slender collarbone.

Izlyn's eyes widened at the beautiful necklace. To her, pearls and garnets looked like the greatest treasure of the most favored queen. She felt beautiful and regal in a way she'd never felt before and she fingered the necklace, awestruck, before looking to Keller in shock. He smiled at the girl, nodding his head.

"It is for you," he said. "Do you like it?"

Izlyn was overwhelmed with the gift. She threw her arms around his waist and squeezed him tightly before swiftly releasing him and darting off. Her right hand remained on the necklace while the left hand held the marvelous scarf. They were gifts beyond compare to a girl who had known so little generosity. As Keller and Chrystobel watched, Izlyn snatched the mirror from her sister and stood close to one of the lancet windows, inspecting her necklace in the weak morning light. The look on her face was all of the thanks Keller needed.

"She is madly in love with the necklace," Chrystobel said softly, turning to her husband. Her expression was deeply sincere. "Thank you for making her so happy. If I were not already married to you, I would marry you now just to show my gratitude."

He gave her a lazy smile. "And I would let you," he said, giving her a saucy wink that made her giggle. Then he turned back around to the remaining items on the wooden chest and pulled forth a corked gourd and an alabaster phial. He extended them both to her. "The small phial is perfume and the larger container is something called 'waters'. It is used for washing hands or cleansing. It even has some medicinal purposes. I thought you might like it."

Curious, Chrystobel took both items, inspecting the containers before setting the gourd down on the nearest table so she could smell the perfume. The scent made her gasp aloud with joy and she immediately put it on her arms and neck, just so she could smell it every time she moved. Setting the perfume down, she then popped the cork on the gourd and smelled the fragrant waters inside.

It was a pungent smell, strong and earthy. She looked at Keller curiously. "And I am supposed to wash my hands with this?"

He nodded. "That is what the merchant said," he replied. "You may wash your hands and face with it, he said. It is also good to drink for medicinal purposes."

"What *kind* of medicinal purposes?"

He shrugged. "Of that, I did not ask," he said. "But there is wine in it, so mayhap it is used to settle nerves or for general malaise."

She grinned as she sniffed the gourd again but decided against tasting it. As she sniffed it again, she caught a whiff of Keller's slightly rotted scent as the result of his clothes being unable to properly dry after being caught in the rain yesterday. He smelled most foul and a thought occurred to her. She went in search of a bowl.

"Mayhap you should be the first person to try this," she said. "Mayhap you would like to wash before we leave?"

He frowned. "I bought that water for you."

She smiled brightly. "And I am sharing it with you," she said, not wanting to offend him but thinking that at least a quick washing and a change of clothes was in order. "Would you not allow me the privilege of helping you to wash?"

He just looked at her, a vaguely wry expression on his face. "I am sure it is not necessary."

Chrystobel wrinkled her nose, trying desperately to couch what she was trying to say. Unfortunately, she couldn't quite come up with a tactful approach.

"I realize that you were caught in the rain yesterday and your clothes have not been properly dried," she said, "but you smell a bit..."

She trailed off and he lifted his eyebrows to encourage her. "Wet?"

"Rotted."

He cocked his head but there was a smile on his lips. "Rotted, am I?" he said. Then he shrugged his big shoulders again. "Then mayhap I had better wash so I do not shame my well-dressed wife. But my clothes are upstairs where Rhys and Gart are sleeping, I believe. On the day I arrived, I took most of my possessions up there. I shall retrieve clean clothing and return."

He quit the room and they could hear his big boot falls heading up to the second floor above them. Chrystobel, wanting to be alone with her husband in order to help him bathe, sent Izlyn off on an errand to the kitchens to pack some food for their journey, simply to get the girl out of the room. Izlyn went happily with her lovely necklace and beautiful scarf. By the time Keller returned, Chrystobel had poured the "waters" into a big bowl and was awaiting him. He closed the door behind him, tossing the clean tunic onto the bed.

"I brought my razor," he said, holding up what looked like a dirk in a sheath. "I have a feeling I could use a shave as well."

Chrystobel smiled. "You do look a bit ragged."

With a grin, Keller pulled the smelly tunic off and tossed it to the ground. "Then I am in your hands, Lady de Poyer. Do with me as you will."

She did. She had Keller bend over the table, over the big bowl of scented water, and proceeded to scrub him with a horsehair brush she had that was used solely for bathing. She also used a bar of lumpy white soap that smelled of roses because it was the only thing she had, and she scrubbed the man's head, face, and upper torso with it. Using a linen rag, she wiped the soap off his skin, rinsed out his hair with the heavily-scented "waters", and proceeded to use the soap on his face again to lather up his beard. But that was where she stopped.

"You will have to shave yourself," she said. "I have never shaved a man before."

His dusky eyes glittered. "Then perhaps you should learn," he told her, removing the razor from its sheath. He handed it to her. "I will sit down. The best way for you to learn is to stand over me, with my head against your belly, and drag the blade up my face towards you."

Chrystobel wasn't too sure about it but she did as he asked. When he was seated, she came up behind him and he rested his head back against her breasts. Holding his chin with her left hand, she proceeded to drag the sharp razor up his left cheek, scraping off a portion of his beard. With a few more drags, she grew confident and proceeded to very carefully shave his entire face without a single nick. She even shaved his neck. Thrilled at her first attempt, she used more of the "waters" to wipe off his face, cleaning it of the slimy soap, and stood back to inspect her handiwork.

It took Chrystobel a moment to realize that it was the first time she had ever seen her husband clean-shaven. His skin was rough and weathered, but removing the sprouting beard gave her a clear view of his full, smooth lips and square jaw. She found the entire vision extremely handsome and her heart beat perhaps just a bit faster in her bosom. Keller didn't have the overt beauty that Rhys had, or the smoldering sensuality that Gart had, or even the gentle good-looks that William had, but he certainly had something that made her heart race.

"Well?" Keller said, breaking into her train of thought. "Am I presentable yet?"

Chrystobel nodded, setting the damp linen rag onto the table. "You are indeed," she said. "Thank you for allowing me to help you bathe."

He stood up, picked up his tunic from the bed, and bent over to kiss her gently on the lips. "My thanks to you, Lady de Poyer," he murmured against her mouth, kissing her again because she tasted so good.

"I have a feeling this will not be the last time."

Chrystobel blushed furiously, giving in to his kisses so much that when he pulled away to put the tunic over his head, she nearly fell over. She had to catch herself. A bit addle-brained from his sweet kiss, she struggled to focus, collecting the wet linen and taking the bowl of used water and setting it aside so the servants could use it. Soapy, fragranced water, even though it had been used by the lord, was a prized commodity to the servants who liked to bathe in the sweet-smelling water as well.

As Keller straightened out his tunic and ran his fingers through his dark, damp hair, Chrystobel went to her dressing table and collected the emerald and pearl necklace he had given her. Holding it out to him, he fastened it around her neck and she put her new pale green scarf over her head, draping it elegantly over the single, heavy braid that cascaded over her right shoulder. When she collected the dark brown cloak on the bed, the one she had been mending, and turned to Keller to signal she was ready to depart, he just stood there and looked at her for a moment.

"By God's Bloody Rood," he muttered. "You are by far the most beautiful woman I have ever seen."

Chrystobel blushed. "Thank you, my lord," she said, bobbing a little curtsy for him. "It is the necklace, I am sure."

He shook his head, giving her a somewhat reproving look. "It has nothing to do with the necklace," he said. "You could be dressed in rags and you would still be the most beautiful woman in Wales."

Chrystobel didn't know what to say. She was unused to flattery in any form, so she simply grinned demurely and lowered her gaze. Keller reached out and took her hand, kissing it sweetly.

"There is a morning meal awaiting us in the great hall," he said, his voice low and gentle. It was so deep that it was nearly a purr. "May I escort you, Lady de Poyer."

Chrystobel lifted her eyes to him, her expression shining up at the man. "I would be honored, my lord," she replied.

Keller kissed her hand again before escorting her from the room. In fact, his hands never left her the entire time – down the stairs, out of the entry, or across the bailey. He couldn't seem to stop touching her, as if finally realizing she belonged to him. No more emotional walls to break down, no more fear of heartbreak. He'd passed that milestone long ago. Chrystobel had managed to heal what the widow had broken. And Keller knew he was better for it.

He felt whole again.

CHAPTER SEVENTEEN

Machynlleth

T HE SUN WAS just starting to rise over the eastern hills that flanked the small berg of Machynlleth. The River Dovey ran to the north and the River Dulas ran to the east, while hills surrounded the town for the most part, enclosing and protecting it. It had been those hills that had masked the Welsh raiders who had attacked the English the day before, and even now they still held Welsh rebels. Only today, there were more, and they were waiting for the English from Nether Castle to make another appearance.

Gryffyn had managed to confiscate a small home on the edge of town by thrashing the farmer, his wife, and their young son who normally inhabited it, throwing them out into the dead of night. He needed their abode far more than they did as a place to conceal more Welsh who had come down from Castell Malwydd, men who served Colvyn but who were more interested in food, money, and shelter than the great Welsh resistance against the English. Gryffyn had to promise those men a cut of whatever wealth they confiscated off the English this day, should it come to that, so men had gathered on the southern edge of Machynlleth, heavily armed, and waiting for the funeral procession of Trevyn d'Einen to appear. Once the small farmer's home was full of Welshmen, the rest spilled over into the fields beyond until over one hundred Welshmen lay in wait in the cold and in the dark, waiting for the word to come down from Gryffyn d'Einen to move into the town.

Inside the home with its warm fire and sturdy walls, Gryffyn sat at a small table with Colvyn on the opposite side of him. After hearing Chrystobel discuss plans to bury Trevyn at St. Peter's Church, it had taken a good deal of persuasion to convince Colvyn to return to Machynlleth for another try at the English, mostly because Colvyn's first try against the English had resulted in six dead men with a seventh man dying later that day of his wounds.

Like most Welsh, Colvyn's tactics were hit and run, not great organized armies to fend off invaders. After his skirmish with Keller and the English, Colvyn was not eager to take them on again, but Gryffyn had been influential. He was sure with enough men they could easily overcome a funeral party.

"It might make more sense to try and penetrate Nether Castle while the English are in town attending a funeral," Colvyn said as he toyed with a cup of stale ale, also stolen from the farmer. "You said you were able to slip into the castle via a concealed passage. Why can we not take fifty men and use the same passage? We could take the castle that way."

Gryffyn shook his head. "You saw how many English were at Nether," he reminded him. "Fifty men would do nothing against that horde. Nay, it is best to catch them out in the open, here in the town, where they will more than likely have my sisters with them because they will be attending our father's funeral. That is what we are ultimately after, is it not? My sisters?"

Colvyn wasn't entirely sure what they were after any longer. Gryffyn seemed to have taken control of everything, including his men by promising them the spoils of war, and he wasn't happy about it in the least. Gryffyn's motives were still unclear, especially his obsession with regaining sisters that, under normal circumstances, he had no use for. Now, Colvyn was no longer leading his men. It was Gryffyn and his promises of riches and vengeance against the English. As Gryffyn asked the final question, Colvyn simply shook his head.

"I am not entirely sure what is important to you any longer," he muttered. "You went to the church earlier today to ask the priests about the funeral and when they told you what they knew, you killed all of them. You *killed* men of God."

Gryffyn remained cool. "Because they would have told de Poyer I had been there," he said. "It would have put the man on his guard."

Colvyn hissed in frustration. "What difference does that make?" he demanded. "If you truly want to save your sisters, then it would be much easier to slip into the castle and steal them away. As it stands, you have us attacking a convoy of heavily armed knights. This cannot end well, Gryffyn. Or is it feeding your pride to do this?"

Gryffyn's friendly expression tightened. "It would not be easier to slip in and steal my sisters away," he said, his voice hardening. "I went there and tried, but both women are closely guarded. It would be stupid to try such a thing. It is better to catch the English unaware."

Colvyn sat forward, his dark eyes intense as he glared at Gryffyn. "I thought you wanted your castle back," he hissed. "When you first came to me, you begged me to help you rid Nether of the English because you feared their foothold in Powys. What is it now? To save your sisters?"

"It has always been to save my sisters from the English," Gryffyn fired back. Knowing that Colvyn's men were mostly following him and his promises of riches gave him such confidence. "Once we have the women safe, we can move on the castle. I have told you all of this before."

Colvyn simply grunted at him and looked away, frustrated that he had become swept up in Gryffyn's scheme. He shook his head and growled. "I should have turned you away when you came to me with tales of English at Nether," he muttered. "I should have punched you in the face and sent you away."

Gryffyn was watching the man carefully, smelling Colvyn's defeat. It fed his courage. "But you did not," he said. "You did the right thing, Colvyn. You are helping me rid Nether of the English. Once we have my sisters back, we can recruit more Welsh to help us purge the castle. What Welshman would not live for the opportunity to kill English?"

Colvyn wouldn't answer him, mostly because whatever he managed to say, Gryffyn would twist to his own advantage. There were over one hundred men now waiting to ambush the funeral party from Nether and Colvyn would not interfere with that plan. Perhaps they would be more successful with more men than he was yesterday with just a select few. A few of those big English knights were as formidable as the devil himself and Colvyn didn't look forward to facing them again.

As the morning began to deepen and the minutes ticked away, Gryffyn finally gave the orders to move on the town but remain concealed. He didn't want the English spooked, so the men had orders to hide and wait for the signal. That signal would be as the knights gathered at St. Peter's church and moved Trevyn d'Einen's coffin into the entry. With the knights focused on the coffin, and the funeral in general, it would be a perfect time to strike.

With eager anticipation, they laid the trap.

☙

As THE MORNING dawned bright and cold, the party from Nether Castle set off for Machynlleth. The sky was surprisingly clear and birds were singing as the group of four knights – Keller, Rhys, Gart, and William – two ladies, and fifty men-at-arms plodded down the muddy, rocky road. George and Aimery had been left at Nether to man the castle's defenses.

It was one of Izlyn's very few trips out of Nether and she was excitedly inspecting the world around her as she sat next to her sister on the wagon bench. On the wagon bed behind them was their father's coffin, into which Izlyn had asked Keller to put a note she had written to her papa. He may not have been much of a father but he was the only one she had, so she had written him a note telling him that she was sorry he had died. Keller thought it was rather touching.

The smell of wet grass was heavy in the air as they traveled and, at one point, they passed a field of Nether sheep that were being guarded by four d'Einen men and two black dogs. The spring lambs were several months old now, fat and fluffy, and Izlyn kept pointing to them as they played in the early morning sun. Gart figured that she wanted one so he spurred his charger forward, galloping across the field, and jumping the rock barrier that kept the sheep contained. As Keller and the others watched, he herded a few of the little sheep into a cluster but the moment he dismounted, the sheep bolted away. Everyone laughed at Gart's expense as the man mounted his charger again and gave chase.

Izlyn was practically standing up on the wagon bench in raw anticipation as she watched Gart chase down frightened little sheep. He finally managed to capture one, returning to the wagon with the sheep slung across his thighs. It was bleating with fright but he brought it up to Izlyn so that she could pet it. Even though sheep was the primary revenue of Nether, Izlyn had never been allowed contact with them. Therefore, the opportunity to pet the little sheep thrilled her.

Gart eventually put the sheep back with its flock as the party continued to travel onward towards Machynlleth. The land was very mountainous and the scenery dramatic, and birds of prey flew high overhead, searching for their morning meal. Chrystobel was enjoying the journey immensely, enjoying the landscape and enjoying watching her husband up at the head of the party. The last time she had seen him dressed in full battle regalia, he had been entering Nether's bailey as the new lord of the castle. At the time, the sight had frightened her. Now, it thrilled her. He looked so proud and strong and handsome riding on ahead. As she admired him from afar, Izlyn grabbed her hand and pointed frantically to the roadside again.

A family of cotton-tailed rabbits were foraging in the morning sun and there were several babies. Izlyn was beside herself with glee and Gart, riding just behind the wagon, saw what she was pointing at. He rode up beside her.

"Lady Izlyn," he said. "If rabbits excite you, I can only imagine you want to eat one."

Izlyn looked at him in horror, shaking her head. Gart teased her. "I'm sure you have had many rabbits to eat," he said. "They are quite delicious. Mayhap I shall capture all of them, make a rabbit stew, and then use their hides to make a cape for you. I will put their little white tails on the front of the cape as an ornament."

He was indicating his neck and Izlyn frowned terribly at him, scowling to the point where Gart had to look away or risk laughing in her face. He was looking at the rabbits again, who were coming up on their right as the party passed down the road.

"Ah," he delighted, seeing Izlyn making faces at him out of the corner of his eye. "I love roast baby rabbit. I think I shall go and catch one for myself."

He pretended to spur his horse forward and Izlyn threw out her arms to prevent him. But the most surprising thing of all was the sound that came out of her mouth. It was something between a grunt and a yell, bursting forth, and everyone turned to look at her with great surprise. Especially Chrystobel. She stared at her sister with shock.

"Izzie!" she gasped. "You… you made a sound!"

Izlyn was torn between embarrassment and surprise herself. She had indeed startled herself with the outburst but it seemed like the most natural thing in the world. Her voice, bottled up for ten long years, had made an astonishing return. She looked at Gart, who was smiling at her. The man had the expression of encouragement on this face and his smile broadened when he made eye contact with the girl.

"Do you want me to catch the rabbit and eat it?" he asked softly. "I will not do it if you do not want me to."

Izlyn's heart was pounding so hard in her chest that she could hardly breathe. She was excited, thrilled, and joyful. Life was joyful to her now, a life with English soldiers who were so very kind to her. Especially Gart. She had indeed decided to marry him but he would never know it unless she told him. Fear had kept her silent for ten horrible years. There was no longer any reason to be fearful. There was no longer any reason to remain silent.

Izlyn shook her head to Gart's question. He was smiling openly at her and she knew he was teasing her. The attention had her happy and content. She pursed her lips, struggling to form words that she hadn't formed since she had been a toddler, and it wasn't easy. She was afraid that she had forgotten how. Her lips twitched and her tongue moved. She was trying so very hard to say something to Gart, struggling to bring forth words that had been bottled up inside of her for so long.

Gart could see that she was laboring to speak. His manner turned surprisingly gentle for the man who, most believed, utterly lacked that quality. Perhaps he did, but not where it pertained to a terrorized twelve-year-old girl.

"Tell me, Izlyn," Gart said softly, encouragingly. "Do you want me to eat the rabbit?"

Izlyn slapped her hand on the wagon bench as if forcing herself to speak, pushing the words out and feeling as if she was vomiting as she did it. She wasn't used to things coming out of her mouth, but out it did come. She slapped the bench again as if compelling herself to project, fighting with every fiber of her being to bring forth a sound. It was on the tip of her tongue... *she could feel it on her lips*!

"N-nay," she finally spit.

Chrystobel burst into tears, throwing her arms around her sister and hugging the girl tightly. Gart, grinning like a fool, came alongside the wagon and reached out, taking Izlyn's little hand and kissing it sweetly. The men-at-arms surrounding the wagon had no idea why the child's word was such a great feat, but Rhys, on the other side of the wagon, understood. He had been told the child was mute, too, so he began to clap, applauding the great effort, as Chrystobel hugged her sister and wept. Up at the head of the party, Keller and William heard the commotion and reined their chargers back to the wagon.

The first thing Keller saw was Chrystobel holding her sister and sniffling. He threw up his visor and looked at her with great concern.

"What is wrong?" he demanded gently. "Why are you weeping?"

Chrystobel looked at her husband, wiping the tears on her face. "Izzie spoke!" she exclaimed. "Gart asked her if she wanted him to eat the rabbits and she told him 'nay'!"

Keller looked at Izlyn, surprised. "She *did*?" he asked, awe in his voice. "Izzie, is this true?"

Izlyn looked at Keller, her young face rosy and full of delight. She was thrilled with the attention and the praise. She nodded but she didn't verbally answer him, so he looked over at Gart.

"I do not suppose she wants me to eat those rabbits, does she?" he asked the man.

As Gart grinned, Izlyn looked straight at Keller and shook a finger at him. "N-*nay*!" she barked.

The knights roared with laughter, as did Chrystobel. She hugged and kissed her sister, giggling as the girl soaked up the praise. They were so happy, thrilled with life, thrilled with what the future would hold. It was a day of blessings and of sorrows with Trevyn's funeral looming, but at the moment, they were mostly counting their blessings. It was a momentous day, indeed.

The rest of the journey into Machynlleth was pleasant and uneventful after that. Izlyn didn't say another word, but it didn't matter. She'd already made a great achievement, at least in her world. In truth, it couldn't have been a better day in spite of the fact that they were heading for a funeral mass. There was joy among the sorrow.

Surprisingly, the air seemed to be warming a bit in the bright sunshine and everyone seemed to soak up the warmth and sunlight as they traveled the road that was growing less muddy by the minute. The ground was drying up as the sun soaked up the moisture, and as they began to reach the outskirts of the town, they began to see farmers in their fields or shepherds with their flocks. There were a few orchards about, mostly apples, pears, and plums, and being that it was fall, the fruit was being harvested before the colder weather could ruin it.

A young boy herding several goats ran alongside the party of soldiers, directing his goats with a stick by slapping them on the rump or on the shoulder, depending on what he wanted them to do. Izlyn was very interested in the boy, since he was around her age, and she watched him intently. When she lifted a hand to timidly wave at him, he waved wildly, stuck his tongue out at her, and then tore off into another field with the goats running after him. Chrystobel had seen the lad stick his tongue out and she watched Izlyn's face shift from interest to outrage and then back to interest again. She thought she even saw a hint of a smile.

Hiding a grin at her sister's reaction to the cheeky youth, she turned her attention to the town up ahead as the party drew close to the eastern end of Machynlleth. They entered the town proper and ran head long into a busy avenue filled with people going about their morning business. As the mud from the rains dried up, the smells came out, and the heavy scent of animal dung and human waste was prevalent on the moist air.

Chrystobel and Izlyn, having lived rather isolated lives, were quite interested in all that was going on around them. People darted around them, carrying baskets laden with vegetables, or other goods, and they even saw a woman carrying piglets in a basket. Izlyn was quite interested in the piglets until she spied a man leading four goats, each one tied to the next in a string of goats. The knights had fanned out and took position at both the rear and the front of the column as they headed towards the church, watching for any threat. Villages in particular were hazardous because there were so many places to hide, and since they'd been attacked yesterday on this very road, they were well on their guard.

At the head of group, Keller had his visor up, his dusky eyes taking in every detail; every word, every breath, every movement was noted. He was especially edgy because they were approaching the part of town where the merchants were and where they had been ambushed. He almost thought to put Chrystobel and Izlyn in the bed of the wagon to better protect them, but he veered away from that stance. They were safe enough on the bench next to the wagon driver should something happen, and he knew that he could get to his wife very quickly if he needed to. Therefore, he allowed the ladies to remain in full view as they passed through the heart of the busy burg.

Nearing the vendor stall where he had purchased all of the beautiful finery, he noticed the old merchant coming out to greet him. The old man waved a hand at him, almost frantically, and Keller raised a fist, indicating for the column to stop. Behind him, men and animals ground to a halt.

"Fy arglwydd!" *My lord!*

Keller leaned forward on the saddle to address the man. "Greetings," he said in Welsh. "Have you more jewelry to sell me?"

He meant it as a jest but the old merchant appeared nervous and grim. He waved a dismissive hand at him. "I could see you coming from the crest of the road to the east," he said, pointing to the rising sun. "I went to the alley behind the shop where the view is better. I must warn you, my lord, that I saw many men back in the fields, men with weapons and crossbows. They have gone into hiding now."

Keller's mood turned serious. "Are you sure?" he asked. "How many did you see?"

The merchant shook his head. "*Too* many," he said. "They were moving through the fields and trees. Mayhap these are the same men who attacked you yesterday."

Keller's gaze moved around the avenue without moving his head. He kept it pointed towards the merchant. If they were being watched, he didn't want to give away the fact that they were being warned by looking around as if hunting for someone or something. He wanted to appear as casual as possible, at least for the moment. But inside, his heart began to race. *We have women with us... my wife is with us!*

"Mayhap," he said nonchalantly. Then, he motioned to William, who was nearest to him, to come closer. William brought his steed alongside and Keller leaned in the man's direction, his voice quiet. "The merchant says he has seen men with weapons around the town. He says they went into hiding when we approached. Spread the word and make sure my wife and her sister are well protected down in the wagon. Use the coffin as a barrier if you have to. I am sure Trevyn would not mind."

As William nodded and moved off, Keller returned his attention to the merchant. "We are going to the church to bury my wife's father and then we are returning home," he said. "I will be at the church should you need to send a message to me."

The merchant nodded nervously and darted back into his stall. Keller gave the signal to move and the column lurched forward. As William moved back among the men, spreading the ominous word, Rhys moved forward to ride point with Keller. He reined his big black and white charger close enough so that he wouldn't have to shout.

"What are your thoughts, Keller?" he asked, his gaze studying the town, the people, just as Keller was. "Do you think they are the same rebels who attacked you yesterday?"

Keller didn't look at Rhys. "It is possible," he said. "If it is not, then that is very concerning."

"What do you mean?"

Keller glanced at him. "I mean that if these are not the same men, meaning that they are somehow indigenous to this village, then it would stand to reason that we are either being followed unaware, or that someone told local rebels that we were returning today so that the rebels would be here to greet us." He shook his head. "The only people who knew we were returning were the priests."

"I doubt the priests would have been party to setting up an ambush."

Keller wriggled his eyebrows. "I would hope not," he said. "Which leads me to the second possibility; we're being followed. If so, by whom? I've not seen any sign of being followed and I am fairly astute at that kind of thing."

Rhys wasn't sure how to answer that. "There are a myriad of possibilities," he said. "For one, we look, act, and smell like *Saesneg*. Of course the locals would know that we are not Welsh. It would not take long for word to get around."

Keller turned to look at him. "You are half-Welsh, are you not?"

Rhys nodded. "My mother is Welsh," he said. "But only by name and by blood. Our heart and our family culture is more English than most."

"Then what do you think of the situation, as a man with Welsh blood in him?"

Rhys exhaled calmly, looking around the town at the peasants dressed in heavy wools and durable, if not well-used, clothing. "I think that the Welsh have conveniently shown up both times in a town you happen to be visiting," he said. "To me, that reeks of a traitor."

Keller cast him a long glance. "Someone is informing the resistance of my movements?"

"It is possible."

Keller turned around to look at the women in the wagon, now being moved to the bed of the wagon by William. He watched Chrystobel as she carefully followed her sister into the back of the wagon. After a moment, he faced forward, wracked with thought.

"Not my wife," he said. "I do not think she would be capable of that kind of deception."

Rhys was careful with his words. "But you have only known the woman three days," he said quietly. "She is Welsh, Keller. Is it possible she has been deceiving you?"

The mere thought made Keller sick. He shook his head firmly. "Nay," he said. "She would not do such a thing. There are other possibilities more viable than that."

Rhys didn't pursue the wife. He moved on to the next possibility. "What about the sister?" he asked. "Gart tells me she can write. Is it possible she has been sending messages?"

Keller shook his head, more firmly this time. "You are chasing phantoms," he scolded softly. "With what went on at Nether before we arrived, do you truly think either of those women would want to chase us off so it would be as it was before? That's madness."

Rhys shrugged. "I am simply listing possibilities," he said. "Eliminate the improbable and, no matter how impossible, whatever remains must be the truth."

"Find another truth."

"Very well," Rhys was undaunted. "What about the brother? You said that he escaped and you have mentioned your fear that he is lurking about, watching the activities at Nether. Mayhap he is behind the Welsh rebels that appear in this town every time you do."

Keller sighed heavily. "That is as good an explanation as any," he said. They were drawing near the church so he shifted his focus to what lay ahead. There would be time for speculation later. "We are nearly to the church. Assign six men to remove the coffin from the wagon. I want to get inside the church as quickly as possible."

Rhys nodded and reined his horse around, heading back into the column of men. Keller could hear him making assignments, calling out men and rearranging the defensive line around the wagon. The church of St. Peter loomed large off to the right, the gray, squat building that Keller became acquainted with yesterday. Before they entered the structure, he would send some men in to make sure no Welsh were lying in wait for them. At this point, he didn't trust anyone or anything. Bad tidings were on the wind and he would not be caught unaware, especially with Chrystobel and Izlyn with him. He would never forgive himself if anything happened to either one of them, and he was positive he would never recover if harm befell Chrystobel.

As the column pulled up to the church, he made sure that the men-at-arms created a defensive circle so that the coffin and ladies could be moved into the church with ample protection, and he had William send a few soldiers into the church to clear it. Even as Keller dismounted his charger and headed for the wagon, he felt distinctly uneasy. He didn't like that they were being watched but he was very thankful that the merchant had the courage to warn him. At least now they would not be caught off guard. Or, at least, that was the hope. Still, he could feel the tension rising. Everyone was uneasy.

When he reached the wagon, he smiled at Chrystobel as he lifted her out of the wagon bed and set her on her feet. Izlyn followed shortly and he took both women politely by the elbow, steering them clear of the coffin that was just being removed from the wagon. As they stood by and watched, the men-at-arms heaved the coffin off the wagon bed and turned for the church. The pace was slow because the coffin was heavy, and as they approached the entry, the soldiers that had been sent in to clear the sanctuary emerged to signal that no danger wait beyond.

That was good enough for Keller. Taking the women by the arms, he moved in front of the coffin, heading for the protective innards of the church. It was cool and dark in the sanctuary beyond, and he could smell the pungent scent of incense. Just as he reached the doorway, he heard several high-pitched noises, sing-song, and he knew immediately what they were. He'd heard them many times before, in battle or in conflict of some kind. Keller knew the sound of an arrow when he heard it.

He shoved Chrystobel and Izlyn into the church as several arrows rained down upon them. As everyone began to run for cover, two of the soldiers holding the coffin were hit and they went down in the street. The coffin, now unbalanced, fell heavily and tipped onto its side, knocking open the lid and spilling Trevyn d'Einen's body out into the mud.

Chrystobel and Izlyn, watching this terrible scene from the entry to the church, screamed in horror as their father's corpse lay askew in the street. Keller was bellowing at his men to get under cover as more arrows rained down, but just as quickly as the second wave fell, men began running at them from all directions, weapons held high. Before Keller could take a second breath, they were entered into the throes of mortal combat.

And the women were right in the middle of it.

CHAPTER EIGHTEEN

KELLER REALIZED EARLY in the fight that the Welsh were aiming for him. As soon as he shoved Chrystobel and Izlyn back into the church for a second time, he was overrun with attackers. He could hear Chrystobel scream and his broadsword came out, flashing wickedly in the dim light and slashing at the nearest man as he made his way to his wife and her sister. But the doors to the church were open and the Welsh were pouring in, creating a deadly situation in an instant.

At least a dozen Welshmen had followed him into the sanctuary and the mighty de Poyer broadsword was in full swing. The Welsh weren't particularly skilled fighters but there were many of them, so Keller backed the women into an alcove lit with dozens of candles and blocked them in with his big body in order to protect them. Men were coming at him from all sides, some with short blades, others with clubs. He lashed out a big boot to kick one man with a club right in the groin, sending the man to the ground as his colleagues tripped over his groaning form.

There were three men to his left who were slashing at him with smaller swords, fat-bladed, and ones that were easily made by Welsh smithies. Keller kicked out again, hitting another man in the gut and sending him to the ground while he used his broadsword to fend off the others. He'd managed to seriously gash one man and stab another, and the Welsh body count in the sanctuary was growing. But more were flooding in and he knew, with sickening certainly, that it would only be a matter of time until he was overwhelmed by sheer numbers if he didn't get help soon. His men knew he was in the sanctuary and he expected help to come at any moment, so he continued doing battle against men that were determined to kill him.

He was fighting off a man on his left and one directly in front of him when another man, this one with a spear, came at him from his right. Keller saw the man moving towards him and he fell back slightly to give himself the opportunity to turn and fight him off, but as he turned, the strangest thing happened. He heard a female grunt, a yell really, and suddenly a big iron bank of candles went crashing into the man with the spear. Hot wax and fire sprayed everywhere and the man screamed as his clothes ignited.

Shocked, Keller turned to see Chrystobel on the other end of the iron candle sconce. She was wielding it like a weapon, swinging it again when another Welshman got too close. When she turned to look at Keller, all he could see was terror and determination in her eyes. Courage in the face of fear was not a quality everyone possessed, but Chrystobel evidently did. The sweet, bright woman who had been abused her entire life was finally learning to fight back.

That brave gesture from her bolstered Keller's courage more than God himself could have. He gave her a half-grin, one of great approval, as he continued to fight off a swarm of Welsh. He managed to dispatch two more attackers when some of his men, led by Rhys, burst in through the church entry.

Rhys' double swords were flying furiously, killing or maiming anything they came into contact with. The man plowed into the collection of Welsh holding Keller and the women hostage and, with Keller's substantial help, managed to clear out the group. Still, it was a brutal battle until the end. Those who weren't injured finally ran off, leaving the dead and wounded littering the cold-packed floor of the church.

"Are you well?" Rhys asked both Keller and the women. "Is anyone hurt?"

Keller shook his head, turning to his wife, who was still standing there with the iron sconce in her hands. She looked terrified. He went to her and gently unpeeled her fingers from the iron, letting it fall to the ground. Cupping her head with one big hand, he forced her to look at him.

"All is well," he told her softly. "You were very brave, my lady. I owe you much."

Chrystobel was trembling, white with fear and rage. "They... God's Bones, they were trying to *kill* you," she breathed. "I could not let them do it."

Keller put a big arm around her shoulders, kissing her forehead. "With you as my defender, they do not stand a chance," he said. He kissed her again before focusing his attention on Rhys. "How is it outside?"

Rhys sheathed one of his swords, keeping the other in his hand. "Still fighting for the most part," he said. "Mayhap we should see if the priests have somewhere to lock the ladies up safely so we can return and clean up the dregs."

Keller shook his head. "I cannot be entirely sure the priests were not the ones who helped set up this ambush," he said. "The ladies stay with me."

Rhys didn't argue with him, mostly because he agreed with the logic. The priests had been strangely absent throughout the battle. "Where *are* the priests?" he asked, glancing at the big empty church behind him. "Have you even seen them?"

Keller looked around the dark, dank sanctuary. "I have not," he said. "Mayhap you should find them and bring them to me. I want to hear what they know of this attack."

Rhys went off into the darkness, taking several soldiers with him. As he headed off, Izlyn came around to Keller's opposite side and slipped her hand around his big arm, holding on to him. Keller glanced down at the girl, winking at her when they made eye contact.

"I suppose you were going to jump into the fight, too?" he asked her, teasing her softly. "Those fools had better run if they know what's good for them."

Izlyn grinned, laying her cheek against his arm in a sweetly affectionate gesture. Keller merely smiled, standing with the two ladies, hearing sounds of a battle outside the door. He found himself wondering if Trevyn was still lying in the street outside, hoping the body wasn't being damaged by the fight going on around it. No matter what the girls felt about their father, he didn't wish for Trevyn's desecration. It might be a bit traumatic for the ladies to deal with.

"Stay here," he told the women. "I must see what is happening outside."

Chrystobel and Izlyn let him go and he made his way to the church entry, gazing out at the activity in the street beyond. He could see the dumped coffin and Trevyn's body still where they'd left it, but there didn't seem to be much activity. He could still hear sounds of a battle going on but he couldn't see where it was coming from. As he stood there, listening to the fading combat, Rhys emerged from the rear of the church.

Rhys made his way over to Keller, unsheathing the second broadsword as he went. "I found the priests," he said as he came to a halt. "They are in the cloister in the rear. Their throats are slit."

Keller's eyebrows lifted as he struggled to conceal his shock. "*All* of them?"

Rhys nodded, glancing at the women over in the alcove to make sure they hadn't heard him. "I counted four priests and at least six acolytes. All dead."

Keller thought seriously on those facts. So much of this situation was puzzling and the mystery seemed to be deepening. "Is it possible that the priests weren't siding with the Welsh?" he whispered. "Is it possible that the rebels killed them so they would not warn me of the impending ambush?"

Rhys nodded. "My thoughts exactly," he agreed. "Keller, we must return to Nether immediately and lock it up. Something bigger may be brewing and we do not need to be caught outside of the safety of Nether's walls."

Keller couldn't disagree. "Then we take d'Einen's body back with us and bury it at Nether until such time as we can return," he said, urgency in his manner. "Let us gather the men and depart."

"What do we do about the priests?" Rhys wanted to know.

Keller didn't like leaving a church full of dead priests but, at the moment, he was more concerned for the living. "Once we have the ladies back to the castle, I will send a contingent of men back to clean up the mess and bury the priests. I shall send word to the Bishop of Welshpool to let him know what has happened, as that is the nearest diocese. Meanwhile, let us put d'Einen back into his coffin and get the women to safety."

The knights swung into action. Rhys went outside to spread the word of retreat while Keller returned to the women. There were only pockets of fighting now, including Gart and William, who had managed to kill several Welsh who were more poorly armed against the big broadswords. Gart in particular had taken fiendish glee in dispatching anyone he came across, lending credence to the *Sach* nickname. It came to the point that when the Welsh saw the big knight coming with his bloodied sword, they scattered. That's the way Gart liked it.

When the fighting finally tapered off, Gart split the forces into those gathering the wounded and those putting d'Einen back into his coffin. Quickly, the coffin was loaded onto the wagon, along with eleven wounded men, and the women were loaded up as well. With no more signs of the Welsh, Keller ordered the funeral party to flee, and flee they did. What had been a leisurely ride to Machynlleth was a harried return to Nether Castle.

Keller was thankful for their very lives, but one thing was certain – Rhys was correct. Perhaps the next attack would be on Nether. The Welsh were cunning and sly, and he would have to be on his guard every moment from this point forward. It was clear that someone was watching him and knew his every move.

He would have bet money that someone was Gryffyn d'Einen.

☞

THE BIG KNIGHT with the dual blades had nearly taken his head off. As it was, Gryffyn suffered a nasty gash to his shoulder, enough so that it caused him to flee the fighting, fearful that something worse would befall him. It was a bad wound that bled a good deal, and it hurt him to lift his left arm, so he needed to have it treated. The problem was that there was no available physic and he didn't trust the dirty, crude Welsh soldiers. He didn't want those dirty hands touching him.

Therefore, he burst into one of the first homes he came across where a woman and her two children were going about their chores for the day. Bolting the door behind him, he beat the woman fairly severely as her children stood by and screamed, beating her to the point where she begged for mercy. Gryffyn was only satisfied when those around him were submissive and once she behaved in a surrendering fashion, he stopped hitting her and demanded she tend his wound. Bloodied and wounded herself, the woman did as she was told.

With shaking fingers, the woman cleaned the gash and stitched it, but she hurt him as she stabbed him with the needle and Gryffyn hit her so hard that her left ear began to bleed. But she finished sewing him, whimpering with fright. When she was done, Gryffyn simply left. No words of thanks, no exchange of any kind. He simply swept out of the hut and headed over to the farmer's cabin he had confiscated because he had left his mount there, a shaggy brown pony borrowed from Colvyn.

As he made his way back to the farmer's dwelling, he made sure to stay low to the ground and move swiftly. He dodged behind houses and jumped over fences. He could hear the distant sounds of what he thought might be combat but he didn't return to find out. His destination was Castell Mallwyd. Whatever men were left after the skirmish with the English would also return there, as they'd been instructed to do. He didn't even know what happened to Colvyn. He'd not seen the man since he set out after Keller, who had been inside the church with Chrystobel and Izlyn.

Like a coward, Gryffyn had fled the scene. He returned to Castell Mallwyd before the nooning meal and it was deserted, so he set about scrounging together a meal from whatever Colvyn had in his food stores and waited for Colvyn and his men to return. It wasn't a long wait. He hadn't been back an hour yet before men started trickling in.

For as many men as the Welsh had against half as many English, the wounds upon the Welsh were bad. It was clear that the English had been the victors, but Gryffyn waited with hope – hope that Colvyn had managed to wrest one or more of his sisters from Keller, but by the time Colvyn returned shortly before sunset, it was clear that he didn't have the women with him. He was empty-handed.

Gryffyn, who had been watching from the derelict battlements, could only feel great disappointment and great fury. He met Colvyn down in the bailey as the man, astride his shaggy pony, wearily entered the grounds of his destitute castle.

"What happened?" Gryffyn demanded. "Where have you been? And why are my sisters not with you?"

Colvyn didn't say a word as he dismounted his steed. But once his feet hit the muck of the bailey, he walked up to Gryffyn and punched the man right in the face. Gryffyn staggered back, falling to one knee has he put a hand to his stinging cheek. When he looked up, it was to see Colvyn looming furiously over him.

"That is for being a coward and fleeing a battle that *you*, in fact, instigated," Colvyn seethed. "I lost twenty-seven men. Twenty-seven! And what did you do? You ran like a woman!"

Gryffyn was livid but he was wise enough not to strike Colvyn in return. The man was a Welsh prince, after all, and the men at Castell Mallwyd were loyal to him. At least, they were for the time being. Gryffyn had been trying for three days to change that.

"I was wounded," Gryffyn hissed, indicating his torn tunic and the stitches on the skin beneath. "I was bleeding all over the damn place and went to seek aid. By the time my wound was tended, the battle was over, so I returned here. Are you telling me that it was *not* over? Was there more fighting that I missed?"

Colvyn growled and turned away. He was disgusted, exhausted, and enraged, which was a nasty combination, and Gryffyn fleeing the battle had only fed that anger. He'd always known the man to be dramatic and cowardly, but this was more than even Colvyn believed him capable of. After pacing a few feet away, he abruptly stopped and turned to Gryffyn.

"This is the last time," he said, his voice low and hazardous. "We will not attack the English again. Twice we have tried and twice we have been defeated. There will not be a third time, at least with the amount of men I have. This is a task for a much bigger army than what I have."

Gryffyn could see his cause slipping away. He could not lose Colvyn's support, not now. He could not face defeat in any fashion and quickly, his mind began to cook up an alternative scheme. The English were too powerful against the under-armed Welsh. Other than a massive Welsh army, which was highly unlikely, Gryffyn had to be smarter than de Poyer. There had to be another way to best him.

In the past, Gryffyn had free reign of Nether and it was easy to do what he wanted to with his sisters. Beat them, jail them… he could do as he wished. Now, de Poyer was there to protect them… *he was there*. What if de Poyer was *not* at Nether? An idea began to bloom, forming in desperation because Gryffyn could not let this go. *He could not fail!*

"There is a simple way to solve this issue once and for all," Gryffyn said, saying it loud enough so that Colvyn's men could hear. "The English have already proven that they can best us in combat, so we must choose another tactic. If force does not work, then mayhap a lack of force will. Mayhap it will be as simple as walking into the castle, regaining my sisters, and reclaiming the wealth that the English have stolen from me."

Colvyn wasn't agreeing with him. "This is another trick, d'Einen," he muttered. "You speak in foolish riddles."

Gryffyn shook his head violently. "I am not, I assure you," he said passionately. "There is a secret passage by which to enter Nether. I used it myself the other day to gain access. We can use it to get into the fortress."

Colvyn threw up his hands in frustration. "Get in for what purpose?" he demanded. "The English will be inside, waiting for us, and this time they will kill us all."

"They cannot kill us if they are not there."

Colvyn was about to fire a retort but Gryffyn's softly uttered statement had his curiosity. He knew he shouldn't ask. God knows, he knew he shouldn't. But he couldn't help himself.

"Explain."

Gryffyn tried not to sound too excited, knowing that convincing Colvyn would not be easy. He motioned to some of the soldiers standing nearby to come closer, to hear his plan. He would build a case of public opinion for his scheme and then Colvyn would have no choice but to agree to it. Gryffyn was astute that way.

"If another *Saesneg*-held castle is being attacked by Welsh, then other *Saesnegs* will ride to their aid," he said, sounding quite logical. "Hen Domen Castle is the closest English castle. It is a day's ride from here. If we send de Poyer word that the lord of Hen Domen needs assistance, then we can lure the man out and away from Nether. He will take his army with him and once they are gone, we can sneak into Nether and reclaim the castle."

In truth, it was a reasonable plan. If the English were removed from Nether, then the matter of taking the castle and saving the sisters would be a relatively simple thing. But the scheme was almost *too* simple. Surely there was a hole in it somewhere.

"Hen Domen is the seat of the Earl of Shropshire, Robert de Boulers," Colvyn said, torn between interest and refusal. "I have had dealings with them before, as has my father. They are rather warring towards the Welsh."

Gryffyn leapt on that bit of information. "Do you have a missive from Shropshire?" he asked. "Does your father? We will need to see the de Boulers seal in order to duplicate it on the feigned message."

Colvyn shook his head. "I do not but I am sure my father or brothers might," he said. "My father had some dealings with de Boulers' father several years ago when they were trying to set boundaries of the earl's properties."

Gryffyn was excited at the prospect. "Then we must have a missive with a seal that is intact or at least repairable," he said. "You have a smithy here. Mayhap the man can recreate the seal. Then we can send a missive to de Poyer, lure him away from Nether, and claim the castle and her riches while he is gone. We can *do* this, Colvyn! Can you not see the possibilities? We can rid Nether and this region of the English that so badly want to conquer both."

Colvyn still had his doubts, although they were fading. "So we lure the English away from Nether," he said. "There will still be English at the fortress. Are you truly convinced we can overcome them, even if we enter from the hidden passage?"

Gryffyn had an answer. "If we can get one man from the passage to the postern gate near the stables, he can open the gate for the rest of your men," he insisted. "Believe me when I tell you that this will be the best way to gain control of Nether. With enough of your men overrunning the place, we should be able to easily subdue the English left behind."

Colvyn looked at the man, seeing the light of excitement in his eyes. In truth, it was a viable plan and, if Colvyn thought hard on it, he was looking forward to the reward of regaining Nether for Gryffyn. Coin, food, perhaps even a few sheep would be his reward. He was tired of being so poor and desolate. He was tired of being hungry, of living a pitiful existence from day to day. He had no future and only a sorrowful past because at Castell Mallwyd, there was no hope. It was a doomed place. But what Gryffyn offered was optimism, no matter how unattainable the scheme. At least it was something, and Colvyn was willing to take a chance on something if it meant extracting him from his soulless existence. It was a weakness he had. With a sigh of resignation, he nodded his head.

"Very well," he said. "I will send a message to my father and ask him for a Shropshire seal and explain the circumstances. But this will take time, you know. We will not be able to accomplish this in a matter of days. And this missive, when you send it, must be written in English. I cannot write in English."

Gryffyn was nearly weak with relief in the knowledge that his battle against de Poyer was not yet over. They had one chance left and he was going to take it.

"I can write in English," he said. "I fostered in England in my youth because my father thought it would be wise for me to learn their ways and I learned their vile language, so you needn't worry over that."

Colvyn still had doubts. "What about your sister?" he wanted to know. "Wouldn't she know your writing? What if she sees the missive?"

Gryffyn shook his head. "I am sure that de Poyer would not share his business with my sister," he said. "She is a mere woman, after all. Why would he confide in her or discuss it with her? Nay, it is a chance we must take."

Colvyn wasn't so sure about the risk of Gryffyn's writing being recognized but he let it go. There was no use fighting d'Einen because, in the end, he would only persuade him otherwise. So he backed off, with nothing more to say, and headed towards the great hall where a meager amount of food awaited. *That is the first thing I am going to do upon reaching Nether,* he thought to himself. *I am going to eat myself into oblivion.* He justified his compliance by focusing on his end reward.

Hunger had a way of making strange bedfellows. The wheels of deceiving the English were now in motion.

CHAPTER NINETEEN

Early November

IN THE BIG master's chamber that she shared with her husband, Chrystobel was helping one of the house servants tend freshly washed clothing. Since their marriage almost three weeks ago, Chrystobel had come to learn that her husband was somewhat slovenly. Not in the literal, terrible sense, of course, but the man didn't keep his clothing clean in the least. Therefore, he had several tunics that had hardly been washed, if ever, and that included two heavily padded tunics he wore under his mail coat.

Upon acquiring such knowledge, as it wasn't difficult considering how badly some of his clothing smelled, she was able to coax him into turning over all of his clothing to her so she could wash it. Keller was embarrassed that his wife had to wash his filthy laundry, but Chrystobel was thrilled to do it.

As she was ironing freshly washed and dried tunics with a hot stone upon a smooth, worn tabletop, she kept hearing what sounded like strained voices outside. Sticking her head from the lancet window that faced north over her garden, she was able to look down and see George and Aimery wandering through her garden, evidently chasing something. She called down to them.

"Watch out for my garden," she said. "Do not step on anything!"

The knights looked up at her. "We are being careful, Lady de

Poyer," George said, pointing. "There is a rabbit in your garden."

"And you want to catch it for supper?"

George shook his head. "Your sister wants it for a pet!"

Chrystobel fought off a grin when Izlyn, who had been standing just out of her line of sight, suddenly appeared and waved up at her sister. The young woman was thrilled to have the high-strung Ashby-Kidd brothers as playmates, which they had been for well over a week now. They treated Izlyn like a princess and because of it, she had spoken at least four more words. It was amazing what respect and happiness could accomplish. As Izlyn waved her hands happily at her sister, Chrystobel waved back.

"Be cautious," Chrystobel warned again. "I do not want to see my flowers trampled."

The knights didn't mention that most of the flowers had long since bloomed and were already dead or dying. They simply waved her off and Chrystobel returned her attention to her laundry. It was a clear November day, not particularly cold, and as she focused on her task. Her husband had tasks of his own.

The tallymen were downstairs in the small hall with Keller providing updated tallies and information about Nether's vast sheep herds. That information had always been Trevyn's domain and Chrystobel knew little about it, so Keller and his razor-sharp mind took to the business aspect easily. He seemed to enjoy the financial side of Nether's empire and she was content to run the castle as chatelaine just as she always had. The past few weeks had seen Keller and Chrystobel form a very comfortable and extremely affectionate working relationship as each one settled into their new roles as Lord and Lady Carnedd of the Carnedd Barony.

As Chrystobel carefully rolled up an ironed tunic, her thoughts lingered on Keller. Surely a sweeter, more attentive man had never existed. She was sure of it, in fact. He was always thinking of her first, bringing her a few late-fall posies or a pretty bird feather he had managed to come across. Since their rather rough beginning, there had been no more misunderstandings or harsh words between them, and they had settled into a symbiotic relationship as man and wife. Every night, Keller would make love to her and every morning, he would kiss her awake and do more of the same. He had become very confident in his role as husband and she swore she hadn't seen him nervously pop his knuckles in weeks. That bad habit seemed to have faded away the more comfortable he became with his wife.

As Chrystobel tucked away the rolled tunic into the large wardrobe that had once belonged to her father, her thoughts were lingering more heavily on Keller and she decided to go downstairs and visit him. It seemed that they were never far away from each other and she left their warm, comfortable chamber and headed down the steps to the entry level below.

As soon as she hit the landing, she could hear voices in the small hall. There were several men in the room, standing around the table that Keller was seated at. He had parchment in front of him and a quill in hand, speaking to one of the shepherds about a young flock that was off to the east. The flocks were heading into winter and their wooly coats were filling in, and Keller was curious about the amount of wool each sheep would produce, but his conversation ended the moment he saw Chrystobel standing in the doorway. At that moment, he had eyes only for her.

He extended a hand to her, inviting her in, and Chrystobel smiled brightly as she entered the room, reaching out to take his offered hand. Keller excused the men standing around him, telling them to go to the kitchens for food, and they eagerly obeyed. Once the men quit the keep and it was just the two of them remaining, Keller reached up and pulled Chrystobel onto his lap.

His big arms went around her, his face buried in her neck. He inhaled deeply, smelling her sweet, musky scent. He'd come to depend on that scent, keeping him a sane and happy man. These past few weeks with her were just how he always imagined a contented relationship would be, only there was more to it. Somehow in the past several days, he realized that he loved her. He hadn't told her yet, of course, for things like love and emotion were treacherous waters, indeed. He hoped to summon the courage to tell her soon, but until then, he was content simply to feel and breathe her.

"How long has it been since I last saw you?" he whispered.

Chrystobel smiled, her arms around his head and shoulders. "Hours," she said dramatically. "Mayhap even days."

He chuckled. "Sometimes it seems like that," he said, pulling his face from her flesh and gazing at her. "What have you been doing?"

She toyed with his dark hair. "Finishing the last of your wash," she said. "I spied George and Aimery out in my garden chasing a rabbit for Izlyn."

Keller grunted. "Those two are supposed to be tending to the collection of horses I have confiscated from your brother," he said. "I do not intend to keep all of them and would like an inventory and surmised value. And you say they are chasing a rabbit?"

Chrystobel shook her head at him. "Do not become angry," she said. "It is for Izlyn, after all. I suppose she could always go find Gart and force him to chase the rabbit for her."

This time, Keller shook his head. "Forbes has more important things to do."

"Like what?"

"Like manage the battlements," he said, feigning sternness as he gently pinched her nose. "Rhys is in the gatehouse and William is sleeping because he had night duty."

She grinned at him, letting him know that she had been jesting, but quickly sobered. "How long are Gart and Rhys planning to remain here?" she asked. "Of course, Izlyn will be crushed when Gart leaves. She says she is going to marry him."

Keller snorted rudely. "She will have to set her sights on someone else," he said. "Forbes is not the marrying kind."

"Why not?"

"Because his wife is whatever directive David de Lohr dictates," he said frankly. "Gart lives and breathes de Lohr blue. He will never let anything distract him from that."

Chrystobel thought on that. "It is a sad state, then," she said. "He seems as if he would make some lady a fine husband."

Keller shrugged. "Mayhap," he said. "But tell Izzie to focus her attentions elsewhere. Gart Forbes is not meant for such a sweet and gentle soul."

"That is a kind way of saying she is not even a consideration."

"Well, she is *not*."

Chrystobel laughed softly. "What about George or Aimery?"

Keller rolled his eyes and stood up. "Those two?" he said, making a face to convey his distaste. "I suspect they would only marry her for the money and if that was truly the case, I would have to kill them, so put those two out of your mind as a husband for your sister. She is only twelve years old, for Christ's sake – she does not need a husband for another six years at least."

Chrystobel eyed him, teasing him. "It will be your duty to find her one."

Keller nodded rather comically, resigned to the inevitable. "They shall all have to pass tests of my choosing before I will even consider them."

"What *kinds* of tests?"

He shrugged. "Seeing how fast they can run with a raging bull chasing them," he said, pretending to be thoughtful. "Seeing how well they can fend off six bulky knights and six equally big broadswords. Gart will help me with that test, of course. Mayhap I shall see if they can beat me in a fist fight with one of their arms tied behind their back. You know, *tests*."

Chrystobel was laughing by the time he was finished. "That is terrible!" she exclaimed softly. "She will never find a husband that way."

He smirked at her, pulling her close for a sweet kiss. "It will certainly narrow the field," he said. "Only the worthy will survive."

Chrystobel giggled, wrapping her arms around his neck. "Either the very worthy or the very persistent," she said. "But none of this answers my original question. How long are Gart and Rhys going to stay?"

Keller didn't particularly want to talk about his knights with Chrystobel in his arms. He could think of much better things to talk about but he dutifully answered her. "When we returned from the ambush at the church those weeks ago, you will recall that I sent out several missives, one of which was to William Marshal," he said. "I informed him of my first few days at Nether and told him that, for the time being, it is wise to keep Rhys and Gart here with me. The two attacks against me could be local rebels or it could be something bigger. We simply do not know, so I would rather err on the side of caution and keep Rhys and Gart at Nether until we can determine if there will be more hostilities. The Marshal will inform de Lohr that I intend to keep his knights."

"Is William Marshal de Lohr's liege?"

"William Marshal is *everyone's* liege."

Chrystobel thought on the man who seemed to control every fighting man in England, the very man who had brokered her marriage. She realized that she owed him everything.

"When do you think William Marshal will send his reply to you?" she asked.

"It could be months."

It seemed like a very long time to wait for an answer, but Chrystobel supposed the Marshal was a busy man and would get to it when he could. "What about those other missives you sent out to local warlords?" she asked. "Have any of them replied?"

Keller shrugged. "The missives I sent to my allies down around Pembroke have seen responses," he said. "My old friends will be coming to Nether at some point to help me establish relationships with some of the local Welsh chieftains. As for those local chieftains, however, I have not had any responses. It has only been a couple of weeks, however, so I am not concerned. They will respond, eventually."

She smiled faintly. "Do you think it would help if I went to call on the warlords personally?" she asked. "I know a few of them. I may be able to help you."

It wasn't a bad idea but he didn't want to play up his marriage to a Welsh wife just yet. He wanted to see how the local chieftains would react to him and him alone, as the new lord of Nether.

"I appreciate your offer," he said as he pulled her close once again. "I will certainly let you know should I decide to accept it."

He kissed her again. The taste and smell of her filled him and he wrapped his big arms more tightly around her, kissing her deeply as she turned weak and pliable in his arms. He loved it when she went limp. It made him feel powerful and dominant. His kisses grew more forceful but they were interrupted when the entry door opened, slamming back on its hinges. Keller released his wife as Rhys entered the small hall.

The man was dressed in full armor, which was now required by anyone manning the gatehouse. But it wasn't the fact that he was in full armor, it was the expression on his face. Before Keller could open his mouth, Rhys held out a big gloved hand. Within it was clutched a large piece of sealed parchment.

"A missive for you, Keller," he said, his expression grim. "The messenger who delivered it said that Hen Domen Castle is under siege. They are requesting assistance."

The mood of the room darkened. Keller's brow furrowed as he reached out and accepted the missive.

"The messenger told you this?" he clarified. "Where is he?"

Rhys shook his head. "The man handed it to our sentries and swiftly departed," he said. "He said he had to return immediately. What messenger would do that? He should have waited for a response from you at the very least."

Keller was growing increasingly puzzled as he noticed the seal on the message. The dark green wax bore the stamp of Shropshire – a shield crest with a diagonal line through it and the words "Deum super omnia." *God above all.* Keller gazed at the seal a moment before breaking it and unrolling the parchment.

As Rhys and Chrystobel stood by in tense silence, Keller read the carefully written missive. It looked as if an educated man had written it. The seconds ticked away as he digested every word. By the time he got to the end of the parchment, he began to speak.

"De Boulers has been attacked by a local Welsh warlord," he said. "He asks for help. Hen Domen, if I recall correctly, is near the town of Trefaldwyn on the marches. I must see my map to be sure."

Since Keller had been conducting most of his business in the small hall, the maps, parchment, and writing instruments he had brought with him were stored on a rather large writing table that had been brought into the room for just that purpose. He set the missive on the small feasting table and went over to his collection of maps and other items, rifling through them until he came to the map he had been looking for. As he turned back for the feasting table, he glanced at Rhys.

"You had better find the other knights and send them to me," he said. "And wake William. He will need to hear this, too."

Rhys nodded and was gone, quitting the keep as Chrystobel stood there in fearful silence. Her gaze was fixed on her husband.

"What does this mean?" she asked, trying not to sound frightened. "Are you leaving to go to battle?"

He had his map half-unrolled but went to Chrystobel and put an arm around her shoulders, kissing her temple. "It is not as bad as all that, I am sure," he reassured her. "By the time we get there, the fighting will more than likely be over."

He kissed her again and dropped his arm from her shoulders, taking his map over to the feasting table and unrolling it, anchoring the ends with fat tapers. As he hunched over it, studying the map that depicted all of Wales and the entire stretch of the marches, Chrystobel came up behind him. She studied his broad back, his powerful form, as he scrutinized the map. He was thinking of the marches and she was thinking of him. God's Bones, how she would crumble if something were to happen to him. She was so very frightened for him. Reaching out, she touched his back, her hand moving across his broad body until it came to rest on his hip. Laying her cheek against his upper arm, she held her husband to her, feeling his warmth and life, trying not to let her fear get the better of her. Instead, she focused on the map to take her mind off her disquiet.

"That is a lovely map," she said quietly.

Keller's eyes were on the mid-marches. "It belonged to my grandfather," he said. "When I was assigned to Pembroke Castle, my father gave it to me. It has been invaluable."

Chrystobel noted the lovely designs and clean lines. She also noted the de Poyer family crest – a big red shield with three birds of prey in yellow. She'd never seen it before.

"My father has maps," she said. "They were in his chamber and I packed them away."

Keller nodded. "I found them," he said. "I went through his possessions before they were stored and took the maps. They are mingled with mine now. His maps of the interior of Wales are more detailed than mine."

Chrystobel's gaze moved to the pile of maps and papers over on the writing desk against the wall. She could see her father's smaller maps neatly stacked on the table with Keller's bigger ones. Not wanting to further distract her husband with chatter, which was really just nervous chatter on her part, she remained silent, leaning against him as he continued to study the map.

Too many sorrowful things were going through her head. She knew Keller was a knight and had fought many great battles. Perhaps, foolishly, she had hoped that would end when they married and they could live in peace for the rest of their lives. Aye, it had been a foolish thought, she knew.

Sighing sadly, she moved away from Keller, wandering over to the end of the small feasting table where the missive from Shropshire lay partially opened. She wasn't trying to be nosy, nor was she particularly curious about the missive, but she happened to look at it as she moved towards the end of the table. As her gaze moved over the letters, she noticed something suspicious about them. She'd seen letters like that before, many times, and she reached out, snatching the parchment and unrolling it completely. As she read the scribed characters, her eyes widened with both shock and dismay. *Dear God... it couldn't be!*

"Keller!" she gasped. "This... this missive!"

Keller looked up sharply from his map at the sound of her voice. "What is it?"

Chrystobel's mouth popped open. She couldn't help it. Horror flushed her veins as she held the missive out to Keller.

"This is my brother's writing!" she hissed. "Gryffyn wrote this!"

Keller snatched the missive from her, peering at it. He could feel the woman's terror and it bled over onto him. But, more than terror, his most predominant emotion at that moment was rage. Pure, unbridled rage.

"Are you certain?" he demanded, aghast.

Tears popped to Chrystobel's eyes and she nodded furiously, so much so that her careful braid began to unravel. "Aye," she said, her voice tight. "I would know his writing anywhere. I have seen it enough to know that Gryffyn wrote this missive!"

Keller stared at her, seeing her complete sincerity. But he still had his doubts, futile doubts clawing at him in the face of something quite shocking. Could it really be true?

"It is still possible for more than one man to have similar writing," he said, having difficulty disputing her. "An educated man wrote this. I can tell from the words."

Chrystobel wiped at her eyes. "Gryffyn is educated," she insisted. "My father made sure all of his children could read and write. God's Blood, my sister can write in three languages and so can Gryffyn. Believe me when I tell you this is his writing. He is trying to mislead you!"

After a moment, his focus moved back to the missive. The more he looked at it, the more disgusted and enraged he became. By the time the knights joined him in the small hall, he had been working on a steady simmer for at least a half of an hour.

Woe betide the man who truly enraged Keller de Poyer.

03

"It bears the seal of Shropshire," Keller told his knights. "I can only assume that d'Einen either stole a seal or had one made. Who's to know how he came across it in the first place, but he evidently has. This is the last time this man will try to deceive me. If he truly believes I am stupid enough to fall for this, then he is in for a rude awakening. I will play his game but I will win it, once and for all."

Rhys was reading the missive as Keller spoke. The other knights were looking rather disgusted by the entire thing, enraged and frustrated as Keller was that Gryffyn d'Einen was going to such lengths to destroy him. As Keller fumed, Rhys glanced over at him.

"Are we completely sure this was written by d'Einen?" he asked. "No disrespect intended towards your wife, but I have seen Shropshire's seal and this is it. What if this truly came from Shropshire and the handwriting is from someone else who scribes similarly to Lady de Poyer's brother?"

Keller wasn't offended. In fact, he nodded his head in agreement to everything Rhys was saying. "I have thought on that myself," he said. "My wife is convinced it is her brother's writing and given that we've been attacked twice now by Welsh rebels, with no true knowledge of how the rebels always seemed to know our every movement, my suspicion has been that Gryffyn d'Einen has been behind it all along watching everything we do. This missive, if indeed written by him, would only confirm that suspicion. The man is trying to destroy me."

Rhys drew in a long, slow breath. "I cannot disagree with you," he said. "But unless we have someone who comes to us and confirms that he saw d'Einen write this missive, we must go on the assumption that it indeed came from Shropshire and that Shropshire is calling for aid. We cannot refuse the call."

Keller sighed heavily. "I am aware of that," he said. "But let us assume it is *not* from Shropshire and that d'Einen indeed sent it. For what purpose? The only logical assumption is that he is trying to get me out of Nether, but why? To attack my army on the road?"

Behind him, William shook his head firmly. "Nay, Keller," he said. "I had dealings with d'Einen, lest you forget. I saw the man in action. It would be my guess that he is trying to remove you from Nether altogether. With you away, the castle will be vulnerable to a rebel attack. He is trying to get you *out*."

Keller looked at William, pondering his statement. With another heavy sigh, he turned away from his knights and began pacing. The knuckle-popping started again, in earnest, as it usually did when he was frustrated. It was his habit of choice. Carefully, he considered the situation.

"So he is trying to remove me," he muttered, more to himself than to the others. "He wants to remove me so he can claim Nether and, more importantly, claim his sisters. He knows I would not take the women with me on a battle march, so I can only assume he wants to get at them."

"He will kill them, Keller," William said quietly. "You know this to be true."

Keller nodded, his gaze lingering on William. "I cannot go the rest of my life fighting off my wife's brother," he said. "Eventually, I may fail and the results could be devastating. He would reclaim both Nether and my wife, and this I could not stand for. It would therefore stand to reason that I must eliminate him. I have been spending all of my time on the defensive. Mayhap it is time to go on the offensive and eliminate the man once and for all."

William and Gart, who was standing next to William, nodded in agreement. "He means to destroy you," Gart insisted. "You must destroy him *first*."

Keller knew that. He paused a moment, staring up at the ceiling as he thought over the situation carefully. He had the finest knights in all of England on his side. It was time he used them to his advantage.

"Very well," he decided, finally turning to look at the group. "If d'Einen wants me out of Nether, then mayhap I shall go. At least, to his eyes, I shall be taking my army to Shropshire, but in reality, I will be here at Nether, waiting for him to make his move."

"A trap?" William cocked an eyebrow. "An excellent idea. What did you have in mind?"

Keller scratched his head in thought. "How many men do I have here at Nether?"

"Five hundred and fifty," William replied.

Keller absorbed that number. "I have to send more than just a few men out in response to the Shropshire missive," he said. "If the Welsh are watching, and you know they will be, they will be suspicious if I only send out one hundred men. It has to be more than that to make a good show of things."

"Agreed," Rhys said from behind him, still holding the missive. "Send the Ashby-Kidd brothers out with two hundred and fifty men, and dress some of those men up as knights so that any observers will count more than two knights. The rest of us will remain here, lying in wait for d'Einen and his men to make their move."

Keller nodded thoughtfully to that suggestion. He liked it, but he had more to add. "If d'Einen is trying to remove me from Nether, then it is because he wants to clear the way for an easy conquest," he said, scheming as he went along. "Being that he has lived here most of his life, he knows the fortress better than most. He knows that Nether is nearly unbreachable because of the Gorge of the Dead that surrounds her walls. There is no place for a man to get a foothold to mount the walls, which makes the gatehouse the most vulnerable point of entry."

"The gatehouse is nearly impenetrable," Gart said. "All we have to do is burn the wooden bridge that spans from the gatehouse across the Gorge of the Dead, and then there is no way to reach the gatehouse."

Keller turned to look at Gart. "But there is that passageway that leads from the kitchens down to the gorge," he reminded him. "You were supposed to block it off. Did you?"

Gart nodded. "I took barrels from the stores and clogged the passageway," he said. "It is blocked off by all manner of heavy obstacles now. It would be virtually impossible to get through."

Keller's dark eyes glimmered. "Remove them," he said quietly.

Gart's brow furrowed. "But why?"

A flicker of a smile crossed Keller's lips. "I can only assume d'Einen plans to use that passageway," he said. "Let him. Let him come up those narrow stairs where I will be waiting at the top to take his head off. If I want to destroy the man, then I have to make it easy for him to come to me."

Gart understood then. "Of course," he agreed with approval. "That passageway is only big enough for one man at a time to enter. Let them all come."

Keller was feeling extremely confident with his plan. It wasn't the fact that Gryffyn was trying to kill him. Men had been trying to kill him for years, so that didn't bother him in the least. What bothered him was that Gryffyn seemed determined to get to Chrystobel and Izlyn. Any man who would target women was a vile man indeed, but Keller already knew that. More than that, he had been correct when he said he couldn't live with the threat of d'Einen hanging over his head for the rest of his life, and neither could his wife. At some point, Keller was going to have to take a stand, and the stand would come now. He was finished playing games.

It was time to win, once and for all.

CHAPTER TWENTY

THE RAINS HAD returned with a vengeance.

Two days after the Shropshire missive was received, the army intending to ride to the aid of Hen Domen was gathered in the bailey in the early morning hours in the midst of a horrible rain storm. All of the knights were in the bailey, outfitting the army, including four soldiers who were now dressed as knights. Keller had brought out four chargers from Gryffyn's collection, mounting the soldiers on the expensive beasts to create more of an illusion of knightly power. As the rain poured and the thunder rolled, two hundred and fifty men were made ready for the ruse that would hopefully bring Gryffyn d'Einen into the jaws of defeat.

In case there were any rebel eyes inside the castle, which was always a possibility, Keller and the knights dressed as soldiers, all except for Gart, who refused to be brought to that lowly level. He dressed in a padded tunic, leather breeches and boots, and wore a woolen cap over his head to conceal his bald skull. His big concession to their charade was not to wear his armor, which made him feel positively naked and contributed to his nasty mood. Consequently, there was a lot of bellowing going on as the army assembled.

Chrystobel and Izlyn were awake, dressed in their warmest as they watched the activities from the keep entry. Rain pounded on the stone in front of them and overhead, where a corbel at the top of the door arch stood out far enough to provide some shelter from the rain. Chrystobel was clad in a heavy dark blue cloak, made from wool and oiled, so it acted like a water repellant. It was the best thing she had for days such as this. Izlyn was also clad in an oiled cloak of pale green that had once belonged to their mother.

Both ladies knew exactly what was going on. Keller had been honest with them about the plans for circumventing the forged missive, but still, they were nervous, fearful that somehow the plan wouldn't work and, somehow, they would find themselves at the mercy of Gryffyn. Chrystobel knew her brother would kill her if given the chance, but Izlyn wasn't quite so informed. They had been careful to keep such talk away from her. Still, her fear was quite healthy. Anything involving her brother terrified her.

As the rain pounded and the thunder rumbled in the pewter sky above, Izlyn broke away from her sister and headed down the entry stairs. Puzzled, Chrystobel called after her sister but the young girl ignored her as she headed around the side of the keep. Curious, Chrystobel followed, dodging mud puddles and rain as it poured off of the keep, until she found her sister back in her flower garden which, by now, was more of a muddy soup with dormant plants sticking out of it. There were, however, a few sprigs of green that still had blossoms on them, now limp with rain, and Izlyn pulled at one of the last purple thistles, tearing it free of the plant.

Chrystobel continued to follow her sister as the girl returned to the bailey where the army was nearly formed. The knights were yelling and a quartermaster's wagon was being moved into place. Men were soaked, and unhappy, but there wasn't much that could be done about it. Izlyn headed straight for the army, peering at the men she came across. It was clear that she was looking for someone and as she stood there, looking rather lost, George came through a row of men and nearly ran into her.

As Chrystobel watched, Izlyn's face lit up and she smiled brightly at George, who smiled in return. He had genuinely become fond of the girl over the past few weeks, as they had spent a good deal of time together chasing rabbits or trying to fish from the small, overgrown pond near the garden. When George smiled at her, Izlyn extended the thistle to him, giving him the bud, and he took it graciously. He even tucked it into his armor in the folds near his neck. Then he patted her on the cheek and turned away, heading to the front of the column where his charger was.

Izlyn watched him go, an aura of happiness and longing on her face. Chrystobel had seen the exchange, as sweet as it was, but she called her sister over to her once George walked away because she didn't want to see her sister get trampled with the men still moving about. Izlyn scooted over to her and they headed back towards the keep, where it was dry, until a shout caught their attention.

It was Gart, heading towards them from the gathering of soldiers. He was completely soaked through, rain dripping off of his face as he approached. His attention was focused on Izlyn.

"Lady de Poyer," he glanced at Chrystobel, greeting her, but his focus quickly returned to Izlyn. "What's this I hear? You have given George a posy and not me? My lady, I am sincerely crushed. I thought you liked me best of all."

Izlyn grinned broadly and flushed furiously. She was much better with her speech these days but still not completely comfortable. She struggled to bring forth her reply.

"He… is going," she said haltingly. "You will… will stay here."

Gart's eyebrows lifted as he was horribly offended. "Is that all?" he demanded, although there was no force behind it. "You give him a flower because he is leaving? I will not stand for it. I will go fight him right now for your affections. I will not allow George to be your favorite."

Izlyn was giggling, as was Chrystobel. It was so wonderful to see her sister happy, with affection and attention lavished upon her by knights who understood how terrible her life had once been. They seemed determined to make up for every horror Gryffyn had ever inflicted upon her, which made Chrystobel feel a good deal of respect and admiration for these men. They were near and dear to her heart, men of honor and compassion, and she would defend them to the death. She came to realize some time ago that she was more loyal to her English husband and his English knights than she was to the Welsh people. She'd only known pain and suffering from the Welsh. With the English, she'd only known joy, as had Izlyn. It wasn't difficult to be loyal to them.

As Gart postured and threatened to fight George, Izlyn put up a hand and grasped his wrist. "N-nay," she said, sounding firm. "You... cannot fight George. I... I will be angry with you."

Gart stopped in the middle of his rage and looked at her, his expression conveying the best dramatics of a broken heart. Then, he turned away from her, wiping his eyes as if weeping. As he headed back towards the army, he kept turning around to see if she was watching him. When he saw that she was, he would resume wiping his eyes. Chrystobel sighed heavily and looked at her sister.

"You had better go give the man his own posy before he embarrasses himself with his sobbing," she said, pointing to the garden. "Go along and find Gart a flower so he will not feel so bad."

Izlyn nodded and turned in the direction of the garden, but paused a moment to grasp her sister's fingers in order to get her attention.

"I am marrying George now," she said haltingly.

Chrystobel laughed softly as Izlyn ran back to the garden to find Gart a flower. As she stood there, watching her sister disappear around the side of the keep, a big body walked up beside her and grabbed her around the waist.

"Greetings, my lovely," Keller said as he kissed her on the cheek. Then, he hissed when he realized how wet she was. "By God's Bloody Rood, woman! You are soaked through."

She giggled. "I know," she said. "I am returning to the keep, have no fear. But I should tell you something."

"What?"

"Izlyn just told me she is marrying George and Gart is very upset that her affections have turned."

He pursed his lips wryly. "Gart will overcome."

"Gart said he is going to fight George."

"Then George's days are numbered."

Chrystobel grinned at the jest, noticing that Keller kept turning around to see to his men's state of readiness. She found herself looking at the army as well.

"Are they nearly ready to depart?" she asked.

Keller nodded, his gaze lingering on his men for a moment before turning to his wife. "Aye," he replied. "Once they leave, you and Izlyn will stay to the keep and keep it locked. You will not come out, no matter what, and you will not open the door for anyone but me or my knights. Is that clear?"

The conversation had taken a serious turn and Chrystobel nodded. "Aye," she said. "I had better go and make sure there are enough provisions in the keep."

Keller nodded. "That would be a good idea," he said. "I have no way of knowing just how long you are going to be trapped in there, so you'd better make sure you have everything you need."

Chrystobel eyed him. "And you?" she asked softly. "Where will you be during this time?"

He heard the wistfulness in her tone and pulled her into his arms again. He had to get his fill of her before they were separated by necessity. This was a serious business they were about to face and although he was confident of victory, there were always unknown factors. It was those factors that concerned him.

"Keeping to the shadows," he said softly. "I have no way of knowing when your brother will decide to make his move, but I have a feeling I will not have to wait long. Therefore, I will be keeping to the shadows, in the kitchen mostly, waiting for him to make an appearance. You and I must be clear on this, Chrystobel – you must stay to the keep no matter what you see or hear. Is that clear? If you open that keep door, you expose yourself to terrible danger and I will not be able to focus for fear of your safety. If I cannot focus, then your brother might have the opportunity to gain the upper hand. He might even have the opportunity to kill me. Do you understand how serious this is?"

Chrystobel nodded solemnly. "I do," she said sincerely. "I promise I will stay to the keep no matter what."

He kissed her on the tip of the nose. "Good," he replied. "Now, make sure you have enough provisions. I will return to you as soon as the army is gone to seal you up in the keep."

Chrystobel headed off, moving for the kitchens that were now filled with heavily armed men because the passage to the gorge had been unblocked. After giving Gart a small purple flower that had lost most of its petals, Izlyn joined her and together they finished gathering what they needed and had a few servants carry it all into the keep. There were dry stores, of course, beneath the small hall, which would hold them for quite a length of time, but Chrystobel made sure they had enough water to cook and wash with, and pots and utensils to eat from.

In all, the keep was fairly self-sufficient, as it was meant to be. By the time they were moving the last water barrel into the keep, the last of the army was just leaving the gatehouse. Chrystobel stood at the top of the keep, watching the army trickle out and the portcullis slam down behind them. There was something very ominous about the finality of that event. Now, they were open to prying eyes. They would be watched. Gryffyn would be watching. The very thought made her shudder.

Down in the bailey, Keller, Gart, Rhys, and William stood in a quartet near the portcullis. They, too, were watching the army as it faded down the road, blending in with the rainstorm. When the last man faded off, Keller turned to his knights.

"And so it begins," he said quietly. "D'Einen thinks he can easily retake Nether but I will assure him that he cannot. William, make sure we have a heavy presence of men around the postern gate. It is my fear that if one of the Welsh happens to break free of the passage, they will head straight for that gate to open it up. Rhys, make sure the gatehouse is secured. Once William has the postern gate secured, he will join you in the gatehouse. The walls and the gatehouse, and the postern gate, will be your domains. Make sure they are sealed. Gart, you will come with me to the kitchen. You and I will wait for the first foolish Welshmen to come through that passage."

The knights nodded, having their assignments given to them. "How far out will George and Aimery go before they turn around and come back?"

Keller lifted a thoughtful brow. "They are undoubtedly being watched, so they must at least make a good show of heading in the direction of Hen Domen. I told them to head out six hours and then camp. My guess is that d'Einen will move upon us this day, but if not today, then tomorrow for certain. I have told George and Aimery to head back to Nether tomorrow before dawn. We must give d'Einen a chance to move, and we may need George's reinforcements by the time they return."

"And if d'Einen has not moved yet?"

"Then I send a messenger to George and tell him to wait until further notice," Keller replied. "If George returns too quickly, it will spook the Welsh."

The plan was clear and the men headed to their posts, but not before moving to the keep where their armor was held. Now that the army was gone and the fortress was bottled up, they could dress in their protection without fear of someone sending word to d'Einen. Nothing was coming into the castle and certainly nothing was going out, especially a messenger. Nether was as secure as they could make it.

Chrystobel was standing in the keep entry as the knights began to file in, heading for the armor they had stacked up in the small hall. A pair of young squires, the ones that had been part of Rhys and Gart's troops, followed the knights from the gatehouse and began helping the men with their protection.

As the small hall became crowded with knights preparing for battle, Chrystobel and Izlyn stood in the doorway, watching the men as they put on their layers of protection – padded tunics to avoid the itchiness of the mail, which went on top of the padding. Then came a heavy neck scarf to ease the weight and irritation of the hauberk for head and shoulder protection, and then another tunic on top of that one which usually helped secure the scabbard for the broadsword.

It was quite a process although Izlyn in particular was watching the squires, who were about her age. They had mostly stayed to the gatehouse with the soldiers so she'd not seen too much of them. Now, she was watching the competent young men with interest as Gart noticed where her attention was. When she would look at Gart, he pretended to weep, jealous of her attention to the squires. Izlyn just giggled.

Chrystobel, however, was completely focused on Keller as the man efficiently dressed. He was preoccupied, his mind on what lay ahead, and Chrystobel knew he was mostly focused on Gryffyn. Certainly, there was anxiety involving the Welsh that would be coming along with Gryffyn, but Keller was focused on Gryffyn alone.

He should have killed the man the day in the great hall when he came upon Gryffyn as he prepared to kill Chrystobel and, had it not been for Gryffyn knifing him in the back, Keller was certain that Gryffyn's life would have ended on that day. But Gryffyn had not made an easy catch or an easy kill, and Keller was tired of chasing the man. Granted, he had a new wife and a new castle that had cornered his attention, but the time had come to focus on Gryffyn once and for all. The time had come to eliminate the threat.

Rhys and William were finished dressing first, saying their farewells to Chrystobel and Izlyn as they walked past the women and headed out of the keep. The squires soon fled, having nothing else to do, and Gart eventually came to say his farewells also. He accepted a smile from Chrystobel and a kiss on the cheek from Izlyn before heading out into the driving rain with his usual stalking gait.

Finally, it became Keller's time to say his goodbyes and as he came to stand before his wife, words seemed to fail him. He stood there a moment, gazing at her, before taking her by the hand and leading her back into the small hall and away from Izlyn's big and curious ears. Izlyn started to follow but Chrystobel held out a hand to the girl, stopping her in her tracks. Chrystobel, too, wanted a few private moments with her husband. When they neared the feasting table, covered with maps and other things related to the administration of Nether, Keller came to a halt and lifted Chrystobel's hand to his lips.

"I am not an eloquent man," he admitted, kissing her fingers. "I do not know what this day or even what tomorrow will bring, but I will leave you with these words – the day I met you was the day I started to live again, Chrystobel. I was terrified of you and you know that, but I learned to overcome my fear and I am so thankful that I did. Loving you is the best thing I have ever done."

Chrystobel's eyes widened. "You... you *love* me?"

He nodded, kissing her hand again. "I do," he murmured. "Remember what I wrote to you? *When I look at you, I see all things bright and pure. I see the magic of a new beginning.* Every word of it is true and I love you more than words can express."

Tears popped to Chrystobel's eyes and she threatened to crumble but she fought it. It was such a spiritual moment, so ripe with the glorious beauty that was love, and she wanted to savor every second of it. Keller opened his mouth and she heard angels singing. This place, this darkened Netherworld, had never heard such exquisite words uttered. Suddenly, it was a darkened place no longer. It was a place of hope.

"What you have said to me," she breathed, watching him kiss her fingers. "I have never thought to hear those words in my life. And I love you, too, so very much. You have shown me the glory and excitement and beauty of life. Everything I ever dreamed of, I found in you."

Keller pulled her into his arms, kissing her deeply and feeling every emotion and every dream she ever had pouring into him, sustaining him. He was fortified now, more than he had ever been in his life, and he would see this task through. He would emerge the victor. There was no other alternative. Kissing her one last time, he hugged her tightly.

"Remember what I told you about staying to the keep," he whispered. "Do not open the door no matter what you see or hear. You will only open it for me or Rhys or Gart or William. Is that clear?"

Chrystobel nodded, suddenly very fearful for Keller's safety. "It is," she breathed. "You will be careful."

"I will."

She pulled back, gazing into his rugged face a moment before leaning forward, her forehead against his cheek.

"Be well and be safe, husband," she whispered. "Remember that I love you. I pray it gives you strength."

He pulled back, looking into her eyes with a knowing smile on his lips. "It gives me life," he said softly. "Everything you are to me... it gives me life."

With another kiss, he left the hall, moving past Izlyn as the girl stood at the doorway and touching her cheek affectionately with a big hand. Moving out of the keep, he turned one last time to see Chrystobel and Izlyn coming up behind him in preparation for bolting the entry door. He couldn't take his eyes off of his wife, the woman who had become his all for living. He'd never felt more powerful in his life.

When Chrystobel blew him a kiss, he gave her a brief wave and quit the keep, hearing the door slam behind him and the big iron bolt being thrown. The women were safe now and he could focus on what needed to be done. He had a man to settle a score with.

He had an enemy to kill.

CHAPTER TWENTY-ONE

B Y COVER OF darkness, the Welsh finally made their move.

It was raining heavily as Gryffyn, Colvyn, and one hundred and eight men made their way towards Nether Castle. Their scouts had returned earlier in the day to inform them that the English had taken the bulk of their army out of the castle, presumably heading for Hen Domen, and it was just as Gryffyn had predicted. He was confident that his plan was progressing as he had intended so as the rain pounded and the thunder rolled, he and Colvyn set out for Nether Castle.

They set out from Castell Mallwyd on their shaggy ponies, racing down a rocky, uneven path that led from the heights of Colvyn's castle down to the valley below. It was a small road that led southwest from Mallwyd, through a narrow valley until they came to the crossroads. The road to the left went on to Nether Castle while the road to the right went on to Machynlleth. As the rain poured and the dark night grew darker, they dismounted their ponies and hid them in a small vale near the crossroads, as they wanted to make their approach to the castle on foot. There was less chance of them being seen that way. It was another two miles to Nether from the crossroads.

So they ran through the night, soaked to the bone by the cold Welsh storm, sliding on wet grass and passing near fields where wet sheep were huddled up for warmth. There were soldiers watching these sheep, Nether soldiers, so Gryffyn had warned Colvyn's men to stay clear of those fields because the soldiers would launch their crossbows at them for fear they had come to steal the sheep. Colvyn's men obeyed for the most part, sliding by the fields and staying low against the mossy stone walls to avoid detection.

Nether soon became evident, high upon the crest of a hill that divided two great valleys. As Colvyn and Gryffyn drew near, Gryffyn called a halt and the men gathered. Coughing, wet, and uncomfortable, they tried to hear Gryffyn's voice over the driving rain.

"When it rains heavily like this, the Gorge of the Dead fills with water," he said to those who could hear him. "It is possible that the gorge will fill up past the hidden entry in the rocks and if that is the case, we will have to swim underwater to get into the passage.

The men looked at each other, thinking a swampy moat to be less than pleasant. "You never said anything about swimming in the moat," one man said loudly. "We will be drowned!"

Gryffyn shook his head. "It will not be deep enough for you to drown," he assured them. "In fact, it will work to our advantage. As you make your way to the postern gate, stay low in the water and the sentries will have a difficult time seeing you. The path to the postern gate is clearly marked so you will have no trouble locating it. Once the gate has been opened, you will go directly to the keep. If we can take the keep, we can take the castle."

It seemed like a sound plan and the men settled down somewhat. Gryffyn turned to Colvyn. "We will take ten men with us to breach the passageway," he said. "That should be all we need. We shall kill anyone in the kitchen and remain there, hiding, and send a man out to unlock the postern gate. I would do it myself but for the fact that if I am seen, I might be recognized."

Colvyn eyed him. *Is it another trick to keep himself out of danger?* "I will go unlock the gate," Colvyn said. "I have been to Nether and know where the gate is."

Gryffyn was satisfied with that. The more he remained out of sight, the better. Waving an arm at the men, he motioned for them to follow his lead, across the rocky hillside, camouflaged by the wet gray rocks, before reaching the eastern side of the keep where the battlements had a blind spot because of the height of the parapet. Gryffyn took the lead, sliding down the side of the hill and stalking his way over to the Gorge of the Dead.

Fortunately, there was only about three feet of water in the bottom of the gorge but it was filling quickly. It was terribly dark as they began to climb down the rocks into the moat but for a brief flash of lightning off to the north that illuminated the land for a split second. To a sharp sentry upon the wall walk of Nether, however, it was enough of a flash of light for him to catch sight of dozens of Welshmen entering the Gorge of the Dead.

He went on the run for William.

C3

THE WORST PART of an ambush was the wait.

Keller and Gart had been in the kitchen since leaving Chrystobel in the keep, and that had been almost twelve hours ago. The sun had set and the kitchen was now dark but for a small fire in the hearth, and Keller had remained fixed by the hidden door that concealed the passage that led down into the gorge, waiting patiently. On the other side of the hidden door, Gart leaned against the wall, still and silent. He had, however, been yawning for the past hour, the only sign that the man was actually alive and breathing. Other than that, there had been no conversation and little movement. The knights, as well as twenty soldiers, were crowded into the dark kitchen in utter and complete silence.

It was a waiting game. All day, Keller had been wracked with doubt. What if he had been wrong? What if Gryffyn hadn't written that message, the one that Chrystobel had been positive that contained her brother's handwriting? What if this had all been a horrible miscalculation and now here they were waiting on the receiving end of nothing. No Gryffyn, no Welsh, merely Keller and Gart, wasting their time.

Keller could only pray it wasn't true and that indeed he would be looking into Gryffyn d'Einen's face soon. He had to rid his life of this evil that threatened everything he loved.

A day of uncertainty turned into an evening of the same. Time passed with painful slowness. More waiting, and more silence. But that silence came to an abrupt end when William showed up in the kitchen a few hours after sunset. Having run all the way from the battlements, he was understandably winded.

"The Welsh have been spotted, Keller," he hissed. "As of two minutes ago, they were descending into the gorge from the northeast. Be ready!"

Keller perked up, as did Gart. The yawning stopped. What they were waiting for was actually coming to pass and the smell of a battle instantly filled the air. They fed off it, bolstering their courage for what was to come. All of Keller's doubts fled as he realized his instincts had been correct. *Gryffyn was approaching!*

"Excellent," Keller whispered with satisfaction. "So our ruse worked. Notify the postern gate and the gatehouse, William. Tell the men to be prepared."

William nodded sharply. "I have already sent men to inform them," he said. "I will wait here with you."

Keller didn't argue with him, mostly because he welcomed the fighting power of William's sword. He found that he was very edgy, watching the hidden door, waiting for it to move. Slowly, silently, he unsheathed his broadsword and a few feet away, pressed against the wall, he saw Gart do the same. The steel blades glimmered weakly in the dim light as the rain outside continued to pour.

It was madness, truly, waiting for that one small movement, that hint of an enemy, throwing them all into the maelstrom of battle. Keller was anxious to get down to it, so much so that he actually began to sweat. All he could see was Gryffyn's face, the cold and terrible face that had looked down upon Chrystobel so many times as he beat the woman senseless. A mindless beast of a man who did not deserve to live. The more Keller thought on him, the more enraged he became. *Come to me, Gryffyn*, he thought as he stared at the hidden door. *Come to me so that I may take your bloody head off!*

The moments dragged by, elongated, surreal in their slowness. Keller turned to see all of the men crowded into the kitchen and it suddenly occurred to him that they would be seen the moment the door opened, so he waved his hand swiftly at them, motioning them out of the kitchen, a directive to which they swiftly replied once they understood his meaning. All twenty of them piled out of the kitchen and out into the rain, hovering just outside the door, prepared to go charging back in and massacre the Welsh.

And they waited. The thunder crashed and lightning blared, but still, they waited. Keller was about to move to the hidden panel to see if he could hear anything beyond when the door suddenly jerked. Startled, the English faded back into the shadows. The door jerked again, shifted, and slowly began to open.

Keller was pressed flush against the wall, no more than a foot or two away, watching the panel slowly open up. His heart was thumping against his ribcage and anticipation filled his veins just as a head stuck out of the open door, peering around the extremely dark room. *Come out just a little further*, he thought. *Just a little further so I can grab hold of you.* But the figure didn't emerge any further, at least not right away. The head turned in Gart's direction and Keller was fearful that the big knight was spotted because he wasn't too adequately concealed. But Gart was still, and the kitchen was dark, so the intruder evidently didn't see him right away.

The door opened wider, scraping against the floor of the kitchen. The head peering out was attached to a body that quietly stepped out onto the hard-packed floor. The minute he emerged into the room, Keller lashed out a big hand and grabbed the man by the hair, yanking him in his direction.

The man started to yell but Keller rammed a broadsword into his back, between his ribs, killing him instantly as Gart jumped forward and grabbed the next man, making quick work of him. The English soldiers that were waiting outside the kitchen saw the fight commence and they rushed in, crowding the door as more Welsh tried to push through. From a silent, dark room one moment to a crowded mass of chaos the next, the kitchen was upended in unholy style.

It was so dark in the kitchen, and so crowded, that two of the English soldiers nicked each other with their swords because it was difficult to see who they were fighting. Welsh were charging in through the open door, one at a time, being met with the English and their sharp blades. Because of the darkness and chaos, however, it was difficult to tell who was an enemy and who was a friend.

Men fell down onto the floor, being trampled and stabbed at, as the mass in the kitchen swelled. There was absolutely no room to fight so it was like being compressed in a big crowd with no opportunity for movement. Keller had dispatched four Welshmen but he was looking for Gryffyn, who he knew was amongst this group. He could see William near the door, doing battle with a Welsh rebel, but suddenly, he could see men spilling out from the kitchen into the yard beyond. The Welsh were escaping and the fight was following them.

"William!" Keller roared. "They are entering the bailey!"

Wellesbourne, in turn, bellowed into the bailey. *"Breach!"*

Men came running from all corners of the castle. Rhys, on the second floor of the gatehouse, watched as men began spilling out of the kitchens, dark forms racing into the bailey on to be met by English troops. But the Welsh were cleaver. Rhys could see that they seemed to be driving in the direction of the stable yard and he knew what was there – the postern gate. His jaw ticked as he hissed at the men around him.

"They are going for the postern gate," he growled. "I am going down there to fight them off. You men hold the gatehouse. If they manage to take this, all will be lost. Hold fast."

The soldiers of the gatehouse nodded firmly as Rhys descended the stairs to the ground floor, unsheathing his dual blades as he headed out into the dark bailey. His target was the postern gate as well. He would kill anyone who tried to open it.

More men poured out of the kitchen, both Welsh and English, fighting in the extreme dark as the rain poured around them. There was grunting and yelling over the sound of the rain and by the time Rhys reached the stable yard, he could see pockets of fighting around him. The men assigned to guard the postern gate were doing their duty by preventing the Welsh to get to the gate. In fact, as Rhys entered the yard, there were only two active fights going on and before he could get to them, the soldiers managed to subdue them.

Six Welsh littered the muddy ground, speared by their English counterparts. Rhys still had his swords in his hands as he went to a couple of them, rolling them over to see the extent of the damage and to make sure they were dead. He gazed down at one young man, who couldn't have been older than twelve or thirteen years. He must have gazed at the youth for an extended length of time because beside him, an old soldier spoke.

"They grow younger all the time, m'lord," the man muttered.

Rhys nodded slowly. "He should be sitting at his mother's hearth still," he said quietly. Then, he began looking around the yard. "Is this all there is?"

The old soldier nodded. "Aye, m'lord," he said.

Rhys turned his back on the young man and headed for the bailey to see how the fight in the kitchen is progressing. The rain was loud so he couldn't hear anything of the outcome. He needed to have a visual sighting. He was even thinking about joining the kitchen fight if it seemed as if it was still going strong. Eyes on the skirmish near the kitchens, he had no idea what was transpiring behind him.

The youth with the stab to the chest was not dead. He was fading, but he wasn't dead. He was still mobile enough to roll to his knees when the English knight's attention was elsewhere. The postern gate was about eight feet from him and he crawled towards it, on his hands and knees, unable to breathe for the hole in his chest but knowing he had to complete his mission. He knew he was going to die and he didn't want it to be in vain. Just as he reached up for the bolt that secured the postern gate, Rhys happened to turn around and see what was happening.

"*Nay!*" he roared.

Rhys bolted for the postern gate just as the dying young man managed to throw the bolt. The gate swung open and all of Wales began to pour through. Rhys' double blades began swinging in earnest as the soldiers who had been guarding the gate raced forward to block the flow, but men were streaming in and the battle was bad from the onset. Now, the English had a serious problem with two points of entry and they hadn't been able to stem either one of them. The Welsh were, if nothing else, determined, and one of the English soldiers who had been guarding the postern gate ran out to the bailey to announce the turn of events.

"Breach!" he screamed.

William, over by the kitchens, was the only one who heard the cry. He could see men fighting in the stable yard as it began to spill out into the bailey. Dispatching the man he had been fighting, he began shoving men out of the way as he made his way into the kitchen.

"Keller!" he bellowed. "The postern gate has been compromised!"

Keller was still back near the open hidden door, still fighting Welsh who were trying to enter the kitchen. He yelled over to Gart.

"Forbes!" he boomed. "To the postern gate! William and I will handle the kitchen!"

Gart broke the neck of the man he was fighting and charged out of the kitchen, killing another Welshman when the man happened to get in his way. Gart roared and beat at his chest, fueled by the blood lust, as he plowed through the crowd and out into the bailey. He could see the fighting going on over by the postern gate and made haste to join Rhys as the man tried to prevent a larger tide of Welsh from entering the castle. When Gart entered the fray, it became more horrific than before. It became a blood bath.

Keller was now the only knight inside the kitchen but he was handling the Welsh efficiently enough. There were several dead sprawled out across the kitchen floor and the tide coming in through the hidden passage had stemmed somewhat. Either there were no more men or the ones that were coming through had guessed the carnage beyond and had turned around. Doing away with his last opponent, Keller managed to shove the hidden door closed and, with the help of several English soldiers, blocked the door up with a heavy butcher table and a barrel of water, which made it nearly impossible to move. Satisfied that no more Welsh could come through, he left four men guarding the door while he headed out into the bailey.

There was a massive fight near the postern gate as the Welsh had come through but had been effectively stopped. Now, it was just close quarters fighting, but a few Welsh had managed to make it through the fighting and were heading for the keep. Keller wasn't too terribly concerned about the keep being breached because it was a nearly impenetrable structure, but he did want to prevent the Welsh from making an attempt on it. Glancing over his shoulder, he could see William battling a fairly large Welshman so Keller came up behind him and shoved his broadsword between his ribs. The Welshman went down and William stepped over his former opponent, pointing to the keep.

"They are heading for the keep, Keller," he said, wiping the water from his eyes.

Keller nodded. "I know," he said. "But they cannot get into it. The only way they could marginally breach it is if they set fire to the door, which they cannot do because of the rain. I am not concerned with a few paltry men. What I am concerned with, however, is finding Gryffyn. He is here, somewhere. You and I are the only knights who will know him on sight so it is up to us to find him."

William nodded, looking around the bailey where the Welshmen who had been running for the keep were now being fended off by soldiers from the gatehouse.

"You did not see the man come in through the kitchens?" he asked.

Keller shook his head. "It was very dark in there," he replied. "If he did, I did not see him. Go to the postern gate and see if he is there."

William nodded and fled, into the rain, into the night that was filled with pockets of fighting. Keller's gaze lingered on the bailey for a moment longer before thinking he should perhaps check the identities of the Welsh who had been killed in the kitchen. It was quite possible that one of them was Gryffyn and it had been too dark for him to see. His eyesight wasn't particularly good, anyway. Just as he took his gaze off the bailey and turned for the kitchen, something hit him so hard on the back of the head that he pitched forward, onto his face. He struggled to push himself up but something hit him again, a second time, and the world abruptly went black.

CHAPTER TWENTY-TWO

G RYFFYN HAD BEEN positioned two men behind Colvyn when the man shoved the hidden door open and was subsequently gored by an English knight. The next man, too, had been killed, making it instantly and abundantly clear that the English had set a trap.

With that knowledge, Gryffyn fell back and began screaming at the Welsh, urging them onward, watching them push their way into the black kitchen and subsequently engage the English that were prepared with big weapons. Gryffyn wasn't about to put himself in harm's way. He let the other rabid Welsh battle the English while he pushed in with the crowd and immediately fell to his knees, creeping across the dirt floor and pressing himself between a corner of the wall and a big wooden cabinet that contained things like utensils, bowls, and other kitchen implements. It was so dark in the kitchen that hiding hadn't been difficult. He had been able to watch the entire battle unfold from his vantage point.

In truth, he was shocked that the English had been waiting for them. More than that, he had been embarrassed. What he considered to be a perfect scheme had somehow been circumvented, by de Poyer, he was sure. Somehow, someway, the man had discovered his plans and had countered them. Now, Gryffyn was ashamed and furious. So he went off to hide as the English made bloody work of Colvyn's Welsh-men, but Colvyn was dead and didn't see how his men were abused.

Gryffyn did, however. And the chief abuser was none other than de Poyer himself.

He could see the man in the darkness, killing one Welshman after another. There was no mistaking de Poyer's size, nor his power, so Gryffyn watched from the shadows as de Poyer and his men put down most of the Welsh. Some of them ran outside. He didn't know what became of them and it was difficult to hear anything for all of the rain that was coming down. He did, however, hear of a breach at the postern gate and he watched de Poyer send a very large knight out to combat it. That left just de Poyer and Wellesbourne, whom Gryffyn could see just outside of the kitchen door. Gryffyn remained in his hiding place and waited.

Eventually, the fighting died down in the kitchen with most of the Welsh either dead or run off. There were several soldiers still in the kitchen, plus de Poyer, and the men were inspecting the Welsh dead surrounding them. There was a dead Welshman about three feet away from Gryffyn and when one of the soldiers came near to kick the man to see if he was really dead, Gryffyn pressed himself deep into the black corner in his attempt not to be seen. Still as stone, he waited until the soldier moved away and they blocked off the hidden passage with a heavy table and other heavy items. Then, the soldiers filtered out as de Poyer remained behind.

The rain had lessened somewhat at this point, enough so that Gryffyn could hear the sounds of battle in the bailey. He could see de Poyer standing in the doorway, surveying the situation, and as Gryffyn watched, the wheels of his mind were in motion. The very man he hated was standing just a few feet away, the man who had stolen his entire legacy. The man who had stolen his sister... *his sister!* Surely Chrystobel and Izlyn were in the keep, bottled up and safe. Gryffyn knew he could never take Nether Castle. All he really wanted were his sisters, anyway. The ultimate goal, the feat of ages... having control over Chrystobel and Izlyn, watching them die by his hand. It was his right, wasn't it? They belonged to him. In his twisted mind, they had always belonged to him. It was his right to take their lives or save them.

He would take them.

But he had to be logical about this. If the women were in the keep, then the keep was locked. He could bang at the door all he wanted to but it would never open for him. His gaze moved to de Poyer... but it would open for Keller. If he held his sister's husband hostage, then most likely, the English, and Chrystobel, would do anything he asked. Chrystobel would even exchange her life for her husband's, of that Gryffyn was certain. Mad ramblings of a mad man. The mind grew darker, and so did the plot.

As de Poyer stood in the kitchen door, Gryffyn moved out from his hiding place. Over near the hearth, he could see a small, heavy iron pot with a handle on it. In the darkness, any sounds he made drowned out by the rain, he made his way to the pot and took hold of it, coming up behind de Poyer in stealth.

Don't turn around, de Poyer, he thought. *Stay where you are... just a brief second more....*

The pot came down on the back of de Poyer's helmed head, hard enough to nearly crack his skull. De Poyer fell face-first out of the doorway, into the muddy ground beyond, but he was still moving. He was trying to push himself up. Straddling de Poyer's supine body, Gryffyn used both hands to bring the pot down on Keller's head again. This time, the man went still.

Exhilarated with his quarry, Gryffyn rolled the man onto his back and kicked the broadsword several feet away. Then, he rifled through Keller's tunic until he came across an assortment of small daggers, which he systematically tossed away until he came to the last one. It was a big dagger, and very sharp. That one, he kept. Rolling the man onto his belly again, he yanked off his now-dented helmet and grabbed de Poyer by the hair as the man started to regain consciousness. The dagger went against de Poyer's jaw, just below the ear where the blood vessels flowed heavily.

Now, he had him. It was time to move.

CR

THE RAIN HAD been incessant, blinding at times, but it seemed to be easing slightly as the storm blew through. High in the keep. Chrystobel and Izlyn had spent the day sewing, or in Izlyn's case, building her little structures from pieces of kindling as she liked to do. She had always been fond of that. Chrystobel merely sewed, passing the time as she carefully stitched a new tunic for her husband from some eggshell-colored linen that had been meant for her father. Trevyn didn't need it any longer, temporarily buried near her flower garden as he was, so Chrystobel had confiscated it for Keller.

He didn't know about it, of course, as it was meant to be a surprise. She smiled when she thought of his reaction to a new tunic, hopeful that he would appreciate it. Even if he didn't, he would never let her know. He was sweet that way. She tried to maintain positive thoughts as the day passed into night, but it was difficult. An uncertain future always was, and worry over Keller's well-being compounded the anxiety she was struggling not to feel. When night finally fell, Chrystobel's angst deepened. She simply couldn't help the way she felt.

The first sign that anything was amiss was when Izlyn, standing at the lancet window that faced the bailey, began waving to her sister frantically. Concerned, Chrystobel put her sewing aside and went to the window only to see a big fight near the postern gate. The gate was open and she could see men battling all around it. Blood was being spilled. Frightened, she put her arms around Izlyn as they both stood and watched the chaos unfold.

"Keller was correct," Chrystobel murmured to her sister. "The Welsh were indeed coming. The missive they sent was a deception."

Izlyn was watching the battle below with big, frightened eyes. She had never seen a fight before. "Gryffyn?" she asked softly.

Chrystobel hugged her. "Aye," she said. "I am sure it is. But he shall be defeated. Keller and the other knights will not let him in, nor will they let him harm us. You must not be afraid."

Izlyn couldn't help but be afraid of her brother. She'd been afraid of him all her life and it was difficult to change the innate behavior. She knew, however, that Keller and Gart and the other English knights would never allow anything to happen to her, so in that respect, she wasn't afraid. But the thought of Gryffyn naturally had her fearful. She couldn't help it.

Chrystobel knew that. It made her fearful, too, no matter how much she told herself otherwise. She hugged her sister, kissing her on the top of her blond head.

"We will never fear him again," she said softly. "But if he does happen to come to us, then we will never allow him to hit us again, do you hear? Gryffyn only means harm, Izzie. If he were to come to us again, then it would be to kill us and we cannot allow that, can we?"

Izlyn shook her head, moving away from her sister and boosting herself up into the window so she could see the battle outside from a better angle. There was a lot of fighting down below, pockets of men trying to kill each other. She could see Sir Rhys near the postern gate with his double swords and as she watched, he cut a man in half. Izlyn clearly saw two pieces of the man fall to the ground. Shocked, Izlyn turned to her sister and pointed out of the window.

"Sir Rhys!" she exclaimed. "He kill... killed a man in half!"

Chrystobel went to the window to see what had her sister so shocked, but she wasn't able to discern what, exactly, Izlyn was talking about. Izlyn's speech was growing better by the day but she couldn't quite make sense out of killing a man in half.

Still, it was ominous and violent out in the bailey. She and Izlyn continued to watch as men fought, and men died, and somewhere in the process of watching, she realized that men were coming away from the gatehouse, rushing over towards the kitchen yard, which she couldn't quite see because it was just out of her line of sight. In fact, she could see Rhys coming out of the stable yards, moving for the kitchen as well, followed shortly by Gart, his big bald head reflecting what little light there was.

All of them seemed to be heading towards the kitchens but they stopped just short of the kitchen yard. Everyone seemed to be hovering, waiting and watching, and Chrystobel had no idea what they were looking at, but whatever it was certainly had their attention. In fact, they were now starting to turn towards the keep. She could clearly see the movement of their directional focus. Curious, she strained to catch a glimpse of what they were looking at. Then, through the rain and wind, she heard something.

Someone was yelling at the door of the keep. It was a loud, angry bellow. Concerned, she climbed down off the window sill.

"Someone is at the door," she told Izlyn. "I must see who it is."

Izlyn scampered after her, following her sister as they moved to the master's chamber where there was a window that had a much better view of the keep entry. Chrystobel moved a stool next to the window, which was a bit tall for her, and stood on it, looking down at the entry. What she saw startled her to the bone.

Her eyes widened at the sight of Gryffyn holding a knife to Keller's throat. Gryffyn had Keller by the hair, the dagger aimed just beneath Keller's right ear. It was Chrystobel's worst nightmare and she shrieked, drawing Gryffyn and Keller's attention upward. They both saw her in the window. Keller was the first one to yell to her.

"Do not open the door!" he boomed.

Chrystobel burst into tears as Gryffyn kicked Keller in the back, causing the man a good deal of pain. Gryffyn yelled up at her.

"If you want your husband to live, you will open the door," he shouted. "Do you hear me? Open this door or your husband will die!"

Chrystobel staggered away from the window, toppled off the stool, and fell to the ground. Izlyn ran forward to help her sobbing sister, but Chrystobel was nearly hysterical. Izlyn, unable to get a coherent word from her sister, thrust herself up into the window, gazing down on the horrible scene.

Gryffyn yelled at her, too, as Keller bellowed in unison. One was telling her to open the door while the other one was telling her to keep it bolted. Gryffyn was so frustrated that he nicked Keller's neck with the dagger, causing bright red blood to pour. Izlyn watched, her eyes as wide as trenchers, as Rhys and Gart and William tried to move up behind Gryffyn.

The English knights were stalking him but Gryffyn saw them coming and made a point of turning Keller around so they could see the blood flowing from the man's neck. With the knights focused on Keller and Gryffyn, one of the Welsh rebels managed come up behind Wellesbourne and nick him in the torso with a short Welsh blade. It would have been worse had William not seen the man move from the corner of his eye. As it was, he had a few seconds to move away and attempt to defend himself.

Bedlam followed as more Welsh moved upon the knights and soon the three of them found themselves in serious combat as Gryffyn held Keller at knifepoint at the keep entry. In the bailey of Nether, chaos and terror reigned.

Izlyn fell out of the window much the way her sister had, shocked and horrified at what she had seen. She looked at Chrystobel, who was now picking herself up off of the floor. Chrystobel, in fact, seemed to be calming a great deal as she reached out to grasp her sister.

Chrystobel's face was pale, her hands shaking, but her expression was something Izlyn had never seen before. There was an intensity beyond anything Izlyn believed her sister to be capable of. Somehow, someway, Chrystobel had calmed herself to the broad point of determination. Hysterics would not save Keller. She had to keep her head about her if she was going to be of any use. With that in mind, Chrystobel focused on Izlyn.

"Listen to me, Izzie," she said, grabbing her sister by both arms. "Gryffyn is here. Did you see him?"

Izlyn nodded, terrified. "There is... blood."

Chrystobel couldn't think about that. All she could focus on doing what was necessary to save their lives. That is what it came down to now; her survival, or Gryffyn's. She had to make sure it would not be Gryffyn.

"He will kill Keller if we do not open the keep to him," she said to Izlyn. "But the only reason he wants to come inside the keep is to get to you and to get to me. He wants to kill us. Do you understand?"

Izlyn nodded fearfully, her eyes welling, but Chrystobel shook her gently. "Nay," Chrystobel said firmly. "No tears. We do not have time. We *cannot* be afraid anymore. We must save Keller and we must kill Gryffyn. We have no choice. All of those years that he beat us, we never fought back, but tonight that will change. Tonight, we *must* fight back. If we do not, all of our happiness will be destroyed. *We* will be destroyed, and I am not ready yet to die. Are you?"

Izlyn shook her head. "N-nay," she whispered.

Chrystobel drew in a long, fortifying breath, thinking of what had to happen. The time had come for her to save herself, her husband, and her sister, and she would not fail. It was time for her to take a stand against a man who had spent most of his life beating on helpless women, knowing they wouldn't fight back.

Tonight, all of that would change. They had no choice if they were going to survive.

"Listen to me, Izzie," Chrystobel said, cupping her sister's face with her hands. "I know you are frightened. I am frightened, too, but we must do this to save ourselves and to save Keller. I will not allow Gryffyn to terrorize us any longer. It is time we fight back."

Izlyn nodded again, her tears fading somewhat. It was clear that she was trying very hard to be brave. "What… what should I do?"

Chrystobel thought a moment. She'd never had to do this kind of thing before. She didn't think like a killer, but for the moment, she had to. She had to do something exceedingly final, something that would rid her of her brother forever. As she took her sister's hand and headed for the chamber door, her gaze fell on a big iron sconce, about four feet tall, with great spikes on the end to hold the tapers with. She remembered using a similar weapon at the church on the day they had gone to bury her father, using the wax and candles against men who were attacking her husband.

Dropping her sister's hand, she raced for the sconce and removed the tapers, revealing five inch long iron teeth, sharp as daggers.

She headed down to the first level below with the sconce in hand and deadly intentions on her mind.

She had a plan.

CB

KELLER KNEW HE was in a bad way the moment someone grabbed his hair and pulled him off the muddy ground. Dazed, his ears were ringing and the world was rocking slightly, and he felt something very sharp against the side of his neck. The next voice he heard in his ear was not unexpected.

"Greetings, de Poyer," Gryffyn said. "It seems that we were destined to meet again under somewhat violent circumstances."

Keller's heart sank when he realized who had him. He was also quite furious. "Damn you, d'Einen," he snarled. "Release me immediately."

Gryffyn laughed, although it was not a humorous laugh. "Hardly," he said. "If the situation was reversed, would you release *me*?"

"If the situation was reversed, I would have killed you by now."

Gryffyn's smile faded. "That was my first thought, also," he said. "But I want something and I suspect I will not get it unless I use you as a bargaining tool."

Keller didn't even have to ask what Gryffyn wanted. That was abundantly clear. But he sought to distract the man, anything to help him gain the upper hand. Threatening d'Einen wouldn't work because, clearly, the man had the advantage. Therefore, Keller had to resort to another tactic. He had to stall enough to disorient or confuse the man. Then, maybe he would have a chance to turn the tables. At the moment, he couldn't think of anything else to do.

"What is this obsession you have with your sisters?" Keller demanded. "By God's Bloody Rood, d'Einen... what is this sick fixation you have for them? Why breach an entire castle to get to them?"

Gryffyn yanked on Keller's dark hair. "Because they are *mine*," he growled. "They belong to me, as does this castle. It all belongs to me and you stole it!"

"I saved it from you."

"It is mine!" he shrieked. "You have no right to it!"

Keller could see that he had Gryffyn off-balance. He pushed. "With you here, Nether was indeed a living hell," he said. "You made it a Netherworld in every sense of the word. This place is much better off without you and your brutal ways."

Gryffyn growled, coming out something of a yell. He began to half-shove, half-drag Keller in the direction of the keep. As the rain pattered and the thunder rumbled, they made their way across the bailey but Keller wasn't going willingly. He slipped more than once, purposely falling to his knees, buying time until one of his men could gain sight of him and figure out something was wrong. At one point he even fell to his belly and Gryffyn yanked viciously on his hair until he labored to his knees, standing wearily.

By that time, both the English and Welsh combatants were noticing that something was very, very wrong. The soldiers began shouting to Rhys and Gart, who emerged from the postern gate area to see Keller being dragged across the bailey by a man who had him by the hair, pointing a dagger at his throat. William, who had just finished off a particularly wily Welshman, saw what was happening. Rhys and Gart heard him hiss.

"That is d'Einen," he said. "That is the man we hoped to kill to-night."

Rhys sighed heavily. "And we will," he said. "Spread out and approach him from the rear. He cannot fight off all of us at once."

"He has a dagger at Keller's neck," William reminded him. "I have seen this man in action. He will not hesitate to use it."

Rhys wriggled his dark eyebrows, watching Gryffyn as steadily as a cat tracking a mouse. "Then we must make sure he does not get the opportunity," he said. "Find me a crossbow and I can take him from behind."

William snapped quiet orders to the nearest soldier, who went on the run. Meanwhile, he moved into stalking position alongside Rhys and Gart, waiting for the right moment to strike. He prayed they could take Gryffyn down before the man had the chance to ram the dirk into Keller's neck. He wasn't so confident that they could, and that thought sickened him.

But Gryffyn wasn't paying attention to the knight stalking him and even if he was, it wouldn't have mattered. He had the advantage so the posturing knights had no power against him. Dragging Keller up the slippery steps of the old, gray keep where he was born, he began yelling to the occupants. He knew his sisters were inside. He continued to yell until he heard a shriek overhead.

Looking up into the dark sky as rain pelted his face, he could see Chrystobel's head emerging from a lancet window on the second floor. But Keller spied her, too, and before Gryffyn could shout, Keller was bellowing at his wife.

"Do not open the door!" he boomed.

Frustrated, Keller kicked the man in the kidneys, listening to him grunt with pain. Then he returned his attention to his sister, glaring up at her through the inclement weather.

"If you want your husband to live, you will open the door," he shouted. "Do you hear me? Open this door or your husband will die!"

Chrystobel's head disappeared after that. Shortly afterwards, Izlyn appeared and both Keller and Gryffyn shouted at her, confusing the girl. Frustrated with Keller's behavior, Gryffyn kicked Keller again and when the man bent over, he hit him on the head with the butt of the dirk, sending Keller to his knees.

As Keller saw stars and struggled not to pass out again, he began to hear sounds of fighting behind him. He could hear song of broadswords as they met with metal upon metal, and he knew there was no way he was going to allow Gryffyn into the keep or near his wife. He didn't know where the dirk was that Gryffyn had been holding against him but at the moment, it didn't matter. He was no longer willing to play the dazed victim.

Keller was unsteady, and his ears were ringing badly, but the time had come to fight back. When he caught a glimpse of Gryffyn's legs off to his left, he lashed out a massive boot and swept the man's legs out from under him.

Gryffyn hit hard on his back on the wet stone surface of the entry and the dagger in his hand went flying. Keller pounced on him, using his big fists to pummel the man's head. The first blow shattered Gryffyn's nose and the second blow dislodged six teeth. Gryffyn threw up his hands, trying to defend himself, but Keller was all over him, beating him senseless.

Unfortunately, some of the Welsh that were in the bailey also saw the beating and ran to help. Gryffyn was the man who had promised them riches from Nether and they assumed that saving the man's life against his bitter enemy would garner them more reward. Keller soon found himself swamped with Welshmen and, without his broadsword, it was his bare strength against six or eight of them. The Welshmen pulled Keller off Gryffyn, but d'Einen was seriously dazed and bloodied. He lay there a moment, watching Colvyn's men beat away at Keller.

Keller and the writhing mass of Welshmen rolled down the keep's steps, ending up in a muddy pile at the bottom. William, having just fended off several Welsh, ran to Keller's aid and began slashing away at the Welshmen who were still beating on him. Some of them had weapons and at least two of them had slashed Keller, wounding his right forearm fairly seriously as the man fought for his life. Because Gryffyn had stripped him of all his weapons, he had nothing to fight back with except his bare hands, and those were taking a serious lashing.

As Keller battled the Welsh, Gryffyn was struggling to sit up when the door to the keep suddenly lurched open. Startled, Gryffyn looked up to see Izlyn standing in the doorway. She just stood there, looking weak and vulnerable. When their eyes met, Gryffyn's expression was a mixture of surprise, glee, and fury.

"Izlyn!" he gasped, struggling to his knees. "You little fool! How good of you to let me in. Where is your sister?"

Izlyn stood just inside the doorway, backing up as Gryffyn labored to his feet. "Inside," she said. "Come in."

Gryffyn froze, his eyes wide at her. "You *speak*?" he said, astonished. "You actually speak? By all that is holy, I *knew* you could! All this time, I knew you could but you were simply being difficult, weren't you, you little chit? In fact, I am very angry at you for it and shall punish you severely for your insolence!"

Izlyn was still backing up as Gryffyn, now on his feet, began to move towards her. He was utterly focused on the young girl, furious to hear her speak after all this time. Izlyn continued to back up, luring him in through the doorway. The moment he set foot into the keep, the fates of retribution enveloped him in their discourteous fold. He was trapped and he didn't even know it yet. He had no idea that a lifetime of brutality against the weaker sex would now cost him his life.

While Gryffyn was focused on Izlyn, the form of vengeance was Chrystobel. She emerged from the shadows off to his right, charging out of the darkness with the iron sconce wielded like a spear. Five dagger-sharp points meant to secure tapers rammed into Gryffyn's back, puncturing deep, and sending the man crashing over onto his left side.

Chrystobel was mad with panic. She knew if she didn't kill her brother, he would rise up and murder her, so she yanked the sconce out of his body and stabbed him again, listening to him wail with pain and anguish.

Kill him or he will kill you!

His cries of pain held no meaning for her. She pulled the sconce out of his body one more time, using it to beat him over the head. The sconce was blood-covered, and very heavy, and she pounded it over Gryffyn's skull, repeatedly bashing his head, until the man stopped struggling and finally lay still. Even then, she continued bashing, beating the man's head, caving his skull in. Every blow had her name on it, or Izlyn's name, or her father's name. Every blow for the dozens of times Gryffyn had abused them, breaking bones or drawing blood. Every blow was meant for her life, Izlyn's life, and now her husband's life.

She was mad with the feeling of freedom, free forever from the fear of Gryffyn, and now it had become a frenzy. She was slashing him and beating him right into the stone, and with every strike, her terror seemed to fade, further and further, until it was nearly gone. But Chrystobel didn't stop beating Gryffyn's head until someone came up behind her and grabbed the sconce, preventing her from leveling yet another blow on a clearly dead man. Finally, her vengeance had come to a halt. Finally, it was over.

Keller stood behind his wife, holding her wrists as she wielded the sconce. His hands and arms were bloody and torn, his face bloodied from the fist fight outside the door, but it didn't matter. When Chrystobel turned to see who had prevented her from turning her brother's head into pulp, a gasp of genuine joy escaped her lips. The sconce crashed to the floor, next to Gryffyn, as she threw herself into her husband's arms, weeping tears of terror and relief.

Keller held his wife tightly, his face buried in the side of her head, his eyes stinging with tears. She was safe. He was safe. They were *all* safe. Words of alleviation defied him at the moment.

"Are you well?" he asked tightly, a lump in his throat. "He did not injure you in any way?"

Chrystobel shook her head adamantly. "He never had the chance, not this time," she wept, pulling away from the man to run her hands over his face, inspecting the damage. "But you are bleeding."

Keller shook his head to downplay the damage, leaning forward to kiss her as deeply and as passionately as he had ever kissed her. His joy, his relief, went beyond words.

"I will survive," he muttered.

"Please," Chrystobel begged softly, trembling as she touched his face. "Let me tend you."

He kissed her fiercely. "Later."

With that, he glanced over her shoulder to the bloody, brain-splattered mess that used to be Gryffyn. It was horrifically gory and he caught movement out of the corner of his eye, seeing Izlyn standing there, looking impassively down at her brother's remains. She had been a party to this just as much as her sister had and Keller wondered at the depths of relief as well as confusion they must have been feeling. To finally have ended their brother's reign of terror must have been an overwhelming realization.

But their joy in such things would have to wait. Grasping both women and trying to keep them away from the sight of Gryffyn's bloodied corpse, he directed them toward the stairs. He wanted to get them back up to their room and lock them in so he could return to chasing the Welsh from Nether. D'Einen was dead, but there was still the matter of the men he brought with him. Keller couldn't truly celebrate the man's elimination until everything was under control.

As they reached the steps, William entered the keep. He looked at Gryffyn with surprise, a rather gruesome sight on the floor, before calling out to Keller.

"D'Einen is dead?" he pointed to the body.

Keller paused. "Indeed he is," he said, his gaze moving over Chrystobel. He truly wasn't surprised by her actions. He was very proud the woman had learned to fight back. "If there is any justice in this world, it has just been served here today."

William pondered that a moment. Of course, he wanted to know how it happened, but such details would have to wait. There were more important things at hand.

"The Welsh are leaving, Keller," he said. "You'd better come."

Keller looked at the man with some surprise. "Leaving?" he repeated. "Last I saw, they were battling quite strongly."

A flicker of a smile crossed William's lips. "I know," he said. "But reinforcements have arrived in the form of George and Aimery.

Evidently, they didn't listen very well. They have returned early from their jaunt to Shropshire, and thank God for it."

Keller shook his head in both frustration and approval, an odd combination. "Return early, indeed," he grumbled. "George never was very good at telling time. Tell the man to stay away two days and he stays away one."

"Fortunate for us," William grinned. "Rhys just had the men open the gatehouse and another two hundred and fifty English soldiers are pouring in. It would seem that the Welsh are afraid of that."

Keller grinned, saying a quick prayer for the early return of the Ashby-Kidd brothers. Timing was everything. He sighed heavily and waved William off.

"I will be there in a moment," he said. "Let me settle the women first."

William ducked out of the keep, heading into the bailey where the two hundred and fifty fresh soldiers were making short work of any remaining Welsh. Men were bottled up, chased off, and otherwise defeated.

Keller, inside the keep, continued to direct the ladies up the stairs. In truth, he could hardly believe the course the night had taken. The results were as he had hoped but the means to get there had been somewhat complex. As they hit the second floor landing, Keller paused and pulled Chrystobel into his arms once more. He just had to feel her, safe and whole, against him once more. Chrystobel clung to him.

"Are you sure you are well?" he whispered.

Chrystobel nodded. "I am," she confirmed, gazing up into his dusky eyes. "I simply... I cannot believe it is over. I have never feared anything so much as I have feared my brother and now that he is gone... I still cannot believe it."

Keller smiled at her. "As I said to William," he said quietly, "if there is any justice in the world, it has happened here tonight. Your brother took everything from you – your dignity, your peace, your life. Tonight, you took it back. It was your right."

Chrystobel thought on that a moment. "In truth, all I could think of was saving you," she said. "I could not let Gryffyn hurt you. There was such rage when I attacked him, Keller. So much rage...."

Keller kissed her on the forehead. "That rage is gone," he assured her. "Gryffyn is gone. You did what needed to be done to save yourself, to save me, to save Izlyn, and ultimately to save Nether. You are a brave woman, Lady de Poyer, and I am very proud to be your husband."

Chrystobel smiled modestly, absorbing his adoration, perhaps absorbing all of the events that the night had brought. There was much to take in, much to deal with, and much to reconcile.

As Chrystobel and Izlyn retreated to the smaller chamber and bolted the door, Keller went back down to the keep entry where Gryffyn lay, blood and brains coagulating around his bashed head. Keller just looked at the man, resisting the urge to kick the corpse. For all of the terror he had caused, for the patricide had had committed, Gryffyn d'Einen deserved everything that had happened to him and more still. His evil had infected Nether Castle, creating a Netherworld that Keller had managed to bring into the light.

Keller crouched down next to Gryffyn's body, his gaze moving over the man. After this moment had passed he would never look upon him or think of him again.

"I hope you are enjoying Hell, you worthless bastard," he muttered. "I hope you are enjoying the real Netherworld, which I am sure is now your happy home. For all of the pain you have caused this family, I sincerely hope that Satan has a special place reserved just for you."

With that, he stood up and walked from the keep, out into the night where the rain had started to clear up and the English were now corralling the Welsh stragglers. The stars were peering out from behind the parting clouds and he looked up at them, seeing their brightness and feeling as if the world was suddenly bright and new. No more threat, no more terror. Finally, the Netherworld was no more.

Finally, Nether Castle would know peace.

The magic of a new beginning.

EPILOGUE

1204 A.D.

I T WAS A bright day in August and surprisingly warm. The door to Nether's keep was open and a balmy breeze blew through the cold stone rooms, warming them. Keller was sitting at the feasting table in the small hall, peering at an updated map of the marches he had purchased in Gloucester a few months ago. He had taken his two oldest children with him, Caledon and Stafford, and the boys had gotten into a good deal of trouble that Keller still hadn't told his wife about. The twins reminded him a good deal of George and Aimery Ashby-Kidd in that if there was disorder to be had, those two would find it. He never thought he'd see the day when he'd have two troublemaking twins.

Even now, they were under the table trying to light the dogs' tails on fire. He kept having to stamp on the small pieces of kindling, extinguishing the fire, before the boys could get to the dogs.

"Lads," he finally muttered, his gaze still on the map. "If one of those dogs ignites, I will blister you both. Is that clear?"

Two blond heads popped up from underneath the table. Identical brown eyes looked at their father innocently. "We were not lighting the dogs, Papa," Staff insisted. "We were just playing."

Keller looked up from the map, his eyes narrowing at his six-year-old son. "I know you were playing," he said. "You were playing with fire."

Cal nodded his head seriously. "We were practicing, Papa."

Keller didn't believe his child for a minute. "Practicing what?"

Cal was animated. He stood up and raised his arms in emphasis. "When we are great knights, we will capture a castle," he said. "We must know how to burn the drawbridge down."

Keller fought off a grin. His boys had a wild imagination, but they were sweet little terrors and it crushed him every time he had to discipline them, which was often. Everyday saw them stealing chicken eggs, or fist fighting each other to the point of bloody noses, or pulling their sisters' hair, which often garnered their mother's displeasure as well.

"You will not be burning down drawbridges any time soon," Keller said, holding out a hand. "Give me your kindling."

Unhappy, Cal came out from underneath the table, begrudgingly placing a few sticks of kindling in his father's hand. Staff, on his brother's heels, did the same. But Keller kept his hand outstretched.

"The flint, please."

Cal frowned terribly, producing a small piece of flint he'd been keeping in his other hand. Both boys started to walk away but Keller grasped Staff, preventing him from going any further, and frisked him until he found a second flint stone. He eyed his boys sternly.

"No more fire," he told them, calmly but firmly. "If I find that you have been playing with fire again, I will punish you. Is that clear?"

The boys nodded, frowning faces and averted gazes. As Keller leaned forward and kissed both boys, Cal on the forehead and Staff on the cheek when the child squirmed, he heard footsteps coming down the stairs from the second floor above.

Chrystobel descended the stairs with a baby on her hip, a small girl in one hand, and another small girl trailing after her. She helped her second youngest child off the stairs and the little curly-haired lass ran straight for her father, who picked her up and hugged her. Chrystobel stood at the base of the stairs as her middle child, a daughter with her blond hair and Keller's blue eyes, carefully made her way down the steps. When the little girl got to the bottom, she ran to her father just as her younger sister had. Four-year-old Iselle and three-year-old Genevieve were quite attached to their father, and he to them. He hugged his little girls happily, forgetting all about the map and his naughty boys.

Chrystobel, with her one-year-old son Tallys on her hip, smiled as she watched her husband with the girls. He was really quite sweet with them, spoiling them with hugs and kisses and gifts. In fact, he did that with all of the children. The man was a giver, in every sense. But he could also be very stubborn and she braced herself for that possibility as she prepared to deliver some news.

"I have something to tell you," she said, watching him bounce Genevieve on his knee.

Keller glanced at her. "What is it?"

"George is here," she said. "I have been watching him for quite some time. He is now heading up the hill and should be here shortly."

Now, Keller's gaze fixed on her. "How do you know it is him?"

"Who else could it be?"

Keller shrugged. Already, Chrystobel could see the scowl coming. "It does not have to be George," he insisted. "It could be anyone."

"He is coming from the south, from Pembroke Castle where he is now stationed."

"It is probably just a bachelor knight, wandering from castle to castle."

Chrystobel sighed faintly. "Keller," she admonished softly. "You told George and Izlyn that they had to wait until she was eighteen. She turned eighteen almost a year ago. George wrote you six months ago and said he would be coming for Izlyn around her nineteenth birthday, which is next month. You must face facts, my love. George has come for her."

As Keller sat and looked at the two babies in his lap, pondering the fact that George had finally come to marry Izlyn, the young lady in question came bounding down the steps. Keller could tell her steps. She always sounded as if she was scurrying. Izlyn scurried down the great stone steps from the floor above, racing into the small hall and throwing her arms around her sister and baby nephew.

"He is here!" she exclaimed. "George has come!"

Chrystobel was thrilled for her sister but still aware of her husband's feelings. Keller had been terribly protective of Izlyn since the day he married Chrystobel and basically treated the girl like a daughter. Izlyn had spent her formative teen years not fostering in a cold household, but living with her sister and husband, deeply loved. Therefore, Keller felt as if he was losing a daughter.

"Mayhap you should go to the gatehouse," Chrystobel said helpfully. "The sentries have a much better view of the road and will know for sure. Where is William?"

"He should be at the gatehouse," Keller said, his voice sounding sad and dull. He sighed heavily. "I will go and see if it is indeed George."

Izlyn took Genevieve from Keller's lap as he set Iselle carefully on the floor. As he headed out of the hall, Iselle whimpered and ran after him, so he picked her up and carried her out with him. Chrystobel and Izlyn watched him go, feeling his melancholy mood.

"Is he upset?" Izlyn wanted to know. "Surely he is happy for me."

Chrystobel nodded. "Of course he is happy for you," she said. "But you know he is very attached to you, to all of his girls. It will be difficult for him to turn you over to another man, even another man as wonderful as George."

At the mention of George's name, Izlyn broke into a big smile. A woman grown now, she was blond and beautiful and elegant, and the speech that had evaded her for so long had returned with a vengeance after her brother's death. She was eloquent and articulate now, and very much in love with George Ashby-Kidd, and he with her. That fondness from years ago had developed into something much, much more.

"Keller will send word to St. Peter's, won't he?" Izlyn wanted to know. "He said he would when the time came. I would like to be married there."

Chrystobel nodded patiently. "He will, I am sure," she said. "If he does not, then I will do it. Have no fear that you shall be married, Izzie. Even if I have to drag my husband kicking and screaming to the church, I swear you shall be married there."

Izlyn laughed softly, very excited to see George. She hadn't seen him since Christmas of last year and it was a very long time to be separated from the man she loved. With Genevieve still on her hip, she left the keep, standing on the steps just outside of the entry, watching the activity at the gatehouse. Chrystobel came out to stand behind her, noticing that Keller was ordering the portcullis to be raised. Beyond, straddling the Gorge of the Dead, was the big wooden bridge that connected the castle to the road. As the ladies watched from the vantage point in front of the keep, men began to appear on the bridge, heading for the gatehouse.

George was riding at the head of the small army. There were forty men behind him, including his brother Aimery, who had been married the previous year to William Wellesbourne's eldest daughter. William had moved his family to Nether several years ago, his wife and three children, and while the two younger children had gone off to foster, Aimery had married the very pretty Rose Wellesbourne. But Rose moved back to Pembroke when the Ashby-Kidd brothers were stationed there, so it was a bit of a wonderful surprise for William, in the gatehouse, to see that Rose had accompanied her husband to Nether for a visit. It was even more of a surprise when William saw his daughter's gently swollen belly and realized she was pregnant with his first grandchild.

As Rose and William hugged happily in the gatehouse, George entered the bailey and dismounted his big black steed. As he passed the horse off to a soldier and headed towards Keller, who was moving towards him from the direction of the keep with a small girl in his arms, the de Poyer twins made an appearance.

Cal and Staff had been playing over near the corner of the keep, specifically because William had told them to stay away from the busy gatehouse. Unhappy, they were building something with the stones that were scattered all over the bailey, but when they saw George, they focused in on the man. They remembered George when he had visited at Christmas time. He had a brother that looked just like him, but the brother was starting to bald whereas George wasn't. That's how they recognized him. Furthermore, George had tied them up to a chair when they stole his coin purse out of his saddlebags. Worse yet, he had told their father, who had promptly spanked them. Nay, the boys weren't happy with George's appearance in the least. It was time to get even.

As George made his way towards Keller, Cal and Staff gathered handfuls of small pebbles. George was several feet away from Keller, lifting his hand in greeting, when he began to feel a stinging sensation on his legs and arms. It took him a few moments to realize that Cal and Staff were throwing rocks at him. He came to a halt, scowling at the boys, who continued throwing the pebbles. With a shake of his head, frustrated and resigned, George dodged flying pebbles as he closed the gap to Keller.

"Greetings, my lord," he said to Keller. "You and your young daughter are looking quite well today."

A pebble smacked him right in the cheek and his hand flew to his face, turning to scowl menacingly at the boys. Keller, however, was rather pleased with his sons' aim. He was hoping that if they threw enough rocks, perhaps George would leave and Izlyn would remain unmarried. But he knew that was a foolish thought so he held up a hand to his twins, admonishing them to stop. Cal and Staff ceased their assault, at least for the moment. When their father returned his attention to George, Cal fired off a pebble that hit George in the back of the head.

"The boys have not forgotten how you punished them for stealing your coin," Keller commented as George rubbed the back of his head. "Even at their young age, they have a sense of vengeance."

George eyed the naughty twins. "They are going to have a sense of my hand to their backside if they are not careful," he grumbled, then looked quickly at Keller. "With your permission, of course."

Keller fought off a grin. "Of course," he agreed. "But I seem to remember two brothers in my service a few years ago, twins of course, who fought and threw punches at the slightest provocation. Do you remember those two?"

George sighed heavily, grinning reluctantly. "I believe I do," he said, trying not to laugh because Keller was. From the corner of his eye, he caught sight of Izlyn standing at the keep entry and suddenly, his attention was diverted. The young woman filled his field of vision and his smile turned appreciative. "She has grown more beautiful since the last time I saw her."

Keller turned to see what had the young man's attention. In fact, he didn't even have to guess. He knew. Izlyn was standing several feet away, holding little Genevieve, and she was gazing at George with the same expression that George had. It was the same expression Keller had when he looked at Chrystobel. It was love. Clearing his throat softly, Keller headed for the castle.

"Let us go inside and share some wine as we discuss marriage details," he said to George. "But I suppose you would like to speak with your intended first."

George's eyes were riveted to Izlyn as he followed Keller. "May I even take her hand?"

Keller cast him a long look over his shoulder. "Nay," he said flatly. "You may not touch her until the wedding."

George was disappointed but not deterred. Ultimately, he would get what he wanted and that was all that mattered in the end. As he followed Keller, he felt the resumption of little stings on his back and legs as Cal and Staff commenced throwing pebbles at him again. When Keller was well enough ahead of him, George stopped, whirled around and picked up a handful of dirt and rocks from the bailey in the same motion, and fired off several pebbles of his own that sent the naughty twins running for cover. Then, he dropped the dirt, brushed off his hand, and trotted after Keller, catching up with the man just as he was ascending the steps into the keep. The twins remained in hiding.

Chrystobel greeted George warmly and stood aside when George greeted Izlyn. The two lovers stood there, staring at one another dreamily, until Chrystobel shoved Keller into the keep and followed the man so her sister could be alone with her intended. Izlyn and George could hear Keller voicing his strong objections and then Chrystobel telling him that if she had no objections to leaving them alone, then he should have no objections. Keller grumbled and they could hear a door slam. Izlyn giggled at the fading sounds.

"He is very protective," she said. "But, certainly, he has nothing to worry about. You are always perfectly behaved."

George didn't want to disillusion her, not just yet. That would come later when he was legally and morally allowed to do whatever he damn well pleased to her. He smiled saucily as he began to dig into his blue Pembroke tunic.

"For now, anyway," he said, adding a bold wink. "You look well and beautiful, as always."

Izlyn blushed prettily. "Thank you," she said. "Have you been well?"

"I have," he said quietly. "I have missed you very much."

"And I have missed you. The longing has been dreadful."

"For me as well," he said. He continued to rummage around in his tunic, finally pulling forth what he was searching for. He held something up between them, pinched between the thumb and forefinger of his right hand. "I was packing my belongings the other day and came across this, wrapped in a small piece of linen I had tucked into my saddle bags. I thought you might like to see what I have been carrying for luck ever since you gave it to me."

Izlyn peered at the object. It looked like a dried weed, flattened by time and age, but when he turned it more in her direction, she realized that she was looking at the thistle she had given him the day before Gryffyn had been killed. She gasped as realization swept her.

"You gave this to me years ago," he said softly, watching her astonished expression. "Do you recall?"

She nodded vigorously. "I do," she replied. "I gave it to you back during the time when Gryffyn was killed. And Gart.... do you remember Gart Forbes? He was very upset that I had given you a flower and had not meant one for him."

George grinned as he pressed the flower into her open palm, watching her inspect it. "I remember Gart," he said. "I have not seen him in years, though. He was in France fighting for de Lohr for a while but I have heard he is back in England. If he comes to visit you, I will have to kill him."

Izlyn laughed softly. "Gart moved on from me long ago," she said. Then, she sobered, holding up the flower. "But I am very glad you did not."

George met her gaze, his eyes glimmering warmly at her. Then, he did what Keller told him he could not do. He took the flower from her, took her hand, and kissed it gently.

"Never," he whispered. "Now, let us retreat inside before Keller has a tantrum. Your brother-in-law and I must discuss your dowry."

Izlyn held his arm tightly as they disappeared into the cool innards of Nether's keep, heading for the small hall where Keller was in the process of brooding. He and George spent two days negotiating Izlyn's dowry which, in the end, had been quite generous of Keller and even included a plot of land from the Carnedd Barony to provide them with income. When all was said and done, the only matter left was the wedding itself, and on a warm August day in the year of our Lord twelve hundred and four, Lady Izlyn d'Einen because Lady Ashby-Kidd. Three out of Keller and Chrystobel's five children cried through the entire ceremony. The naughty twins had brought hollowed straw from the stable and tiny little pebbles, using them like blow guns and shooting the groom through most of the ceremony until their mother realized what they were doing and took them both outside to a sound spanking. Then, Keller and Chrystobel had five children who cried through the ceremony.

But it didn't matter, for the mass was beautiful and the couple, very much in love. It couldn't have been a more perfect day in spite of the commotion. The bride had violets woven into her hair while the groom wore the faded thistle his bride had given him so long ago pinned to the collar of his tunic. When it came time for the final vows, Izlyn had remembered something Keller had said to her once, something the girl had written to her sister on behalf of her new husband.

Somehow, the words had always stayed with her so when it came time to repeat their vows, Izlyn had added a line that meant as much to her as it had to her sister. Back in those days, those terrible dark days, they discovered that men by the name of Keller de Poyer, Gart Forbes, Rhys du Bois, William Wellesbourne, and George and Aimery Ashby-Kidd could heal what Gryffyn had damaged. Angels in the form of English knights had changed their lives forever.

I see the magic of a new beginning with you.

Now, it was Izlyn's turn for a new beginning.

CB THE END &O

AUTHOR'S NOTE

This novel, at times, dealt a lot with different languages – Welsh and English, mostly. Now, English is generalized in novels from the High Middle Ages so that the readers can relate to what's being said, because around this time in history, England was transitioning from Old English to Middle English, which are complex languages and not at all like the English language you and I know. Example:

Old English from Beowulf:
Hwæt! Wē Gār-Dena in geārdagum,

Translation:
Lo, praise of the prowess of people-kings

See why authors such as myself don't write in Old English, which would have been true to the period? Because you wouldn't have a clue what we were saying – and neither would we! Therefore, we use colloquial English so you can understand what's being said, but we try to keep the proper syntax of the period. Of course, the Norman's spoke Anglo-Norman when they arrived and that was the preferred language at court until the 1400's, but again, when I write of kings and queens, they speak English for the most part so the reader is at ease. England in the High Middle Ages was a true mix of French speakers and English speakers.

As for Wales, they have an extremely difficult language that they still speak today, and it is still taught in schools much like the Irish teach Celtic in their schools. I've written about Wales – a lot – and even I'm still confused by their language at times. As my husband calls it, the language with no vowels!

Thank you so much for reading. I truly hoped you enjoyed Keller and Chrystobel's story. You can find all of my novels online, in eBook, in paperback, and in audiobook format.

The Ancient Kings of Anglecynn Series contains the following novels:

The Whispering Night

Other novel where this name or same characters appear:

Devil's Dominion

For more information on other series and family groups, as well as a list of all of Kathryn's novels, please visit her website at www.kathrynleveque. com.

Now, please enjoy bonus chapters from ARCHANGEL, Gart Forbes'
novel. ARCHANGEL is available in eBook, paperback, or in
audiobook format.

CHAPTER ONE

Year of Our Lord 1204 A.D.
The Month of May
Dunster Castle, Somerset

H E WAS SEEING ghosts.

It was true that he was weary after having spent the last seven
days traveling from Kent to the shadowed edges of the Exmoor Forest.
It was also true that the wilds of Somerset and Cornwall were said to
breed wraiths and other netherworld creatures, and Dunster was right
in the middle of dark and mysterious lands. But being a man of logic,
Sir Gart Forbes wasn't one to believe in ghosts or phantoms or fairies.
Still, he wasn't quite sure what he had seen.

He was standing in the darkened bailey of Dunster just after sunset.
The castle was perched on the top of a hill, fortified and old even in
Saxon times, and the battlements were lined with men standing guard,
sentries with big dogs and big torches to keep away the night. Gazing
up the wooden steps that led into the second floor of the enormous
square keep, Gart swore he saw something at the top of the stairs that
had just as quickly vanished.

All around him were sounds of the bailey as the men settled in for
the night. He had brought one hundred men with him from
Denstroude Castle in Kent, seat of Baron Thornden, Sir David de Lohr.
Lord de Lohr was in the keep up in the third floor great hall and these

wraiths, these wispy creatures, were between Gart and his liege. With a weary sigh, knowing he must have lost his mind somewhere back on the dusty road, Gart slowly mounted the steps.

The stairs were dark and old. Gart's enormous boots tested the weight of each plank as he made his way up and could hear the wood groan. Normally, he would have been focused on the meal awaiting him, but at this moment, he had to admit he was curious to see if the wraiths would make another appearance.

He didn't have long to wait. The moment he stepped inside the great Norman arch that embraced the entry, something small and white jumped into his path.

"Boo!"

Before Gart could open his mouth to speak, the phantom darted off and hid. It wasn't so much a phantom now that he had a closer look – it was a child, completely white from head to toe. Gart watched the child disappear into a darkened room, a solar that was directly off the entry to the right. His brow furrowed and he shook his head, undecided as to whether he was irritated or amused. He settled for amused until two more wraiths jumped out at him with sticks.

Gart was in armor so he didn't feel the blows, but his amusement quickly turned to irritation when one of the sticks landed a blow a little too close to his groin. He reached down to grab one of the children but his hand came away completely white. They were covered in something white and powdery.

Gart grabbed a stick that came flying at his groin again, yanking it out of the child's hand and tossing it out the door. He locked gazes with a boy no more than seven years of age and he would never forget the look of fury on the boy's face.

With a yell, the child charged him and tried to bite him, but all he came away with was mail to the mouth. Gart grabbed the child by the hair and the boy screamed.

"Let me go!" he howled. "I will have you arrested if you do not let me go!"

Gart's hand was bigger than the child's head as he gazed down at him. "Is that so?"

"It is!" The lad tried to kick him, struggling to dislodge the iron grip. "If you do not let me go, I... I will have you boiled! I will have you flogged! I will have you...!"

Gart put up a hand, cutting him off. "I understand your meaning," he said, noticing that the two other white-covered children were beating at his armored legs. He shoved one away by the head and kneed the other one across the floor. It wasn't a kick as much as it was a good push with his kneecap. Then he let go of the child in his grip.

"Let me pass and you can assault the next fool who walks in the door," he told them.

The three boys were not so easily dissuaded. They rushed back at him with their fists and sticks and Gart shoved them all away again, only to have them rush him once more as he tried to mount the stairs to the third level.

Irritation growing, he managed to grab all three of them, carry them over to the dark and empty solar, and shove them inside. Slamming the door closed, he noticed there was no exterior bolt as the boys beat at the door and yelled from the other side. Gart stood there as long as he could, holding the door shut as delicious smells taunted him from the hall above. He didn't have time for this foolishness. Daring to let go of the latch, he made a break for the stairs.

The solar door flew open and the three boys charged out, catching Gart as he was halfway up the spiral stone stairs. They grabbed at his feet and he kicked back, attempting to dislodge them. He didn't want to outright hurt them but they were annoying and beastly, so he finally kicked out and sent one boy crashing into the other two.

The whole lot of them slid down the stairs, leaving a trail of white powder as they went. They hit hard in a group, the older ones falling on the smaller one. The little lad at the bottom of the pile began to wail loudly and rub his head where he had smacked it.

Gart smirked at the screams, thinking now they would finally leave him alone. He hadn't taken two steps before he started to feel some remorse. They were just children, after all. He had been a child once, thirty years ago during times he could hardly remember. These children were just playing games. At least, he hoped so. Maybe they were really murderers in disguise. Taking another step, the cries prevented him from continuing.

With a heavy sigh he turned on the stairwell, peering down at the pile of boys at the bottom. The two older ones were attempting to pick the younger one up and convince him that he wasn't injured. Gart took a couple of steps down, watching the boys who seemed much less aggressive than they had been moments earlier.

"What are you three doing?" he demanded softly.

Three pairs of big blue eyes looked up at him as if startled by the question. He could see the hostility seep back into their expressions but, so far, not one of them had made a move against him. They seemed to be posturing an awful lot.

"Brendt hurt his head," the tallest child said angrily. "You did...."

Gart waved the boy off. "That is not what I meant," he took another step down. "What are you three doing attacking men who enter the keep?"

The tallest boy's brow furrowed. "Robbing them!"

Gart couldn't help it as his features screwed up in confusion. "*Robbing* them?"

"Aye," the boy insisted. "This is our castle. Whoever comes in this door belongs to us."

Gart stared at the lad a moment before finally shaking his head. Truth be told, he was fighting off a grin. The lad was deadly serious.

"Who are you?" he finally asked.

The boy stood tall. "Romney de Moyon," he announced. "These are my brothers, Orin and Brendt. Our father is Julian de Moyon, Baron Buckland, and this is our castle. Who are you?"

Gart came down the rest of the stairs and stood in front of them, massive fists resting on his hips. He avoided the question. "Why do you have white powder all over you?"

Romney looked at his brothers before returning his attention to Gart. "Because we are ghosts. You cannot see ghosts and it makes it easier to rob people."

Gart rubbed his hand over his chin and mouth so the boy would not see his grin. It was really quite dastardly and very humorous, he thought.

"I see you quite clearly," he ran a finger across Romney's chest, peering at the white powder. "What is this?"

"Dust from the stone," Romney told him. "Father is building a house for the soldiers and this is the dust from the white stone."

Gart inspected it a moment longer before wiping it on his tunic. His gaze moved to the youngest, who was no longer crying, but still rubbing his head.

"Had you not attacked me, you would not have hurt your head," he was looking at the smallest boy but lecturing all three. "Does your father know what you are doing?"

Romney lifted his shoulders, for the first time losing some of his confidence. "He does not care," he said. "Will you give me your money or will I have to fight you to the death?"

Gart bit his lip to keep his smile from breaking loose. "Are you sure you want to fight me to the death?"

"I am sure."

"I do not have any money on me."

Romney's fair brow furrowed and he looked to his brothers with uncertainty. "Well," he said reluctantly. "We will wait until you return for it. Come back with your money."

"I will not," Gart said flatly. "Why do you want my money, anyway?"

"Because," Romney said. "We want to buy nice things for my mother and sister."

Gart scratched his head. "Your mother and sister?" he repeated. "Surely they have enough nice things."

Romney shrugged. "It makes them happy. When Mother is crying, it will make her stop."

Gart scratched at his chin again, a little puzzled at the last sentence but he didn't pursue it.

"I see," he said. "I am afraid that I am going to disappoint you, your mother and your sister. You will have to get your ill-gotten gains somewhere else."

Romney didn't like that answer at all. It was clear he wasn't used to having his wishes denied. Gart eyed the children one more time before turning for the stairs and the three were on him in an instant with their fists and sticks. Gart rolled his eyes with frustration as he grabbed Romney by the arm and twisted it behind his back. Romney screamed and the other two lads stopped their onslaught.

"Oww!" Romney howled. "You are hurting me!"

Gart lifted an eyebrow. "I am getting tired of being attacked simply because I walked into this keep," he said in a low voice. "If you promise to cease your assault, I will let you go. Otherwise, I will bind all three of you and toss you into a closet."

Before the boy could reply, they heard a voice from the floor above. It was a female voice, soft and sweet, and soon the swish of a voluminous surcoat could be seen and heard. Great yards of crimson fabric descended the stairs, calling for Romney and Orin. As Gart stood there with Romney's arm twisted behind his back, a vision in red appeared.

"Romney!" the woman gasped. "What has happened? Are you injured?"

Gart stared at the woman in surprise, although his stone-like features did not give him away. He was actually stunned speechless for a moment as a vision from his past made an unexpected appearance. Although it had been years since he had last seen her, there was no mistaking the ethereal beauty. There wasn't anything like it anywhere else in England.

"Emberley?" he asked hesitantly. "Emberley de Russe?"

The Lady Emberley de Russe de Moyon came to a halt when she

heard her name, staring at the enormous knight with shock and some fear. He had her son by the arm and the child was in obvious pain, but as she gazed at the man, he began to look vaguely familiar.

From the mists of her memories emerged the face as a very young man, someone her brother had been friends with. She had known that face well, long ago. Now he had grown into a strikingly handsome man. Her deep blue eyes lit up with recognition.

"Gart?" she asked.

Her voice was soft with uncertainty. Gart's green eyes glittered as he nodded his head, realizing he still had Romney by the arm and hastening to release the child. He tried not to feel guilty that this glorious creature had witnessed him roughing up the child.

"It is me." He just stared at her, a rather soft expression coming over his masculine features. "I have not seen you in years."

Emberley smiled broadly, a dimple on her chin and beautiful straight teeth. "It has been some time," she agreed. "I believe the last time I saw you was when I had just returned home from fostering at Chepstow Castle and you and my brother were newly knighted."

He nodded. "I recall," he said. "That was many years ago."

She warmed to the recognition. "Twelve years, at least," she agreed, cocking her head thoughtfully. "I also seem to remember that on the day I returned you and my brother tore through the outer ward on your chargers, slicing up anything that did not have a heartbeat. My mother yelled at you and my brother for an hour after it was over."

Gart was grinning, an unusual occurrence for him. The man had features of stone and cracking a smile was something that did not come easily. He was trying not to appear too embarrassed.

"We could not help ourselves," he admitted. "Erik had a new sword that your father had given him. We wanted to make sure that it worked properly."

Emberley laughed in remembrance. "My mother took it away for a week," she snorted. "Erik and my father were furious."

Gart's smile grew as he stared at the woman. His last memory of her was a slip of a girl barely past womanhood but to see her now, he could hardly believe the change. She was positively magnificent. His eyes moved over her luscious blond hair, arranged into a beautiful style that had it pulled off her face and trailing down her back. She had spectacular dark blue eyes, like sapphires, and ruby lips that were parted in a magnificent smile. The longer he looked at her, the more enamored he became.

"I was banned from visiting Morton Castle for a while," he said, wanting off the subject of his wild youth. "But that was long ago and now I find you at Dunster. Why are you here?"

Emberley lifted her hand as if to embrace the entire structure. "I live here," she replied. "You and my brother were in the Holy Land with Richard when I was betrothed to Julian de Moyon. Did you not hear of it?"

He shook his head. "I will confess, I did not," he said, somewhat regretfully. "My focus was on sand and battles until… well, until Erik was killed. Then I returned home to more battles and more intrigue."

Her smile faded, her dark blue eyes glimmering warmly at him. "I heard that you brought my brother home for burial," she said softly. "I never had the chance to thank you. It meant a great deal to my parents."

"Do they live still?"

She nodded. "Still," she said quietly. "They live at Morton Castle and have never gotten over the death of my brother. The fact that I have sons has eased their grief somewhat."

Gart gazed into her lovely eyes, the same color and shape as her brother's had been. He realized he missed his best friend very much, someone he'd not thought of in almost eight years. It was a sobering realization.

"Erik was a great knight," he said somberly. "He is missed."

Emberley smiled in agreement, in sympathy, knowing that her brother and Gabriel Forbes had been best friends since childhood. In fact, she had practically grown up knowing Forbes, a man known as

Gart because he didn't like to be called Gabriel. To see him now brought her a great deal of emotional comfort in a life that knew little.

He was an enormous man, very tall, with a muscular body and long, muscular legs. He had sculpted cheekbones and a square jaw, and murky green eyes that were mysterious and intense. His hair, a dark shade of dark blond, had been practically shaved from his scalp but it did not detract from his virile, male handsomeness. The man was powerfully and painfully handsome.

Truth be told, Emberley had always been fond of Gart. As a young girl, she would dream of marrying him. But those days were long gone, as were her dreams. As she thought on the faded days of her childhood, she glanced at her boys and realized they were covered in white powder. Her brow furrowed.

"Why are my children dusty white?" she pointed at them.

Gart tore his eyes off her to look at the boys. "These are your children?"

She nodded. "Romney is my eldest," she smiled at the boy with pride. "He is an intelligent lad, sweet and loving. Orin is my middle son and Brendt is the youngest. Boys, why are you covered in white powder?"

She addressed her sons, who had a complete change of demeanor since her arrival and were now innocent little angels.

"We were playing, Mama," Orin insisted. "We were ghosts."

Emberley's delicate eyebrows lifted. "Ghosts? Why on earth are you ghosts?"

Romney took charge of the conversation before Orin blew their cover. "Because," he said simply, hoping that would be enough to satisfy his mother. "Mama, can we eat in the hall tonight? I want to see all of the knights!"

Emberley shook her head. "Nay," she told him. "You must eat in your chamber. Your father has business to attend to and does not want you underfoot." She looked at Gart. "Am I to understand that you have met my sons already?"

Gart wasn't sure how to answer. He looked at the boys, who all gazed back at him quite innocently. He didn't believe it for a moment. In fact, he was resisting the urge to scowl at them with disbelief.

"Aye," he said slowly, reluctantly. "I have just arrived and the boys were... that is to say, they were...."

"Mama," Romney latched on to his mother's arm. "We were going to show Sir Gart to the hall. May we do that, Mama? May we, please?"

"Of course, sweetheart," Emberley smiled at her eldest. "That is quite gracious of you."

Gart eyed the boys suspiciously as the youngest one reached out and took his big hand. "We will show you, Sir Gart," he said politely. "Come with us."

Gart didn't want to pull away from the child because he didn't want to offend Emberley. He stood there dumbly as the boy took his hand and Emberley smiled happily.

" 'Tis so good to see you again, Gart," she said sincerely, her dark blue gaze drifting over his handsome features. "It has been a very long time. Much has happened since you and I last saw one another. I would like to know what you have been doing in the twelve years since I last saw you."

Gart could only nod. Realizing she was the baron's wife dampened his enthusiasm at their re-acquaintance and he was coming to think that he had been very, very stupid as a young man not to have realized her potential. True, she'd always been a lovely girl, but had he known she would have grown into such an exquisite creature, he might have vied for her hand. But that thought was tempered by the fact that she had apparently raised three hooligans who had her completely fooled. The woman was raising a pack of wild animals.

Emberley smiled at him and beckoned him to follow her back up the stairs. He did so willingly, gladly, but the moment she turned her back on the boys and headed up the stairs, the youngest one yanked his hand from Gart's fist and began smacking him on the leg.

Romney, too, waited until his mother's back was turned before shaking a fist at Gart, making horrible and threatening faces at him. Orin still had a stick and he whacked Gart on the back with it. Gart grabbed the stick and tossed it away but when Emberley turned around at the sounds coming from behind her, the four of them froze and smiled innocently at her. Emberley grinned and continued up the stairs.

The attack against Gart resumed and continued all the way into the great hall above.

CHAPTER TWO

"**F**ORBES IS THE one they call 'Sach'."

Baron Buckland looked at the man who spoke. "What does that mean?"

Sir David de Lohr, Baron Thornden, wriggled his blond eyebrows, noticing that Forbes was entering the smelly, smoky hall in the company of a very beautiful woman.

De Lohr and Baron Buckland sat at the far end of the long, scrubbed table, enjoying the heat from the enormous hearth and the fine alcohol. Now their focus was on the pair approaching from the darkened entry.

"It is an abbreviated Celtic name," de Lohr told him quietly. "It means 'insane'."

Julian de Moyon, Baron Buckland, lifted his dark eyebrows. "Insane?" he repeated. "The man is mad?"

De Lohr shrugged vaguely, collecting his half-drained cup of tart port wine. "Not in the literal sense," he said, his voice lowering as Forbes drew near. "But there is no one fiercer on the field of battle or in the face of adversity. He is absolutely fearless and skilled beyond compare."

Julian's gaze moved between the enormous knight with the shaved head and chiseled features, and his wife as they approached the table.

"He is a giant," he commented quietly. "Look of the size of his hands."

De Lohr nodded slightly as he lifted his cup. "Those hands can rip a man's head from his body. I have seen it myself. I pity the man who truly enrages Forbes."

Julian looked at him, shocked, as Gart and Emberley reached the table. Emberley's warm smile turned into something forced as she focused on her husband.

"My lord," she addressed him. "This is Sir Gart Forbes, a man who was friends with my brother long ago. Gart and I knew each other when we were very young."

Julian eyed Gart, more focused on his wife. "Get out," he snapped. "The men have business to conduct."

Emberley's smile faded and her cheeks turned red, reflexive reaction to her husband's humiliation. He hadn't even acknowledged her polite introduction, which wasn't unusual. Still, she was embarrassed even though she should have been used to the treatment after all of these years.

"I will bid you gentlemen a good eve," she said politely to the table, turning to Gart one last time. "I hope to see you before you leave so we may finish our conversation."

Before Gart could reply, Julian slammed his fist against the table. "I told you to leave, woman. Go before I take my hand to you."

Gart eyed the baron, looking to Emberley and seeing how ashamed she was. He didn't like the way the man spoke to her. His first impression of the baron was not a good one. He smiled at Emberley, a gesture that those who knew him did not believe he was capable of. Gart Forbes was not a man who smiled, in any case.

"I will not leave before speaking with you, my lady," he said kindly. "Good eve to you."

Emberley's trembling smile turned real as she silently thanked him for his graciousness. Gathering her skirts, she fled the hall as Gart watched. His gaze lingered on the empty doorway a moment, thinking of Emberley and her three wild, beasty boys before returning his attention to the table. Seeing the baron and his crass manners, he was coming to see why the boys behaved as they did. He was coming not to like what he was seeing.

But he was a mere knight and his opinion was not of issue. He did what he was told to do and served whoever his liege directed. Without a word he sat down, collecting his cup and taking a large measure of wine only to realize that Julian was staring at him. Gart stared back, noting the small, dark-haired man with the bushy mustache.

"You are Forbes?" Julian confirmed.

Gart nodded shortly. "Aye, my lord."

"I have heard much of your abilities."

Gart simply nodded and Julian sat forward in his seat. He seemed to be taking a good deal of interest in studying him. The man was enormous, no doubt. Everything about him was big, from the top of his shaved head to the bottom of his massive feet. His voice was so deep that it seemed to bubble up from the ground. But it was his eyes that had Julian's attention – they had a sinister and calculating look about them.

As Julian gazed at the man, he could see why the soldiers had nick-named him "Sach". From what he could see, it suited him.

"I understand you have been in Normandy for the past year, fighting on the king's behalf," Julian finally said.

Gart regarded the baron, his hand tightening around his cup. "I have, my lord," he replied.

"How did the battles fare?"

"My lord?"

"Were they well supplied and well commanded?"

Gart wasn't sure of the motivation behind the question but he nodded. "They were, my lord."

Julian digested the answer and, satisfied, moved on. "Am I to understand that you know my wife?"

"I do, my lord," Gart answered. "Her brother and I were the best of friends until his death in The Levant."

Julian snorted as he collected his wine cup. "Then you know she has always been a beautiful girl," he took a long drink of wine and smacked his lips. "She has provided me with three fine sons, perhaps the only thing that keeps her useful to me other than her obvious beauty."

Gart didn't react to the statement although he didn't like the way the man said it. Having nothing to say to him, he returned to his drink as Julian turned to the baron seated to his left.

"Does he know that you are sending him back to France?" he asked.

David glanced at Gart. "That has not been decided yet," he said evenly. "I am here to discuss the possibility. You and my brother are allies and he has asked me to come to Dunster to hear of your situation. I was told there was an issue with your lands in France."

Julian shook his head. "Not my lands," he said. "The queen's lands. Even as John fights to regain what he has lost in Normandy, his wife also has lands that are compromised. She needs protection and I have sworn to help her."

De Lohr wasn't too quick to support his claim. "What do you have to do with the queen?"

Julian smiled lazily, toying with his cup. "Have you not heard, my friend?" he flicked a careless wrist. "The queen and I are madly in love. She has my heart and I would do anything for her, including defending her lands against Philip Augustus. The French king envies her properties near Angouleme and I have sworn to keep them safe, which is why I need your assistance."

De Lohr sighed faintly. He had heard from his brother, the powerful Earl of Hereford and Worcester, that Baron Buckland was something of a political player and an opportunist. The man had rich lands, however, and a great deal of money and manpower, and spent a great deal of time in London soliciting the favor of the king. It seemed that he had garnered the favor of the queen instead.

"Surely she has enough troops," David said. "She cannot possibly need more men."

Julian poured himself more wine. "She is afraid," he said. "Afraid of the French king, afraid of her own mother who rules similar lands… the woman needs help and I have sworn to obtain it. Will you not supply me with men and knights for this purpose?"

It was evident that David was resistant. Gart stayed out of the conversation, listening to his liege and Buckland go back and forth on what was, and was not, appropriate support. Gart had served de Lohr for six years and knew the man and his family were rigidly opposed to John. They had been strong supporters of Richard until four years ago when the man was killed in France. Then, they had no choice but to support John as the rightful king. It was something that still left a bad taste in their mouths.

Gart sat at the table for quite some time listening to the arguing and pleading. He ate, he drank, and he generally grew weary of the bickering. Finally excusing himself just after midnight, he intended to return to the stables to collect his bags and then find a warm corner of Dunster to sleep in. He was exhausted and decided to let the barons do their bickering alone. He had no say in it, anyway.

Taking the spiral stairs down to the entry level, he could see remnants of white powder on the floor and steps. He half-expected the three little hooligans to come jumping out at him again and knew, reasonably, that they would be in bed and long asleep by now. Quitting the keep, he took the wooden stairs to the bailey and proceeded across the dark, dusty ward.

The moon was full overhead, casting the landscape in an eerie silver glow. Gart glanced up at the sky, seeing a million stars spread across the dark expanse. It was a beautiful night and unseasonably clear.

As he lowered his gaze in search of the stables, he could see the sentries upon the battlements as pinpoints of torch light moved through the darkness. Somewhere, a dog barked. Just as the stables came into view to the northeast section of the castle, his gaze fell upon a small and lone figure near the northeast tower.

He wouldn't have paid any attention except the figure turned and began to walk, and he noticed immediately that it wasn't a soldier. It was too small and too finely wrapped. Drawing closer, he realized he was gazing up at a woman as she walked the battlements.

Not only was it very late for a lone woman to be taking a nightly stroll, it was also unsafe. Only someone very comfortable with her position within the castle would show such confidence walking alone.

Curious, he made his way to the northeast turret and took the stairs to the battlements.

The battlements were long and narrow, perched high on the walls of Dunster. There was a thirty-foot drop to the bailey below as he made his way along the narrow walkway. He could see the cloaked figure ahead of him, heading in the direction of the gatehouse. He picked up his pace, passing a couple of sentries, to catch up with her.

"My lady?" he said when he came to within a few feet of her.

Startled, Emberley spun around and nearly lost her balance. Gart quickly reached out to grab her so she wouldn't topple over the side. When he was sure she was steady, he immediately dropped his hands.

"God's Bones," Emberley cursed softly, patting her chest as if to restart her heart. "You frightened me."

He smiled, his strong feature shadowed in the moonlight. "My apologies," he said. "I did not mean to."

Emberley wasn't truly upset and she returned his smile to let him know. "I know you did not," she replied, studying him for a brief moment. Her gaze moved over his features in a warm, comforting manner. "I was lost in thought and did not hear you approach."

"Surely there are safer places to lose oneself in thought. Why are you on the battlements?"

She gazed across the wilds of Somerset beyond the castle walls. "I do not sleep well and walking helps me to relax," she told him. "Many are the nights I have spent upon this wall walk."

His eyes glimmered in understanding. "I know the feeling well," he said quietly. "I do not sleep well, either. Even now, I am exhausted from a week in the saddle but I do not know if I will be able to sleep."

Her smile grew. "Perhaps if you stay here any length of time, you and I will keep each other sorry company on nightly walks."

He flashed his teeth, big and straight and white. "There are worse things I can think of."

She laughed softly, leaning against the battlement wall as a night bird sang overhead. In the still of the night, it was calm and soothing.

Emberley seemed to be staring at Gart quite intently. From the expression on her face, there seemed to be more on her mind than sleepless nights.

"May I ask you a question?" she finally asked.

"Of course."

"How much did my children steal from you?"

His smile faded and his eyebrows lifted. "Why would you ask that?"

She sighed heavily. "I know what they were doing in the entry earlier this eve," she said softly. "You do not have to pretend. I know they were robbing you."

He shook his head. "They did not rob me."

She cocked her head as if she didn't believe him. "Gart," she lowered her voice reprovingly. "Do not lie for them. I know what they do. They do it to everyone that enters the keep."

He chewed his lip thoughtfully and averted his gaze, leaning on the battlements just as she was. His eyes moved out over the shadowed land.

"How would you know this?"

She sighed with exasperation. "Because many visitors have told me this," she said. "They give them money simply to keep the peace. But I make the boys give it back. If they have stolen from you, please...."

He put up a hand to stop her, turning to look at her lovely face. She was a positively exquisite creature, made more beautiful by the haunting moonlight. As he gazed into her lovely eyes, her beauty nearly erased every thought in his head. It was a struggle to speak rationally.

"They did not steal from me because I did not have any money on my person," he told her. "Therefore, I am not lying to protect them. They did not rob me."

"But they tried."

He reluctantly nodded. "They did."

She held his gaze a moment longer before looking away and shaking her head. "Their motives are so complex," she said. "Romney believes that money will buy things to make Lacy and I happy."

"Lacy?"

"Their two-year-old sister," she explained softly. Then she started throwing her hands around as she spoke. "They rob anyone who enters the keep or, as Romney explains it, they exact a toll from visitors, and then the boys escape the castle and run off into town to purchase things. One time they purchased perfume for me and another time it was a belt, which I am sure they stole. Unless they robbed the king, they could not have afforded it. It terrifies me that they do this. I am afraid that one of these days, they will fall victim to bandits or wild animals. It is not safe for them outside of these walls."

"Nor is it safe for visitors inside of the walls with those three on the loose."

She looked at him and burst out in giggles. "This is serious," she chided him, although she was grinning. "I am nearly at my wits end with them. I apologize that they tried to rob you, Gart. You must think me horrible for raising such terrible children."

He looked at her, a smile playing on his full lips. "I think your children are bold and clever," he said, although it was not quite the truth. "Why do they feel the need to buy you nice things?"

Her smile faded and he could sense her manner becoming guarded. She looked away, off towards the forests to the east. The silence that followed was heavy as she thought on her answer.

"Things… things are not entirely pleasant here," she said, vaguely. "I suppose they think that gifts can make them better."

He watched her profile in the moonlight, a long and pregnant pause. "You are not happy."

It was a statement and not a question. Emberley shrugged. "I have four beautiful children," she said with feigned enthusiasm. "There is much to be thankful for."

He shifted, inadvertently moving closer to her in the process. "I did not question your gratitude," he said. "I questioned your happiness."

She shrugged again, still not meeting his eye. "It does not matter if I am happy or not. My children are healthy and we have much to be thankful for."

He sighed faintly, knowing he shouldn't involve himself in something that did not concern him, but unable to resist. He had known Emberley since childhood. He had seen her grow up for the most part. With Erik gone, he almost felt compelled to act in the man's place, to perhaps advise or console her. It was a foolish thought but he couldn't help himself.

"Does your husband always speak to you so rudely?" he asked quietly.

She looked at him as if startled by the question. "It is his way," she said rather lamely. "It is his right."

"I know what his rights are," Gart said. "I would suspect by the way he spoke to you that he does it quite regularly."

In the moonlight, Emberley's cheeks flushed dully. "It is his way," she repeated softly.

"Perhaps it is, but I do not like it," Gart said. "Based upon that observation, I will ask another question."

"What question is that?"

"Has he ever struck you?"

She hung her head, refusing to look at him. "Gart, I am sure you are asking out of concern, but it truly is none of your affair."

He watched her lowered head, her lovely profile, seeing tears pooling in her eyes. He suddenly felt very, very angry as he realized the truth. She didn't even have to tell him. He knew.

"So he takes his hands to you," he rumbled. " 'Tis a vile, foul man that would strike a woman."

Emberley took a deep breath and wiped quickly at her eyes before the tears could fall. When she turned to look at him, he could read the anxiety on her face.

"I appreciate your concern," she whispered, laying a soft, white hand on his wrist. "I truly do. But you must not ask me any more questions. You would not like the answers and if Julian found out, he would not like that I have told you."

His jaw flexed. "Your husband was quite eager to announce to the men in the hall that he and the queen were lovers," he said. "Is this true?"

She yanked her hand away from his wrist and he would never forget the expression on her face. It was something between disgust and shame. Turning on her heel, she tried to rush away from him but he was on her in an instant, his colossal hands grasping her slender arms. She tried to shrug him off but he wouldn't budge.

"Leave me alone," she snapped. "I do not see where my husband's affairs are any business of yours."

He cooled, releasing her. She stepped away from him but she didn't run. She faced him defensively and he backed off.

"You are correct," he agreed calmly. "They are not my business. I suppose since your only brother was my best friend, perhaps I was showing interest on his behalf. It is simply that I look at you and see that young girl who used to follow Erik around and...forgive me. I should not have overstepped myself. I was only concerned."

Emberley gazed at the man, cooling significantly at his placating words. Then she sighed heavily as if all of the fight suddenly left her. Her defensive mechanism was always close to the surface, preparing to defend her tender heart from her cruel husband and his cruel words. She realized she need not be defensive with Gart. For as long as she'd known him, she'd never once heard of him showing women any manner of cruelty.

"You need not ask forgiveness," she said, remorseful. "It is I who must ask for your grace. I should not have snapped so. I know you are only asking out of concern."

He gazed steadily at her. "Great concern," he corrected gently. "Erik would ask this of me."

She smiled gratefully. "I know," she whispered. "I miss him very much."

"As do I."

"You are a good friend, Gart," she said. "When you were not upsetting my mother, I know she looked upon you as a son."

He gave her a lopsided grin. "I am thinking that Erik and I were much like your boys – into great mischief and mayhem in our youth."

She laughed softly. "Then perhaps you will not think me such a terrible mother that my boys rob anyone who enters the keep."

He was glad to see she was no longer tense and angry with him, thinking he would try yet again to get at the truth of the matter now that he seemed to have broken her defenses down.

"I never thought you a terrible mother," he said quietly. "But I would like to know the truth of your husband's treatment of you."

Her smile faded as she gazed up at him. "Why?" she lifted her shoulders. "There is nothing you can do. He is my husband and may do as he pleases."

Gart knew that and somehow, it hurt his heart. He knew it would have hurt Erik's. "Is he truly the queen's lover?" he asked quietly.

She nodded without emotion. "They have been lovers for almost a year," she replied. "I do not know what she sees in Julian other than his wealth. He is a terrible character and a horrible…."

She trailed off, embarrassed at divulging more information than she should, and Gart's expression grew serious.

"I am truly sorry," he said in his soft, deep voice. "You do not deserve such disrespect. The man is a fool."

Her smile returned, weakly. "You are very kind."

"Kindness has nothing to do with it. It is true."

Her smile grew, now modest. "I appreciate your concern. It has done my heart good to see you, Gart. You remind me of better days."

Her words, kind and sweet, softened him. His heart began to beat strangely in his chest as he reached out and took her small hand in his, bringing it to his lips for a gentle kiss.

"It has done my heart a world of good to see you," he said softly. "I see Erik in your eyes and it comforts me."

Gart's warm kiss on her hand made Emberley's breathing quicken. She was taken back to the days when he was a handsome, very young man and she was his adoring public. He had grown into such a magnificent man she could hardly believe it. She wondered how different her life would have been had she had not married Julian. If only Gart could have been her husband… *but no.* She chased the thought away as quickly as it came. It would do no good for her to long for a man she could never have. That opportunity was long gone.

"I am glad," she squeezed his hand and let it go. "Perhaps we will have more opportunity to speak in the next few days. Do you know when you are leaving?"

He shook his head, wishing she hadn't let go of his hand. Her touch had been magic.

"I do not," he told her. "My liege and your husband are debating that as we speak."

She pulled her cloak more tightly around her slender body. The evening was growing cool and damp in spite of the bright moonlight.

"Then perhaps tomorrow we may…."

She was cut off when something hit the wall just behind Gart. Startled, he jumped forward and threw his arms around her to protect her. But it was the wrong move. Standing several feet behind him was Julian. The arrow he held in his left hand, the second of two he had collected from the armory after spying his wife and Forbes upon the battlements, went sailing in Gart's direction. Gart put up an armored arm and easily deflected it.

Unwinding his arms from Emberley and turning to face Julian as the man approached, Gart could tell by his face that they were in for a good deal of trouble.

"Whore!" Julian screamed.

Gart remained cool, keeping Emberley protectively behind him. "My lord," he said evenly. "Your wife and I were discussing days past when we knew each other. We were discussing her dead brother."

Julian's thin face was livid. He approached Gart and slugged him in the chest, although with Gart's size and Julian's diminutive stature, Gart hardly felt the blow. Still, the implication was obvious.

"You are alone with my wife," he snarled. "You had your arms around her in a disgraceful embrace. How dare you violate my hospitality by taking my wife and... and wooing her."

Gart shook his head. "I did not violate anything, my lord," he was calm and steady. "Your wife and I knew each other as children and were discussing...."

Julian cut him off by shoving him back and reaching around to grab Emberley by the wrist. He pulled hard and she stumbled, nearly toppling over the side of the wall railing. Gart grabbed her to keep her from going over but Julian was wild with fury – he pounded on Gart's steadying arm even as he yanked at his wife.

Emberley didn't put up a fight but she was trying to keep her balance as he yanked. Sensing her hesitation as resistance, Julian slapped her hard across the face.

"I will deal with you, you treacherous whore," he snarled, lifting his hand to strike her again. "You are a...."

Before he could bring the hand down, Gart reached out and grabbed it. Julian turned to scream at him but was faced with an expression so tense, so deadly, that the words died in his throat.

De Lohr was suddenly on the battlements, as were several other de Lohr soldiers, and they were moving for Gart in a group, trying to pull him away from Buckland. Even Emberley, her right cheek stinging from the slap, reached out and grasped Gart by the arm.

"Gart, no," she whispered, begging. "Please let him go."

Gart heard her, as he also heard his liege behind him, firmly and quietly ordering him to let the baron's arm go. But at the moment, Gart could only see Buckland. From a man he had initially found distasteful and displeasureable, that displeasure had grown into full-blown loathing quickly. All he could see was a weak, bully of a man and he hated him for it.

"You will not strike her ever again," he growled. "Is that clear?"

Julian was torn between fear and outrage. "You cannot make demands of me!" he howled. "I will do as I please with my own wife!"

Emberley's soft voice infiltrated Gart's rage. "Please, Gart," she begged softly. "Please let him go."

Her sweet, pleading voice broke through his haze of rage and he tore his eyes away from Buckland long enough to look at her. She mouthed the world "*please*", her big eyes beseeching him, and he reluctantly let the man's hand go. But Julian wasn't a smart man – he slugged Emberley in the jaw simply to demonstrate his power and Gart went straight for his neck.

Emberley screamed as she fell onto the wall walk, trapped beneath Julian as Gart tried to break the man's neck. But soldiers and knights were swarming over them and someone pulled her free of the fighting. Shaken, she looked up to see that it was de Lohr. His handsome face was taut as he made sure she was secure before diving into the fray.

Terrified for Gart, Emberley positioned herself back against the wall as she watched eight men pull Gart off her husband. He was such a big man and fed by such anger that his strength had been astounding. Julian was unhurt but he was furious, screaming threats at Gart. Knowing his wrath would eventually be turned against her, Emberley wisely fled the wall walk and raced for the keep, hearing the angry voices behind her filling the night with foul language and brutality.

Heart pounding, Emberley mounted the steps into the keep, running up the spiral stairs until she reached her children's chambers on the third floor. Scooping sleeping Lacy out of her bed, she fled into the boys' bower and closed the door, throwing the heavy bolt behind her. It would take an army to break the old door down and all of the pounding and screaming Julian would do could not breach it. She knew she was safe, at least for the moment.

With her daughter still sleeping heavily in her arms, Emberley sank to the floor and wept.

CHAPTER THREE

"THANKS TO YOU, I had to pledge men to Buckland's cause whether or not I agreed with it." De Lohr was rightfully seething. "What on earth possessed you to touch another man's wife?"

Gart stood in the dark, dusty stables, silently and stoically taking a verbal lashing from his liege. He deserved it, he knew, but he didn't regret his actions. Not one bit. De Lohr knew this, which was why he was so furious.

Gart Forbes was the best knight he had ever seen, and he had seen a lot of good men in his life. Many talented men had passed beneath his command or his brother's command at one time or another. But Forbes was different – they didn't call the man "Sach" without good reason. He was power, strength, cunning and brutality all rolled into one but, more than that, he was grossly unpredictable, as evidenced by the scene on the wall walk.

Gart could have easily snapped Buckland's neck but he hadn't – he just wanted to scare the man. Forbes had bouts of volatile fury but he was as cunning as a fox. He knew exactly what he was doing when he wrapped his hands around Buckland's throat.

"I did not touch her, at least not in the manner you are suggesting," Gart told him. "I swear upon my oath that we were simply talking."

David gazed at him a moment, trying to read the unreadable face, before letting out a heavy sigh.

"I believe you," he said, with less anger than he had been exhibiting earlier. "But Buckland has used this entire circumstance into blackmailing me for support."

"Blackmailing?"

De Lohr nodded with some disgust. "If I provide him with four

341

hundred men, he will not have you thrown in jail," he said, throwing up his hands. "I have no choice. Unless I want to lose my best knight, then I must support him. I hope you liked France because you will be heading back there shortly."

The last sentence was spoken with some irony. Gart stared at de Lohr for a long moment before breaking down into a puzzled, disgusted expression. He just shook his head and turned away, pacing over to his charger. The beast was tethered in a far stall because he was so vicious, but with Gart, the black and white steed was as tame as a kitten. The animal nickered softly as Gart approached and began stroking the big neck, giving it an affectionate slap.

"My apologies, my lord," he finally said. "It was not my intention to put you in an awkward position."

De Lohr sighed with regret. "What were you doing with her alone up on the battlements? Did you not stop to think that it was a compromising position to say the least?"

Gart shook his head. "We were speaking," he reiterated. "I have not seen her in twelve years, this lovely young girl who was the sister of my best friend. Seeing her… it is as if I am seeing him again. I simply wanted to speak with her. Perhaps old memories are clouding my judgment but I do not believe so. We did nothing wrong."

De Lohr nodded his head in resignation. "Even so, you are not the one who will ultimately suffer in all of this. It will be her. Buckland is a vicious fool with a mean streak in him. She will be lucky if he does not beat her senseless for this."

Gart knew that but it didn't help the raging fury he felt, starting in his toes and rising up through his big body. By the time it reached his head, his face was red and he was sweating. De Lohr caught his expression and he put his hands up as if to stop the building tide. He knew that look well.

"There is nothing you can do about it," he told him sternly. "Your interference is what caused all of this in the first place. Had you simply walked away…."

"He struck her," Gart cut him off. "Could you have stood by while he did that?"

David rolled his eyes. "She is the man's wife, Gart. He can do with her as he pleases."

"Even assault her?"

"Aye, even assault her."

"You did not answer my question. Could you have stood by and watched him beat her?"

De Lohr eyed him, finally shaking his head after a moment. "Nay," he admitted, looking away. "But it is different with me. I am a man of rank and you are a mere knight. What you did, in most circles, would land you in the vault for the rest of your life."

Gart's jaw ticked dangerously. His face was still red and sweating, never a good sign. "I will not let him take out his anger on her. I cannot."

De Lohr threw up his hands. "You have no choice," he said. "Gart, I will send you home this night if you cannot control yourself. You are already in enough trouble. Any more from you and I may not be able to placate Buckland. He would throw you in jail and bury the key."

Gart didn't reply. Anything more out of his mouth would get him in deeper trouble. De Lohr was only trying to help him and he knew it.

There was a big pile of dry hay on the other side of his charger, stacked there by the grooms. He made his way over to the hay and plopped down into it, lying back against the clean, scratchy stuff. Folding his hands over his chest, he closed his eyes.

David watched him a moment, knowing that Gart was doing what he needed to do to calm down and stay on an even keel. Without another word, he quit the stable for his own quarters in the keep, a small room that Buckland had allocated to him.

Even as de Lohr made his way through the cold, bright night towards the distant keep, he knew that this was not the end of it. He could feel it. Gart felt as if he were protecting his best friend's sister and unable to process that the fact she was another man's wife took precedence.

David wondered what horrors awaited them come the dawn.

☙

GART AWOKE TO three little faces staring at him. Startled, he sat up, hay stuck to his back and arms. It was just growing light outside, the sky in shades of pinks and blues as the sun pierced the veil of night. It was cold in the stable as the animals began to stir, hungry for their morning meal. Gart rubbed the sleep from his eyes as Romney, Orin and Brendt gazed back at him.

"What are you doing here?" he asked them, shaking the sleep from his mind.

The boys were not particularly well dressed against the cold and Romney looked particularly pale, which concerned him. They all looked a little lost. Gart also noticed something else – without all of the white powder on him, Romney's ashen face bore a striking resemblance to his long-dead uncle. The mirror image was uncanny.

"We are sorry we tried to rob you yesterday," Romney said somberly.

Gart rested his arms on his up-bent knees. "You did not rob me. I did not have anything for you to steal."

Romney and Orin looked at each other, bewildered. "We tried to rob you," Romney looked back at Gart. "Mother told us to apologize."

Gart thought on that a moment, studying Romney. More and more, he could see Erik in the boy, even down to the expressions on the child's face. He couldn't help but think how thrilled Erik would have been with his three nephews.

"I see," he said. "Then your apology is accepted."

Romney cocked his head. "She said that you and Uncle Erik were friends."

Gart nodded. "We were," he said, eyeing the brown-haired, blue-eyed boy. "In fact, I was just thinking that you look a good deal like him. He was a great knight."

"Mother said he died in the Holy Land for Richard's damn crusade."

Gart fought of a smile. "She said that?"

Romney nodded solemnly. "She said it was damn foolish and damn stupid."

Gart bit his lip to keep from smiling. "Your uncle was a great knight on the crusade," he said. "We fought together for almost two years."

"How did he die?"

Gart didn't feel like smiling anymore and the grin faded from his lips. "A Saracen arrow pierced his helm," he said quietly. "It lodged in his eye and it killed him."

"Oh," Romney looked thoughtful, distressed. "Did it hurt?"

"I would imagine so."

Romney continued to look distressed as Orin and Brendt decided the charger was more worthy of their attention. Gart saw the boys moving towards it.

"Do not touch him," he admonished. "He will stomp you."

The boys drew back in fear, gravitating back towards their eldest brother. Romney was still looking at Gart.

"Since we are sorry that we robbed you, will you give us money anyway?" he asked.

Gart gazed steadily at the boy. "Why?"

"Because Mother needs a present."

"Why?"

"She is unhappy."

Gart's good humor faded completely. "Why is she unhappy?"

Romney seemed to lose some of his confidence. He looked at Orin and Brendt, who gazed back at him with wide eyes. Suddenly, Orin rushed Gart and grabbed the neck of his wrinkled tunic.

"Becausth," Orin had an extremely lazy tongue and a bad lisp. He yanked at Gart's tunic and began hitting him with his little fists. "He did thisth... and thisth... and she cries."

Gart put his hands on the lad to both steady him and pull him off.

Even Romney moved forward to pull his violent brother away from the enormous knight. But Gart didn't miss the gist of what the boy said. In fact, he began to feel the familiar fury build in his feet again and start to work its way up. *She will be lucky if he does not beat her senseless for this.* He wondered if de Lohr's prophetic words had come true.

"Who?" he had Orin by the arms but he was looking at Romney. "Who made your mother cry?"

Romney wouldn't look at him. He was more interested in pulling Orin away from the man. "Father," he muttered. "He hits her and she cries."

The slow build of fury began to gain speed. Gart could feel the sweat popping out on his forehead and he struggled to control the brewing anger.

"Did he hit her last night?" he asked quietly.

Romney shook his head. "Nay," he replied, giving Orin a good yank and sending the boy off of Gart and onto his bum. "He did it this morning. She cried and cried."

The rage reached Gart's head and his cheeks began to turn red. "Where is your mother now?"

Romney shrugged, either losing interest with the conversation or afraid to say much more. He fidgeted uncomfortably. "In her bed," he said. "Father is leaving for London. Will you give us money now so we can buy her a present?"

Gart stared at the little boy, feeling a great many emotions in his heart that he was unfamiliar with. He'd spent most of his life allowing only one emotion to infiltrate his mind, and that emotion was fury. It worked well for his purposes. The soldiers didn't call him insane for no reason. They called him that because it was the truth.

But now he was feeling something more than fury. He was feeling great sadness and grief, feeling as if he had failed somehow. When he'd meant to protect Emberley, it seemed as if he'd only gotten her into more trouble. He had no reason to believe that the boys were lying to him and he muttered a silent prayer to Erik, begging the man's forgiveness for what he had done. It was a struggle to keep a rein on what he was feeling.

"Where is your father?" he asked, hoping he didn't sound as angry as he felt.

Romney shrugged. "In the hall," he said. "I heard him tell people that he was leaving for London today to see the queen."

Gart stood up from the hay pile, brushing pieces of hay off his arms and back as he went to the bags that were lodged against the wall next to his charger. The grooms began coming into the barn to feed and water the animals but he ignored them as he began to rummage through his bags. Although he wanted very much to go charging into the keep, he kept his cool. He knew that would only make the situation worse. He had to keep his wits about him. But he noticed as he dug through his bags, his hands were shaking.

As he rummaged through his possessions, he realized he had company. He glanced to either side and noticed that Romney was on one side of him while Orin and Brendt were on the other. They were watching him dig through his satchels with great interest. Surely the knight had many wonderful things in that dark and mysterious bag. Finally, they could stand it no longer.

Romney reached in and grabbed a strip of carefully rolled leather, pulling it out to look at it as Gart took it away. As he was distracted with Romney, Orin reached in and pulled out a very sharp razor. Gart snatched it before the boy could injure himself and told the boys not to stick their hands where they did not belong. As he packed away the razor and rolled up the leather strip, little Brendt literally climbed into the largest of his satchels.

He gleefully tried to bury himself in the clothing that had been carefully rolled up and packed. Gart removed the boy from his satchel but in doing so, it opened up the door for Orin to plunge head-first into another bag. Soon, Gart was occupied removing the boys from his bags rather than searching for clean clothes. He would remove one and another would take his place. He swore there were twelve children and not just three, so fast they moved. Finally, he stood up and spread his big arms.

"Cease," he roared softly, jabbing a finger at Brendt, who was back in his satchel and trying to pull one of Gart's enormous tunics over his head. "You – out. And stay out. All of you stay out."

Brendt started to weep and Romney turned his big, blue eyes to Gart. "He wants the tunic," he told him.

Gart waved his hands impatiently. "Fine," he snapped without force, lifting the boy out of his bag. "He can take the tunic. But you other two – get out and stay out. I do not have time for this foolery."

Dejected and scolded, Romney and Orin actually began to repack one of Gart's bags. He looked at their sad faces and began to feel like an ogre for scolding them. But he didn't apologize. He helped them replace what they had pulled out. With both bags repacked, he removed one carefully rolled-up tunic, removed his dirty tunic, put it back in his bag and then sealed everything up.

Meanwhile, Brendt had managed to pull the tunic he stole from Gart over his little blond head and was trying to walk with it. The tunic was far too long for him and he tripped, laughing as he wallowed in the dirt. Romney and Orin giggled at him and Gart couldn't help but crack a smile as the lad tried to get back to his feet without tripping again. He couldn't quite seem to manage it, which sent Romney and Orin howling with laughter. Even Gart was snorting, his gaze moving over the three boys. They were good boys even if they were mischievous. Erik would have been proud. Gart was starting to realize what Erik's mother and father must have gone through when Erik and Gart were into mayhem. Now, he understood.

Pulling the fresh tunic over his head, he proceeded to reclaim his armor. The boys watched with great interest as he pulled on his mail coat, his hauberk, and proceeded with pieces of plate armor that were still fairly rare. He wore great, well-crafted plate armor on both forearms that bore the crest of de Lohr. He also had a big piece that fit over his chest and back, hung from his shoulders by big leather straps.

Romney inspected the piece curiously and even tried to lift it, but Gart discouraged him. It was an expensive piece and too heavy for the boy to play with. Leaving the chest piece in the stable next to his bags, Gart headed out into the dusty courtyard.

Dunster Castle was a massive place built in a long, rectangular configuration which positioned the stables on the far north side, away from the keep but near the kitchens and the well. There were two blocks of stables and as Gart emerged from the block that extended on the northeast wall, he could see that there was great activity from the block lodged against the north wall.

Two chargers and several other horses had been brought out and were being prepared, as well as a big wagon that was being loaded down with goods. The animals were excited and their breath puffed up in great clouds in the cold morning air. Gart's gaze lingered on the group, knowing it must be the baron's escort to London. Just as he passed from the stable yards into the big bailey beyond, he caught sight of de Lohr heading towards him.

Gart was surprisingly in control as he and David came together. Romney, Orin and Brendt were clustered around Gart, following him like puppies, something that didn't go unnoticed by de Lohr. He eyed the boys as he came upon Gart.

"Are you summoning your own army?" he asked.

Gart had no idea what he was talking about until he followed David's gaze and saw the boys standing around him. He grunted.

"Do not let their small size fool you," he told him. "They are brave beyond measure."

David lifted an eyebrow at Romney. "I know," he said. "They were unafraid to rob me yesterday when I entered the keep."

Gart lifted an eyebrow at Romney, who looked both fearful and defiant. "Mother only said we had to apologize to you. She did not say we had to apologize to everyone."

Gart just shook his head, resigned. "What did you steal from the baron?"

Romney's brow furrowed deeply. "Not much."

David fought off a grin. "I gave them a pence each to let me pass," he said. "I was afraid for my life."

Gart's eyes narrowed at Romney. "You will give him back his money. That is not a request."

Romney was deeply displeased. "It is upstairs."

"Go and get it. *Now.*"

The boys darted off, scattering like frightened chickens at Gart's deep and growling tone. They weren't used to such commands but the instinct for survival bade them to obey it. David waited until they were well away before looking at Gart with a grin.

"Brave and bold boys," he commented. "I thought it was quite humorous."

"Did they hit you with a stick?"

"They tried. I paid them before they could whack me."

"Yet I did not," Gart wriggled his eyebrows. "They were not afraid to attack me when I would not pay their demands."

David snorted. "I would like to have seen that. The mighty Gart Forbes being set upon by three small bandits. Those children did what grown men are afraid to do."

Gart shrugged, his gaze trailing up to the enormous dark-stoned keep to the right. "Their mother interrupted what would have surely been a bloodbath," he said. "Speaking of their mother, I am told that the earl beat her this morning."

David's smile faded and he sighed heavily. "That is why I have come to find you," he said quietly. "Knowing how you feel, I wanted you to hear the news from me."

"Did he kill her?"

David shook his head sadly. "From what I can gather, she barricaded herself in her children's room last night after the incident on the wall to avoid her husband's wrath," he said quietly. "My chamber is on the floor below theirs and I could hear him banging at the door a good portion of the night. Then it faded away until dawn when, apparently, one of her sons unbolted the door and the earl was lying in wait. He locked the children out of the room, including the crying two-year-old girl, and proceeded to beat his wife. I could hear the woman screaming. By the time I reached the floor, I found four crying children staring back at me. Even the servants were crying. So I took everyone down to the hall, made sure the children were tended, before returning to the chamber. By the time I returned, all was silent and the earl was just emerging. He told me that if I wanted to remain a trusted ally, I would leave well enough alone."

By this time, Gart was the familiar shade of red. The veins on his neck and temple were standing out, throbbing. De Lohr knew that look. It was always the calm before the storm.

"Did you see Lady Emberley?" Gart asked through clenched teeth. "Is someone at least tending to her injuries?"

David shook his head. "The earl will not let anyone near her," he explained, sickened. "He says she must be punished. The servants are too afraid to go against his wishes and I cannot do it because he would not only break his alliance with my brother but more than likely accuse me the same way he accused you. The man has a warped and dangerous mind."

Gart couldn't stand it any longer. He began to walk towards the keep. David reached out and grabbed him.

"Wait," he snapped softly. "The earl is in the hall and if he sees you ...."

Gart turned on him, his face red with rage. "I am going to see to Lady Emberley's health and well-being, and her husband be damned," he snarled. "Her brother was my best friend and I will not...."

De Lohr put up a silencing hand. "Listen to me," he cut him off. "I knew you would not be stopped but I also know that if Buckland sees you, there is no telling how volatile this situation will become. Do you not understand that your actions have brought this about? What do you think will happen if you do not understand your place and continue this behavior? It appears as if you are attempting to come between the baron and his wife."

Gart was so angry that he was sweating, his big hands working much in the same manner they did right before he plunged into battle. He was starting to reach the point that every man feared, the insanity that would soon overtake him. It was at that point that he would start ripping heads from bodies, Buckland's included, and to hell with the consequences.

"I am not trying to come between the baron and his wife," he said in a manner that suggested the whole idea ridiculous.

"It appears that way. Can you swear to me that there is nothing more to this than the concern of an old friend?"

"I can swear it."

De Lohr sighed softly. He wasn't sure if he believed him, given the fact that the man was acting in a way he had never seen before, but he would not dispute him. At least, not yet. "Very well," he said quietly. "But you must show restraint, Gart. This situation is delicate to say the least."

"I am going to see to her," Gart repeated, his jaw gnashing. "I must see what has happened. If you cannot understand that, then I cannot explain it to you any more than I already have."

David just shook his head, tightening his grip on Gart's arm. "I understand," he lowered his voice. "I also understand that whatever I say, you will do as you please."

"That is a fair assessment."

David sighed in resignation. "Then we must act carefully. You and I will enter the keep and I will distract the baron so you can slip to the upper floors to tend the lady. Meanwhile, I am going to tell Buckland that I have sent you away and hopefully that will appease him. But in doing so, you need to make every effort to stay out of the man's way until he leaves for London. If you hear him coming, hide or all will be lost, including his trust in me. Is that clear?"

Gart was agreeable with the plan for the most part. "It is," he replied. "My charger and possessions are still here, however. What if the earl sees them?"

David shook his head. "He would not know your possessions or charger from the next man's. He does not seem particularly bright or observant."

Satisfied, Gart could feel himself calming now that there was a plan, something that would enable him to see to Emberley. Taking a deep breath, he struggled to calm himself. "And once the baron has left Dunster? What then?"

David shrugged. "You can remain here if you wish, at least until I send for you. I suspect we will be mobilizing for France in the next three or four weeks, so be prepared. If you leave Dunster, go back to Denstroude because that is where I shall look for you."

Gart nodded, the dull, red tone of his face fading to a normal healthy color. David eyed the man one last time, just to make sure he was going to do as he was told, before finally nodding his head.

"Very well," he turned for the keep. "Let us make our move."

Gart was right behind him.

Read the rest of **ARCHANGEL** in eBook or in paperback.

ABOUT KATHRYN LE VEQUE

Medieval Just Got Real.

KATHRYN LE VEQUE is a USA TODAY Bestselling author, an Amazon All-Star author, and a #1 bestselling, award-winning, multi-published author in Medieval Historical Romance and Historical Fiction. She has been featured in the NEW YORK TIMES and on USA TODAY's HEA blog. In March 2015, Kathryn was the featured cover story for the March issue of InD'Tale Magazine, the premier Indie author magazine. She was also a quadruple nominee (a record!) for the prestigious RONE awards for 2015.

Kathryn's Medieval Romance novels have been called 'detailed', 'highly romantic', and 'character-rich'. She crafts great adventures of love, battles, passion, and romance in the High Middle Ages. More than that, she writes for both women AND men – an unusual crossover for a romance author – and Kathryn has many male readers who enjoy her stories because of the male perspective, the action, and the adventure.

On October 29, 2015, Amazon launched Kathryn's Kindle Worlds Fan Fiction site WORLD OF DE WOLFE PACK. Please visit Kindle Worlds for Kathryn Le Veque's World of de Wolfe Pack and find many action-packed adventures written by some of the top authors in their genre using Kathryn's characters from the de Wolfe Pack series. As Kindle World's FIRST Historical Romance fan fiction world, Kathryn Le Veque's World of de Wolfe Pack will contain all of the great storytelling you have come to expect.

Kathryn loves to hear from her readers. Please find Kathryn on Facebook at Kathryn Le Veque, Author, or join her on Twitter @kathrynleveque, and don't forget to visit her website at www.kathrynleveque.com.

Made in United States
Orlando, FL
12 January 2022

13335137R00202